BAD SUMMER PEOPLE

EMMA ROSENBLUM

THORNDIKE PRESS
A part of Gale, a Cengage Company

GALE
A Cengage Company

Copyright © 2023 by Emma Rosenblum.
Thorndike Press, a part of Gale, a Cengage Company.

ALL RIGHTS RESERVED
This is a work of fiction. All of the characters, organizations, and events portrayed in this novel are either products of the author's imagination or are used fictitiously.
Thorndike Press® Large Print Core.
The text of this Large Print edition is unabridged.
Other aspects of the book may vary from the original edition.
Set in 16 pt. Plantin.

LIBRARY OF CONGRESS CIP DATA ON FILE.
CATALOGUING IN PUBLICATION FOR THIS BOOK
IS AVAILABLE FROM THE LIBRARY OF CONGRESS.

ISBN-13: 979-8-88578-996-7 (hardcover alk. paper).

Published in 2023 by arrangement with Flatiron Books.

Printed in Mexico
Print Number: 1   Print Year: 2023

To Monty, Sandy, and Charles,
my best summer people

PROLOGUE

Danny Leavitt, a gangly eight-year-old with a severe peanut allergy, was the one who discovered the body. It was early, maybe 7:30 a.m., and he'd been riding his black Schwinn bike around town to search for snails after the big storm they'd had the night before. The boardwalks were wet and slippery and covered with leaves and small branches blown off by the strong winds. It hadn't been a tropical storm, but it'd been close — an intense microburst that had hit the island unexpectedly, sending deck furniture flying and doing some light damage to several roofs around the village. Danny's house, which was right on the beach, was fine, the power intact, but his mom yelled after him to be careful as he left, warning of potential downed wires.

He'd ridden for about ten minutes, going from the ocean down to the bay on the walk that he lived on, Surf. Then he decided to ride over to Neptune Walk, where the playground was, to see what shape it was in. He turned on Harbor from Surf, passed Atlantic, Marine, and Broadway, and then turned left on Neptune. Something shiny caught his eye in front of the Cahulls', a friendly couple with one little kid, Archie. He stopped and got off his Schwinn to see a bike, nearly hidden in the woody, shrubby area that lined the boardwalks, about a three-foot-drop down. The town had lifted all the walks after flooding from Hurricane Sandy, and Danny's dad, along with many other people in Salcombe, thought they'd gone overboard. "Someone could break their neck," he remembered his dad muttering.

Danny figured the bike had been blown away by the wind, so he grabbed its wheel and dragged it up onto the boardwalk, no easy feat — it was a grown-up's bike, and Danny was small for his age. It was then he saw that the bike had been covering something else: a person, facedown in the reeds. The body was angled strangely and not moving at all. Danny felt his throat close, almost as if he'd eaten a peanut. He hadn't, had he? He ran to the Cahulls' house and banged on the door loudly, shivering and scared. Marina came quickly, in her pajamas

8

and glasses, holding Archie, a concerned look on her face. Marina was very pregnant.

"Danny Leavitt? Are you okay?"

Danny could barely get the words out.

"There's someone out there on the ground, I think they fell off the boardwalk on their bike. They're not moving."

Marina put her son down and called for her husband, Mike.

"Come inside now. Mike and I will handle it. You just stay here."

Mike, in sweatpants and a sleep-rumpled T-shirt, passed them by and went out to look at the find. Marina smiled at Danny. They were silent for a minute. Mike came back into the house. He seemed tense, like when Danny's dad had a bad day at work.

"Take Danny back to his house, and take Archie with you. Don't look at the body. I'm going to call the police. Or whoever it is out here that they call police."

The body? Danny had only heard that phrase in TV shows his parents watched. Marina grabbed her son, who was fussing, and led Danny down the walkway toward his bike, redirecting him away from *the body,* as Danny now thought of it. She told Danny to ride home and then put her son in the baby seat of her bike and took off after him.

Danny wasn't part of the excitement after

that, but he did get to speak to two police officers that day (they were real police officers, weren't they?) and tell them what he'd found and how he'd found it. His parents seemed upset; he'd overheard them speaking in a loud whisper in their bedroom after the cops had left.

"Great, now he's going to be the 'dead body' kid — this is going to be the talk of Dalton," said his mom, Jessica.

"I wonder if there's a way we can sue the town," said his dad, Max. "I'm not paying two million dollars for my beach house, plus fifty thousand in property taxes, for my son to find a corpse. Someone needs to pay for this."

But overall, Danny felt pretty good about discovering the first murder victim in Salcombe, like, ever. He was looking forward to telling all his friends at camp about it. How cool was that?

■ ■ ■ ■

PART I

■ ■ ■ ■

June 26

Part 1

June 26

1
LAUREN PARKER

Lauren Parker was in desperate need of a great summer. This winter had been awful. First of all, it had been freezing since December. Lauren hated the cold. If she could move to Miami, she would — it seemed like everyone else she knew was doing just that. But Jason's job was based in New York, and he needed to occasionally stop by the office. He was the boss, after all. ("If you're the boss, why can't you just *declare* you're moving to Florida?" Lauren kept asking. "You don't go in during the summer!" She never got a good reply.)

Secondly, the Upper East Side school that Lauren's kids went to, Braeburn Academy, had been embroiled in a public scandal, and for months, it was all anyone within a twenty-block radius could talk about.

It started in February, when the school's board received an anonymous email about Mr. Whitney, Braeburn's revered headmaster of twenty years. Mr. Whitney was a Braeburn legend — British, in his late sixties, fond of bow ties and fountain pens, he'd taken the academy from B-list to a true competitor on the scene. Braeburn was now the preferred choice for the most discerning New York City parents, including the Parkers, who bragged to all their friends about Mr. Whitney's unwillingness to bend to the winds of social change.

So, when the board received the accusatory email, it was as if a bomb had gone off on Ninety-third Street and Madison: Mr. Whitney wasn't who he said he was. He was a fraud, according to the widely forwarded screed, a community college dropout who'd forged his résumé two decades ago and tricked Braeburn's leadership into hiring him. They'd all been had by a swindler, a guy from New Jersey who'd pretended to be from England, who'd created a character that specifically, smartly, preyed on the status-obsessed dupes of the Upper East Side.

The story leaked, ending up as a cover in *New York* magazine ("How Francis Whitney Tricked New York's Upper Crust"). Lauren and her mom friends were completely mortified. They'd all gone to great lengths to secure spots for their children at Braeburn and shelled out $50,000 per kid for the privilege of attending. To have it all revealed as a scam, as the rest of the private school circuit sniggered, was a real blow.

"I still can't believe this happened to us," said Lauren's friend Mimi Golden recently, sighing. They were having a glass of wine at Felice, on Eighty-third Street. Mimi had come from a Botox touch-up, and her forehead was speckled with red dots where the needle had entered. "I don't want to talk about it for one more second. We're decamping for the Hamptons next week. When are you heading out to Fire Island?"

"On Saturday," said Lauren. "Jason's been busy with work, so we haven't had a chance to open the house yet."

"How's everything going with you two?" Mimi asked, staring at Lauren with what Lauren imagined Mimi thought was a "concerned look," but the toxins wouldn't allow for that. Lauren, after three wines and no food at a fundraiser, had mentioned that Jason had been completely ignoring her. Mimi had pressed her about it since.

Lauren looked down at her glass of chardonnay. She strived to project an image of perfection and stylish ease; messiness and vulnerability had always been weaknesses to avoid. But this year had been a doozy, and

15

for the first time in her life, she was struggling to keep up the charade. "Fine, fine. All good." She quickly changed the subject — Mimi was fun, but you couldn't trust her as far as you could throw her. "I'm also done with this year," Lauren continued. "I need to go sit on a beach, read a book, and never hear the word *scammer* again."

She and Jason had discussed pulling Arlo, seven, and Amelie, five, out of Braeburn, but ultimately, the board was able to salvage the school's reputation by stealing the headmaster of Collegiate, Mr. Wolf, a veteran who brought clout and legitimacy. None of the parents cared that tuition was raised to fund Mr. Wolf's wildly high salary. They'd pay anything for this nightmare to end. The Parkers put next year's deposits down at Braeburn for Arlo and Amelie. All was right again on the Upper East Side.

The temperature in the city had started to warm, and the tulips had already bloomed and died on Park Avenue. Lauren couldn't wait to get to their beach house in Salcombe, on Fire Island, which had been sitting empty since last Labor Day. (Salcombe, named after a British seaside town, was pronounced "Saul-com," with a silent *b* and *e*. The townspeople liked how refined it sounded and scoffed when outsiders called

16

it "Sal-com-BE.") The Parkers usually started going for weekends in late April, but because of a glut of birthday parties, plus Jason's packed work schedule, they hadn't yet had a chance. Lauren had a team of cleaners arrive at the house the week before to open it up — get rid of a winter's worth of accumulated dust, make sure the bike tires were filled with air, unpack the multiple deliveries she'd had sent from FreshDirect and Amazon, plus the cheeses, olives, and meats from Agata & Valentina.

Once they went out to the house, they stayed through the summer; Jason used to travel back and forth just for weekends, but the new world order allowed everyone to work remotely, so all the dads were there, too (a development the wives pretended to be thrilled about). The kids attended camp, and Lauren spent her days hanging with girlfriends at the tennis courts and the beach — there was really nothing more to do than that. They also brought their nanny, Silvia, a Filipino woman who had raised three children of her own, to live with them for the summer. During the rest of the year, Silvia worked from 8:00 a.m. to 7:00 p.m., commuting to Manhattan from Queens. Occasionally, Lauren wondered if Silvia, who was just the right combination of self-sufficient and unobtrusive, hated it in Salcombe. But having her there meant Lauren and Jason were free to go out with friends, be on their own schedules, and not have to deal with the hassle of making breakfast, lunch, and dinner for the kids, even on weekends.

In truth, buying a house on Fire Island hadn't been Lauren's choice. It was Jason's thing, this island, this tiny town, Salcombe. His best friend from childhood, Sam Weinstein, had grown up spending his summers in Salcombe, and Jason used to stay at Sam's house for months at a time. He was a built-in playmate for Sam, an only child whose parents were eternally in the midst of contentiously breaking up and getting back together. The boys had a group of Salcombe friends they palled around with, and Sam and Jason continued to use the house long after Sam's parents ended up getting a divorce and buying separate vacation spots in the Hamptons (his dad) and Nantucket (his mom). Sam and Jason spent their teenage summers together in the Salcombe house, working as camp counselors, drinking at the beach at night, sailing and capsizing Sunfish for fun. Lauren had heard *all* about it.

Twenty years later, Sam still had the

house, a blue-shingled stunner that over-looked the Great South Bay and had the best sunset views in town. He and his wife, Jen, and their three kids, Lilly, Ross, and Dara, came out in June and left in September, just like Lauren and Jason. Sam and Jason were still best friends, though Sam lived in Westchester (Scarsdale; full of strivers but the best schools around) and Jason and Lauren were in the city. But Salcombe remained their special place.

When the kids were small, and it became clear that Jason's job was going to earn them some real money, he began talking about finding a spot to buy in Salcombe. Lauren had spent her twenties partying in the Hamptons, and all her friends were starting to settle there, buying beachfront in East Hampton and Amagansett and Sag Harbor. She resisted the idea. Why would she want to be stuck on Fire Island all summer, where she knew no one? They'd had a blowup about it one night after the kids had gone to sleep.

"I feel like you're forcing this on me, and I don't want to do it," Lauren had said to him. This was two apartments ago, in the modest two bedroom they lived in on Eighty-eighth Street and Third Avenue (they'd since upgraded to a four-bedroom

19

on Park).

"Lauren, listen to yourself," said Jason calmly. It always pissed her off when he answered her anger with moderation. "I'm saying we can afford to buy a summer house! My only ask is that it's in the town that I grew up going to. The kids will love it, I'm one hundred percent sure."

"*You* didn't grow up going there," Lauren spat back. "Sam did. You were always just a guest."

"Lauren, the Hamptons are a nightmare. You know that. The crowds, the overpriced restaurants, the traffic to get there. It's like the worst parts of the Upper East Side transported three hours east. Four if you take the LIE."

"Yes, I'm aware of what the Hamptons are; I've been there a million times. I've also spent summers with you and Sam and Jen on Fire Island. I'm bored there! What will I do all day?"

"You'll figure it out," said Jason. "You'll play tennis. You'll make friends. The people who have houses in Salcombe are as rich and powerful as your friends in the Hamptons — they're just not wearing shoes."

Lauren had known she'd lost the argument before it had even started. And she knew she was acting spoiled. But she'd

20

finally found a community in their neighborhood; at that point, Arlo was in kindergarten at Braeburn, and Amelie was at the Brick Church preschool. The thought that all her mom friends would be spending the summer together without her made her anxious and jealous, and she hated that Jason needled her about it. "You need to stop doing things just because everyone else is," he'd say, after she'd insist on going to a certain vacation spot in St. Barts, or hiring the most sought-after tutor, or joining the golf club in Westchester that half of Braeburn belonged to. It's not like Jason was some renegade. He'd grown up on the Upper East Side and had returned to the city after college, he worked in finance, he wore the same Brooks Brothers button-downs that all the other dads did. Where did he get off telling her she was a sheep? Jason had gotten a big bonus that year, and so that had settled the conversation. They'd bought a gorgeous, upside-down modern-style house in Salcombe, right on the ocean. Lauren had pretended to be happy about it. And though she'd never admitted it outwardly, Jason had been right. Now she loved it there.

Fire Island was just a sliver of land off the south shore of Long Island. A barrier island, flanked by the Great South Bay on one side and the Atlantic Ocean on the other, it was approximately thirty miles long — its widest point, which happened to be in Salcombe, was only about half a mile. Small towns dotted the island, the most famous of which were Cherry Grove and the Fire Island Pines. If you weren't from New York and you'd heard of Fire Island, it would have been in this context — as a gay party haven, a wild summer retreat filled with fit homosexual men.

Each community on Fire Island had its own ferry line from the mainland — the only way to get there, as the island didn't allow cars — and its own personality. Ocean Beach was a bustling town with restaurants, bars, and hordes of twentysomethings from the city doing share houses. Point O' Woods was an exclusive hamlet with large homes that passed down through the generations (no Jews allowed). Then there was Salcombe, a tiny family place filled with a mix of Jews, WASPs, and Catholics, with the commonality of success and a studied, lowkey vibe. Like the rest of the island, Salcombe was 99 percent white. (In fact, Lauren could think of only one Black person she'd met in Salcombe, and like her, he'd married into it.)

Salcombe was an incorporated village of

about four hundred houses, some traditional summer cottages dating back to the 1920s and some, like Lauren's, newly built, modern and beachy, with open floor plans and rooftop decks with water views. Everyone knew everyone (and everyone knew everyone's business). There were eighty-year-olds who'd been coming to Salcombe for fifty years, plus their adult children who'd been coming their entire lives, plus their grandchildren who were now the inheritors of the sailing lessons and the day camp. You could see a little face on the playground and know, just from the shape of his nose or the swoop of his hair, that he belonged to the Rapner family or the Metzner family or, God forbid, the evil Longeran clan. The village was made up of a web of connecting boardwalks leading back and forth to the beach and the bay. Everyone rode bikes — rusty, squeaky things — to get where they needed to go. You had no choice. A bike ride from the bay on one side of the island to the beach took less than five minutes. Because there were no cars, just some village pickup trucks to transport packages and tote garbage to the dump, children were set free at an early age. Packs of seven- and eight-year-olds roamed alone, riding bikes to each other's houses or bringing fishing rods to the dock, no parents in sight.

Salcombe had one general store, referred to as "the store," which carried basic groceries and prepared foods, and that charged about double what you'd pay off island. For years, the store held residents hostage to its outrageous prices, but now mainland superstores delivered to the ferry, and so you could stock your house at a reasonable cost, which is what Lauren and her cohort did. There was a connecting liquor store, a closet filled with wine and vodka, basically, for those who hadn't the foresight to bring enough booze from the city. Down Broadway, Salcombe's main boardwalk drag, were a quaint white, wooden town hall and an adjoining library that smelled of oak and dust and was filled with well-worn summer reads and children's books from the '70s and '80s. A little farther toward the beach was one baseball field, which hosted an avid adult softball league on the weekends and was the scene of the kids' camp during the week. A small playground sat next to the field, home to a rickety jungle gym, likely not up to current safety standards, and a swing set that croaked with every push.

The only other communal area in town, really *the* communal area, was the Salcombe Yacht Club, which sat on the bay, right near the ferry dock. "Yacht club" was truly a stretch. It consisted of a small marina, with about twenty spaces to dock sailboats and motorboats, plus a petite beach area for kayaks and Hobie Cats. The main yacht club building, on the other side of the boardwalk, looked somewhat like a large beach house and had two interior rooms: a restaurant set up with a bar in front, and a bigger, open area in back with a little stage, a pool table, and space enough for toddlers to run around while their parents ate dinner. There was also an outer deck that overlooked the bay, perfect for sunset drinks. Five tennis courts appeared around back, all clay, four smooshed together in stacked pairs and one outlier closer to the club. All in all, it was an unimpressive affair, as these things go, but it fit with the shabby chicness of Salcombe just fine. Crowds gathered there every night for drinks and dinner, and every day for tennis and gossip. And Lauren felt good telling her friends in the city that she hung out at a "yacht club" all summer. Let them think what they wanted to.

It was now late June, and she was finally sitting on a painted blue bench on the top of the Fire Island Queen ferry, headed for Salcombe. She'd spent the previous week in the city dealing with the kids' graduations, getting a haircut at Sally Hershberger, getting a wax, getting her nails done, and seeing friends for "until September" drinks. The sun was shining on the Great South Bay, and the black-and-white Fire Island Lighthouse stood in the distance, welcoming the Parkers back to their summer home. Arlo was next to Lauren, messing with his iPad, and Amelie and Jason were sitting behind them. Amelie had spotted one of her little friends, Myrna, and had insisted they sit together. Lauren could hear Myrna and Amelie having a five-year-olds' chat, talking about the names of their teachers and discussing their favorite kinds of animals.

Lauren closed her eyes behind her Tom Ford sunglasses. She felt the breeze ruffle her newly shorn, newly highlighted blond bob. She heard Jason say hi to Brian Metzner, Myrna's dad, and Brian slide into the seat next to Jason.

"Hey, dude, how are you?" Brian asked, clapping Jason's back in greeting.

"Not bad," Jason said. "How was your winter? You guys make it out to Aspen this year?"

Brian was a hulking guy. His checked button-downs strained at his stomach, and he'd shaved his head when he'd started to bald in his twenties. He was a hedge funder, a very successful one, and whatever he spoke about, no matter the subject, he framed in financial terms.

"Oh, man, yeah, we killed it in Aspen," Brian said. "At first, I thought we'd only have marginal success, with Myrna especially, but then we got her to level up and get her game on. By the end of the trip, she was racing down black diamonds. Her execution was high, dude."

"That's awesome," said Jason flatly. Lauren could tell he was dreading the boat-ride-long conversation. Jason and Sam tolerated Brian, but they didn't like him. She wondered where Brian's wife, Lisa, was. Lauren and Lisa were friends — they all lived on the Upper East Side — but their kids went to a different school (Horace Mann, all the way up in the Bronx), and so they mainly communicated over text during the winter, exchanging occasional gossipy tidbits and DM'ing each other Instagram posts in which mutual acquaintances looked fat or old. Lisa was "studying" to be a life coach, the trendy new career of choice for bored stay-at-home moms who may have once chosen to become interior decorators or handbag designers. Lauren thought it was ridiculous — what advice could Lisa give?

Marry rich? Lauren took her AirPods out of her Celine bag. She'd listen to a true-crime podcast and tune out Brian and Jason. Before she had the chance, she felt a tap on her shoulder.

"Lauren, oh my God, hi! I love your hair!"

Standing to her right was Rachel Woolf, a longtime Salcombe resident who'd be-friended Lauren, by force, when Lauren had first arrived. Rachel's family owned a house right by the yacht club, and she'd inherited it when her mom died a few summers ago (her dad had died in a car accident when she was barely a teen). In a town of gossips, Rachel was the reigning queen, and you couldn't do anything — from having an af-fair to having a new tennis partner — without her knowing about it. Rachel was forty-two and still single, unhappily, though she'd dated about half of Salcombe in her youth. Lauren suspected she'd even slept with Jason at some point, but if that was the case, Lauren didn't want to know.

Rachel was thin, almost too thin, with brown straight hair and buggy blue eyes. Some men thought she was attractive, perhaps in a puppy dog kind of way, but Lauren didn't see it. Even if Lauren hadn't wanted to be friends with Rachel, which often she didn't, she was an impossible person to avoid. Rachel went to every party, hosting many, and you had to stay on her good side if you wanted to have any Salcombe social life whatsoever. Lauren patted the seat next to her, motioning for Rachel to sit down.

"How was your winter?" Lauren asked as Rachel settled in, pushing her L.L.Bean monogrammed tote under the seat. Rachel was embarrassingly unfashionable. "Have you been coming out here a lot?"

Though nearly all Salcombe's summer residents lived in the city, they rarely saw each other outside its confines. The relationships were very much June through September, and the townspeople kept it that way through an unspoken pact. Rachel lived about ten blocks from Lauren and Jason in Manhattan, but Lauren never socialized with her there. Their friendship existed in this very specific bubble.

"Good! I mean, fine. I was dating this guy for about six months. Divorced, lawyer, two kids. But we broke up last month. He didn't want to get married again and, well, you know how I feel about that," said Rachel.

Lauren did.

"How about you?" Rachel continued. "I read that stuff in *New York* magazine about your kids' school. Sounds like a nightmare."

29

Lauren cringed at the thought that Braeburn's stain had even reached childless Rachel Woolf.

"It was," said Lauren. "Thankfully it's behind us now. We have a new headmaster, Mr. Wolf, and the school is now in good — heavily vetted — hands."

The boat was chugging along, cutting through the water at a clip. The ferry ride took about twenty minutes from Bay Shore, on Long Island, to Salcombe, just the right amount of time to switch your mind from city to beach mode. Brian was still rattling about his family ski trip, and Lauren looked back to check on Amelie, content to stay silent as Myrna pattered on about nothing. Like father, like daughter.

Rachel was checking her phone; Lauren thought she caught sight of a dating app — men's smiling faces — before she quickly put it down.

"Have you been playing much tennis?" Rachel asked. Rachel was seriously competitive about tennis, though she wasn't very good, and always wanted to know who'd been practicing over the winter and how much. The yacht club held annual doubles tournaments for its members, and Rachel was determined each year to win. She and her partner, Emily Grobel, generally made it to the semifinals or finals before being knocked out by one of the stronger teams. Lauren wasn't an amazing player, but she wasn't terrible. She'd been on her high school team and had a decent backhand and a terrific lob. Rachel, who played all year round, resented that Lauren could pick up a racket after months and easily play at her level.

"Not really," said Lauren, truthfully. This year she'd gotten really into the Tracy Anderson Method. She'd had to schlep all the way down to a studio in midtown for it, so hadn't had the time to join her usual league at Roosevelt Island. "But I'm planning to take a few lessons this week to get back into it."

"There's a new pro at the club," said Rachel. "I took a lesson with him last weekend. His name is Robert, and he is totally hot."

"Who's hot?" Brian leaned over, having heard them during a brief pause in his own monologue.

"You, Brian, of course," said Rachel, giggling. All the wives hated how much Rachel flirted with their husbands, but no one said it out loud.

"Yeah, I've been working out, maximizing body profits, investing in myself," he said.

Lauren couldn't tell if he'd realized Rachel was kidding. Brian turned back to Jason, launching into another earful about his Peloton obsession.

"The pro was at some fancy country club in Florida before this. I'm not totally sure what he's doing up here now, but he's definitely going to be a favorite with the women," said Rachel. "Plus, he already helped fix my janky serve." Rachel was known for her janky, loopy serve.

"Looking forward to meeting him," said Lauren, bored of the conversation. Why was Rachel annoying her so much? She was in for a long summer if she couldn't even stomach a boat ride with her. Rachel sensed Lauren's disinterest, so she dropped a nugget of gossip to lure Lauren back in.

"Did you hear about the Obermans?" Rachel bent closer to Lauren, lowering her voice.

Lauren shook her head.

"They're splitting up. Apparently, Jeanette caught Greg having an affair with their dog walker."

"Their dog walker? How weird," said Lauren.

"She's also an aspiring actress, I think," said Rachel. "Anyway, Jeanette will be out here with the kids, but Greg is spending the summer in exile. He's trying to work it out, but Jeanette wants nothing to do with him." Lauren had always thought Jeanette and Greg hated each other. She must have been right.

The boat lurched, pulling into the dock in Salcombe. It jutted out from the bay, one hundred yards long, crafted from the same boardwalk that laced the town. Lines of old-fashioned wagons were locked up near the end of the dock, waiting for owners to pile them with the summer's goods. Lauren felt relief. She'd made it.

She took Arlo's iPad from him ("Mom! I wasn't done!"). Jason helped gather Amelie and the rest of the bags. The view from the top of the boat encompassed the entire shoreline of Salcombe, including the bay-beach area — a square of sand and a life-guard chair, perfect for little kids to search for crabs and take seaweed-y swimming lessons — plus the yacht club and surrounding bayfront homes. People were pulling wagons and riding their bikes, and a small crowd had gathered to greet the arrivals. It could have been 1960 or 1990 or 2022. That's what Jason said he liked best about the island, that sense of timelessness, that nothing had changed, that the modern world didn't exist. Lauren was fine with this so long as they had fast internet and good satellite TV.

"I'm going to have some people over for drinks tonight," said Rachel as they disembarked. "Are you guys free?"

"Sure," said Lauren. "Sounds great." Why not just rip off the Salcombe Band-Aid on their first night? Silvia was coming on the next boat, and Lauren would have to get it over with at some point. As they stepped off onto the dock, Rachel forcefully tugged Lauren's arm.

"Look! There's the pro, Robert," she whispered into Lauren's ear, too loudly to not be overheard. Rachel physically turned Lauren's head toward a man standing in front of them, carrying two tote bags filled with groceries and wearing a white polo shirt and khaki shorts. Lauren could only see his back. He was about Jason's height, maybe six foot two, with light brown, close-cropped hair. He walked like an athlete, fully in control of his body. Lauren noticed how nicely tanned his legs were. Someone called his name to say hello — Lauren couldn't see who — and he turned to look for who was greeting him. Instead, he made eye contact with Lauren, meeting her gaze with deep blue eyes, a straight nose, and a smile of perfectly white teeth. She looked away immediately, pretending to be searching for something in her bag, and he walked on down the dock toward the yacht club.

"See, I told you he was hot," said Rachel with a giggle. "He's coming tonight to my house for drinks — we can flirt with him there." Lauren felt her cheeks flush. She rolled her eyes playfully at Rachel and started to think about what she was going to wear.

2
ROBERT HEYWORTH

Robert Heyworth was not as rich as he looked. He'd grown up in Tampa, the third in a family of three boys, all super athletic. His oldest brother, Mack, played baseball, making it to the minors, and his middle brother, Charlie, ran track for the University of Florida. Mack was now a contractor, married with two little girls, and Charlie was a mortgage broker, married with a son and a baby girl on the way. They all still lived in Tampa, near his mom, a retired schoolteacher. Their father, handsome in his youth like his sons, had been a cop. The boys were all gorgeous — tall, lanky, their eyes sparkling.

Robert's thing was tennis, always had been. There were public courts down the road from his house, a tidy, squat, white ranch with palm trees out front, and he'd walk over every day and hit with whomever was there. When he was nine, a coach teaching a local rich kid noticed Robert had talent and had recruited him into a program that met daily after school. He'd given Robert's parents a discount, a big one, and from there, Robert was absorbed into the tennis circuit, competing in USTA tournaments around the state, his mom toting him to and fro. All his friends had been tennis friends, and his girlfriends in high school were tennis girlfriends. It was basically all he thought about aside from schoolwork, occasionally, and sex, constantly. At his peak, when he was seventeen, he was ranked third in Florida in his age group. Good, yes, but not enough to go pro. Oddly, Robert had been sanguine about this. He'd heard too many stories at that point about ATP journeymen, paying their way to lose in tournaments around the world, to not want that kind of life. He'd always seen tennis as a means to an end, a way to get out of his middle-class life. He thought his brothers were stupid for choosing track and baseball (he thought they were stupid for other reasons, too); people who played tennis had *money.* He'd had no interest in being a cop like his dad. He loved his parents but felt superior to his family. He was so good-looking, so talented in his sport, he walked with such grace for a teenage boy. He felt he was destined for better things.

But when he'd graduated from Stanford, fresh from his full-ride scholarship, and his mixed record playing as number five singles, and his recent breakup with Julie Depfee, whose connections Robert had been banking on, he'd been at a loss. What now? He didn't know anything other than tennis. He'd met friends' fathers along the way, powerful guys in their industries who might be willing to get Robert an entry-level gig if he'd asked. Otherwise, his major, history, was a joke in terms of anything lucrative. He'd thought Stanford was going to be his golden ticket, but he hadn't capitalized on it soon enough; he'd been head down, playing tennis, tennis, tennis. And then it was over. He was just as dumb as his brothers were, apparently. This thought caused Robert physical pain.

He'd met Julie when they were sophomores, and they'd dated for two years, during which Robert had been exposed to the kind of wealth that they don't tell you about when you can't afford to go anywhere on vacation other than Disney World. Julie's father was a venture capital guy who'd gotten in early at PayPal, LinkedIn, Yelp, and Uber, among others. They owned homes in Atherton and the Hamptons and Sun Valley, and apartments in London and Paris. They flew private. They had a staff. Julie was beautiful, blond, willowy. Robert had never had a problem getting girls — they flocked to him. Men, too. It wasn't just about his face and body. He was cheerful and easy, and he knew how to look at people, really *look* at them, in a way that made them melt. But even he was surprised that Julie made it her mission to lock him down, to make sure he was hers. She was out of everyone's league.

They'd met at a house party, one of the rare ones Robert had attended — he couldn't drink during the tennis season, so going out was pointless. But he'd been dragged there by his roommate, Todd, who promised he'd get to meet the rarefied crowd there, the rich kids (Stanford was filled with rich kids, but these were the *rich* kids). Julie was there with her group of lackeys, carbon copies but not quite as pretty as she, and when they'd started to talk, or, rather, she'd started to talk, Robert had immediately fallen for her magic. They'd slept together that night, in her room in an off-campus house that was leagues nicer than Robert's childhood home. They were inseparable after. Julie attended all of Robert's matches, and he accompanied her home for holidays and long weekends. During the summer, they'd lived at her parents' house in the Hamptons, loafing about, hanging at the pool, and eating out on her dad's credit card until Robert had to go back to California to start early practice.

Robert had thought that maybe they'd get married. He'd known it was a silly idea — they were only twenty-one. But he loved being with her, and more importantly, he loved her life. It was so easy. He fit in with her friends and family. Most of them didn't know he didn't come from money. He was a handsome tennis player at Stanford; people assumed what they wanted to. And Julie had liked that he was middle-class. It was *interesting* to her. Though they never went to visit his family. He wouldn't have her to that ranch house, no way. It was all too embarrassing.

By the end of senior year, when their friends had either secured first-year banking jobs, been accepted to law or med school, or been recruited by Google or Apple, it occurred to Robert that he should've thought of his career beyond tennis. Julie had plans to move to New York and intern at an art gallery, the owner of which was a friend of her mom's. She thought maybe her dad could help Robert get a job at a boutique finance firm, doing something or other, even though Robert was wholly unqualified for any such position.

"We can live together in my parents' apartment for the first year," Julie had said. They were eating sushi at a nice Japanese place off campus. As usual, Julie was footing the bill. Robert had just had a tense conversation with his dad, who'd warned him of relying too much on his "rich girlfriend." He'd hung up with a bad feeling in his stomach. He knew, to a certain extent, that his dad was right. But he didn't know how to act otherwise.

"I'm not sure," Robert said, eyeing Julie as she stuck an entire piece of spicy tuna in her delicate mouth. "John Badner is moving to LA for the year to teach tennis at a club. He told me he could get me a job there if I wanted to. Apparently, there are lots of celebrities there. He said he was already booked to give Ashton Kutcher a lesson."

Julie stared at him, a piece of salmon paused in midair.

"Ashton Kutcher? Ew. Why would you do that? Why don't you come to New York with me and get a real job?"

"That is a real job," Robert said defensively. "Maybe I don't need your dad's help." He didn't even know why he'd said it

41

— he didn't feel that way, did he? But once he'd spoken the words, it was too late to back down.

They'd left the dinner unhappily, not holding hands on the walk back to Julie's off-campus home. Something had opened up between them that Robert was pretty sure would never go back.

He thought about that conversation as he sat atop the ferry to Salcombe, the sleepy beach town on Fire Island where he was working this summer. It was eleven years ago that he'd split from Julie, following John Badner to Los Angeles to work as a pro at the Brentwood Country Club. He'd stayed in LA for eight years, his clientele a regular rotation of actors, directors, and big-time agents. It was good money, pretty great money from where he came from, a couple of hundred thousand a year. His parents had never made that much combined. And he'd topped it off teaching private lessons to the celebrities' spawn, bratty kids who couldn't hit a forehand to save their lives, playing on gorgeous private courts. The women in LA were beautiful and available, and he'd spent his twenties sleeping with a lot of them. They were grown daughters of his clients, or aspiring actresses who were working as waitstaff, or well-kept women in their thirties who played doubles, whose older husbands ignored them.

He'd lived in a little bungalow with John in the hills, and they were either working or partying. Occasionally, Robert would be struck with the anxiety that he wasn't "living up to his potential," as his mom put it. He'd miss Julie and her fancy life in New York among the art snobs and finance bros. He didn't want to be a tennis pro for the rest of his life, did he?

Then when he was twenty-nine, his dad got sick. Stage 4 lung cancer from smoking Marlboro Reds for his whole goddamn life. Everything started to feel less fun. LA was too competitive, there was too much traffic. He'd been at Brentwood for nearly a decade, but there was nowhere to go from there — he'd basically topped out on the scene, unless he wanted to become the head pro and deal with all the administrative stuff, which he didn't.

So, at his mom's urging, and against his better judgment, he quit abruptly and moved back to Florida. His clients were devastated; they'd all begged him to stay, to put extra money in his pocket to keep teaching them how to serve and volley, master their one-handed backhands. But Robert had gone home. His dad died weeks later, quickly, so quickly, and so he'd stayed with his mom at their ranch, helping her clean and mourn.

After a few months, he'd gotten bored. This life was not for him. He was used to being surrounded by good-looking, wealthy people, and Tampa was filled with losers. His oldest brother, Mack, offered him a job at his contracting company, an office gig filing paperwork and dealing with complicated and often shady permit situations. His mom asked him to take it, to find a little place nearby and build a life there with them. He'd turned thirty; he needed to settle down, find a wife, have a baby. He'd gone to Stanford, for fuck's sake. This was all wrong.

But Robert had tried it, he really had. Mostly because he hadn't felt he had better options. He'd gotten up every day and gone into Mack's office, he'd filed papers, he'd answered the phone, he'd sent emails. He'd rented an apartment in a condo complex ten minutes from his childhood home. He couldn't stand it. He missed tennis, he missed chatting with important, powerful people, he missed the looks he got from all those women.

Robert had stuck it out for two long, depressing years. At thirty-two, he had a breakdown. He'd invested some money, basically all his savings from Brentwood, in a company his friend Todd Anderson from Stanford had recommended, some start-up that sold life insurance to millennials. "The Warby Parker of insurance," Todd had assured him. Todd lived in San Francisco and worked at Facebook. Todd had lots of money to waste. The company, called Lyfe, tanked. It turned out the CEO was using the capital he'd raised to fund his very expensive OnlyFans addiction, in which he paid women wild sums to verbally abuse him. Robert had lost everything. He had nothing to show for those years of work, just his biweekly salary from Mack, hitting his bank account with a small thud, saving him from eviction. His mom offered to loan him some money, but the idea made him want to kill himself. Instead, he ran his credit cards to their limits paying his monthly bills, then told her and Mack that he was quitting his job at the contracting company and going back to being a tennis pro. He didn't belong there.

He'd quickly found a job at the Boca Country Club in Boca Raton. It wasn't as flashy as Brentwood — more old wealthy macher than young Hollywood player. He'd stayed for a year and a half, living in a room on the grounds — it was a Waldorf Astoria property, and the staff were put up in the fancy digs. Robert had finally felt like himself again. He'd started sleeping with one of the waitresses, Taylor, who was putting herself through law school. She was superhot and *very* adventurous in bed. But a better life was always on the horizon. Every now and then, he thought of Julie, who was married to some hedge fund guy, splitting her time between her town house next to Sarah Jessica Parker's in the West Village and an estate next to Tory Burch's in Southampton.

He'd gotten hooked up with a new client named Morty Friedman, a retired investment banker who'd made a bunch of money in the '80s. Morty was a terrible tennis player, he could barely hit the ball, but he loved the game and booked time with Robert nearly every day. They'd struck up a casual friendship, and Morty took a fatherly interest in Robert, giving him unasked-for life advice during water breaks.

"You've got to get to the East Coast, son, if you want to go anywhere in life. You'll meet connected people there, find something exciting in the city. You went to Stanford! You're talented, handsome, smart. Florida is a wasteland. I'll help you find something up there you can use as a launching pad."

Robert had nodded along politely. Everyone always promised him things, but few, he'd learned, truly delivered.

But true to his word, two weeks later, before the start of a particularly pointless backhand lesson, Morty came to him with an idea.

"Have you ever heard of Fire Island?" Morty asked. He had curly salt-and-pepper hair and wire-rim glasses over big brown eyes.

"I think so — it's the gay island," said Robert.

"No, no," said Morty. "Well, it does have a couple of gay towns. But mostly it's just families from the city. Hamptons-y people, but quirkier. There's a village there, Salcombe, that one of my former partners has a house in. He told me they're looking for someone to run the tennis program at their little yacht club. It's nothing fancy, but the community there is intense, obsessed with tennis, and they're willing to pay someone a lot to come in and revamp their system. I think around a hundred K for the summer, plus a percentage of any private lessons." A hundred thousand dollars for three months of work? He'd be able to pay off his debts and then some. It sounded good to Robert. Too good.

"What's the catch?" he asked Morty.

"Got me," he said. "My former partner, Larry Higgins, is a nice guy. His whole family has been going out there for decades. I think they had some issue with the last tennis pro — he was a drunk or something. Anyway, I'll put you in touch with Larry, yes?"

Robert nodded. "Come on, old man, let's go hit some balls," he'd said, heading out to the court, the Florida sun beating mercilessly on his exposed neck.

He'd gotten the job. He always got the job. Taylor had wanted to come with him, but he'd broken it off before he moved. He needed a fresh start in New York, and he wasn't going to take a girlfriend — a *waitress* — with him to live in this beach town for the summer. The yacht club was putting him up in a small house near the town playground, a shabby two-bedroom bungalow with ants in the kitchen and a ceiling fan that rattled the whole place. The tennis pros lived there every year, and there were still remnants of the last occupant, Dave, the former pro whose drinking problem had lost him this cushy position. Robert had found a yellow-striped beach towel, a pair

48

of Nike shorts, and an old bottle of gin under the sink.

Larry Higgins, Morty's former partner who headed up the Salcombe Yacht Club Tennis Committee — apparently a vaunted position within the town's hierarchy — told Robert that Dave had been caught drinking vodka out of his water bottle during a group clinic for seniors. Someone unnamed, possibly with a vendetta, had snitched on him to Susan Steinhagen, the woman who oversaw the tennis program for the members.

"You should have seen how livid Susan was," said Larry, who'd found Robert on the top of the ferry. Robert had been in Salcombe for a week and had gone off island to buy some groceries in Bay Shore. The ones in "the store," as the villagers called it, were so overpriced it took Robert's breath away. Ten dollars for a pint of milk?

"Her head nearly exploded. She screamed at him in front of everyone at the mixed doubles tournament. Huge town drama," Larry continued. Larry had a reedy build, with thick, white, expressive eyebrows that reminded Robert of poplar fluff. He'd been the one to hire Robert, and for that, Robert liked him very much. Dave had been asked to leave immediately, Larry said, with Susan publicly dragging him out like a hardened criminal.

Robert had met Susan this week; she'd stopped by the courts to introduce herself and to discuss the upcoming round robin tournament. She was in her seventies, he guessed, a former accounting professor who now put all her kinetic energy into making sure that Salcombe's tennis programs ran smoothly (also making sure everyone knew who was in charge). She was tiny, maybe five foot two, with papery skin and a beak nose. Her voice boomed louder than any-one's Robert had ever encountered. Robert was slightly scared of her. This story about Dave solidified his fear.

"Poor guy," said Robert. He knew of a few tennis pros who'd become alcoholics. It was a tough career, generally filled with people who had dashed tennis dreams, and Robert felt bad for this Dave character.

"There was also a rumor that he'd been stealing from the club," said Larry. "But that was never confirmed. I think Susan had her suspicions but couldn't find anything concrete, and so she used the drinking thing as an excuse to get him out."

This piece of information was interesting to Robert, and he wanted to keep asking Larry questions. But he was distracted by a pair of women sitting to his left, a brunette, whose name was Rachel Woolf, and a blonde, probably in her midthirties. Rachel, whom he'd given a lesson to this week, was a bit of a mess, but Robert liked the look of the blonde, with her sharp bob and toned shoulders. She was clearly the mom of the boy sitting next to her, maybe of one of the little girls sitting behind her, too. Something about her reminded Robert of Julie. A poise, he thought, the air of someone who knew she deserved everything. Rachel had invited Robert to her house that evening for a drinks thing, and he'd tentatively accepted, though he'd been tempted to cancel. Was it smart for him to be socializing with clients before he'd even started the job? This opportunity had potential to set him up for bigger things. It was his last shot; he couldn't fuck it up. But maybe he'd go for one beer. It was part of the role to fit in with the crowd and encourage them to play. And perhaps the blonde would be there.

The boat docked, and Robert shook Larry's hand, promising to meet him at the yacht club later that week for a welcome drink. As Robert disembarked, he heard someone calling his name. He looked around to see who it was. Instead, he locked eyes with the blonde, and he liked her even better from the front. She blushed. Robert felt his familiar power. He'd see her later that night.

52

3
RACHEL WOOLF

Rachel Woolf knew how to get people drunk. Entertaining was her specialty, something she enjoyed doing and was actually good at. She wasn't good at much. She'd done so-so in college (Middlebury; her family had used connections to get her in, as her SAT scores surely hadn't). Then she'd bounced around afterward from marketing job to marketing job, never truly finding her path. She was currently stuck in middle management, while most of her friends were VPs, or SVPs, or even EVPs, if they were lucky. Or smarter than Rachel.

She wasn't great at finding boyfriends, either. She'd lived with someone once, Benji Malin, in a small apartment in Murray Hill. That was when she was twenty-eight to thirty-one, during that prime time when her social circle was getting married. But Benji had broken it off when she insisted they get engaged. She'd been aimlessly dating since, a couple of six-month-long boyfriends followed by breakups when they couldn't (or, rather, wouldn't) commit. She'd tried everything — setups, apps, a matchmaker that cost way too much money and who connected her with only one guy, a grumpy ad exec who was five foot four. Now, at forty-two, she was only finding men who'd been divorced, twice, had custody issues, and/or were impotent. Thank God for Viagra.

So, here she was — middle-aged, single, childless, still living in Manhattan in a one-bedroom apartment while all her friends had moved to the suburbs with their families long ago. But at least she had her house on Fire Island, in Salcombe, the small town in which she'd grown up spending summers, causing trouble with her three sisters. She had a life there. She was someone there. No one in Salcombe knew how sad her existence really was. She always had a story about so-and-so, whom she'd just been dating, or such-and-such job, which was just around the corner. She had tons of friends, way more than she had in the city, and she looked forward to the summer each year like a kid counting down till Christmas. On Labor Day, she spiraled into a depression that didn't end until the next Memorial Day.

And then there was tennis. Rachel loved playing — she was on the courts at least three days a week, more in the summer. She enjoyed everything about the game — the cute outfits, the exercise, the winning (she hated losing). She and her doubles partner, Emily Grobel, often made it to a late round of the women's doubles tournament in August, and Rachel was hoping that this would be their year. She'd heard Cici Maclean had a wrist injury, that Lauren Parker hadn't picked up a racket all winter, and that Vicky Mulder had to collect her daughter at sleepaway camp the weekend of the tournament. So that gave Rachel and Emily a shot of going far, maybe even winning it all. She was supremely dedicated to making this happen. She'd already had one lesson with the new pro, Robert, and he was talented. He'd worked on her serve, which was admittedly weird, and she could tell his tweaks were making a difference. Plus, he was extremely handsome and charming. He made her feel like a star.

She thought about this while she set up her house for drinks later that night. She'd invited four couples, plus Robert, over for watermelon margaritas (a recipe from the *New York Times* cooking section) and appetizers. As a festive twist, she'd decided to have Micah Holt bartend for the evening, even though she didn't really need the help. Micah was the gay, college-age son of Judy and Eric Holt, who lived on Navy Walk. He worked as a bartender at the yacht club, and Rachel had known him since he was a baby. He probably would have done it for free — Micah always added to the fun and made the adults feel cooler just by gracing them with his stylish, upbeat presence. Rachel was giving him a hundred dollars to hang, keep everyone's glasses filled, and help her tidy up afterward.

The party was called for 6:00 p.m., but she assumed people would come at more like 6:30. At 5:45, Micah arrived, looking very Timothée Chalamet in fitted white jeans and an electric-blue sweater. Rachel thought back to when she was in Middlebury, the guys in baggy khakis and roll-necks doing keg stands. Boys nowadays were a different species.

"Hi, Rachel. Thanks for having me! I got Willa to fill in for me at the club, so I'm all yours. Let me know how I can help with the setup," said Micah, smiling amiably.

Rachel didn't have much left to do, so she sent him off to the kitchen, instructing him to create a makeshift bar on her porch with whatever nice-looking booze and stemware he could find. She went into her bedroom to finish getting ready, studying her face critically as she applied a final brush of bronzer, angling it up her cheekbones as she'd been taught by a Trish McEvoy makeup artist at Saks.

She found Micah perched on a wicker chair on her porch, having artfully arranged her alcohol on a small foldout table pushed off to the side of the room. He stood as she entered.

"How's that? Need me to do anything with the food?"

"Looks great, thanks," said Rachel. "How's school going?"

Micah was only twenty, but he struck Rachel as older than his age. Growing up, he liked to hover near the adults, listening to their conversations and occasionally piping in with an adorable aside. Rachel had always suspected he was gay. He was too beautiful and clever not to be. When he came out in high school, and Judy and Eric began quietly telling their friends in Salcombe, no one seemed to care (people *did* care when he got accepted to Yale; an Ivy League education was more important, to Salcombe residents, than one's sexual orientation).

"All good," said Micah, hooking his

thumbs in his pockets. "I'm an English major like everyone else. I'm going abroad this year to Madrid. I can't wait. Otherwise, happy to be out here bartending. I suppose I should have gotten an internship this summer, but I'm genuinely not feeling stressed about it all. I'm trying to enjoy the moment, you know?" Rachel didn't know, and it made her feel old.

At 6:30 on the dot, the first of her guests arrived. It was Sam and Jen Weinstein. Rachel had known Sam forever; he'd also grown up coming out to Salcombe. He was younger than she was, forty to her forty-two, but they'd hung in the same circles. Which meant that she'd dated him long ago, when she was twenty-one and he was nineteen. Sam had been a counselor at the day camp, and Rachel was working at the yacht club, waiting tables and helping with events. By that point, Sam's parents were divorced, and he and Jason Parker stayed alone in his bayfront home. They all played adults together, drinking wine with dinner and doing laundry loads of sheets and beach towels. Sam had been having some anxiety in the wake of his parents' battle, and Rachel helped him through it. She'd been proud of that. At the end of the summer, she'd floated the idea that she and Sam stay together — he was back to Dartmouth in the fall, and she was returning for her senior year at Middlebury. But he politely rejected her offer, citing the need for freedom at college. Rachel had been devastated but played it cool. That was her thing, even then.

The following year, the summer after Rachel graduated, she'd attempted to get back together with him. He was older and broader; another year away from home had made him even more appealing to her. He was in Salcombe for a week before his law firm internship started, and they were at a party at their friend Ben Connolly's house. She'd followed him upstairs when he went to the bathroom and pushed him against the hallway wall when he came out. He turned his head when she tried to kiss him.

"I'm sorry, but no," he'd said. "I do like you as a friend, though." Her face stung with embarrassment, and she'd slunk home without saying goodbye to anyone. She still felt the shame of it every time she saw him, the press of her lips on his hair instead of his mouth.

"Sam, Jen, hi!" Rachel said, welcoming them in. Sam was still so handsome; he had curly, thick, prematurely graying hair and wore trendy black plastic glasses. He was in a breezy white linen shirt and was somehow already tan, even though it wasn't even July. Jen handed Rachel a bottle of expensive-looking sauvignon blanc, which she passed along to Micah, who stuck it in an ice bucket on the bar. Sam gave Micah a bro-y hand clap, and Jen went over and gave his shoulder a squeeze. He retreated to the kitchen.

"It's great to see you again," Jen said as she embraced Rachel in a small, awkward hug. "I hope you had a wonderful winter. I'm so glad to be out here."

It was impossible to hate Jen, even though Rachel surely tried. She was so *good.* Pretty, with shoulder-length brown hair, large hazel eyes, and porcelain-smooth white skin, Jen was also annoyingly kind to everyone. She was a psychologist, with a private practice she ran out of their large home in Westchester, treating wealthy disgruntled housewives. Sam and Jen were a golden couple in Salcombe, beloved by the whole town. Even their three little kids were beautiful and well-mannered. At least Rachel was a better tennis player than Jen, who'd only taken up the game recently. This gave Rachel some comfort. Also, she'd fucked Jen's husband first.

"I know, I'm so excited for summer," said Rachel. "Have you been playing much tennis this year?"

"I actually have," said Jen. She was wearing an elegant white shirtdress and had accessorized with a simple gold chain necklace. She was always so put together. Rachel felt dumpy and childlike in comparison in her floral smocked J.Crew number. "I took on fewer clients this year, and we joined a country club — I know, gross, but it was really for the kids. But it meant that I was able to play tennis almost every day. Maybe you'll take pity and invite me to an A-level game one of these days," she said. Rachel inwardly seethed.

"Yes, for sure," said Rachel. "Emily and I are always looking for games. You could partner with Lauren? She told me she's rusty, so maybe it'll be a nice warm-up game for everyone."

Micah brought over a whiskey for Sam and a white wine for Jen. Rachel's house was small and bare-bones compared to her friends', but she had a nice open front parlor area with a screened-in porch on which guests could chat and lounge. And she always had colorful specialty drinks on hand, as well as ample food for snacking. The key to a good party, she knew, was to keep people's glasses full without them even knowing they'd finished the last drink.

That's when things got interesting.

The rest of the guests arrived couple by couple. After the Weinsteins came the Metzners (Brian and Lisa), then the Grobels (Emily and Paul), and finally the Parkers (Jason and Lauren). By 8:00 p.m., everyone had eaten some kebabs and had at least two drinks. Brian was holding court, his Lacoste polo ringed in underarm sweat.

"So, I told him, 'You know who's the boss? It's not you, it's *me,*'" he boomed. Rachel caught Sam and Jason giving each other an eye roll. Paul Grobel was staring off into the distance; maybe he was already drunk. Lauren, dressed in a gorgeous deep-green silk camisole, was off in a corner chatting with Emily and Jen. Rachel thought Lauren looked particularly pretty that night. She felt the constant urge to please and amuse Lauren, even though she could be cruel. She reminded Rachel of the popular girls in high school who'd ignored her. Rachel's screen door squeaked open, and Robert walked in, wearing a light blue button-down and khaki shorts, the color of his shirt bringing out his eyes. Everyone turned to look. Rachel felt a jolt of excitement run through the little familiar group. She immediately went to greet him.

"Robert! You made it! Come in, come in.

Let me get you a drink and introduce you to everyone." He was wearing a cologne — musky, not too heavy, just the right amount — that reminded Rachel of her dad, who'd died nearly thirty years ago. She took his arm as she led him to Micah, manning the bar, hoping no one saw that her eyes suddenly, to her surprise, had filled with tears.

"Thanks so much for having me," Robert said. "It's been a great week meeting so many people." Micah, as captivated as the rest of the group, handed Robert a sugary watermelon margarita, which he politely took a sip of, stifling a small grimace. "It's been interesting coming into a community where I know absolutely no one. But everyone has been really welcoming. And there are some great players here!" Rachel hoped he was referring to her.

Rachel led Robert to the group of men. "Robert, this is Jason, Brian, Sam, and Paul. They're like the Goodfellas of Salcombe. Though not criminals. I think," said Rachel. No one laughed.

"Nice to meet you, Robert," said Jason, extending his hand. Jason was tall, about Robert's height, with black hair and eyes, full lips, and a look of engaged intensity. "Can't wait to get to know you. My wife, Lauren" — he gestured to the women, who were staring at them silently — "is the tennis player of the family. But I occasionally get out on the court." Rachel saw Lauren perk up at the mention of her name, rolling her bare shoulders back and standing up straighter.

Robert chatted with the guys for a while, each one going through his name and tennis level (Sam was the best, Jason was scrappy, Brian thought he was great but was barely good, Paul only played softball). They all showed off, one-upping each other with cringey jokes, even Sam, who was normally the center of attention. Jason asked Robert some questions about his background (everyone was impressed by his childhood ranking and playing at Stanford) and how he'd come to Salcombe. Robert explained the Morty-Larry connection, and that he'd been vetted by the Salcombe Yacht Club Tennis Committee, and everyone groaned at the mention of Susan Steinhagen.

"Susan used to scream at us when we were kids," said Sam. "If we were riding our bikes too fast, or jumping off the lifeguard stand after hours, or drinking at the yacht club when we were teenagers. She was always just . . . there. Watching and judging."

Robert nodded, taking in this information without adding to it. He was adept at fitting in with his employers socially, which meant humoring them but not joining in any shit-talking. He didn't particularly care what had happened to these rich adults back when they were rich children or teenagers. Plus, everyone was a potential client, and Robert couldn't be seen to be taking sides or partaking in gossip.

Rachel tapped him on the shoulder, handing him a glass of whiskey. "This more your speed than a pink margarita?" she said. Rachel liked the feel of his skin on her hand, and so she kept it there for a second too long. "Come meet the ladies," she said, leading him to the other side of the porch, where Lauren, Emily, Jen, and Lisa were perched around her wicker coffee table, which her mom had bought in the '80s.

"Everyone, this is Robert. He's the tennis genius who's going to be improving our game all summer," said Rachel.

Jen stood up from her chair and shook his hand. "Hello, Robert!" she said warmly as the others crowded in.

Lauren positioned herself directly to his right. Robert gave them the same spiel about his background and how he got to this town. They were rapt, pleased to be in the presence of a man, an extremely good-looking man, who wasn't one of their husbands. Rachel took leave for the guys, with whom she always felt more comfortable. She'd known Sam and Jason for nearly her entire life. And men just weren't as competitive or bitchy as women. They gave her much-needed attention that the women out here didn't.

Unfortunately, they were discussing taxes, which bored Rachel, so she did a quick drive-by and headed for her kitchen to get a refill of olives for the spread. Micah would make sure to keep guests' glasses topped off. The kitchen was a small space, filled with old cast-iron pans and her mother's dishes and oven mitts. She'd get around to redoing it one of these days, but it wasn't top priority. What little extra cash she had went to paying for tennis lessons. This house was really her only asset — she'd bought her sisters out with the money from her mom's will. They'd been kind enough to know how much it meant to her. Besides, they were scattered all over the country, married with children. All Rachel had was this place.

She took a bowl of olives into the party area. Still hidden by the kitchen door, Rachel saw Jason walking toward her bathroom, through the small hallway that led from the parlor to Rachel's bedroom. He knocked and Jen emerged, lipstick fresh, and as they passed each other, Rachel noticed Jason's hand brush against Jen's, then give it a small squeeze. He said something to her, but Rachel couldn't hear it. Neither of them saw her standing there, and she stepped back into the kitchen to make sure it stayed that way.

What had she just witnessed? Maybe it was just two old friends teetering too close after a few too many drinks. But maybe it was more than that. The idea that there could be something going on between Jason and Jen — *Jason and Jen* — was almost unfathomable. Jason and Sam were like brothers, and Jason had Lauren, beautiful Lauren. There's no way he'd do that to her. Would he? She'd always suspected that Jeanette and Greg had been living separate lives, so it was no surprise when she'd heard they'd split. But Jason and Lauren and Sam and Jen all seemed so rock-solid. Whatever she'd seen, it thrilled her to know that drama was on the horizon, that possibly some of the people she thought were happiest were as miserable as she was.

She'd been gone too long, so she continued out with the olives, hoping her face didn't betray how unsettled she felt. Robert was still holding court with Lauren and Emily. Lisa had drifted over to the bar with Jason and Sam, peppering Micah with questions about what it was like to be young and desired. Jen was chatting with Paul and Brian.

Rachel went over to them, standing next to Paul, who was in shorts and a vintage-ish Strokes T-shirt. Paul's thing was that he was "cool." He worked in marketing at a record label and fancied himself the creative in the group, though they all knew that he was a corporate shill like everyone else. He was always talking about new bands, or the cult TV show from Israel or Denmark that only he'd heard of, or bragging about the fact that they still lived in the East Village (in a shiny new development near Union Square, but that point wasn't mentioned). Emily, who stayed home with their two kids, playing the part of "downtown hip mom," came from family money. Her mother's side had some sort of steel fortune. Rachel was mostly friends with them so that she could stay in Emily's good graces, be included in her tennis life, and remain her partner for the women's doubles tournament. Rachel found Paul to be insufferable. He was the only husband she didn't enjoy flirting with, to be honest. He was also short, maybe five foot six, which Rachel viewed as a character flaw.

"Everything has become so Disney-fied," Paul said. "I hate to say this, but even the East Village has lost its soul."

"I agree with you, but hasn't that been happening for the past twenty years? Sam and I were worried that by moving out of the city we'd lose that energy and excitement, but it seems to me that the city has become interchangeable with where we live in the suburbs. You just get less space there," said Jen.

"And more homeless people," chuckled Brian. "De Blasio was a disaster."

Brian and Lisa lived in a town house in the '90s. She'd been home with their kids for years and was now training to be a "life coach," whatever that meant. Rachel found it funny to be around all these women who didn't need to work for a living. She wondered what that must feel like.

"Don't be so insensitive. Many of those homeless people are suffering from mental illness," said Jen.

"Oh, sorry, Saint Jen, I didn't mean to offend you. I know you and Sam are roughing it out there in Scarsdale, so you can relate," Brian sniffed. Jen's face darkened. The more Brian drank, the ruder and more full of

69

himself he became.

Sam walked over and put his arm around Jen's waist, pulling her in close. Rachel felt a pang of jealousy.

"Brian, stop being a dick to my wife," he said lightly, smiling. Sam was a master of defusing tension.

"Yeah, yeah. Sorry, Jen. I lost a lot of money this week, so I'm in a shitty mood." He wiped some sweat off his forehead.

"It's true," said Lisa, joining the group, pouting. Something looked different about her, Rachel thought, studying her face. Lisa caught her and narrowed her eyes.

Rachel floated away from the conversation, grabbing a piece of truffled gouda and making her way over to Lauren and Robert, who were speaking alone, heads bent toward each other. They looked up to see her at the same time, flashing identical annoyed looks at the interruption. Robert expertly converted his irritation into a smile. Lauren didn't.

"What are you gossiping about here?" Rachel asked, raising her eyebrows at Lauren, who continued to give her a death stare. "Must be juicy."

The image of Jason and Jen popped into Rachel's mind.

"We're just discussing doubles strategy,"

said Robert with a chuckle. "Pretty boring, actually." He looked a little flushed. Maybe Rachel's Japanese whiskey was going to his head.

"Robert promised he's going to fix my forehand," said Lauren. The green silk of her camisole brought out the green flecks in her eyes, and Rachel saw Robert was watching her as she spoke.

"Can I get either of you another drink?" Rachel asked, eyeing Lauren's empty glass.

"Not for me," said Robert. "I've got to go back to my place now and get some rest. I have lessons tomorrow starting at 8:00 a.m. But thank you so much for having me. It was really nice getting to know everyone."

Robert smiled at Lauren and went over to say goodbye to the others, leaving Lauren standing with Rachel. Rachel took a step closer to her and lowered her voice. She could smell Lauren now, an appealing mixture of Chanel No. 5 and natural bug spray.

"What were you two *really* talking about? You looked cozy," Rachel said in her best conspiratorial voice. She wanted Lauren to open up to her, and she hoped to act as her non-judgy confidante. Lauren didn't take the bait. She took a step back from Rachel, leaning attractively against the wooden shingled wall of the screened-in porch.

"Doubles. We told you," Lauren said.

"Isn't he so cute?" prodded Rachel. The screen door banged as Robert left, and the buzz went out of the room.

"Yes, obviously, he's ridiculously cute. He told me about where he's from in Florida and that his dad died a few years ago. He went there to help his mom and then just kind of got stuck," she said.

Jason approached; he looked shiny and drunk. "All right, honey, let's go. I've had like four drinks and am ready for bed," he said.

Lauren nodded. Rachel hated this part, when people started to leave.

The couples trickled out together, saying their thank-yous and goodbyes, leaving Rachel with Micah, who'd started to tidy the mess. Wineglasses were strewn around the porch, and the dregs of the appetizers were awaiting cleanup.

"Thank you so much for everything. Please feel free to go home. I'll do the rest," said Rachel, not really wanting to make conversation. "I'm sure you've had enough of the grown-ups for one night."

"Oh, no, it's totally fine. I can help," he said, picking up the bowl of olive pits. "Anyway, it's fun for me to hang with your

72

group — I get to see and hear things I normally wouldn't." He looked her straight in the eyes as he said it. What did he mean?

"Please, go have fun with your friends. I'm all good!" She handed him a hundred dollars in twenties. He nodded cordially, his duty done, leaving Rachel all alone. She was always alone.

She didn't feel like clearing up quite yet, so she poured herself a glass of cabernet (she always started the evening with white and finished with red) and walked out to the boardwalk. Maybe she'd go sit on the dock for a bit by herself.

She lived on a walk called Marine, right across from the tennis courts and connecting yacht club, closer to the bay side of the island than the ocean. The moon was out, and it was cool. Rachel wished she'd worn a sweatshirt. There were no lights on the boardwalks, so the only guidance came from lamps in people's homes. The later it got, the harder it was to navigate without a flashlight. As she walked toward the bay, she could hear a few people standing on the raised outdoor deck of the yacht club, drinking and chatting. She didn't want anyone to see her, as then she'd be obligated to go up and join the fun. She wasn't in the mood.

She turned around and instead walked in

the direction of the ocean, the path getting increasingly less visible as she got farther from the constant flashing of the Fire Island Lighthouse. Though it was quiet and dark, she felt safe. There hadn't been a violent crime in her forty-two years coming out to Salcombe. Likely because no one kept any valuables in their beach homes, and you had to take a ferry back and forth. How would a criminal escape? Occasionally, bikes were stolen from people's homes or the yacht club, but that was the work of rowdy local teens (or drunken, confused adults). The bikes were usually found discarded in a neighboring town after the guilty party's adventure ended.

One boardwalk, Harbor, cut through the middle of town, equidistant between the bay and beach. Rachel walked across it to Neptune, peering into the small house on the corner, where her old friend Leah Thomas used to live. It was now owned by a new family, the Cahulls, who had one toddler, with a baby on the way. Rachel had spent so many nights there when she was a kid, sleeping over in Leah's room, Leah in the top bunk, Rachel on the bottom, talking about boys and life. She missed having her own best friend in Salcombe. All that was left of their crew were the guys — Jason and

Sam — and so Rachel was forced to befriend the wives and new couples. Leah lived in California now with her husband and three kids.

Rachel could see the Cahulls on their couch, watching TV. Mike was giving Marina, who must have been about seven months pregnant, a foot rub. Rachel had heard that Marina had dated women before marrying Mike, but from the view she had now, all looked very traditional. She continued toward the beach, enjoying the lonely walk, the wind ruffling her dress. She felt younger than forty-two in the cover of the Salcombe night, like she was a teenager ambling home after a rager on the dunes. The air smelled fresh, the stars were out overhead, and she spotted a deer crossing the boardwalk just up ahead. They were everywhere on the island, spreading Lyme disease, no doubt (the kids in town even referred to the reeds lining the walks as "tick grass"). But it still amazed Rachel that such wild, large, beautiful creatures lived in such proximity to the people there. There had been a political fight some years back about the legality of killing deer to control their population, but Rachel couldn't remember which side won. Either way, they were still there every summer, munching on grass and scaring the bejesus out of small dogs.

The beach, reached by a thinner board-walk path leading to a wooden stairway, was deserted. The moon was shining on the gray water, small waves lapping the shore. She walked about thirty feet to the right and plopped down on the cool sand near the dunes, finishing the last drop of wine in her glass before placing it down beside her. She hugged her legs and looked at her phone. It was 10:22. She should really head back.

Just then, she heard footsteps on the stairs heading down to the beach, a light clomp-ing, maybe two people. She slid farther into the tick grass that edged the back of the beach, hiding herself not out of fear but the fact that she'd be humiliated to be caught drinking by herself at this hour. She was sure she'd know whomever it was; she knew everyone. She could see it was a couple, now, a man and a woman. Her chest tight-ened as she recognized their shapes: Jason and Jen. Her white shirtdress was unmistak-able. They walked toward the water, contin-ually looking behind them to make sure they were alone. Rachel hunched smaller, willing herself to be invisible, trying not to so much as breathe. They were about forty feet in front of her.

"I can't do this all summer," said Jen, taking Jason's hand in hers. They were facing away from Rachel, but she could hear them as well as if they were still at her party.

"I can't see you and not be with you," Jason said. He stroked Jen's hair and kissed her, Jen leaning into him, arms around his back. Rachel didn't know what to do. Should she make a run for it? She could go all the way to the next town, Kismet, and walk back from there.

"We just have to keep it quiet for now," said Jen. "We can't do it while we're all out here. Think of the kids. Think of the town scandal this will become. We have to get through until Labor Day, and then we can make a plan."

"It just sucks so much," said Jason. "I can see you, but I can't touch you."

"We really shouldn't even be here — some teenagers could be out with their friends; someone could walk down. We should go home," said Jen.

Jason, looking tortured, ran his hands through his hair. "Okay, let's go back. I told Lauren I was heading to the club for a drink, but I'm going to say I just walked around for a while and changed my mind."

"Sam is already passed out. I'm not worried about him," said Jen. "You go first, and I'll wait here for ten minutes before I leave, in case anyone is around."

They kissed one more time. It reminded Rachel of when she used to make out passionately with her high school boyfriend in front of her back door. What was wrong with them?

"Can you imagine if Rachel found out?" said Jen as Jason started back toward the steps. Rachel felt her heart beating so hard she was sure they could hear it. Jason laughed. Then he disappeared into the dark.

Jen did as she said, standing at the water for another ten minutes, arms crossed, pacing. Rachel thought she might explode from stress. She also really had to pee. Finally, Jen made her way back off the beach, leaving Rachel alone again. She waited another few minutes before creeping back to her house carefully, empty wineglass in hand.

4
MICAH HOLT

Micah Holt knew who was fucking who. It was his gift, honed as a closeted boy, to suss out social dynamics before anyone else. He used that power, when he was young, to protect against bullies. "I know who you have a crush on," he'd say to anyone who seemed like a threat. "And I know who she likes." No one would beat up someone who had such precious info.

Now, out for many years, handsome and smart, beloved by men and women, Micah had no need for games. But he still saw everything. It was partly why he enjoyed being a bartender in Salcombe. He didn't do it for the money; his parents gave him plenty. But he loved mixing drinks and getting people tipsy and hearing all their secrets.

And everyone had so many. He knew that Brian Metzner's hedge fund had imploded this year and that he was on the verge of bankruptcy. He knew that Brian's wife, Lisa, was into recreational drugs. He knew that Jeanette Oberman told people that her husband, Greg, was having an affair with the dog walker. That was true. But what she didn't tell people was that the dog walker was a guy. (Micah could have told you Greg was gay; he'd come on to Micah numerous times.) And, based on what he'd witnessed that night, he thought there might be something going on with Jason Parker and Jen Weinstein.

He'd noticed them together while he was working at Rachel Woolf's cocktail party. Jason had followed Jen back to the bathroom, clearly intent on seeing her alone, and Micah had seen him whispering something into her ear.

Jason and Jen! Micah could only imagine how big this would be if it got out. Sam, Jason, Jen, Lauren, Rachel, and their crew were about ten years younger than Micah's parents, Judy and Eric. Micah had always looked to that crowd with admiration. The guys were hot and seemingly successful; the women were pretty and fun. They all liked to get drunk at the club. They made being an adult seem not so bad (as opposed to Micah's mom and dad, who were generationally dull).

Micah considered an affair between Jen and Jason. Everything in Salcombe hinged on delicate social webs, and this would unravel many of them. Also, why would Jen want to fuck Jason over Sam? She was a mystery.

Micah was on his way to the beach. He'd finished up at Rachel's (poor Rachel), swung by the club for a vodka soda, and was set to meet Ronan, the lifeguard he was hooking up with, at 10:45 by the dunes. Ronan was a beauty. Six foot three, perfect body, tanned, sandy-haired. Exactly the kind of guy Micah had always wanted, had looked at from afar with a longing familiar only to homosexual boys.

Ronan's family had a house in Kismet, the next town over. They lived on Long Island and were less wealthy than Micah's parents by a long shot. Ronan and Micah were the same age, twenty. They'd met last year, at a party thrown by Micah's best friend, Willa Thomas, who lived on Anchor Walk. She'd invited all the lifeguards, and Ronan had arrived in a blue hoodie and Levi's, bumping fists with the other straight guys. He'd locked eyes with Micah, and Micah had thought: *Aha!* Micah liked how retro it was — sleeping with a closeted lifeguard. It felt very '90s, and Micah was

81

totally into it. His group of friends at Yale were genderless, pronoun-less, and confident. Ronan was sweet and confused. He went to Villanova. Poor guy couldn't tell his family he was gay. It was so old-school.

Micah was happy to engage in illicit acts with this gorgeous, willing man. He did occasionally feel bad, as if he were taking advantage of a lamb. But not to the point that he wasn't going to blow him by the dunes tonight. That was definitely happening.

He crossed Harbor and continued up Marine. It was hazy and silent out. He saw a figure, a man, turn down Marine from Lighthouse, heading toward him. Probably someone coming back from drinks in Kismet or Salcombe's other neighboring town, Fair Harbor. As he got closer, Micah recognized Jason's shape; tall and sturdy, his arms swinging with purpose. Micah could sense when Jason caught sight of him. He slowed, his body stiffened. There was nowhere to escape to. They reached each other a few seconds later. Jason's face was shadowed, but his black eyes were shining through the darkness.

"Hey, Micah, you heading home?" Micah couldn't think of the last time he and Jason had spoken to each other alone. Sam was much friendlier, asking Micah about his life, cracking jokes. Jason was always just there, standing next to Sam, brooding.

"Yep, I'm done with tonight," said Micah, lying. "I hope you had fun at Rachel's. She always throws a good party."

"Yes, it was very fun," said Jason, shifting from his left to his right.

Micah wanted to end the conversation. Ronan was waiting, and Jason was acting weird. Micah assumed it had something to do with Jen.

"I'm off, then. See you later!" Micah went to pass Jason, but he put his hand on Micah's shoulder, holding him back.

"Uh, I'd appreciate if you didn't mention to anyone that you saw me tonight. I like to wander the boardwalks sometimes when Lauren goes to sleep. It relaxes me."

"Sure, no problem. I totally get it," said Micah. "I love being out at night here alone, too. Though you have to watch out for the deer. They'll scare the shit out of you."

"Don't I know it," said Jason, smiling tightly.

The two men nodded goodbye and headed in opposite directions. Micah, relieved to be free, continued up to the beach.

5
JASON PARKER

Jason Parker had always hated his best friend, Sam Weinstein. Maybe *hated* was too strong a word. Resented, more like. Felt jealous of. Was annoyed by. No, hated *was* probably the right way to describe it.

No one knew this. Not even Lauren, Jason's wife, would have suspected it. Jason and Sam had been friends since they were kids. They'd met in their first-grade class at Dalton and bonded over their love of Superman. Jason was chubby and shy. Sam was not. They were at each other's apartments almost every day after school, playing Nintendo while their moms drank coffee and watched *Oprah* together. Both Sam's and Jason's parents were well-off — Sam's dad was a prominent litigator, and Jason's father ran a company that manufactured high-end rugs. Jason's mom and dad were happily married; Sam's home was a mess of screaming and slamming doors and accusations of infidelity. When they had sleepovers, it was always at Jason's. As Sam's parents' situation devolved, he became a constant presence in Jason's apartment, eating every meal there, hanging out all day on the weekends. When they were in sixth grade, Sam's mom fell into a long depression while his dad jetted off to Aspen for the winter. Jason's parents became Sam's de facto guardians.

He moved in, sharing Jason's room, fighting with Jason's sister, coming with them to Thanksgiving, traveling with them over Christmas break. Jason knew his place was to be the dutiful son and friend, so he stayed silent while it felt like Sam took over his life. Jason and Sam, Sam and Jason. Always, always, always.

Jason even had a sneaking suspicion that his mom preferred Sam to him. Sam would sit with her while she folded laundry and ask her questions about her friends and tennis game. As Jason and Sam became a package deal, it was clear who was the favorite child. But Jason was stuck with him.

Sam's only redeeming trait — more a real estate perk than a trait — was his house on Fire Island, in Salcombe, to which he invited Jason to live with him every summer. Jason loved it out there. He loved riding his bike by himself all over town, swimming in the rough ocean, learning how to sail out on the bay. As they got older, he managed to make his own friends in Salcombe, had his own summer crushes, his own little life while living rent-free in Sam's perfect bayfront home. He felt relaxed there in a way he never fully did at home. By the time Jason was a teenager, he'd lost his baby fat. He wasn't quite as good-looking as Sam, but he was getting there. He grew taller and thinner, his eyes settled into his head, large and brown. Women started to look at him with interest.

At that point, they had the run of the joint themselves. Sam's parents had finally divorced, letting him use the house, solo, as a gift for ruining his life. Sam and Jason became perma-summer-roommates, through high school, college, and into their twenties, Jason integrating himself into the community until no one could remember a time without him there.

The last summer that Jason spent with Sam in the house at 6 West Bay Promenade was when they were thirty. Jason was doing well at his private equity job, which allowed him to lean into his aggressive personality, and Sam was on the partner track at his law firm, Sullivan & Cromwell, where he worked on high-profile white-collar-crime cases.

They'd both just met girls they really liked. Sam was dating Jen Paulson, a button-cute brunette, as he described her, who'd just finished her graduate degree in psychology. And Jason was with Lauren Schapiro, a hot blond snob from Northern California, who worked as a buyer at Bloomingdale's. Jason was relatively sure he was going to marry Lauren. She checked all the boxes — pretty, from a good family, chatty, fun. They clicked in bed, and she seemed to tolerate Jason's moodiness.

He was happy, he thought. He had a great job, an attractive girlfriend; he was young with everything ahead of him.

And then he met Jen. Sam brought her out to the beach one weekend toward the end of that summer, after it became clear that the relationship was more than a fling. They came on a Saturday morning; Jason was cooking eggs for breakfast on the Viking stove in Sam's mom's country kitchen when they arrived. Jason turned around to say hi, not knowing what to expect from Sam's new girlfriend. Sam had hardly ever dated anyone seriously. Jason figured it had some-thing to do with Sam's parents' fucked-up relationship. So, when he'd said he was with a psychologist, of all things, Jason had been surprised.

"Jason! This is Jen. Jen, this is my best friend, Jason. I've known him since I was five, and I've obviously told you all about him already."

"So nice to meet you," said Jen. Jen was the most beautiful thing Jason had ever seen. She had a throaty, mature voice and lovely, pearly teeth. Her eyes were large and hazel, nearly the size of a Disney Princess's, and she had clear skin that glowed. She was wearing a plain white tank top and cutoffs, her body smooth and thin.

"I've heard all about you, too," said Jason, turning the oven off. He suddenly felt stupid cooking eggs in front of this perfect person. "Sam never brings girls out here, so he must really like you," he continued, feeling awkward. Jen blushed. He could feel her staring at him for a second too long as he averted his eyes.

"I do!" said Sam, oblivious. "I'm going to show her around Salcombe, and then we can go to the beach later. What do you think?"

Jason nodded dumbly. The happy couple left and Jason remained standing in the kitchen, his breakfast burned and bitter.

Later that day, the trio went up to the beach together, laying out towels and baking in the sun. Jen was wearing a white bikini, and Jason had a hard time looking at anything but her. Why did Sam always get everything that Jason wanted? Jason hadn't thought of Lauren once since Jen had arrived. But he could also sense that Jen was looking at him, too. He could feel her interest. At least he thought he could.

Sam wandered off to go chat with some of the lifeguards, buff and tan in their red swimsuits. Jen looked up from her *New Yorker* and propped herself up on her side, facing Jason, who was lying on his back, eyes closed.

"Are you asleep?" she asked, knowing the answer.

Jason smiled. "Nope," he said. He felt her hand move up his leg toward his waist. He kept his eyes closed.

"Sam hadn't told me that his best friend was so cute," she said, leaning closer into him. "It sounds like you two have a very complicated, codependent relationship."

"I wouldn't call it *codependent*," said Jason, putting his hand over hers, feeling its heat. "I sort of despise him, but I'm stuck with him forever."

"Well, if you hate him, you won't mind fucking his girlfriend," she whispered.

Jason's breath came fast. He glanced over toward the lifeguard stand to make sure

Sam was still a safe distance away. He was there, smiling and chatting, handsome as ever, completely unaware of what was transpiring between his most trusted friend and the girl he would eventually marry.

"I definitely wouldn't mind that," said Jason.

They left the beach without a plan. Jason didn't know what to expect, but he assumed Jen would take care of it. She seemed to know what she was doing. They all had dinner together — Sam grilled steak on the outdoor Weber, they had loads of red wine — and then Jason went alone to his room, the former maid's quarters, on the first floor of the house.

He couldn't sleep. The familiar little bed felt lumpy and strange. At 2:00 a.m., he heard the door crack open and felt Jen slip in beside him, in underwear and that sexy white tank, this time without a bra.

This summer was the tenth anniversary of that night. Jason remembered that as he skulked home in the dark from his and Jen's meeting at the beach. Ten long years of wanting something that he couldn't have. Ten years of having to fake his way through his own life, married to someone he didn't really love.

That was the first and last time Jason and

Jen had slept together. Until this year, that is. After that weekend, Jen acted as if nothing had happened, and she and Jason didn't discuss it. He was too humiliated to bring it up, but he thought about it constantly. He continued to date Lauren, and the four of them — Sam, Jen, Lauren, and Jason — became a little unit, going on double dates, taking trips to Italy together, spending summers on Fire Island. Sam proposed to Jen a year later, and Jason proposed to Lauren a couple of months after that. Jason and Lauren got married in California, near her parents' home, while Sam and Jen, ever so chic, did an intimate ceremony on the beach in Salcombe, followed by a raucous party at the yacht club.

Occasionally, over the years, Jason felt that he was over Jen. He'd be having an okay moment with Lauren, or enjoying his kids, or making more and more money at work, and he'd think, *Fuck her, I'm fine.* Sam and Jen had moved to Westchester to get more space, while Jason and Lauren had stayed in the city, Jason's increasingly large income paying for them to exist in a rarefied crowd. As soon as Jason was able, he bought their beautiful home in Salcombe. He was attached to the town, yes, but more importantly, it was the only place he'd get to see

Jen consistently. He loved to look at her, and speak with her, and smell her. He liked the way her jewelry clinked on her wrists, and the stories she told, and the way she licked her lips. Sometimes she looked at him and he knew she was also thinking about that night a decade ago. He just *knew.*

For what seemed like forever, Jason thought that this would be it. He'd pine for his best friend's wife until the day he died. He'd come to terms with it. He was successful, he had a family, nice homes. That was enough. Lauren bugged the shit out of him, but didn't everyone's wife bug the shit out of them?

Then, one night last summer, that all changed. Rachel Woolf had hosted cocktails at her house for the usual group. It was late August, close to the end of the season, and everyone was looking well rested after months of beach time. As usual, Rachel had been plying them with alcohol, and they'd gotten wasted, particularly Lauren and Sam, both of whom had taken themselves home to bed, leaving their spouses to mingle. Jen and Jason had been alone before in situations like this; that wasn't new. The end of the evening was approaching, and the few remaining guests, including Rachel, decided to head to the yacht club for a nightcap. Jason, blurry and buzzed, chose to stay on her porch and finish his drink. He'd thought he was the only one left. He'd thought Jen had gone. But then she was there, sitting down next to him, close, too close, touching her thigh to his as she leaned in to whisper, "I want you. I've always wanted you." All Jason felt was relief.

They'd stumbled up to the beach, taking care to avoid any of the boardwalks with streetlamps, holding hands like teenagers and occasionally stopping to kiss, Jason running his hands greedily up and down her body. She was dressed in white pants and a silk tank top, and she felt the same to him as she did all those years ago. Warm and soft. Exactly what he wanted.

They'd found cover underneath a stairwell leading down to the beach — not the main beach on Broadway but one about a hundred yards away, off a walk called Pacific. They were sitting together on the sand. It was dark and cool, and the ocean looked black.

"Why now?" asked Jason.

"Because I've had it," said Jen. "I've just turned forty. I have three kids. I've spent years trying to convince myself to be happy with Sam. He's so sweet, and he truly loves me so much. He's a great dad. He's everything I knew he'd be when we started dating. And you —" She trailed off, turning to him, and putting her hand on his head, pulling up on his hair. "You were his dark and intense friend, the person he loved the most. And I was so attracted to you. I think about you when I'm in bed with Sam. I picture your body instead of his. I knew I'd do this eventually; I knew I would break. Everyone thinks I'm so good, I get that," she said, pulling harder on his hair. Jason closed his eyes and enjoyed the sensation. "But I'm not."

That was a year ago. Since then, there hadn't been a week without them somehow seeing each other, mostly at hotels in the city, though a few times, in desperation, Jason drove out to the suburbs and they had sex in his car. Jason felt crazed with lust. He finally understood what *crazed with lust* meant. She was all he thought about. He could barely pay attention at work, or when Lauren was droning on about a friend's face-lift or complaining about the headmaster controversy at their kids' school.

At first, Jason didn't think Lauren had a clue. He'd been faking business trips and work dinners, and she didn't even seem to notice, other than to occasionally inquire about his schedule to plan dinner parties

and make sure he could come to fundrais-
ers. She'd become increasingly vapid over
the years, Jason thought, leaning into this
rich-housewife lifestyle in a way that re-
pelled him. She was obsessed with the
school stuff, obsessed with her friends and
what they were doing and wearing and buying, obsessed with looking a certain way. It
was so unattractive. To be fair, he'd known
she was like this when he'd married her.
But Sam had proposed to Jen, and so Jason
was left with no choice but to soldier on
with Lauren, his beautiful girlfriend, whose
worst trait was that she wasn't Jen.

Then this spring, Lauren seemed to get a
whiff that something was up. She kept asking him about his work travel and then
harping on this idea of possibly moving to
Miami. Jason would never move to Miami;
Jen lived in New York.

"The Goldbergs just bought a place in
South Beach, the Adlers moved to Delray.
Everyone is going," Lauren had said to him.

They were in the bedroom of their apartment on Park Avenue. She'd just gotten her
hair cut and colored, and the bob framed
her face nicely. Jason had to admit she was
aging very well; she was even more gorgeous
now than when she was twenty-eight. He
suspected it had to do with those mysteri-

ous charges he saw on their credit card statement to various Upper East Side dermatologists and plastic surgeons.

"Lauren, I'm the boss. I can't just up and leave." He sighed.

They'd been around and around this topic, always landing in the same place: no.

"We can still go to Fire Island in the summers, if that's what you're worried about," she said, sitting down in a huff on one of their yellow velvet lounge chairs from ABC Carpet & Home.

Jason just shook his head.

"What is up with you lately?" Lauren said. She squinted at him. "You're even more absent than usual, if that's possible. I'm not an idiot, Jason."

He could tell she was starting to get riled up, and wanted to deflate her before it became a huge thing.

"Nothing is going on! I'm just working a ton, you know that. Things will get better in the summer. I just need to get through these next couple of months."

And now here they all were. They'd arrived at their house that day, a whirlwind of unpacking and settling in and organizing, mostly handled by Lauren and their nanny, Silvia. Jason knew that Jen and Sam had gotten there the day before; he and Jen hadn't seen each other in nearly two weeks. There had been too much hoopla around the kids ending school and everyone getting packed and ready to figure out how to meet. Jason was desperate to see her.

They communicated with each other over Signal, an encrypted messaging app. Texts disappeared within minutes of reading them, never to be seen again. The joke about Signal was that it was the app for people having affairs and, well, Jason supposed that was true. He checked the app at least once every couple of minutes, a thrill running through him every time he saw Jen's name appear in black letters.

He'd chatted with her on Signal earlier that day, while Lauren was busy banging around their kitchen, putting the imported Trader Joe's snacks in their correct cabinets. Jason went up to their roof deck, which overlooked the ocean; the views impressed him anew. He couldn't believe this place was his. The beach was nearly empty, save a few young couples with little kids. It was too early in the season for the crowds. Jason opened Signal on his phone.

Jen Weinstein: I miss you. How was the trip?

Jason felt a buzz.

Jason Parker: Fine, whatever. I had to sit with Brian on the boat. He never shuts the fuck up. But we made it. When can I see you?
Jen Weinstein: Are you going to Rachel's tonight? I assume she invited you guys.
Jason Parker: Yes, we'll be there. But how will I keep my hands off you?
Jen Weinstein: You'll just have to control yourself. You're good at control.

It was true. Jason was moody, sure, and he'd have months during which he felt angry at, well, everything. But he didn't lose his temper. It was one of the things that annoyed Lauren the most — that fact that he met her outbursts with an eerie calm.

That night, when he and Lauren arrived at Rachel's, he saw Jen standing at the bar. She was wearing a white shirtdress with a gold chain around her delicate neck. Her hair was glossy, her lipstick was red, and Jason wanted to consume her right there. He felt an invisible tug toward her and made his way over, giving Rachel a quick peck on the cheek hello as he did.

This wasn't the first time they'd been together in public — there had been a few group dinners in the city, and Jason and Lauren and their kids had gone to Jen and Sam's house in Scarsdale for two birthday parties. But there was something about being back in Salcombe together, back where they'd first slept together, where they fell back into it last year, that made Jason antsy about the whole thing. As if there was no way they could get through this summer without getting caught. How was it supposed to work? They'd been avoiding that question for months. Truly, they'd been avoiding a lot of questions.

"Hi, Jen. How are you?" Jason said to her, a small smile on her lips. Before she could respond, Sam came over and gave Jason a big bear hug. Jason stood there limply as Sam crushed him with his arms. This was their shtick.

"Here we are again," said Sam warmly, placing a watermelon margarita into Jason's hand. "You get the house unpacked?"

"Yeah, mostly," said Jason. "Lauren's the one doing everything. I'm just standing around and getting in her way."

"Story of my life," said Sam, putting his hand on Jen's arm. She batted him away playfully. Jason's stomach lurched seeing them so comfortable and close. If you didn't know what was going on — and Jason was almost 100 percent sure no one did, including Sam — you'd think Sam and Jen were a happy couple.

Lauren slid up to them. She was wearing a green silk camisole that made her eyes shine, and she'd done her date-night makeup. Why was she so dressed up? Jason wondered.

"Hi, guys. Happy summer," said Lauren, clinking everyone's glass with her own.

"I heard the new tennis pro is great," said Jen. "I've been playing a lot this year, though I'm sure I'm still way worse than you," she said to Lauren.

"Maybe this is the year we actually do a mixed doubles game," said Sam.

Jason thought that was a terrible idea.

The party continued like that, everyone settling into their usual summer selves. Jason had conversations with the other guests, but he was talking just to talk; he didn't really know what he was saying. He was only focused on Jen. Where she was in the room, who she was speaking with. He wanted to somehow connect with her, but he didn't know how.

At a certain point, that tennis pro, Robert, arrived — Jason met him and they'd chatted briefly. He seemed to be a nice guy. Very good-looking. All the women were aflutter.

The guys, too. Jason noticed Paul Grobel standing on his tiptoes to seem taller.

Jason eventually saw Jen make her way to the bathroom, which was farther back into Rachel's first floor, near her kitchen, and away from the gathering. He waited two minutes and then went back that way. The door was still closed, so he knocked; she would surely know who it was. She opened it and came out, looking directly at him, finally.

He knew it was a risk, but he had to touch her, he just had to, so he brushed his hand against hers as she passed, giving it a gentle squeeze. "Let's meet at the beach," he whispered. She gave a quick nod and continued back to the party, smoothing her dress as she went.

Jason felt like the rest of the evening was an endless slog of boring conversations and tepid laughter. He was just waiting for it to be over so he could escape Lauren and see Jen. Paul cornered him for half an hour, telling him about some secret dining club that he and Emily belonged to. Jason was tall enough to see the top of Paul's head, and he noticed the telltale black dots of an in-process hair transplant. Paul *would* spend thirty grand to hold on to his hair for dear life.

"It's by the guys who run Carbone," Paul said, "and you have to fill out this form to apply, then pay a five-thousand-dollar retainer. And they hold the meals in roving locations, like an empty loft in Tribeca or in the basement of a random diner in Queens."

"Sounds like hell on earth," said Sam, who'd snuck up next to them. He laughed.

Paul glared at him. It had always been kind of tense between the two of them. Sam was so fun and attractive, and Paul was a ball of insecurity. They just didn't gel.

Jason chuckled. He loved when Sam bothered Paul. There were moments, still, when Sam reminded him of the five-year-old kid he'd befriended in kindergarten, the one he'd dressed up with in superhero costumes and played endless games of hide-and-seek. He momentarily felt bad that he was sleeping with Sam's wife. Sam was so guileless, standing there in his stupid white linen outfit. But Jason pushed the thought to the back of his mind. Paul walked away, clearly annoyed at Sam and Jason.

"Paul can be such a tool," said Sam. He and Jason were alone by the bar. Jen was with Emily and Rachel on the couch. Brian was in the bathroom. Lauren and the tennis pro were deep in conversation. *Good*, thought Jason. *Someone else can listen to her rattle on.*

Sam then looked at Jason earnestly, his tanned face turning serious. *Oh, shit,* thought Jason. *He knows.* His throat tightened and he felt his mouth go dry.

"I have to speak to you about something," said Sam, his voice soft.

"Do you want to go outside?" asked Jason.

"No, then people will think something's up. I just want us to act casual, like we're talking about the Knicks or something," said Sam.

Jason nodded. *Fuck, fuck, fuck.* Sam's eyes flicked over to Jen. Jason braced for the worst.

"Something happened at work," said Sam. Sam was still at Sullivan & Cromwell, where he oversaw the entire litigation department. "There was this girl, this associate," he continued.

Jason caught his breath. This wasn't about him and Jen; Sam still didn't know.

"And nothing ever happened between us, I swear. We just worked closely together on a couple of cases. I liked her, but only as a colleague. You have to believe me, Jason," he said. He looked scared.

Jason wasn't used to seeing Sam like this.

"She's now making *accusations.*" Sam was nearly whispering now.

"She's saying I made advances and that I forced her to kiss me. It's not true. I would never do that. You know me. But now they're investigating me — they've brought in an outside counsel to do it. And it's getting intense."

Jason was shocked. Sam was so straitlaced. Or as straitlaced as a handsome lawyer could be.

"Jen doesn't know," Sam went on. "I'm not going to tell her if I don't have to. But I had to tell someone. I think this girl just wants a payoff from the firm; otherwise, she would have gone to the police. But she doesn't understand that she's ruining my life."

Jason wasn't sure how to respond. His immediate thoughts went to how and if this information could derail his relationship with Jen.

"So, what's going to happen?" he asked.

"I'm not sure," said Sam. "They're still deliberating on how to handle it. But there are at least a couple of people who aren't friendly to me on the management committee, and I'm worried I'm going to get fucked. If I lose my job over this, I'll be ruined. Please don't say anything to anyone, including Lauren, but especially Jen."

As if conjured by her name, Jen appeared

right then next to Sam, putting her arm through his.

"What are you boys discussing, all secretive?" she said, looking dazzling in the dimmed porchlight. Jason decided right then that he wouldn't tell her about Sam. He worried it would mess with what they had going, and he wasn't willing to put that at risk. Just another secret to add to the pile. He would see her later at the beach and act as if nothing had changed.

6

SILVIA MABINI

Silvia Mabini dreaded summer. It wasn't the weather; she loved heat. She'd grown up in a small village about an hour outside Manila, and she was used to that sticky, heavy humidity. When it was a hundred degrees in the city, walking through the neighborhood near her apartment in Jamaica, Queens, she felt at home. What she dreaded, what caused her fifty-two-year-old skin to crawl, was the idea of spending two months on Fire Island with her boss's family.

But here she was, again, in her little room on the first floor of the Parkers' beach house, bored, lonely, watching soaps on YouTube. The house was nice, of course. Everything about the Parkers' life was nice. Lauren was very particular, including about what the kids wore — designer dresses for Amelie, no sweatpants on Arlo — and ate — only organic, very little refined sugar, no juice *ever.* Silvia had learned Lauren's preferences immediately, as she'd been trained to do. And Lauren was a good boss to Silvia; demanding, but clear with her expectations, generous with Silvia's pay, absentee in a way that Silvia appreciated. It was always better for the nannies when the moms were out of the house.

In all, Silvia was content with her setup. As a boss, Lauren was perfectly fine. She was gorgeous and chic and, Silvia knew, deeply unhappy. They all were.

The Parkers were her fifth and hopefully final family before she could retire. She had a little house in the Philippines that she'd bought with two of her sisters (she was one of twelve siblings, ten still alive), and she was planning to move back there in a few years. Her children, whom she'd raised alone, were all out of the house now — one son was a nurse, one daughter was a physician's assistant, and one daughter, the mother to her only granddaughter, Molly, was a Manhattan nanny just like she was. Silvia's husband had moved back to the Philippines years ago, and they were barely in contact. He called their children on their birthdays, and that was about it. Silvia was fine with that.

In the past, Silvia had enjoyed traveling

with her families. It was a perk of the job. Aruba. Telluride. London. She'd stayed in fancy hotels. She'd even flown private with one of her families, the Jesseps. But before the Parkers, she'd only had summers in the Hamptons. The houses there were so massive, she'd nearly always had her own wing. She could go hang in her TV room, make tea in her own kitchenette, and not have to see anyone until 7:00 the next morning.

But Fire Island was different. More . . . compact. She couldn't escape. And it was harder work, too. In the Hamptons, Silvia stayed at home most days, supervising pool time, dealing with meals, and babysitting when her bosses went out. In Salcombe, she was outside with the kids constantly, dropping them off at the camp (which only went until noon — *why?*), taking them to tennis and then the beach. She would occasionally befriend another nanny, but many families paid local teenagers to watch their children. So, she sat alone on her adult tricycle, which she rode for its large rear basket, big enough for towels and beach bags, waiting for the kids to finish activities, scrolling on her phone. Then she'd watch Amelie zigzag on her training wheels up and down the boardwalks. The boardwalks gave Silvia such stress. They were so far off the ground, and the kids went so fast on them. Someone was bound to break a bone. Then it would be her fault. But how could she prevent it?

The thought sometimes haunted her as she lay in bed, trying to fall asleep. Occasionally, there would be a mosquito buzzing around her room, taunting her, preventing her from her much-needed rest. The mosquitoes in New York loved her more than the ones in the Philippines. They sought her out, bit her ceaselessly, left large, red welts on her skin.

Silvia spotted one in the corner and got up to shoo it away with a magazine. She heard the door open and shut, and then Lauren's footsteps passing by. Jason wasn't with her. Those two were never together. Jason was having an affair. Silvia was sure of it. She'd done his laundry enough times to know that he was sleeping with another woman. His clothes didn't smell like Lauren, who only wore Chanel No. 5. They smelled like someone else's shampoo. And sex. Most of the dads she'd worked for were having affairs, but Jason was the most obvious by far. He didn't even pretend to like Lauren. Even Arlo and Amelie could tell. Amelie once said to her that "Daddy hates Mommy." She wondered if Lauren had said that to her, or if she'd come to the thought on her own. Silvia loved Amelie, who was beautiful and imperious. Like her mother. Arlo she could take or leave. There was always one child in a family like that.

Rich people were miserable, but they didn't know how lucky they were. They paid her $1,450 a week, plus room and board, plus $20 an hour extra to babysit at night when they went out. It was nothing for them. She was at the top rate for a nanny. She wondered how she could squeeze more out of them before she retired.

She lay down on her bed and snuggled into her soft Frette sheets. The mosquito buzzed in her ear. She hit her own head, hard, trying to kill it. Another two months to go in this place.

PART II

July 4

July 4

7
LAUREN PARKER

July 4 was Lauren Parker's least favorite national holiday. It was always hot, always buggy, always chaotic. The town of Salcombe set up a full day's schedule for its citizens, which sounded great in theory, but, in reality, was a long, annoying eight hours to endure. In the morning, there were games and races for the kids at the town field — an egg toss, a potato sack race, a three-legged disaster. Someone inevitably got hurt or had a tantrum, and Lauren ended up sweaty and covered in bites. Afterward came hot dogs and hamburgers and watermelon, set up on long picnic tables at the fire station next to the field. The firemen, or rather "firemen," as Lauren thought of them, were Salcombe dads — lawyers and bankers and media executives — who, as part of their midlife crises, had decided it'd be cool to become volunteer firefighters. They took a training course

113

together at the beginning of each summer, and then the townspeople were left to hope that nothing bad ever happened. You didn't necessarily want Brian Metzner to come to your rescue during a five-alarm emergency. The firehouse was a quaint wooden garage-like structure that housed one smallish fire truck and mostly served as a hangout for said dads to relax and drink beers in the afternoons.

Lauren and Silvia had walked with Arlo and Amelie down from their house for the games and lunch, while Jason had stayed behind. He claimed he had "tons" of work to get through before his noon tennis game with Sam. Work on a Sunday that was *also* a national holiday? Lauren didn't buy it, but she also didn't blame him for not wanting to join in the forced fun with the rest of the town. Arlo and his friend August had won the three-legged race for their age group, and so he was wearing a plastic medal around his neck. Amelie, who'd had her face painted with fireworks, was in her Pink Chicken flag dress, which Lauren had bought specifically for today. Just because she hated the holiday didn't mean she didn't want cute pictures to post on Instagram. Both kids had spent the past week at the Salcombe camp in the morning, which involved art projects and swimming, and had been in various activities during the afternoons — tennis for both, sailing for Arlo, a crafts class for Amelie. Silvia had been escorting them to and fro, and so Lauren had time to play tennis every day. She was starting to feel okay about her game; the muscle memory was returning, and her strokes were getting smoother.

Yesterday, Lauren and Claire Laurell had played against Rachel and Emily. Lauren had been in good form — her backhand was working, and her first serve was going in. Claire Laurell was in her early sixties and had two teenage daughters, Lila and Reb, who occasionally babysat for Arlo and Amelie if Silvia needed a night off. Claire had been a terrific player in her youth but had slowed down considerably over the past ten years, and she couldn't run to the net as quickly as Lauren wanted her to. But her ground strokes were still strong, and Lauren was able to scramble around the court to make up for Claire's leaden feet. They'd beaten Rachel and Emily in the first set 6–4 and had been leading 5–3 when their hour was up.

"That was fun," said Rachel, sweaty and red-faced as they picked up their balls and packed up their rackets. Rachel was the world's sorest loser, and it always amused Lauren to see her try to be polite after she lost. "I really need to work on my follow-through; I'm going down instead of over my shoulder." Rachel could never just say: "You played well, Lauren." It was always couched in the way Rachel had failed, with the idea that if she'd been playing as she normally does, the outcome would have been in her favor.

Claire waddled up to them, her gray hair stuck to her forehead, a line of sweat dampening the area under her large breasts. In her brown tennis skirt and tank, she reminded Lauren of an Idaho potato.

"Nice game, girls," said Claire. Lauren had heard a rumor that Claire and her husband, Seth, were swingers and that twenty years ago there'd been a group of them in Salcombe who'd regularly switch partners after a wild night at the yacht club. She couldn't imagine Claire, and especially Seth, now stout and bald, with oddly hairless legs, having sex with each other, let alone being attractive enough for others to want in on the game. But that's what everyone said had happened, so maybe it was true. If so, good for them. She and Jason barely ever had sex anymore. Maybe once or twice a month. Lauren was fine with that frequency — Jason grossed her out lately. His breath, which hadn't bothered her before, now smelled faintly rancid. Maybe it always had, but for whatever reason, she was finally noticing. And she couldn't even watch him chew. The smacking of his lips, the inhaling of his food. It made Lauren want to vomit.

When they'd first gotten together, she'd thought he was sexy. He'd been a chubby kid, he'd told her, but that wasn't evident in his adult form, which was nicely chiseled. He had full, nearly puffy lips, and dark, deep-set eyes. His hair had nice, thick body, and there was something about his intensity that women, including Lauren, found attractive. But that was then. Maybe her type had changed as she'd gotten older. Or maybe Jason had just curdled.

She spotted Robert giving a lesson to Larry Higgins, a member of the Salcombe tennis committee, on the singles court behind where she'd played.

"Connect farther away, Larry!" Robert said as the old man hit yet another ball into the net. "You're getting there. Remember, move your feet and turn your shoulders. Low to high!"

Robert was wearing black Nike shorts and a white Nike T-shirt, which hugged his slimly defined chest. He looked up and saw Lauren watching him, and though she was already warm from the July sun, she could feel her face burn. He waved to her, and she waved back.

She thought of their lesson a few days before that, her first of the season. Robert had come over to her side of the court to help her fix her forehand grip, which had always been off. She'd been wearing her cutest tennis dress, a white Lacoste number, and had applied a coat of waterproof mascara beforehand. She knew she looked good, and she'd wanted him to notice. He had taken her small wrist in his large hand, holding her racket, and then sliding her fingers onto the handle in the proper position. Lauren's legs had gone soft, and warmth had risen up her torso. On instinct, she'd subtly leaned back into Robert, pressing her back against his solid arm and leg. He didn't resist; she'd felt him get an erection. He continued to give her pointers about how she needed to straighten her arm more to get more power, and Lauren pretended to act interested in what he was saying, pushing her body harder against his as she did. Robert finally took a step back, nudging her toward the bench on the courts next to them. Lauren, snapped out of her own head, looked over to see Susan Steinhagen sitting there, staring at them suspiciously. Lauren gave her a little salute and shook it off. Susan hadn't seen anything, because there'd been nothing to see, she'd thought. She was probably just jealous that Lauren's game was improving so quickly. Susan used to be one of the top female players at the club, but now she was old, with a bum hip, and was relegated to the "seniors tournament," which no one watched or cared about.

Lauren had spent the past two days fantasizing about Robert. Thinking about him constantly, riding by the tennis courts to get a glimpse of him playing, turning the idea of having sex with him over and over in her mind. She'd never cheated on Jason; she hadn't even had a flirtation with a man in years. Where would she have met someone? She'd stopped working when the kids were born and so was only around other women, doing school stuff and exercise classes and dinners. When men were present, they were always with their own wives, looking bored. And it's not like Lauren found any of her friends' husbands attractive. They had potbellies or were too small or too old. Jason was the handsomest of any of them. So, this feeling of *wanting* someone, even if he was just a tennis pro, was completely new and thrilling. She kept coming back to what it felt like to touch Robert. Honestly, would Jason care if she did cheat on him? Lauren wasn't so sure. He'd been so disengaged, so pissy lately. He never looked up from his phone. Maybe he'd just shrug and let her get on with it.

She scanned the July 4 crowd for Robert, hoping that maybe he'd stop by the firehouse for a beer in between his clinic schedule. She hadn't booked another lesson since their last one. On the one hand, she wanted to be close to him again, but on the other, she didn't want to come off as pushy. Or worse, desperate. What if he wasn't actually into it?

They'd had that conversation at Rachel's party, his face close enough to hers to kiss. They'd been talking about Robert's dad — he'd told her he'd died a couple of years ago. She'd acted suitably sympathetic, though she couldn't relate. Her dad was alive and well in California, living it up at the golf course with his buddies. But she loved the way his face looked as he spoke, the small crinkles at the sides of his blue eyes, his jaw square and masculine. There'd been a pause in the conversation, and Lauren, feeling tipsy and bold and furious at Jason for ignoring her for what felt like forever, said to him in a low voice, "I want to be alone with you." What was wrong with her? Her husband was right there! This was a tennis pro! But Robert had just nodded and moved in closer, until, right then, Rachel had come over to offer them a drink, ruining the moment.

Then, at the lesson, he hadn't pulled away. If anything, he'd leaned harder into her. She wasn't imagining it, surely. It wasn't like Lauren to be so insecure. She'd always gotten attention from men — they still turned to look at her on the street. But she was out of practice.

Amelie came running up to her out of the Fourth of July throng, her face paint smudged, her dress covered in ketchup.

"Mommy, Lucy Ledbetter pushed me and spilled ketchup all over me! And then her mommy laughed." She collapsed in Lauren's arms, wailing.

Lauren looked for Beth Ledbetter, whose kid, Lucy, clearly took after her. There she was, standing by the beer, laid out on a folding table in plastic cups. Beth Ledbetter, née Taubman, was a Salcombe lifer. Like Sam and Rachel, she'd grown up there and had inherited her parents' house, a red cottage on the corner of Harbor and Pacific, when they'd retired to Florida. Though she'd been a constant presence in their youth, according to Sam, she'd never really fit in. Then, as now, she was combative, a know-it-all, and, on top of all of that, a huge liar. She literally made stuff up from scratch. (Jen, a psychologist, once clarified to Lauren that Beth was a pathological liar — someone who lied to get her own way or manipulate others — rather than a compulsive liar, who lied out of habit.) She'd flat out deny things she'd done — "No, I didn't take your 9:00 a.m. tennis lesson on purpose; the spot was open when I walked by" — and also stir up trouble where there wasn't any — "I heard Lisa *hates* Rachel."

Beth had disappeared from Salcombe summers from the ages of eighteen to thirty, showing up suddenly one year with a baby and a nearly silent husband, Kevin Ledbetter, in tow. She'd rebranded as Beth Ledbetter, dropping all trace of Taubman (though most other lifers stuck with their maiden names, if not in the real world then certainly here), and attempted to insinuate herself with the new couples who'd arrived in her absence, those who didn't already know her reputation. It semi-worked — she now had a small group of mom friends, people like Jeanette Oberman, Jessica

Leavitt, and Mollie Davidson, all of whom Lauren viewed as B-listers.

A couple of years ago, Lauren and her friends went from tolerating Beth to actively excluding her from drinks events and dinners at the yacht club. Beth retaliated by spreading a rumor that Lauren had been sending her children to camp with forbidden snacks like peanut butter pretzels, causing Lauren to get an angry call from Jessica Leavitt, whose son, Danny, had a deathly nut allergy. It wasn't true! *Once* at the beach, Lauren had allowed Arlo to have a bagel with peanut butter, but she'd made him stand far away from everyone and wash his hands afterward.

Lauren made her way over to the beer table, dragging Amelie by the hand along with her. Beth was standing with some of the firefighters, all of them sipping Coors and eating hot dogs. God knows what would happen if there was a fire today. Beth was wearing denim shorts over her chicken legs, and a ripped black T-shirt, her hair pulled back under a tennis visor. Instead of the cute summer dresses from brands like La Ligne or Gabriela Hearst that were sported by all the other women in town, Beth wore baggy outfits that hid her skeletal frame. It was *weird*. And Lauren hated weird.

Beth glared at Lauren as she approached. Amelie was still sniffling, and Lauren bent down and told her to go find Silvia while Mommy spoke with Mrs. Ledbetter. She shuffled away sadly, her sullied Pink Chicken dress now a throwaway.

Lauren was furious. Who laughs at a crying kid? Lucy was out of control, and Beth was encouraging it. Lauren never made a scene, but there was something about today that felt different. She bit down hard on her bottom lip. She was *angry.*

Beth was smirking now. One of her lackeys, Mollie Davidson, was standing by her side like some lame bodyguard.

"Hey, Beth, I need to speak with you," said Lauren. Her mouth felt like it lost all its saliva at once.

"What's the problem?" Beth shot back, standing up straighter in her ridiculous outfit, more suited to a seven-year-old than a grown woman.

"Did you laugh when Lucy spilled ketchup all over Amelie?"

Lauren couldn't quite believe that she was saying it as she did; most mom fights ended in fake apologies and promises to get a glass of wine later. A small crowd gathered around the two women. Lauren saw Rachel and Emily in the circle and was grateful to have two of her own posse there to help spin the story however it needed to be spun.

"Absolutely not," said Beth. "Little kids get in arguments. Why would I laugh at her? Though that dress *is* kind of funny."

There was an audible gasp from the observers. Lauren's cheeks stung. Her hands started to shake. Even Beth looked surprised that she'd gone that far. Lauren wasn't sure whether to turn and walk away or really go for it. *Fuck it,* thought Lauren. She'd had enough of people mistreating her lately. The surrounding group had grown twofold. Lisa and Brian were now in the mix. Where was Jason when she needed him? Fuck him.

"Oh, fuck *you,* Beth. My daughter is upset. You're such a liar. And a *bitch*!" Lauren yelled.

Beth's homely face turned white. She took a step toward Lauren. Was she going to try to hit her? Brian, hulking in his heavy firefighter's gear, stepped in between them.

"Ladies, ladies, let's all calm down. No one's going to come out of this making the winning investment," he said. *Fuck Brian Metzner,* thought Lauren. *Fuck all of them.*

Rachel swooped over and locked Lauren's arm in hers, leading her away from Beth and toward the field, where the kids were still running races and chucking water balloons at each other. Lauren spotted Amelie and Arlo, eating watermelon with Silvia. Luckily, they hadn't witnessed their mom's mental breakdown. Rachel kept walking until they'd reached the wooden bleachers in front of the baseball diamond. The two women sat down. Lauren felt like she might throw up.

"What *was* that?" said Rachel, still in her tennis clothes from earlier that morning, nearly bursting with excitement and trying to suppress a smile.

"I don't know," said Lauren. "Beth laughed at Amelie after Lucy bullied her, and I kind of just lost it."

"Beth is the absolute worst," said Rachel. Lauren was occasionally irritated by Rachel, but in situations like these, she was useful. Rachel was loyal to Lauren, and Lauren knew she'd spread anti-Beth gossip accordingly. Rachel leaned closer to Lauren. "I heard — and don't quote me — that Beth's been smoking a *lot* of pot lately. Even during the day," she said gleefully. "Maybe she was on drugs."

"Could be," said Lauren. She felt rattled and not at all like herself. Lisa and Emily walked over. They were dressed nearly identically, in white linen jumpsuits and big black sunglasses.

"Oh. My. God," said Emily when they arrived. Her long blond hair was swept up in an artful bun, and her arms looked twiglike. "I cannot believe that just happened. Are you okay?"

"Yes, yes, I'm fine. I think I just momentarily lost my mind," said Lauren.

"I'd love to unpack that with you," said Lisa, putting on her life coach hat. She was shorter than Emily and prettier, with brown shoulder-length hair and brown eyes that were strangely, but not unappealingly, set wide apart. She was a former PR maven who'd stopped working when she had kids, but she still put that loud energy into everything she did.

"I've never seen you like that," continued Lisa. "Did something happen today to set you off?"

"I honestly don't know," replied Lauren truthfully. "I'm still so upset about the scammer scandal at Braeburn. Jason and I have been at each other's throats. Maybe it had something to do with that?" Lauren immediately regretted saying it out loud. She knew better than to reveal anything of note in front of Rachel. Lauren saw her perk up.

"If it makes you feel any better, Brian has also been on my last nerve," said Lisa. "I always forget how annoying he is during the year, because he's off working and I'm doing my thing, and then we get out here for the summer and spend time together, and I'm, like, *Oh, yes: I hate my husband.* And why is he always wearing a fireman's hat around town? He's a hedge fund manager."

Everyone giggled, including Lauren. Lauren was starting to feel a little better. She knew that she held the superior position in town to Beth and that she'd end up coming out on top in all this.

"Speaking of men, there goes your boyfriend," said Emily, gesturing toward the boardwalk. Robert was there with a group of older women, including Claire Laurell, getting slobbered all over.

"Oh, please," said Lauren, who glanced over quickly. "He's like a child." She knew it sounded unconvincing as she said it.

"Come on, we've all seen him staring at you on the court," said Emily.

Lauren just shrugged.

"Okay, girls, let's go back to the food and drinks," said Lisa. "It looks like Beth and her crew have left. So, you'll just have to find someone else to scream and curse at."

Lauren laughed. Maybe she could enjoy this newfound power. The four women dispersed, each going to check on their brood before heading back to the action. Amelie and Arlo were fine — they were in the playground now, playing freeze tag with a group of kids. Lauren decided to walk home — she'd left her bike up there — and so headed up Neptune boardwalk toward the beach. She needed a moment alone before rejoining the merriment. She wasn't sure how she was going to explain the Beth incident to Jason; he hated when she lost her temper, even when it was just the two of them. The boardwalk was deserted and quiet. The whole town was at the field. Lauren heard footsteps approaching and then felt a tap on her shoulder. She turned to see Robert, alone. He was wearing fresh tennis clothes, his tan reflecting off his white Reebok shirt.

"How are you? I saw you got in a fight or something," he said. "Who was that woman? Are you okay?"

He was looking at her with genuine concern. Lauren hadn't felt that kind of attention in ages. It was marvelous.

"Oh, she's just the town bitch, Beth Ledbetter. I think you teach her daughter."

Robert shook his head. "I'm still so new. I feel like everyone here has ancient history together." Had he followed her?

"Do you want to come see my house?"

Lauren asked. She was feeling brave and strange. The Beth incident had unlocked something, though she wasn't yet sure what that was. "It's right there," she said, pointing to it, a two-minute walk away.

Robert hesitated.

"No one's there," she said, making it even awkwarder. It was past noon, and Jason had a tennis match. The kids were with Silvia at the field.

"Okay," said Robert.

He didn't say anything else, just followed Lauren as she walked to her beautiful gray beach home, past the bike rack with Lauren's light pink cruiser parked in it, and up the wooden staircase to the entrance. It was an upside-down house; the bedrooms were on the first floor and the kitchen and living areas on the second, which had the better ocean views. Lauren opened the screen door and felt Robert's hand run down her neck, landing all the way, firmly, on the small of her back. She didn't turn around, just led him through the hallway, lined with framed family pictures from past Salcombe summers, and into her bedroom, decorated in beachy, upscale hues of Hamptons blue and white. They stopped at the bed, and Lauren turned to face Robert. He took both of her shoulders and gently pushed her down.

Thank you, Beth, Lauren thought as Robert took off his shirt.

"Stay there," he said.

8
BETH LEDBETTER

Beth Ledbetter was a victim. That's how she saw herself, at least. The other women in Salcombe targeted her for no apparent reason. She hadn't done anything to them! She had every right to exist and play tennis and go to the yacht club. She'd been here longer than all of them, except for Rachel Woolf, that ass-kissing cunt. Rachel was obsessed with getting Lauren and Lisa and Emily to like her.

Beth couldn't be bothered to win over those cliquey bitches. She had her own friends, including Mollie and Jeanette and Jessica, and that's all she needed. She didn't have to be the most popular person in town. She'd never been popular. But she'd thought, perhaps stupidly, that by spending years away from Salcombe, she could come back and have a fresh start. Not be thought of as "Beth Taubman." She was a grown-up now, not the girl who was always picked last for the kickball games and teased by the boys about her stick legs.

Instead, she arrived at a town ruled by Lauren Parker, Jason Parker's glamorous ice queen wife, who was never going to let Beth in her crowd. Beth had met women like this before. They didn't like her vibe or the way she dressed. They hated that, unlike, say, Rachel, Beth pushed back when someone tried to take advantage of her. Beth wouldn't just shut up and take it, and that killed Lauren, who was used to operating without challenges.

Beth fumed as she rode home from the July 4 games. Lucy was still there, playing with Hazel Davidson, Mollie's daughter. Mollie was watching them both. Beth felt queasy from the midday beer and hot dog; when she got back to the house, she'd pack a small bowl, just to calm down her stomach. She and Lauren had gotten in a fight, a real fight, and now she'd have to deal with the fallout.

She thought about what she was going to say to Kevin. She'd just deny the whole thing. Say that Lauren had started it.

Beth saw Jeanette Oberman riding toward her on her rusty green bike. She slowed down and waved at her to stop. Jeanette, too short to pause on her bike with her feet touching the boardwalk, stepped off and put down her kickstand. She was in short shorts and a black bikini top, her breasts perched inside precariously.

Beth knew Jeanette was a mess — the split with Greg, the slutty wardrobe, the drinking. But Jeanette seemed to like her, so that was enough.

"You'll never believe what just happened." Beth was eager to get her side of the story out as soon as possible.

Jeanette, nodding, was happy to help.

"Lauren just went ballistic on me, for no reason whatsoever. The girls apparently had some little spat, and Lauren came marching up to me at the firehouse and literally almost punched me. You can ask Mollie. She screamed at me and called me a bitch."

"No," Jeanette replied. She shook her head dramatically, and her breasts shook, too.

"I *know,*" said Beth. "I really think there's something wrong with her. Like, I could have called security on her, it was that deranged. Brian had to stop her from physically hurting me."

"That's insane. Over a five-year-olds' fight? I'm just happy you're okay," said Jeanette. "Imagine if she'd actually hit you!"

"It was close," said Beth. "Okay, I have to

get home and calm down. I'll see you later at the club. I just feel a little shaky right now."

"I get it," said Jeanette, getting back on her bike. "Someone needs to teach that woman a lesson. She can't get away with that! I'll see you later." Jeanette rode off toward the field, and Beth continued toward her house.

Kevin would probably be upstairs on his computer. He hated that he didn't have his preferred gaming setup in Salcombe — that ugly black leather chair and all those annoying monitors. He hadn't been like this when they'd met eight years ago (on Tinder — a fact Beth didn't disclose to anyone). He'd loved video games, sure, and had been upfront about that. Most guys liked video games, right? But over the years, it had turned into a kind of mania. You couldn't pay him to play with Lucy, no way. Kevin ran IT at a virtual reality company, which wasn't very lucrative, but Beth's dad had money, so they were fine. He was either working or gaming. He barely even looked at her. Beth had to do everything alone. He wouldn't come to the club with her for drinks, he didn't participate in any of the town activities, he wouldn't go near the tennis courts.

Beth felt like a single mother, though she'd never have expressed that to her friends. It was too humiliating.

She pulled into her little red house on the corner of Harbor and Pacific and looked up to see Kevin in the window of their upstairs sunporch, sitting in front of his computer, eyes glazed. Beth sighed. She was looking forward to her bowl. She'd take a hit, sink into the couch, and plot revenge against Lauren Parker.

9

SAM WEINSTEIN

Sam Weinstein was not a sexual harasser. He was a good person. Sure, he liked to flirt with his coworkers. Who didn't like to flirt with women in the office? He'd done it his whole career. Women *loved* him. That wasn't his fault. Shit, everybody loved him. So, when HR had contacted him, all official, and said they needed to speak to him about a private matter, he assumed that maybe someone in his group was stealing. Or that perhaps he'd have to cut some heads in the wake of soft revenue. Instead, he'd been pulled into Mary Martin's office, where she and Henry Boro, the managing partner of the entire firm, delivered the shock of his life.

"Sam, there's no easy way to tell you this," Mary had said. She was middle-aged, with a no-nonsense gray bun. "Lydia Gross has informed HR that you forced her to kiss you in your office on April 12. We wouldn't normally tell you details about the complaint, especially her name, but because this is so specific, and we're launching an investigation, we're sharing info now."

Sam's stomach dropped. Lydia? He'd never kissed Lydia.

"As of now, she's not filing criminal charges; she's asked that the firm handle it as an internal matter. So, we'll be assigning an investigator, who'll be in touch. In the meantime, you can continue working — and we won't be informing your clients of the matter — but know that if it escalates, you'll be put on leave."

An investigator? On leave? This was too much for Sam to take in at once. Henry had cleared his throat awkwardly. He rarely came to the office anymore and was probably annoyed that this had interfered with that day's golf game.

"Listen, Sam," said Henry, "this is serious." Henry was in a crisp white button-down and slacks, his white hair combed back on his tan head. "We're all lawyers here; we know what this could mean for the firm and for you —"

Sam felt a slick of sweat forming in his armpits. He interrupted him. "Henry, Mary, I didn't do this. I've never even touched Lydia. She's lying. She's lying! If anything,

I think she's mad that I *wouldn't* kiss her."

Henry and Mary both looked at the floor. Sam knew he sounded desperate, but he was telling the truth.

The story was this, the gist of which he passed on to Henry and Mary: Lydia was a first-year associate, an ambitious young lawyer who'd risen at the firm accordingly. She'd wanted to join Sam's litigation team, so he'd given her the opportunity to work on a few cases with them, and she'd impressed him. It didn't hurt that she was attractive. Sam was a butt and boob guy — with the notable exception of his wife, Jen, who had neither — and Lydia was just that. She wore tight pencil skirts and low-cut blouses, to the point that the other male lawyers on their team gave her the nickname "Lydia-tits-a-lot." (Sam didn't participate in their locker room chat, as he was the boss, but more so because he didn't think it was a particularly clever name.) But he certainly noticed and appreciated Lydia's looks. She was hot in that way that the younger generation was — a little too done, with puffy, possibly injected lips and eyelashes that went on for ages.

One night, after a closing dinner at the Polo Bar, they'd all gone out for drinks at Bill's Burgers. Everyone had gotten sloshed, including Sam, which he admitted sheepishly to a disapproving Mary. Sam needed to stop at the office to grab some files before taking a car back to Scarsdale, so he'd peeled off before everyone else to do so. There were probably about six others there, including Lydia, and he'd said his goodbyes and stumbled to his twelfth-floor office at Sullivan & Cromwell's headquarters at 535 Madison. As he was gathering his stuff, the Uber to Westchester waiting outside, Lydia appeared at his door. It was late — probably around 11:30 — and Sam hadn't seen anyone else around as he'd entered. She walked in and shut his door, leaning on the wall in a come-hither manner.

"Lydia! Hi! Did you need to get something?" Sam had purposefully stayed across the room from her. Sure, he'd been tempted to cheat on Jen over the years — there was that woman he met in a bar in London during a business trip, another at a legal conference in Miami — but in the end, he'd always resisted. As a young, good-looking guy, he'd been with plenty of women before meeting Jen. Why take the chance of messing up his marriage? His worst nightmare was ending up like his parents. Granted, he liked to surround himself with pretty women at work, and he liked to joke with them, but it was all aboveboard. He didn't fuck any of them.

"I came here for you," she'd said, slurring somewhat. She started to unbutton her white silk blouse.

Sam didn't move. "Lydia, I don't think this is a good idea," he'd said, as measured as possible. "You're a beautiful girl, but I'm your boss, and I'm married."

Her top was completely open, exposing a black lace bra and very perky young breasts. It was almost too much for Sam to handle, and for a moment he'd thought, *Maybe?* (He didn't mention this in the retelling.) But then she'd turned and run out before Sam could say anything else. His Uber was still waiting, so he went home to Scarsdale, alone, bracing for Monday's awkward team meeting.

The next week was brutal. Lydia couldn't look Sam in the eye and avoided him as much as possible. Plus — and Sam wasn't sure how this happened — some of the younger guys on his team seemed to know that Lydia had a crush on him. Maybe she'd told them after he'd left the bar? He'd heard Jim Hagaen teasing her about it before he came into a conference room.

"Ohhhh, Lydia, here comes Sam! Your older fuckboi!" Jim had said. Sam had

141

entered to see Lydia looking down at her notes, red-faced. By the following month she'd told HR that maybe Sam's litigation group wasn't the right fit and that she'd prefer to work on the corporate side. She was gone shortly thereafter. Occasionally, Sam would see her in the elevator and have a quick, fake chat, and that was that. He didn't think too much of it. He'd been working at the firm for eighteen years at this point and had had his fair share of office weirdness, including the time he'd walked in on Henry Boro, the same Henry Boro standing before him, giving his former secretary a neck massage.

And now here he was, hearing from Henry and Mary that Lydia was claiming he'd basically assaulted her. Sam couldn't believe it.

"Listen, I'm all for #MeToo, I'm a feminist, hashtag believe women, yada yada," said Sam. "I've worked here for nearly two decades. You know me. Lydia is making this shit up." Sam felt spittle fly from his mouth as he spoke.

"Okay, Sam, we'll take your story into account. You'll have to repeat it to the investigator." Mary had sounded stern. Did she even believe him?

Henry stood up and reached to shake

142

Sam's hand. "Sam, we'll figure this out," he'd said. Mary shot Henry a look. "If you didn't do it, you didn't do it."

Sam wondered if Henry was thinking about the massage incident.

Sam hadn't told anyone what had happened, even Jen. He didn't want to worry her unnecessarily, or so he told himself. She didn't need to know he'd been wasted in his office with a younger female colleague, even if he hadn't done anything wrong. For the past month, he'd been chatting with the investigator, a flat-faced woman named Erin, at length, and having what felt like his entire work life torn apart. It was part of why he couldn't wait to get out to Fire Island that summer — he knew he could speak to Jason about it. Jason, his best friend since he was five. Jason, who'd saved him when his fucked-up parents fell apart. Jason, who knew him better than anyone.

It was July 4, and he and Jason had a tennis game at noon. The courts were empty; the rest of the town was celebrating with games and food at the field, including Jen and Sam's three kids, Lilly, Ross, and Dara, who were eight, six, and four. It was hot and humid, and Sam was looking forward to getting a good sweat on. He'd been stressed. He'd gotten word this week that the management committee was going to make a decision soon, and he'd barely slept since. How soon was soon?

He sat on the benches in front of the courts to wait for Jason. He'd told him about it as soon as he'd seen him, at Rachel's drinks thing the first night they were in Salcombe. Sam had been relieved to offload the info, but Jason had reacted strangely. He hadn't really asked many questions and hadn't brought it up with Sam since.

This whole year, really, Jason had been acting weird. Sam had barely seen him since last summer. Normally, they'd meet about once a month for drinks before Sam hopped on the train home, and had quarterly dinners with their wives. But Sam could count on one hand the number of times he'd hung out with Jason this year. Had Sam been so focused on himself that he hadn't noticed that something was wrong with Jason? He wondered if everything was okay with Jason and Lauren. They'd been somewhat frosty with one another at Rachel's that night, and this week, Sam had overheard Lisa and Emily having a tipsy conversation at the club, going on about Lauren and her "tennis pro boyfriend." He didn't know what that was about, but certainly Jason wasn't the tennis pro they were referring to.

Sam vowed to ask Jason what was up. He was likely being a bad friend. His therapist had told him recently that he needed to stop thinking that the world revolved around him. Sam had always thrived as the center of attention. People were drawn to him, and he had taken full advantage of it. As a kid, he'd cultivated his charm — he was funny, he asked questions, he flattered. He used it as a tool to ingratiate himself with anyone who would have him. He still called Jason's mother, Ruth, every week, chatting with her at her assisted living facility in Florida. Did Jason ever speak to her? he wondered. He'd have to ask.

He checked his phone. Jason was three minutes late for their game and had sent him a text.

Sorry, have to bail. Emergency work thing, will explain later. See you at the fireworks.

What the fuck? Just then, Rachel rode by, on her way back from the revelry at the field. She slowed down when she saw him.

"Hi! Who are you playing?" She was still in her tennis clothes from earlier that morning, her racket in her basket.

"No one," said Sam. "Jason just ditched

145

our noon game."

Rachel brightened. "I can hit with you! I had a 10:00 a.m. with the girls, so I'm already warm."

Truthfully, Sam didn't want to play with Rachel, but now he felt like he was stuck. He nodded okay.

Sam and Rachel had both spent every summer in Salcombe since they were children, running in and out of each other's houses, attending movie nights at the yacht club, taking sailing and tennis lessons together. He'd always liked her as a friend — she was fun and easy and up for adventures, the kind of girl you could pal around with but not one you wanted to date. He knew she'd always been in love with him — nearly every girl in town was — but he didn't encourage her; he talked about other conquests in front of her, purposefully, to let her know where she stood.

Then one summer, the summer he was nineteen, he relented. It was a mistake, but he'd been in a bad place. His parents had finally gotten a divorce, after an epic, decade-long legal battle that included having Sam testify in court. He'd thought he'd only feel relief that it was over, but instead, it sent Sam into a tailspin of depression and anxiety. His whole life, his entire childhood, had revolved around the fact that his parents hated each other but stayed together regardless. Without that, he felt destabilized. He and Jason had moved out to his Fire Island house that June, after their first year of college, and he'd started having panic attacks. He'd be on the tennis courts, hitting nicely, and then suddenly he couldn't breathe. Or he'd be swimming in the ocean on a calm day and, out of nowhere, he wouldn't be able to move his legs for minutes at a time. He told Jason, who was sympathetic, but didn't really have any plan other than to call his mother, which Sam didn't want to do. He didn't want to burden Ruth, yet again, with the fact that he was mentally falling apart. And so he'd turned to Rachel, who was a little older than they were, already a rising senior at Middlebury.

They were sitting on the beach together one day, and she asked how he was. He told her the truth. She'd listened and provided what Sam felt was mature advice ("Go to a therapist," "Talk to your parents about it," "Try to practice deep breathing"). In exchange, Sam had slept with her. He allowed her to nearly move in with him and Jason, to share his bedroom. As a bonus, she did his laundry and cooked dinner for him and Jason. It was a sweet deal, particularly because Sam continued to hook up with other girls on the nights that Rachel was with her own friends.

Sometimes he'd feel bad about it all, like when, at the end of the season, she'd told him she loved him and wanted to stay together. He *did* like her. He was drawn to her in a complicated, comforting way. She didn't judge him. And she'd taught him things about sex that, as a nineteen-year-old, he was grateful to try. But he'd thought she'd known all along that this was a one-summer wonder. He couldn't date Rachel, not really. He couldn't introduce her to his friends from Dartmouth, his frat brothers in puffy down vests. He'd let Rachel down gently, explaining that it would be too hard to go back to college tied down to one girl. They'd remained friends, though periodically she'd try to throw herself at him, which he always shot down (nicely! Sam was always nice).

He was sad for her that she'd never found a husband or had kids. It was sort of pathetic, but not unexpected. She was always just . . . *there* . . . waiting for someone — Sam, whoever — to take advantage of her. Sam wondered if she had guy problems because her father had died so suddenly when she was young. That must mess a girl up. He certainly liked Rachel more than Jen did. Jen thought she was a total gossip (Jen was right). And that she didn't have people's best interests at heart (Jen was always right). And that she stirred up trouble. Sam didn't mind. Though that still didn't mean he wanted to play tennis with her on a hot July 4 afternoon.

They hit for about thirty minutes. Rachel was good for a woman, with a loopy serve and a nice forehand. Sam played down to her and ended up enjoying himself more than he thought he would. They finished a set (Sam won, 6–2) and met back at the bench. Rachel was cherry-faced. Sweat beaded on her upper lip, and she was panting. For a quick moment, Sam remembered what it was like to fuck her.

"I'm beat," she said. "Want to come to my house for a Bloody Mary?"

Sam had nothing better to do, and he really didn't feel like joining his family at the sweltering, chaotic field games. They sat on Rachel's porch, cooled by the overhead fan. Rachel disappeared into the kitchen to make the drinks, and Sam texted Jen. She'd been acting funny since they'd arrived on the island. Somewhat distant. Maybe she was just adjusting to summer life, he thought. Rachel brought the Bloodies, which were spicy and strong. Sam hadn't had any breakfast.

"So, how are you?" said Rachel. She settled back into her white Pottery Barn couch.

She seemed happy, and Sam figured it was because she'd finally gotten him to herself. They'd known each other so long. Even the mole on her neck was familiar to him.

"You know, fine." He shrugged and took a big sip. "Jen and the kids are good, everyone's happy to be out here. Work's the same. How was your year? Weren't you dating someone?"

Rachel's face momentarily darkened. "Yeah, for like six months. I met him in September, and we were together through the spring. He's divorced, has two kids, eight and eleven. A lawyer like you, but corporate — at Skadden."

"What happened?"

"The same thing that always happens to me. It started to get serious, and then he bailed. He didn't like that I wanted to get married and definitely didn't like that I expressed interest in having a baby."

"Having a baby? Is that even possible?"

"Don't be a dick. I'm only forty-two, and I froze my eggs years ago. Science is a beautiful thing."

"I'm kidding, I'm kidding. Anyway, it sounds like he was the dick, not me."

Rachel sighed. Sam was starting to feel the vodka now.

"Yes, he was terrible. But I would have married him. I need to marry *someone*, for the love of God. I'm so ready to end my streak as the sad old maid of the group."

"You'll always be my favorite old maid," said Sam.

He'd finished his drink. In a flash, she'd brought him another. She sat down next to him, her thigh, peeking out from her white tennis skirt, nearly touching his.

"As long as we're being honest, how's your anxiety? You seem stressed. Is everything okay with you and Jen?"

Sam took a big, delicious gulp. Rachel made the best drinks. He decided to tell her about work, even though he knew it was a risky move, given her inability to keep a secret. But he had to speak to someone about it, and Jason kept avoiding him.

"I'm not great, actually," he said. "I'm going to tell you something, but you can't tell anyone. Even Jen doesn't know." He saw Rachel's eyes light up.

"Of course! Cross my heart." She x'd her chest as she said it.

Sam went into a detailed retelling of Lydiagate, emphasizing his innocence and eliciting *oh my God*s and *you* have *to be kidding me*s of sympathy from Rachel. This is what he needed. Someone to listen and take his side.

"Sam, I've known you my whole life, and I know you'd never force yourself on anyone."

It felt good to hear that. Very good. "Thanks, Rachel. I appreciate the support."

She paused. She shifted her leg closer to his. "If anything, women are always forcing themselves on *you*. I know I've tried." She gave him her flirtiest smile.

What was Sam supposed to do with that?

"Do you want another drink?" she asked.

"I'm good," said Sam. "It's barely lunchtime, and I'm already kind of toasted."

Rachel had also had two drinks. How strong had she made them? Her face subtly shifted to annoyance. *Here we go.*

"You're the biggest tease of all time," she said. Still playful, but there was an edge to her voice that Sam didn't entirely like.

"Oh, come on, Rachel. Let's keep it friendly. I've just bared my soul to you! Isn't that enough?" Sam tried to pat her on the back, but she moved away from him.

"You have no idea what it's like for me out here," she said. She was getting louder now. She must be drunk. "I'm all alone. Everyone has someone. Jen has you. Jen has *everyone*!" She put her hand over her mouth as she said it. Then she got up abruptly and left the porch, heading toward her bedroom. Sam didn't understand what was happening. What did she mean, "Jen has everyone"?

He followed her back through the hallway to find her lying on her bed, facedown, her tennis skirt flounced out around the back of her legs.

"Rachel, come on, get up. What's going on?" She was acting like a teenager, Sam thought. Or one of his kids.

She turned over but didn't sit up.

"Sam, I'm sorry about your work situation. And I'm sorry you told me instead of your wife. Have you thought about that at all?"

Sam sat down next to her. "You know Jen," he said. "I don't want her to get worked up before she absolutely has to."

"Do *you* know Jen?" she said. She had a nasty tone now.

"Okay, that's my wife. What are you getting at?" Sam had a bad feeling about this. His stomach started to turn.

Rachel took a deep breath. She sat up, her legs dangling off the bed. "I think that Jen might be cheating on you."

Sam felt dizzy. "She's not cheating on me. What are you even saying?"

"I'm almost positive," said Rachel. She looked at the wall and kept going. "I saw her with someone. I definitely saw it."

"Who?"

"I can't tell you."

Sam grabbed her thin wrist, pulling her toward him. He'd never touched a woman like this, and it felt strangely pleasurable. Like he could snap her arm in half. "Rachel. Who?"

There was the sound of a loud knock from outside. They both froze.

"Rachel? Rachel? Are you there?" It was Susan Steinhagen's roaring voice. She rattled the screen door, and Sam heard it open.

"Rachel, are you here? I need your help with the mixed doubles tournament draw. Rachel? You said you'd be here at 1:30. Are you in the back?"

Sam stood quickly, but not quickly enough. Susan's head, led by her prominent curved nose, popped into Rachel's bedroom, took in the scene, and then quickly pulled out.

"Oh, sorry! I'll come back tomorrow," she said as she rushed out.

Sam heard the door bang shut. Rachel was still sitting on the bed. Her face looked white. If anyone found out that Rachel and Sam had been sitting in her bedroom together, alone in the middle of the day, Sam was fucked. Without saying anything, Sam left. He walked through Rachel's porch, past the empty Bloody Marys (which Susan would have seen), out onto the boardwalk, and into the hot sun. He still felt a little drunk. He needed to find Jen.

10
ROBERT HEYWORTH

Robert Heyworth had just had sex with a married woman, a paying client at his very new, very lucrative job. So, that had been a stupid move on his part. But also: inevitable. Lauren wanted him and he wanted her, and they both knew it. No one to blame. And it had been good. And he'd do it again.

Robert had spent the morning of July 4 teaching lessons, starting at 9:00 a.m. First, he'd had the Longeran brats, Milly and Milo, eight and nine, who'd tortured him the entire time. "Robert is a big, fat poop. Robert is a big, fat poop!" they'd chanted, ignoring his calls to hit, follow through, and pick up balls. Their parents, as usual, were nowhere in sight. Then at 10:00, he'd done a 30-minute doubles strategy session with Rachel Woolf and Emily Grobel, who were gunning to win the women's tournament this year (it probably wasn't going to happen, but he'd certainly accept their money to try to help them). At 10:30, he'd had Larry Higgins for an hour. He liked teaching Larry because Larry didn't give a shit. He just enjoyed playing and wanted to keep improving, ever so slightly, into his old age. He hobbled around the court because of an old skiing injury, but he had a great time doing so, cracking jokes with Robert in between points. Afterward, they'd sat on the bench and chatted for a bit.

"So, how are you liking the gig? Is your house okay?" Larry had asked, wiping his face with a towel.

"I'm liking it a lot," said Robert, which was true. "And the house is great," he continued, which wasn't.

"You're shitting me," said Larry, chuckling. "The house is a dump."

Robert laughed. There was something about Larry that reminded Robert of his dad. An endearing, no-BS quality.

"Yeah, it's not perfect. But it comes with the job, and I'm happy to be living there. I just need to figure out how to get rid of all the ants."

"I can have Pete, the exterminator, come by. Don't worry about it." Everyone who worked in this town — who didn't have a house of their own and came in on the ferry to do their job — went by one name. Pete the exterminator. John the bike guy. Anthony the contractor. Luigi the plumber (yes, the plumber was really named Luigi).

"Thanks, Larry, I'd appreciate that. But otherwise, things are good. My schedule is booked up — I barely have time to grab lunch — and people are generally nice. Much nicer than other places I've worked."

"Oh, everyone here is a lunatic. We both know that," said Larry.

Robert laughed again. On cue, Susan Steinhagen marched over from the other court. Larry caught Robert's eye and made a grimacing face.

"Hello, Larry. Hello, Robert. Just the two people I need to speak to." Her voice was two levels too loud, as always.

"What can we do for you, Susan?" Larry said politely.

"I'm going to need both of your help in putting together the tournament draws. It's becoming a bigger and bigger job each year, and I need some additional support. Larry, you're on the tennis committee, so I'll deputize you to handle the sign-ups, and Robert, you can handle administrative tasks, like alerting people to their game times. I'll still be seeding the players."

"Oh, of course you will be," said Larry with a quick wink at Robert.

Susan clocked it. "Larry, this is serious business. You know how out of control people get about these tournaments."

Robert could imagine. For a town filled with mediocre tennis players, they all took themselves very seriously.

"I'm happy to help," said Robert. "Just let me know the best way to go about it."

Susan nodded. "I'm also going to loop in Rachel Woolf, as she knows the women players the best," she said. "Though I'll absolutely not allow her to influence who ends up playing whom."

"Oh, no, you could never," said Larry, continuing to goad her.

She shook her head at him. "Larry Higgins, you can expect my instructions imminently." Then she'd turned and walked back to her game of elderly women.

"Yes, sir!" Larry yelled after her, chuckling. "What a piece of work," he said to Robert when she was out of earshot. Robert feared Susan, particularly after she'd seen him and Lauren standing so closely on the court, and he enjoyed hearing Larry take the piss out of her.

"You never finished telling me that story about the former pro, Dave. You said Susan thought he might have been stealing from the club."

"Oh, yeah, the alcohol thing was a cover for her," said Larry. He picked up his racket and walked off the courts toward the club. Robert followed, nodding hello at Sam Weinstein as he went, stretching in preparation for his noon game. Robert had a break now until 2:00 p.m.

"Apparently, she'd noticed that lessons weren't getting charged correctly. Or, rather, they'd be charged twice. Dave had said it was a clerical error, but something was definitely fishy."

How stupid of that guy, Robert thought. After just a couple of weeks on the job, he could see a much easier way of stealing. All you'd have to do was not "officially" enter a lesson into the ledger and charge the member's card to a different account from the club's. No one checked who was on the court and when. He was the only one keeping track of it. Why hadn't Dave just done it that way? Maybe alcohol had scrambled his brain.

Robert had two hours to kill, so he walked over to the firehouse, where hot dogs and beer were being served, and the volunteer firefighters were all dressed up in their uniforms. They looked ridiculous, like grown men wearing Halloween costumes. There was Brian, snapping his suspenders.

Robert saw Brian's wife, Lisa, standing with Emily. They were dressed like twins in white jumpsuits. Robert was confused by the women in Salcombe, and he'd never been confused by women before. Did they like one another or not? He always heard them gossiping, talking about whose kid was misbehaving and whose tennis game wasn't as good as she thought it was. Henrietta, Larry's wife, didn't invite Claire to her dinner thing; Emily thought she could find a better doubles partner than Rachel; Lauren was vain. But on the flip side, they were all inseparable. They had drinks every night, they spent hours all together at the beach, they sat and watched their kids play corkball at the field in the afternoons. Like Lisa and Emily, they dressed identically in designer brands. He'd never worked — or lived, for that matter — in such a small community. He could see how you could get easily sucked in.

He spotted Lauren in the crowd, wearing a flowy, floral dress. The straps of a pink bikini were peeking out of the top. Against his will, Robert felt himself get momentarily hard. *Pull it together, you idiot,* he thought.

Claire Laurell walked up to him, taking the last bites of a hot dog. Instant erection killer. *Thank you, Claire.*

161

"Robert! How's everything? You're still here, so I suppose we Salcombians haven't scared you off quite yet."

Rachel had told him, in between serve repetitions, that Claire and her husband, Seth, had once been swingers. Apparently, everyone in this town had a secret or two.

"All good, Claire, thanks for asking. I saw you playing the other day — looks like you were doing well."

"I just like to hold my own with the young crowd," she said. "I can't run for shit, but it's nice of them to include me."

Robert heard a commotion near the beer table and turned to see Lauren standing in the middle of a circle of people. "Oh, fuck you, Beth!" he heard Lauren shout. Claire elbowed him, enjoying the show. Claire continued to ramble on about her game ("I just can't get my feet to move anymore"), and they were joined by a few other women of Claire's age. He listened patiently as they introduced themselves, one by one going over her tennis level and history. But he was only paying attention to Lauren, whom he saw walking off on Neptune toward the beach.

"I want to be alone with you," she'd said to him at Rachel's the other night. At first, Robert thought he'd misheard. He'd been focused on her all evening, even when he'd been chatting with the others. And he could tell she was into him. But her husband was right there. Then a couple of days later, she'd booked a lesson with him. She'd worn a fitted Lacoste tennis outfit, her lean, long legs on display. He'd wanted to touch her the entire time, and he finally found the excuse when she asked about her forehand grip. He went to her side of the court and took her delicate wrist in his hand, sliding it up the racket so it sat properly.

As he spoke — some nonsense about power and grip — she'd leaned back into him, nuzzling her warm body against his groin. She'd known what she was doing. He'd allowed her to settle in, enjoying the sensation of her butt pressing against him; he hadn't slept with anyone since he'd left Taylor back in Florida a few weeks ago. A few seconds passed before he'd noticed old Susan Steinhagen, sitting on the bench on the opposite court, watching them. Lauren had quickly stepped away, and they'd both acted casual for the rest of the lesson. Robert had vowed to figure out how to see Lauren alone. Now was his chance.

"I'm sorry, ladies, but I have to run. I look forward to seeing you on the courts!" he said.

They all smiled their most flirtatious old-women smiles.

Robert crossed the field, zigzagging among groups of sweaty kids wearing red, white, and blue, shooting each other with water guns. He passed the bleachers and turned up Neptune. He could see Lauren walking away, a lone figure surrounded by an arc of trees. He hurried to catch up to her. He didn't know what would happen when he arrived, but he felt the need to keep going.

And then she'd invited him to her house. He'd followed her in, impressed by the airiness of the place. It was so immaculate, both beachy and luxurious, hardly a trace of the two children who lived there with her. Robert thought of his own little shack, ants in the kitchen, the lumpy bed. He'd always imagined he'd have a place like this one day. Decorated, pristine, like the houses and apartments he'd stayed in with Julie.

He thought of Lauren's body, her flat stomach, her small, pert breasts, later that day as he walked from his house to the outdoor deck at the yacht club, set up for the annual July 4 cocktail party. After they'd had sex, he'd left her there, naked and satisfied, sneaking out her side door and making sure no one could see which house he was emerging from. He'd spent the rest of his afternoon teaching, distracted and drained. He'd slept with clients before, but this felt different. This town was so small, and everyone talked so much — if it got out, he'd lose his job. Then where would he go? Back home to Tampa? Begging his mom for money? The thought made him feel unwell. Images of Lauren kept popping into his head. Her tongue on his stomach. The top of her head, her beautiful blond hair, as she sucked his dick. He knew he would see her tonight at the party. Jason would be there, too.

The temperature had dropped nicely, and there was a breeze coming off the water. Robert turned onto Bay Prom and walked past Broadway to the yacht club, which was on Marine. Others were headed in the same direction, riding their rusty bikes in dresses or khakis and button-downs. Robert had on a white polo and seersucker shorts. He knew how to fit in with this crowd.

The deck was already packed with people by the time he arrived. It was 6:30 p.m., and the sun was still high in the sky. Waiters were passing hors d'oeuvres — mini quiches, shrimp cocktail, smoked salmon on toast that the women were declining. Robert was handed a glass of champagne. They'd spruced up the club for the occasion, putting tablecloths on the wooden tables and adding floral arrangements for some class. Robert always felt a little awkward at these things. Was he a guest or the help? He looked like these people, but he wasn't of them. In college, he'd gotten good at faking it, especially with Julie on his arm. But he was feeling rusty now, likely due to his recent prolonged stint in Shitsville, Florida.

"Robert! Fabulous to see you!" It was Emily. He'd just seen her that morning, though she greeted him as if it had been a year. She was wearing a white ruffled shirt that looked like an expensive doily, and large green earrings. Her blond hair was slicked back into a sleek bun. She wasn't pretty, but she was pulled together in an attractive way. That's what money could buy, thought Robert.

"Here, come chat with us," she said, taking his arm and leading him to a group that included her husband, Paul, and Jen and Sam Weinstein. Jen was her normal, friendly self. She was in a bright blue, kimono-like dress. Robert felt Sam rivaled him in handsomeness, though, with Sam's salt-and-pepper curls and tan skin, more George Clooney to Robert's Brad Pitt. Sam looked uncharacteristically grumpy. He barely even acknowledged Robert and was standing far away from his wife. Paul had been in the middle of a monologue, and he'd continued on.

"The reason we live downtown is to get the diversity of the city. Our kids are really experiencing the world, you know? If you live uptown, like Lauren and Jason, you're really only exposing them to that white, rich crowd. Also, I work in the music industry, and so my kids know that you can pursue something other than finance to be happy. I think that's so valuable."

For a tiny guy, Paul had a strikingly large ego. Robert could see that Paul was irritating Jen.

"It's somewhat hard to see how living in a beautiful apartment near Union Square and attending a private school is exposing your kids to the diversity of the city," said Jen. She was smiling as she said it.

"Our school is really low-key," said Emily.

Robert got the sense that Emily wasn't the brightest of the bunch.

"There aren't any grades — the teachers evaluate students based on their emotions. It's called a *feelings-led philosophy.*"

Jen raised an eyebrow.

"There are a lot of celebrity parents," Emily continued. "But they're like famous artists and authors and directors — not like

TV actors or anything."

"I thought you said the Gyllenhaal kids were there?" said Jen.

"Oh, you're right, but that's different," said Emily. "The school is so good that they send their kids all the way from Brooklyn for it."

"I used to give Jake Gyllenhaal tennis lessons," Robert offered.

Everyone turned to look at him. Even Sam seemed impressed.

"He was a regular client when I was at Brentwood. We used to go out for drinks afterward. Nice guy," said Robert casually.

Paul, in particular, eyed Robert with admiration. Robert knew a star fucker when he met one.

A waiter came over and offered everyone a gourmet slider. Robert took one. He was starving.

"I was also really happy with the way our school handled Black Lives Matter," said Paul. He was wearing a yellow-and-pink Hawaiian shirt, though Robert assumed it was more "a play" on a Hawaiian shirt than the actual kind that his dad liked to wear when people came over for barbecues. It was probably Valentino or something.

Sam had been silently sipping his drink, but he perked up at that.

"The race stuff, the #MeToo stuff I'm sick of all of it," Sam said. "People need to stop complaining and get on with their lives."

Jen looked at him, surprised. Everyone was taken aback; Sam was always so positive and light.

"I don't disagree with you," said Paul.

Here we go, thought Robert. He'd heard a million and one of these conversations among his clients. Rich people loved to bitch about people who tried to take away their power.

"At our company this year, the only employees who were promoted were Black. It was totally for optics. We'd send out a nice press release, which *Variety* would pick up, and we'd get some good PR for the fact that our leadership was stacking its ranks with people of color. But honestly, it wasn't a great move for the business. You need to promote the *best* people, full stop. Even white women are now getting the shaft!" Paul chuckled.

"Paul, aren't you supposed to be the woke one?" sneered Sam.

At that moment, Theo Burch, the only Black guy in Salcombe, walked by the group. He was with his white wife, Erica Todd, whose family owned a house on

Atlantic Walk and the beach. There was a tense second during which no one knew if Theo had heard Paul's rant. Theo, who dressed at all times like he was about to play golf at Augusta, had just been promoted to COO of a major insurance company. Robert had heard whispering on the court about how Theo had "benefited from the times," but from what Robert could see, Theo wasn't any less deserving than the other wealthy executives in this town.

"I don't know about white women," Sam continued darkly. "They still hold a lot of the cards in my world."

Robert, having finished his slider, drained his champagne glass. How could he get out of this conversation? He scanned the crowd — no Lauren yet. He didn't see Jason, either.

"Well, this chat just took a strange turn," said Jen.

Robert was getting shitty vibes from everyone.

"Robert, why don't you and I go look for stronger drinks?" she said.

Sam glared at him.

"Cheers, everyone," Robert said as he followed Jen into the bar area, leaving Sam and Emily and Paul standing there, looking uncomfortable.

170

Jen slid onto one of the red wooden stools and patted the one next to her. He sat down.

"Sorry about that," she said as she flagged down the bartender, Micah Holt. "Two whiskeys, please, Micah."

Micah's brown hair was parted dramatically on the side, and he was smiling widely, enjoying the power to please all his parents' friends. Robert felt a wave of envy for Micah's position in life; young, rich family, fun summer job. He reminded Robert of all the guys he knew at Stanford.

"Paul can be an asshole, as you might have heard, and I'm not sure what's going on with Sam. I don't think he really feels that way. Just ignore him," Jen said. She was clearly embarrassed. "I think people here forget that not everyone in the world has the means to buy a beautiful second home and live in this privileged place."

"Oh, don't worry about it. I've heard way worse," said Robert. It was true.

The door opened, and Lauren walked in, with Jason trailing behind her. Robert felt woozy. He turned so he was facing Jen entirely, not wanting Lauren to see him yet. She was in a sleek navy dress that hit at her calves and hugged the rest of her body. She looked dewy, her cheeks flushed, her blond bob angled just so. She waved at someone

171

toward the back of the room and headed that way, passing Robert and Jen without seeing them. Jason, meanwhile, made a beeline right to their seats. Robert felt Jen tense up.

"Jen, Robert, hi," said Jason. "How was your July 4? Did you see all the hoopla at the field?"

"Yes, I was there," said Robert. "Quite a day this town puts on." His throat felt tight. Why had Jason come to speak to him?

"Then maybe you saw my wife get into a fight? I heard it was a scene," he said.

Robert couldn't tell where this was leading. "Yeah, I saw something," he said.

"Is she doing okay?" Jen interjected.

"Yes, you know Lauren," Jason said. He seemed to have lost interest in Robert and was fully standing in front of Jen, staring at her. "She's always fine in the end." He waved Micah over. "I'll have a vodka martini, straight up with a twist."

Micah nodded and got to work.

Jen smiled at Jason. There was something going on that Robert couldn't put his finger on, but he was just happy to not have Jason's attention focused on him, the person who'd fucked his wife in his bed earlier that afternoon. No one said anything. Was Robert supposed to make conversation?

"Jason, how's your game coming along? I've seen Lauren out on the courts, but not you so much."

Micah handed Jason his martini. He wiped the condensation from the sides of the glass. Jason was in a blue-and-white-striped button-down, and his eyes looked even darker than usual.

"I was supposed to play today with Sam, actually, but something came up at work," he said. "But I'm definitely going to get out there next week. Maybe you can give me a lesson?"

How had Robert not known that was coming? "Yes, sounds great. I'm busy, but I'm sure I could squeeze you in one morning."

Jen shifted in her stool, and Robert saw this was his moment to escape. "Thanks for the drink, Jen," he said, standing up. "I'm going to go say hi to a few other players."

He left the two of them there, Jason standing and Jen sitting, and walked toward the back room. He took his drink out the back door near the tennis courts and headed into his little hut. It was wooden and compact, maybe five by eight feet, and held his buckets of practice balls, a small restringing machine, and some extra rackets for those who'd forgotten or broken theirs. It was where he hung out during the day in between lessons to cool off. He had a little chair and makeshift desk on which he kept his lesson paperwork and daily schedule. Luckily, there was also a door, which he closed to prevent clients from trying to discuss the ins and outs of their game during off-hours. He closed it now, too, and sat down at his desk, enjoying the silence. He drained his whiskey. He knew he should get back to the party, show his face and market his talents, but he felt anxious. He both wanted to see Lauren and didn't.

But it wasn't up to him. There was a quick knock on the door, and there Lauren was — she stepped in. She was holding a glass of white wine, and her eyes looked a little wild.

"What are you doing here? Someone will miss us," said Robert.

His heart was beating faster than he wanted it to. She put her wineglass down on his desk, sloshing it as she did, and pushed him against the restringing machine. Robert's back pressed uncomfortably against a piece of cold metal. Lauren kissed him hard and slid one of her warm hands down his shorts.

"I followed you," she said. "No one saw me."

"Lauren, Jason is right there, someone could find us," he whispered.

"I don't care," she said, pressing into him.

Her navy dress was riding up her legs, and Robert helped push it up above her waist. He turned her around and pulled her underwear down. His shorts fell to his ankles; he bent her over his desk and fucked her quickly from behind until they both came, fast and easy.

In an instant, she'd pulled her dress down and smoothed her hair. She kissed him lightly on the mouth and grabbed her glass of wine, slipping out the door and shutting it behind her. Robert pulled up his shorts and sat down. The whole thing had lasted maybe six minutes.

He knew he should be happy, but he felt sour and used. He decided not to go back to the party — he didn't think he'd be able to hold a conversation after that. Instead, he flipped through his little lesson book, looking at the lineup for tomorrow.

July 5 — Lesson Schedule

Susan Steinhagen — 9:00 a.m.–10:00 a.m.

Lisa Metzner — 10:00 a.m.–11:00 a.m.

Claire Laurell — 11:00 a.m.–11:30 a.m.

Doubles clinic — 11:30 a.m.–1:00 p.m.

Lunch
Larry Higgins — 2:00–3:00 p.m.
Lauren Parker — 3:30–4:30 p.m.

He'd see Lauren again soon enough. It was stuffy in his hut, and it now smelled like a combo of sex and the metallic scent of tennis ball cans. The little garbage can next to him was filled with power bar wrappers and empty water bottles. He thought of Dave, the poor old pro, and his botched attempt to skim off the top from the lesson pool. He must have been desperate. But how could he have been so careless?

It occurred to Robert, as it sometimes did, that Robert was much brighter than the average tennis pro. He'd been around enough of them to know that. At $200 a pop, all Dave had to do was siphon off one or two lessons a day to another account of his choosing. He'd have made an extra $20,000 on top of his salary. Twenty thousand dollars, tax-free, would be enough to pay Robert's rent for months while he looked for a better job in the city.

Robert stood up and started to fiddle with the restringing machine. Seth Laurell, Claire's husband, had left his Wilson racket this afternoon to be restrung, blaming his loss to Tom Schiller on his loose strings (he

176

lost because he wasn't very good; the strings had nothing to do with it). Robert had agreed to restring it for him, for $50. He picked it up now and started to snap the strings off with scissors, one by one.

Each snap made Robert angrier and angrier. What did Lauren want, anyway? A boy toy she could discard once the summer was over?

He thought about his dad and how he'd always hoped for more for Robert than to be a tennis pro. He thought about Julie and her glitzy life without him. He thought about all the opportunities that had passed him by. Then he threw Seth's racket against the wooden wall; it bounced off and nearly hit him in the face, landing on his desk and sending papers flying.

Robert sighed and picked up his lesson ledger. He sat down and looked at it again. If Dave couldn't steal correctly, maybe Robert could. No one would suspect him, particularly because no one would think he'd be dumb enough to try the same thing that Dave the alcoholic did the year before. He'd just *rearrange* the money. At the end of each week, he charged members' cards for their lessons; on Labor Day, the club would pay him 20 percent of that total pile. He sent copies of the receipts to the Salcombe Yacht Club Tennis Committee for records and tax purposes. So, going forward, he'd just leave off one or two lessons a day from his ledger. He'd still *give* those lessons, but instead he'd charge those cards to a different account, which he'd create tonight. Why *shouldn't* he get 100 percent of what people paid for his talents? He looked at the lineup for tomorrow again.

July 5 — Lesson Schedule
Susan Steinhagen — 9:00 a.m–10:00 a.m.
Lisa Metzner — 10:00 a.m.–11:00 a.m.
Claire Laurell — 11:00 a.m.–11:30 a.m.
Doubles clinic — 11:30 a.m.–1:00 p.m.
Lunch
Larry Higgins — 2:00–3:00 p.m.
Lauren Parker — 3:30–4:30 p.m.

He ripped that page out of the ledger, crumpled it into a ball, and put it in his pocket to throw away later. He turned to a fresh sheet and wrote:

July 5 — Lesson Schedule
Susan Steinhagen — 9:00 a.m.–10:00 a.m.
Claire Laurell — 11:00 a.m.–11:30 a.m.
Doubles clinic — 11:30 a.m.–1:00 p.m.
Lunch

178

Larry Higgins — 2:00–3:00 p.m.
Lauren Parker — 3:30–4:30 p.m.

He'd still give Lisa her lesson, charge her card (to him), and no one would be the wiser. No one was tracking his every move. Even Susan Steinhagen went to the beach and played bridge. With that extra $20,000, he'd feel a lot better about heading into this fall, jobless, in New York City.

Robert closed his ledger and left his hut, heading away from the club before turning on Harbor to loop back to his place. It was darker now, and he could hear pops of fireworks going over the bay. He passed Rachel's house; the light on the front porch was on, though he could tell no one was home. He hated all these people. Robert felt lighter as he continued down the quiet boardwalk. *Fuck all of them,* he thought. He was excited to take their money. Then he headed back to his kitchen filled with ants.

11
PAUL GROBEL

Paul Grobel pitied the other men in Salcombe. They were all so lame. At the July 4
cocktail party that night, he'd heard some
dude describe himself as "passionate about
finance." Passionate about finance! Ha!
"Yes, my name is Jackass, and I just love
moving money from one account to another
and taking it for myself." Paul couldn't
believe someone could be so vapid.

Paul worked in music, at Atlantic Records,
in marketing, where he helped to promote
various musicians and projects across plat-
forms. In truth, it sounded cooler than it
was. He was basically a glorified publicist
and wasn't even the head of his department
(he only made a couple of hundred thousand a year. Emily had no idea. He allowed
her to think he made at least half a million,
which was acceptable, given the creative
nature of his work.) But he enjoyed what it
sounded like to say he worked "in music,"

and Emily's family paid for everything, anyway.

He and Emily had met at a gallery opening ten years ago, and he'd impressed her with his knowledge of the artist. Even though Paul was short, he'd never had much trouble getting women to date him. Emily was small, too. She didn't seem to mind. His penis was big for his size. He was pretty sure that saved him. And he loved her, for real. He thought she was sweet and pretty and that she had good taste. (Case in point: out of all the men in Manhattan, she'd picked him to marry.) He liked the smell of her hair and the way she gave the boys kisses on their noses before they went to sleep.

He'd known she was wealthy but didn't realize quite how rich she was until they signed their prenup paperwork. It was funny for Paul, who'd grown up upper-middle-class on Long Island, well-off but not set for life . . . to be set for life. They'd decided to stay downtown, at Paul's behest, for "the culture," and Emily made a nice group of similar mom friends — creatives with parental support.

They'd built the Salcombe house next. Paul had nixed the Hamptons — too expected — and they'd settled on Fire Island for its quirkiness and charm. None of the homes there were quite right, so they'd decided to buy a house right on Clam Pond, an inlet on the bay, knock it down, and create their own from scratch. The process was truly a pain; the permits involved, the town zoning board drama. But now the Grobels lived in the biggest, chicest house in Salcombe. The sunset views were incredible. Paul had bought a large motorboat last year, which he kept at their personal dock.

Emily loved coming out for the summer. She said Salcombe was "normal" compared to their life in the city. Paul supposed this meant she liked playing tennis with her friends and going to the beach with the kids (Hayden, four, and Dash, six). Fine by him. He liked aspects of it — the house, the laid-back lifestyle, the fact that everyone started drinking at 5:00 p.m. every night. But he didn't really click with the men in town. They were all too macho, too sporty, too tall. They were lawyers and bankers, the kind of people who said they had a "passion for finance." That wasn't Paul's type. He could tell they all looked at his clothes, which cost a shit-ton of money, by the way, with a side-eye. Paul liked to talk about art and movies and music. He felt like this made him a more interesting person. Did he really want to talk to Brian about how often he rode his Peloton? No, he didn't. But it was just a couple of months, and so Paul could deal.

He was sitting on his back deck, sipping a glass of expensive pinot. Emily came out and sat down across from him. The kids were asleep; their nanny, Lucia, had gotten them down while Paul and Emily were at the cocktail party at the club.

It was dark and warm, and the bay was lapping on their dock. Lights from boats dotted the horizon.

"I feel like all my friends hate their husbands," said Emily.

She looked nice in the dim light. Paul hoped they'd have sex tonight.

"Do you hate me?" he said.

She smiled. "Sometimes," she said lightly. "You shouldn't talk about how Black people are getting promoted at work. It's offensive."

"I know, I'm sorry," said Paul.

She was right. He'd just been floundering for conversation at that point and was trying to engage with Sam.

"Something is definitely going on with Lauren," said Emily. "The way she looks at Robert . . . I don't know. I wonder if she'd cheat on Jason."

"I would cheat on Jason," said Paul. "He's a dick."

Emily laughed. "He is such a dick, it's true."

She got up and went over to Paul, standing behind him and massaging his neck. It felt incredible. He loved his wife.

"Honey, let's go to bed," he said, standing up and taking her hand. He caught his reflection in the sliding doors as they went in. He remembered that he really liked his Hawaiian shirt. It was Valentino.

12
JEN WEINSTEIN

Jen Weinstein was a cheat. She'd cheated on tests in school, writing the answers on her hands; she cheated in tennis, calling shots out that were in; she cheated at cards, glancing at opponents' hands when they weren't looking. And she cheated on men, every single one she'd ever dated, including her husband, Sam, who wouldn't in a million years have suspected her of doing any of it.

She was currently cheating on Sam with his best friend, Jason Parker, though Jason was just one in a long line of affairs. She even cheated on people she was cheating with. She'd been sleeping with Jason since last summer, but this winter, she'd had a one-off fuck with Tyler Brand, the husband of her friend Natalie Brand. She'd slept with him in his car, a BMW SUV, outside the Scarsdale Tennis Club, where their kids took lessons. Then she got out and went into the club to fetch Lilly.

Both Sam and Jason would be devastated to know that she'd done that, a fact that amused her. How were men so gullible? She'd married the most gullible of all. She loved Sam, she did. He was warm and funny, and he spoiled her, both with money and attention. He was lovely to look at, was great at parties, and was a fantastic, hands-on dad. They still had sex, maybe once or twice a week, and Sam was nicely forceful and interesting in bed. In short, he was an ideal husband, and all Jen's friends always told her so. But that didn't mean she could be faithful to him. Oh, no, that had nothing to do with him.

The cheating thing was her own thing. As a psychologist, Jen knew she was addicted to the novelty of it, that she thrived on the adrenaline of the secret. It wasn't about the sex, though she did like the sex. It allowed her, as a mother of three small children, to not go insane. She didn't want to leave Sam and start over; the idea gave her hives. She just wanted to feel alive.

And so this thing with Jason was starting to become a problem. Jason was the first person she'd cheated on Sam with, a million years ago. She'd been faithful to Sam for the first couple of months, a record for her, but then she'd met Jason on Fire

Island, and he'd seemed to want her so badly, she just couldn't resist. That he was Sam's best friend added to the titillation (in fact, Sam adored Jason, and Jason barely tolerated Sam, which she'd quickly picked up on). It was a onetime thing for her, but she knew Jason was smitten, to the point that he couldn't stop staring at her at his own wedding to Lauren. Through the years, he'd dropped hints that he was in love — longing looks, finding excuses to be near her — but she'd coolly brushed him off, feeling it would be too complicated and thinking he might be too clingy. Then last summer, she'd turned forty and had an internal meltdown, not that anyone would have known — Jen was always calm and collected. She started to feel suffocated in her own life, suffocated by her children and her beautiful house and perfect husband. Even the affairs didn't help (at the time, she'd been sleeping with her dentist, Dr. Ada).

So, when Jason drunkenly touched her leg at Rachel's cocktail party, she let herself lean in instead of pulling away. It'd now been a year, and their affair had only picked up steam, on Jason's side, at least. He was fully in love with her, which was a dangerous spot to be in. She was worried he was going to do something crazy, like tell Sam or Lauren, and then everything would be ruined. She didn't want to *be* with Jason. This was all getting too messy, particularly because they were now coexisting in such a small town.

For example, this afternoon, July 4, they'd had a quickie at Jen and Sam's house. Jason had been desperate to see her alone, and they'd not really had the chance other than one late-night meetup at the beach after a party at Rachel's the first night everyone was in town. But the amount of coordinating, and the attendant risk, made Jen jumpy.

Jason had agreed to play tennis with Sam at noon, when the kids would be at the field for the July 4 games with their babysitter, Luana. Jason texted Sam to cancel tennis at 12:01, when Sam was already there and waiting, while racing down to see Jen at her house. The hope was that Sam would either head to the field, or the store, or perhaps find someone else to play with while Jason and Jen had a scant ten minutes to have sex. They did, in Jen's son Ross's room, on his *PAW Patrol* bedding. Jason snuck out through the back door, not that anyone would have been suspicious if they'd seen him — he was Sam's best friend, after all. The whole thing had been unsatisfing and, even for Jen, too close of a call. What if one of the children had come home to pee? What if Sam had decided to come directly back to the house and had run into Jason on his way out?

Jen considered ways to extricate herself from her relationship with Jason. She was lounging on the blue-and-white-striped couch on her gorgeous front porch, sipping an iced tea. Many women, or rather, the kind of women Jen knew, would have balked at inheriting her in-laws' house instead of buying something of her own. But Jen loved Sam's parents' house. It was the perfect mix of shabby chic, seaside décor — sailboat paintings, pillows with anchors — with upscale touches like Viking appliances and customized closets. It was airy and sun-filled and homey. Perhaps Sam's mom had been trying to create the kind of environment she desired for her son, as opposed to the chaotic mess he'd lived through. Sam, who'd suffered some major anxiety in his youth, was happiest here. Jen, too, loved being on Fire Island. Before Jason, she hadn't fucked anyone but Sam in this town. It would have felt like too big of a betrayal. This was Sam's place.

And there he was, standing before her in his damp tennis clothes, curly hair sweaty and stuck to his forehead, a strange look on his face. It was 2:00 p.m., way after he'd been set to play with Jason, but Jen had to act dumb about that.

"How was your game? Did you win?" she asked breezily. She was wearing a tasteful black bikini with an oversize white button-down over it; she'd put it on after Jason had left. Sam swayed but didn't say anything. He seemed drunk.

"Jason didn't show," said Sam, weirdly staccato. "I played with Rachel instead."

Jen felt her body tense, though she knew there wasn't yet reason to panic. "Oh, nice, how was that?"

Jen knew Rachel had always been in love with Sam. They'd had a summer-long fling twenty years ago, which Sam had told her all about and which Rachel couldn't seem to let go. Jen didn't care. Everyone loved Sam. Women were constantly throwing themselves at him, sometimes right in front of her. He was a flirt, for sure, and Jen assumed he had slept with one or two other women over the course of their marriage. Who hadn't? But she was never worried about the possibility of him leaving her.

"It was okay; it was Rachel. What have you been up to?" He stared at her, but she refused to acknowledge his gaze.

"Just reading and relaxing. Luana has the

kids through dinner and bedtime — remember we have the cocktail party at the club tonight."

"That's *all* you've been doing? Reading?" His voice had an edge that Jen didn't like. Had he somehow seen her with Jason? Had someone else?

"No, I also went to the store to get milk." At that, Jen got up and walked through the living room, past the stone fireplace, to the country kitchen in the back of the house. She wanted to end the conversation as soon as possible. Sam took the cue. She heard his footsteps creak up the wooden stairs, and then the door to their room shut. Jen picked up her phone and opened the Signal app, which she used to communicate with Jason, among many, many others.

Jen Weinstein: Have you heard from Sam? He's acting strange.
Jason Parker: No, he didn't even respond to me when I canceled tennis. I've been at the beach since leaving your house.
Jen Weinstein: Okay, let me know if he contacts you. Something is up.

Sam didn't emerge from their room until later that afternoon, during the dinnertime ruckus. The kids were shouting and fighting, and Jen was desperate to get out of the house. She didn't know where Sam's attitude was coming from, but she didn't like that he'd been with Rachel beforehand. That woman loved to spin tales, and Jen was worried Rachel had somehow gotten into Sam's head. Jen had already showered and gotten ready for the party in the guest room — putting on the blue dress that Sam liked, which had been hanging in the wrong closet. Sam came down shaven and handsome in a green button-down. He still wouldn't look at her. *Fuck,* thought Jen. *Is this it?* Sam never got cold with her like this.

They said bye to the kids, who were shoveling plain pasta into their mouths, kissing their warm heads one by one, and walked over to the club. Sam kept a few paces in front of Jen, who struggled to keep up. The night was warm, and the bay was busy. Sailboats were tacking their way back to the Salcombe harbor, and there was a 6:00 p.m. ferry pulling into the dock, carrying weekend guests.

They walked in silence, waving at the people passing on their bikes. Jen tried to act as normal as possible, but she was feeling uneasy.

The club was packed when they arrived, a sweaty sea of polos and summer dresses and statement jewelry. They joined a particularly painful conversation with Paul and Emily, as well as the poor tennis pro, Robert, in which Paul managed to be racist and Sam, shockingly, to sound like he was discounting the entire #MeToo movement.

Jen was continually aghast at the lack of awareness many people in Salcombe displayed about their wealth and privilege. She didn't know Robert's deal, but she assumed he didn't come from much. Jen didn't come from money, either. She'd grown up in Ohio; her parents were both teachers at the local high school — her dad in biology and her mom in English. They were *fine,* not poor by any means, especially by Ohio standards, but they didn't have anything extra. Jen was their only child — her mom had her when she was forty-three, after years of trying. Jen was pretty and popular and smart. A cheerleader, for crying out loud. If she'd allowed her darker impulses to flourish more in her youth, would she be quite so shackled to them today? She'd never know. She went to the University of Pennsylvania, the first in her family to ever attend college out of state, and there fell in with a group of New York socialites, who adopted her because she was good-looking and fun. She followed them to New York

City after graduation, opting to attend graduate school in psychology at NYU, hoping to understand herself as much as others. She went into debt to pay for it, trusting that it would all be fine. When she met Sam, she knew it would be.

He was sweet and handsome and had money. He came from a broken family and loved that Jen's parents had been together for forty years. He admired Jen's work ethic and that she'd made her own way in the world — the kind of girls he usually dated had their daddies' credit cards. She truly liked him, too. Liked that he'd picked her out of every girl in New York. Liked that he paid for dinners. Liked that he had a beautiful beach home, all to himself, on Fire Island.

But then she went to Salcombe and met Jason and, inevitably, she was back to being Jen. There was a certain type of guy, moody and dark, that Jen seemed to have magical powers over. Something about her deep voice or kind eyes or fair skin, she truly wasn't sure. But Jason was a goner. She knew as soon as she introduced herself that he'd be obsessed. She'd only slept with him once; Jen had initiated it. Then she'd gone ahead with her relationship with Sam as if it'd never happened. She didn't cheat on him again until after they were married. But then she did. And did and did.

Jen was done with this conversation. Both Sam and Paul were being total idiots. She mercifully took Robert with her to the bar. Jason walked into the club at that moment, heading straight toward her, even though they'd agreed not to do that in public. Robert made small talk and then excused himself, likely sensing Jason's weirdness. Jen was screwed. She watched Robert disappear into the crowd, and then turned to Jason, who'd sat down next to her.

"I told you not to glom on to me in front of other people," she whispered. "Everyone in this town is watching everyone. It's getting too risky."

Micah approached them for a refill, but Jen shook her head.

Jason looked at her with his best version of a puppy dog face. His eyes were so black.

"But I *like* to speak to you," he said. "And I like to touch you." He brushed his hand against hers, and she pulled away.

"Jason, stop. We need to talk about this later, but not now."

Jen got up, annoyed, and walked into the big room of the club, decorated in kitschy Americana for the occasion — mini flags, red, white, and blue streamers. There was food laid out on two large tables, spreads of meats and cheeses and platters of oysters and shrimp.

Jessica Leavitt passed by and grabbed Jen's arm.

"How are you? I feel like I haven't seen you yet this summer."

"Oh, I'm fine. Just the same, really. How's your lot?" Jessica had two children, Danny and Rose, both of whom suffered from food allergies. It was all she liked to talk about.

"We're good. Happy to be out at the beach. Though it's harder here for Rose to keep track of her gluten, and Danny to stay away from nuts. It's really loosey-goosey, and not all of the moms are as vigilant as I'd like them to be."

Jen half remembered Lauren telling her a story about Jessica yelling at her over a peanut butter bagel. All the women out here were insane, thought Jen as she nodded through Jessica's story about Danny's school.

"He tested into the Gifted and Talented Program when he was younger, but the school closest to us was in Harlem, so that was a no-go. It's way too far to travel every day, and also" — here she whispered — "not a great neighborhood. And I don't even know if the school had an official no-nut policy."

Jen felt herself stifle a yawn.

Jessica continued, "Instead, we put him in Dalton, which is where Rose is. We really did consider the public school thing, though! Danny is such a strong student, we felt he could thrive anywhere. But we're so lucky to have so many options."

"Yes, we're all so lucky," said Jen. It came out harsher than she'd intended, but Jessica didn't seem to notice. Beth Ledbetter, dressed in cargo shorts and a raggedy T-shirt, approached them, smiling. Jen had heard about the fight with Lauren earlier that day, and she didn't want to touch that topic.

Jen was a floater among the women in Salcombe, preferring to be friendly with everyone, but not too attached to anyone. She liked that no one could figure out her loyalties. She was like that in Scarsdale, too. People admired her, but they didn't really know her.

"Hi, ladies," said Beth, clinking her beer bottle to Jen's whiskey glass and Jessica's wineglass. "Everyone having a good July 4? Jen, not sure if you heard, but Lauren and I got into a little tiff at the field."

"Yes, I heard. I hope you're all past it now," Jen said with a neutral face.

"She is *out* of control," said Jessica supportively. "It's not like you were doing anything, and then suddenly she's coming up and screaming, 'Fuck you!' "

Beth shrugged. "I'm just trying to be the bigger person. I think we should both move on," she said.

Jen nearly snorted but caught herself.

Jeanette wobbled up to them. She was wearing a tight pink, low-cut dress, and her curly brown hair was frizzing all over the place. Jeanette was here this summer with her two boys, Mason and Luke, but without her husband, Greg. Jen had heard that she'd caught him in bed with their dog walker. Jeanette was small, maybe five feet, but she was a force. Jen could only imagine the scene when she'd walked in on Greg screwing the dog walker, with the love of Jeanette's life, Doobie the poodle, looking on.

"Girls, girls, how is everyone?" Jeanette was slurring, already wasted.

"We're doing great," said Jessica. "Beth was just recounting her fight with Lauren. How are you?"

"As good as I can be, alone with two monster children and no husband to help." Jen thought it best not to bring up that Jeanette did have a live-in nanny with her for the summer. Let her have her moment.

"That must be so hard," said Jessica.

"He's such a loser," said Beth. "Kevin would never, ever do that to me." Jeanette scowled as Beth blew on. "Jen, you're a psychologist — why do men cheat so much?"

It's not just men, thought Jen. "Oh, it's a host of reasons," she said gamely. "Self-esteem issues, anger issues, the need for variety. And then there's the simple answer — one partner isn't in love with the other."

That shut them all up.

Jen took the moment of silence to say goodbye and wander away. She looked out the big bay windows toward the deck to see if Sam was still there. He was, standing with Paul and Emily. Jason was also with them now. Lauren was nowhere in sight. She waved hi to Theo Burch and Erica Todd as they passed, headed inside for another drink. Jen didn't want to go outside to Sam, but she didn't want to chat with anyone else, either. She was tired and irritated by both men in her life. Jason for being too clingy, and Sam for possibly knowing too much. She headed out back toward the tennis courts for some air, sitting on a bench that faced out toward the "stadium court," the only court that had room for spectators, the one on which all the tournament finals were played. The sprinklers were on, wetting the green clay, and Jen felt a second of calm before two strange things happened. First, she saw Lauren coming out from the little tennis hut that the pros used for storage. Lauren was smoothing down her navy dress, and she spotted Jen immediately. Instead of saying hi, Lauren smiled in a distant manner, as if Jen were an acquaintance rather than a good friend. Then she turned around and walked toward the outdoor deck of the club.

A minute or so later, Jen heard a loud crack inside the hut, as if something had been thrown against the wall. What — or who — was that? But filled with enough of her own skeletons, Jen decided not to investigate. She quietly got up and walked back into the club, steeling herself for more inane chat and a husband who possibly hated her.

13
MICAH HOLT

Micah Holt was drunk. He'd overdone it at the club after his shift ended, taking shots with his friends until the lights came up at 1:00 a.m. He was now lying in his bed, at his parents' house on Navy Walk, and his head was spinning. He tried to focus on a spot on a ceiling, but it just kept going around and around, so he shut his eyes tightly. He knew he should probably make himself throw up — tomorrow would be miserable otherwise. But he didn't feel like dragging himself to the bathroom and risking his parents' hearing him retching. He was too old for his mom to chide him for drinking too much.

Micah pulled up his cozy green comforter, inhaling its familiar, fresh Fire Island scent. He'd spent every summer here since he was born. It was where he felt happiest, a fact he was more than a little ambivalent about. At college, he protested against income inequality. He and his friends spent ages circling the question of their own complicity in society's ills. Being gay didn't get him off the hook, especially since he'd grown up in a bastion of gay acceptance. He was wealthy and white, and he did feel guilt accordingly.

And yet, here he was, thrilled to be back in this enclave of privilege. There were barely even any other gay people here! Just one lesbian couple, Karen and Shannon Travis, who'd inherited a house on East Walk from Shannon's parents. Ah, well. Wasn't that just life? Enjoying things you weren't supposed to enjoy?

Micah thought about what he'd seen at the July 4 party. He was now totally convinced that Jen Weinstein and Jason Parker were having an affair. Early in the evening, Jen had been sitting at the bar with the beautiful tennis pro, Robert, whose gaze Micah had been trying to catch for days. Could he possibly be into guys? He was so good-looking and so hard to read. Even Micah wasn't sure what his deal was. Jason had approached them, Robert took off, and Micah saw Jason try to touch Jen's hand. She'd immediately left Jason on his own, angrily sipping his martini, an off putting scowl on his chiseled face.

Micah had been busy; parties at the yacht club were pure chaos for the staff, people packing in at the bar and shouting for his attention. "Micah, get me three chardonnays, two Stellas, and a vodka on the rocks!" "Micah, Micah, we need a round of Casamigos!" "Micah, my boy, where's that whiskey I've been asking for?" And on and on. Rather than feeling overwhelmed, Micah thrived on the attention. He'd done musical theater in high school, and this was the closest he now got to the thrill of being onstage.

Jason sat on his stool for the better part of an hour, eyeing Micah, which Micah noticed but tried to ignore. Finally, during a rare lull, Jason flagged him over.

"Another martini, Jason?" Micah asked, easy breezy.

"Sure, Micah. And also . . ." Jason softened his voice. "I wanted to thank you for keeping my little walk the other night to yourself. I appreciate your discretion. You've always been a good kid."

Micah, a bit creeped out, felt his face get hot. He nodded and went back to his drinks station, determined to avoid Jason as best as possible. (Which, given the nature of this town, he knew was a losing battle.)

A little while later, Micah watched as Sam Weinstein stomped out the front door, followed shortly thereafter by Jen, a neutral smile in place, as always.

Lying in his bed, feeling the warmth of vodka rise in his throat, it struck Micah that maybe it wasn't a question of *if* people were liars but just of how big a liar you were. After Micah's shift ended, he'd texted Ronan to see if they could meet up at the beach. They'd been seeing each other every few days, and Micah was starting to miss him when they were apart. It was a dangerous feeling, bound to end in heartache, he knew. But he couldn't help it. He loved Ronan's sweet vulnerability, that he was so different from the self-consciously clever crowd Micah hung with. But Ronan never texted back. It was the first time that had happened, and Micah felt confused and hurt. So, as typical of twenty-year-olds throughout time, he'd drowned his sorrows in alcohol. He and Willa had stumbled home together, Willa peeling off at Anchor walk and Micah continuing to Navy, lucky to not have fallen off the boardwalk as he did. You could kill yourself that way.

■ ■ ■ ■

PART III

■ ■ ■ ■

July 24

14
RACHEL WOOLF

The Bay Picnic was Rachel Woolf's favorite day of the entire summer. It was always on the last Saturday of July, and they'd gotten perfect weather this year, eighty degrees and sunny, without a lick of humidity in the sea air. This evening, the entire town would gather on the bayfront on the west side of town, in the sandy area between Bay Promenade and the bulkhead. At 4:00 p.m. on the dot, the town security started letting people set up — everyone raced to put down beach chairs at their preferred picnic spot, a ritual that had, more than once, ended in minor violence (couched in "accidental" elbowing). Then, at 6:00, people brought their picnic spreads, the more elaborate the better — grilled steak, gourmet sliders with meat from Pat LaFrieda, huge raw seafood towers piled with pounds and pounds and pounds of shrimp. Families formed picnic pods and had been paired up for years; you couldn't switch who you picnicked with, even if you hadn't spoken to them in ages (or actively hated each other). There was a Beatles cover band set up in the center of it all — four long-haired white guys crooning "Hey Jude" — while Salcombians ate and mingled as the sun set, sampling other families' feasts and drinking copious amounts of premade margaritas and wine. The kids ran around wild.

To Rachel, the annual Bay Picnic represented the best a town like this had to offer — old-fashioned fun, a community feel, and plenty of alcohol. Plus, there was always lots to untangle and gossip about the next day.

This year, as for the past decade, she was eating with the Weinsteins, the Parkers, the Grobels, and the Metzners. Their little crew had a tradition of doing a Mexican theme, and each couple was given a course to take care of. (Rachel was the only singleton in the group, but that wasn't mentioned.) She'd been assigned appetizers this season, and she planned to do nachos, a selection of salsas, and homemade guacamole — no red onions, per Lauren's request.

Jen, Emily, and Lisa were splitting the mains — quesadillas, grilled corn with cotija cheese, and fish tacos. And Lauren was bringing dessert. She'd ordered churros from Boqueria in New York City, which were set to arrive on the boat that afternoon. One of Lauren's mom friends from Braeburn did PR for that restaurant group, and Lauren had called in a favor.

Rachel had spent that morning prepping — assembling the nachos, which she'd stick in the oven at 5:00 p.m., picking the best bowls to display her variety of salsas, ordered from a specialty store in Los Angeles that she'd read about in *Condé Nast Traveler*. She'd make the guacamole last, right before she left, as otherwise it'd go brown. And there was nothing worse than brown guacamole, was there?

At 11:00, she had a tennis game. Rachel and Emily were taking on Lauren and Jen. Jen wasn't part of their tennis crowd, but she'd asked Rachel repeatedly to include her. This was Jen's shot. Rachel had seen her taking some lessons with Robert and also in games with B-level players like Beth and Jeanette. She wasn't sure Jen could hang with them, but she was fine to give her a chance. Any practice for Rachel and Emily was good practice. Plus, the idea of Lauren and Jen being partners amused Rachel in a dark way. She was still the only one who knew about Jen and Jason. She'd told Sam that Jen was cheating on him with *someone* (he had a right to know, didn't he?). But she hadn't yet delivered the blow that it was his best friend.

He'd been hounding her for more information in the few weeks since, pulling her aside at parties, sitting next to her at the beach, trying to wear her down. But she'd held her ground, informing him that it wasn't her place to give him more details. She had to admit, she enjoyed the attention, as well as the stormy way he spoke about Jen with her.

Rachel walked over to the courts at five to 11:00, fresh in one of her Adidas dresses and Oakley sunglasses. They weren't the most flattering, but Rachel couldn't see in the midday sun without them, and her mom had always taught her that when it came to sports, function trumped fashion. Lauren hadn't gotten that memo. She arrived next, in a tight white dress that came down low in the front. Had Lauren pulled her breasts up in her sports bra for even more cleavage? Rachel could tell she'd applied makeup, but it was the "no-makeup makeup" look that only someone like Lauren could pull off. Lauren was more naturally pretty than almost any of the women in town, maybe except for Jen, depending on your taste. Rachel wasn't wearing a stitch of makeup other than lip balm with SPF. As usual, she felt cowed by Lauren's appearance and air. The only time she felt more powerful than Lauren was on the court, occasionally, when her serve didn't abandon her. Rachel reminded herself that for all of Lauren's beauty and style, her husband was having sex with another woman. That made her feel somewhat better.

Emily and Jen rounded out the foursome and the women took to the stadium court and started to warm up, hitting shots to each other from the service line, giving the other opportunities to volley and serve. Jen and Lauren made a pretty pair. They had a Betty-and-Veronica vibe, the blonde and the brunette. Rachel, who played the backhand side, was warming up with Jen, who played forehand. Her shots were much better than Rachel had anticipated; her forehand had nice topspin, and she had a backhand slice that Rachel would have to look out for. Rachel was jealous that Jen had so much time and money to dedicate to the sport — in between sneaking around with her husband's best friend. What a lucky slut.

It was time to start the game, and the women gathered around the watercooler in the middle of the court to hydrate. Rachel thought she and Emily should take this match easily, particularly if Jen was a beginner in terms of doubles strategy. She wouldn't know where to be on the court, and Rachel could take advantage of that.

"Okay, ladies, have fun!" said Emily, faux cheerfully. Women always complimented each other's shots, gave supportive advice, told each other how cute they looked in their outfits. But just below the surface, they all wanted to kill each other.

The first few games went by in a flash, and before Rachel knew it, she and Emily had lost the first set 3–6. Jen was playing great; her first serves were going in, and she also had an unexpectedly sharp net game. *What the fuck?* thought Rachel, banging her shoes with her racket to get out the impacted green clay. Lauren was also making backhand winners and expertly lobbing over Rachel's and Emily's heads when they were both up at the net.

Rachel and Emily huddled in the back of the court to talk strategy before the start of the second set. Lauren and Jen were at the watercooler chatting. Rachel saw Robert sitting on the bench opposite the court, behind the green fencing, to watch them all play. He was leaning back, arms crossed over his chest, his legs spread in a casual but commanding way. Rachel felt a thrill seeing him there. She'd been working with Robert closely these past few weeks, nearly once a day, trying to level up before the tournament. She wanted him to be proud of her and see how far she'd come.

"We need to take Lauren's lobs out of the air," said Emily, cleaning her sunglasses with her shirt. Emily's face had no lines at all; Rachel knew she got Botox but wondered if it was more than that. But what's more than Botox?

"I agree," said Rachel. "We need to crowd them at the net and be more aggressive."

Emily nodded. The plan was set. But, while Robert looked on, it didn't work at all. Lauren and Jen took the second set 6–2. Rachel and Emily, outmaneuvered, missed easy shots and hit volleys into the net. The partners met back at the watercooler to shake hands and say, "Good game." Lauren and Jen were beaming, which made Rachel even angrier.

"Wow, you guys played great," said Emily graciously. "You pretty much trounced us. Jen, I didn't realize you were that good!"

"Oh, thanks," said Jen. "I told Rachel — I've been playing a lot this year. I'm happy it's finally paying off. And it's easy when you have such a great partner."

Lauren smiled.

"Lauren, wait, do you have a partner for the women's doubles tournament?" asked Emily.

"No, I don't. I don't play in the tournaments; I get too nervous. And this town is so intense," said Lauren.

"You and Jen should play together!" said Emily.

Rachel had been hoping she wouldn't suggest that. What a moron Emily was sometimes.

"Oh, no, no," said Jen. "I'm not good enough to play in the tournament. I'm really just starting."

"Well, you've already beaten us, and we got to the finals last year." They'd lost it to Vicky Mulder and Janet Braun in a heartbreaking three set-er, 6–2, 4–6, 5–7. Rachel still thought about what went wrong nearly every day.

She remained silent. She wasn't going to encourage this. Lauren looked at Jen and raised her eyebrows under her sunglasses.

"I would, Jen, if you'd like to," said Lauren.

Jen shrugged.

"Okay, I'm in," she said.

No, thought Rachel. *No.*

They left the court. Robert was still on the bench. Rachel approached him as the other women said their goodbyes and took off on their bikes home. Everyone had picnic prep to finish.

"Did you see our match? What did I do wrong?" She sat down next to him. Rachel admired his square jaw and perfect lips.

"Well, firstly, you kept hitting it to the player at the net," he said, smiling cutely at her. Was he flirting? "Secondly, you were both running up too quickly, and so Lauren kept lobbing over your heads. One of you needed to stay back."

Rachel was taking this all in, filing it away so she could use it when they played Jen and Lauren in the tournament.

"Got it. You're so right," she said. Rachel had a thought. "Are you going to the Bay Picnic tonight?"

"What's the Bay Picnic?"

"You have to come!" said Rachel. "Everyone brings dinner to the bayfront at West Walk. There's a band, people dance and eat lots of food. You should come and sit with us. It starts at six. Our group is me, the Parkers, the Metzners, the Grobels, and the Weinsteins. All your faves."

Robert laughed. "Okay, sure," he said. He got up, standing in front of her with his strong, tan legs. "I'm heading to a lesson now, but I'll see you later."

The rest of the day dragged. This always happened to Rachel the afternoon before an event she was looking forward to. She rode to the beach around 2:00 p.m. and spent the next couple of hours relaxing there, sitting with Lisa, who was watching her kids splash in the ocean. Rachel had brought a book in case everyone was busy with their children. She often felt left out of that part of Salcombe life — the camp stuff, the babysitting dramas, the swim lessons. The other women did their best to include her, but there were inevitably events — and more importantly, gossip — that she missed because she was childless. It made her depressed. She tried not to think about it.

"Lauren and Jen are going to play in the doubles tournament together. Can you believe it?" she said to Lisa. Rachel was sitting on her Tommy Bahama beach chair, facing out toward the ocean.

It was a calm day with barely any waves. The lifeguards, fit and brown, were sitting on their tall white stand to Rachel's left.

"Oh, really? I thought Lauren hated playing in those things. And isn't Jen a beginner?"

One of Lisa's girls, Maryloo, sauntered over. She was only nine, but in a skimpy red bikini more appropriate for an adult.

"Mommy, Rhenn keeps taking buckets of water and pouring them on my head."

Rhenn Davidson was Mollie and Jeremy's boy. He was a terror.

"Honey, just walk away if he's doing that. Go play with your friends in the hot sand."

The kids referred to the area closest to the dunes as the "hot sand," because on warm days it felt like it was burning your feet. Maryloo obeyed, walking back toward the dunes, plopping down close to where Rachel had been sitting when she'd seen Jen and Jason kissing at the beginning of the summer.

"Yes, Jen is a beginner," Rachel continued. "But she's picked it up quickly, and with Lauren, they could be a real threat."

Lisa played tennis, but not with the same drive or intensity as Rachel and Emily. She was in it more for the skirts and shit-talking.

"They have such a funny relationship, don't they," said Lisa.

Rachel still couldn't tell what Lisa had done to her face over the winter. Filler, probably. Rachel got an occasional shot of Botox in her forehead, but nothing compared to what her friends out here did. She needed to catch up.

"I've always wondered if they actually like each other, or just pretend for their husbands' sakes," Lisa went on. "They're so different."

"Totally. They're also both kind of mysterious," said Rachel, who knew more than she was letting on.

"Especially Jen," said Lisa. "I've known her for, what, almost a decade? And I still don't feel like I *know* her. Sam is such an easy, nice guy. But there's something about Jen that feels off to me."

"I know what you mean," said Rachel. She wished with her whole being she could tell Lisa about Jen and Jason. It was practically falling out of her. But for once in her life, she practiced restraint. Maybe this was what *personal growth* meant, Rachel thought.

"Well, hopefully they don't crush you in the doubles tournament," said Lisa, chuckling. "Either you'd die of shame or murder them both, neither of which is a great outcome."

"Don't be a bitch," said Rachel, laughing. But Lisa had a point.

After another hour, the beach cleared out. Rachel went home and put the nachos in the oven and chopped for the guacamole. At 5:00 p.m., she had a quick meeting scheduled with Susan Steinhagen, to help her with the women's doubles tournament draw. Rachel walked over to the courts and entered Robert's little hut. Susan was already there, wearing a neon tracksuit that looked like it was from 1985. Susan had never mentioned seeing Sam in Rachel's bedroom on July 4. It was the worst of both worlds — Susan probably thought she and Sam were having an affair, but they weren't. Rachel felt a pang of self-pity.

Susan was holding a list of twenty pairs of players, everyone who'd entered the tournament. She wasn't as familiar with the newer players and younger women, so Rachel took a pen and wrote notes next to each coupling.

Laura June and Hailey Milotic: Laura has a great net game but is inconsistent with her ground strokes. Hailey can hit a strong backhand down the line, but that's basically her only shot.

Trisha Spencer and Jane Rosen: Trisha's weapon is her serve, which has great spin and hits deep in the box. Jane is a backboard — she gets everything back but dinks it over.

Jenny Jamison and Paula Rudnick: Jenny can't move — she had hip replacement surgery last winter and is still recovering. If the ball is hit directly to her, however, she has a nice forehand. Paula never comes to the net.

And on and on. Susan looked on as she wrote, nodding approvingly.

"Nice work, Rachel. I appreciate it," she said when Rachel was finished. Even when Susan was being kind, she was still intimidating.

Rachel thought that was that. She went to leave the hut, but Susan held her arm and pulled her back in, closing the door. She narrowed her eyes at Rachel, her lips pursed.

"Rachel, I need to speak to you about something, but confidentially," she said.

Rachel immediately steeled herself for a question about why Sam had been in her bedroom. She'd already prepped a story about how she'd been feeling unwell on the court, and he'd escorted her in to make sure she was okay.

But instead, Susan said, "Have you noticed something going on between Lauren Parker and Robert? I know you're her friend."

Rachel shook her head. She hadn't, had she? They'd all been looking at Robert this summer, it was just that Lauren was the only one of them who was pretty enough to get him to look back.

"No, I don't think anything is going on," said Rachel truthfully. "Lauren likes to flirt with him, but all the women do."

"I know," said Susan with a disapproving snort. "I've seen the two of them getting cozy during lessons. The reason I'm saying anything is that I don't want Robert to go the route of Dave, if you know what I mean."

Rachel did. It was unlike Rachel to miss a beat, but maybe she'd been so focused on Sam and Jason and Jen that she'd over-looked this. She'd have to ask Lauren about it later. She knew Lisa and Emily were always giggling about Lauren's obsession with Robert, and it was true Lauren was playing way more than usual this year (and wearing more revealing tennis outfits). Honestly, if Lauren was having sex with Robert, who could blame her? But Lauren should tone it down. Rachel knew Lauren wouldn't want to be thought of as the mar-ried floozy who was sleeping with the pro.

"I get it, Susan," said Rachel. "I'll speak to her. Thanks for telling me."

Susan opened the door to release Rachel, relieved to get out of that stressful, stuffy room. She was behind on her prep. She needed to finish the guacamole, melt the cheese on the nachos, shower and get dressed, and pile everything in the wagon before 6:00 p.m. She'd speak to Lauren at the picnic. She realized she'd possibly made an error in inviting Robert to join their group. But come to think of it, it'd be a good opportunity to observe the two of them in action. That's how she'd spotted Jason and Jen.

She entered her front porch feeling frazzled by it all. Everyone seemed to be in the midst of some steamy, potentially life-changing affair but Rachel. She felt left out. That's when she saw Sam sitting on her white couch, waiting for her to arrive.

"What are you doing here? I need to finish getting ready for the picnic. We're all going to be late," she said to him.

Sam was still in his bathing suit, an old gray T-shirt hanging appealingly on his chest. His curly hair was wild from the ocean air, and he looked upset.

"Rachel, I just got bad news," he said.

Was Sam going to cry? She'd only seen him cry once before, when they were young and he'd told her he'd seen his dad slap his mom across the face during a fight.

"What's the matter?" she said. She sat down next to him, her thigh connecting with his warm leg. He didn't move it away this time.

"I just got a call from our managing partner, Henry. He said that they've decided to ask me to go on leave while they finish the sexual harassment investigation. I don't know what I'm going to do. This crazy bitch is ruining my life. I can't tell Jen. Anyway, according to you" — he nearly spat the words in Rachel's direction — "Jen is having an affair. So, even if I *wanted* to tell her, I wouldn't. It's all such a disaster." He put his head in his hands. Rachel noticed that his neck was sandy. He must have been up at the beach with the kids.

"I'm sorry, Sam. That's terrible. Did they say how long your leave would last?"

"No. It's summer, and everyone is at their fucking Hamptons house, so the investigation is going at a snail's pace." He slid down the couch in defeat, brushing his leg along hers as he did. Rachel sensed an opening. He was in a bad place. His wife was cheating on him. His job was on the line. But she wanted him to want her, not to be depressed and in need of a pity fuck. Rachel stood up. It was nearly 5:30. She didn't have time for sex. It was Bay Picnic day. Her favorite day of the summer.

"Sam, can we discuss this tomorrow? I could have you over for lunch and Bloody Marys. You could tell Jen you're going for a run. It's just that I'm really behind and I need to get everything done before six."

"Who cares about this dumb picnic?" said Sam. "Why does it matter? Do you really have nothing else going on in your life?"

Rachel's cheeks stung. Now he was just being mean.

"Don't take this out on me, Sam. It's not my fault that you're in this mess."

"Come on. You're the one who felt the need to inform me that Jen was sleeping with someone else. And now you've gone quiet. You told me *just* enough to hold it over my head, but not enough for me to do anything about it. So, it kind of *is* your fault."

He was sitting up straight, and his voice was raised. It was a tone Rachel hadn't heard before — dark and threatening. She needed him to be quiet. She couldn't have anyone hear Sam Weinstein yelling at her in her own home.

"You need to leave now. I'll see you at the picnic."

He stood up and put his face directly in front of hers, so that their noses were almost touching. She could smell his breath, which was sweet, exactly the way she remembered it from all those years ago. Then he turned around and took off, gently closing the

224

screen door behind him, leaving Rachel scared and confused. Plus, she still had to finish the guacamole.

15
JASON PARKER

Jason and Lauren Parker had been yelling at each other all day. Lauren was getting churros for the picnic delivered on the ferry — her friend Abby did PR for Boqueria and had arranged everything. Jason thought it was a bit much for the Bay Picnic. What was Lauren trying to prove? Now it had become a super-stressful thing. The churros had gotten on the wrong ferry and had arrived in Fair Harbor, the town next to Salcombe, instead. Lauren had spent the better part of the afternoon hunting down the ridiculous fancy churros. Calling the ferry company, meeting every boat as it arrived, and then finally figuring out that the churros were indeed on Fire Island, but in a neighboring town.

She sent Jason to ride over to Fair Harbor to pick them up, which he did, unhappily. Hence the yelling. Arlo and Amelie were at the bay with Silvia, so at least they didn't have to witness their parents fighting about something this ridiculous.

Jason had had it with Lauren. This summer so far had been the pits. He could barely see Jen — logistically, it was nearly impossible to be alone with her here. Lauren was being a lunatic. She was obsessively playing tennis, like two or three times a day, and then she'd disappear for stretches at a time, doing God knows what, leaving Jason alone with the kids (well, Jason and Silvia). She'd gotten in that fight with Beth on July 4 and since then had been slightly unhinged. Their squabbling had intensified over the past few weeks, to the point that Jason just found himself screaming, "Those fucking churros can go fuck themselves!"

Meanwhile, Sam was being depressive and was hounding Jason for moral support over this sexual harassment mess. It reminded Jason of when they were kids, the summer after Sam's parents got divorced. He was mopey and clingy and not at all his usual fun self. Jason was starting to worry there was something else going on, maybe having to do with Jen. He'd never said anything about it to Jason, but there was a look in Sam's eye that Jason didn't like.

After the summer he'd been having with Lauren, Jason was prepared to tell everyone the truth. He and Jen were in love and were going to be together. It would be the biggest scandal Salcombe had seen since Dottie Hart and Meryl Haggerty, the women's doubles champions in the '90s, announced they were ditching their husbands to move in together. Lauren Parker, queen of Salcombe, scorned? Sam Weinstein, Salcombe's handsomest man, rejected for his worse-looking best friend? Jason imagined the gossip as he walked over to the bay in front of West Walk for the start of that night's Bay Picnic.

He'd already done one trip there with the wagon to transport the lost-and-found churros, as well as some pitchers of palomas to go with the Mexican theme. Now he was walking back alone; the kids had gone with Lauren ahead of him, all dressed up, as usual, Amelie in some full-on Stella McCartney Kids getup that Lauren had insisted on buying for hundreds of dollars.

It was a beautiful night. Clear with a light breeze. The bay water was sparkling in front of Jason as he approached the crowd of about two hundred people. They were gathered around wagons and small tables, drinking, chatting, and bobbing awkwardly to the Beatles cover band, set up in the middle of it all, doing a wobbly rendition of

"Paperback Writer."

Jason found their group easily, as Rachel always claimed the same spot toward the back left, next to the water. Lauren complained about it every year. ("She puts our stuff down so close to the bay, if any of the children sneeze wrong, they'll fall into the water and drown. Rachel doesn't have kids, so she doesn't think about stuff like that.")

Lauren was standing with Arlo and Amelie, pouring them water into plastic cups. She was wearing a sky-blue pleated dress that hit at her knees and had a V neck that showed off her still-pretty-great cleavage. The sun was hanging in the sky behind her over the bay, a big orange ball, threatening to start lowering any minute. He always liked Lauren best from afar.

He saw Rachel there next to her, fussing with the food placement, and the tennis pro, sitting in one of their beach chairs nearby. Jason guessed Rachel had invited him. She was always looking for single guys on the island, though she rarely found any. Jason didn't think Robert, with his model good looks and athletic swagger, would be a willing target for a desperate fortyish woman. Brian and Lisa were also there, taking selfies in front of the water. A large group of kids had gathered around the band, and

Jason saw Lauren direct Arlo and Amelie over, shooing them away with all the maternal care of an ant.

He scanned the crowd for Jen and Sam but didn't see them. It had been two weeks since he'd been able to be with Jen alone — after the brief July 4 meeting, they'd managed to have sex at Jason's house once, in his and Lauren's room, while Lauren was taking a two-hour tennis clinic and Silvia was with the kids at the beach. Jen had told Sam she was taking a bike ride to Fair Harbor. It was quick and not great. Jen didn't seem into it, and Jason came in about a millisecond.

Jason sidestepped a few other groups on his way to their area, nodding hellos as he went. He passed the Laurells and their middle-aged friends, all in chino shorts; Susan Steinhagen and the rest of the oldies, the women in colorful muumuus; Micah Holt and his crew of cool kids, looking trendy in crop tops (he could sense that Micah had been avoiding him since that first night of summer; so long as Micah kept his mouth shut, which he clearly had, Jason didn't care if he couldn't get a martini at the club to save his life). And there were the Ledbetters, the Leavitts, and Jeanette Oberman, alone this summer without Greg, who'd been caught fucking the dog walker. Jason wondered what Lauren would do if she found out about him and Jen. Would she kick him out, like Jeanette did to Greg? Would she scream and yell and cry? Would she be cold, calmly asking him to leave, never letting him see his children again?

"Hey, Jas, how's your week been? I had some *fantastic* wins," said Brian, done with his forced Instagram photo shoot. He was chugging a paloma. Jason reached down and got one for himself, sipping the sweet drink from a red Solo cup.

"Fine, fine. Work's been busy, but I managed to do a couple of jogs to the lighthouse," said Jason, already bored by the conversation. Lauren came over, and for once, Jason was grateful to see her.

"How are you, Brian? You and Lisa get some feed-worthy pictures? Want me to take one?"

She really was so goddamn pretty, Jason thought, looking at his wife. He wished he liked her more.

"Yes, please," said Brian, handing her his phone. He grabbed Lisa, who was eating a nacho. She momentarily bristled at his touch before putting on her Instagram game face, smiling with her husband in front of the beautiful sea view. Lauren snapped from

231

every angle. Jason could see a large bead of sweat drip from Brian's hairline down his forehead to his cheek.

He wondered where Jen was; it was past 6:30, and the party was in full swing. Just then, he spotted Sam headed toward the group, walking from the boardwalk, weaving in and out of wagons and tables, stumbling a little as he went. Was he still in his beach clothes? As Sam got closer, Jason could tell he was wasted. Fuck. What had happened? Where was Jen?

"Is that Sam?" said Brian, mid-chew of a large fish taco. "Why is he still in a bathing suit?" Sam looked like he'd just emerged from an all-night beach rave, sand on his legs, hair going in every direction, a glazed look on his sun-kissed face. He approached almost in slow motion, every head turning toward him as he passed. Jason could hear the swell of whispers as he went.

"Is that Sam Weinstein? What's up with him?"

"Why is Sam wearing that?"

"Where's Jen?"

"Is he drunk?"

Jason's feet felt glued to the ground. Any other year, he'd have gone over to Sam immediately. But right now, he was worried this had to do with him. He saw Lauren

232

looking at him, confused. Robert was the only one who took action, getting up from his chair and helping Sam, stumbling, over to their area, gently placing him in the chair in which he'd been sitting. Robert crouched next to Sam and started speaking to him, but Jason couldn't hear what he was saying.

Lauren came to Jason's side.

"Go see what's wrong. There's something wrong with him. Jason, go," she hissed, pushing him toward the chair.

He went over to Sam and Robert, standing up over them, not sure what to do. Sam was clearly in a bad way.

"What do *you* want?" Sam asked, looking up in his direction but not entirely at him. "You haven't been speaking to me all summer. What have you been up to, Jason? *Work?* What?" His voice was raised in anger now, and people started to wander over to see what was happening. Jason saw the Ledbetters and the Leavitts ambling toward them, salivating at the thought of picnic drama.

Rachel joined Jason, her hands in her mouth, nervously biting her nails.

"Come on, don't make a scene," Rachel said quietly.

Sam stood up shakily, facing the two of them. Robert stood up, too. No one said anything for a moment, and Jason hoped Sam was thinking of taking Rachel's advice.

"Why would I listen to you?" said Sam. "You're the one who told me my wife was fucking someone else. But maybe you're just lying. Maybe you're just trying to ruin my marriage because you're so miserable."

Rachel stepped back as if someone had punched her in the stomach. Jason felt like he might throw up.

"And guess what?" Sam continued. A group of about twenty people had gathered near them, pretending not to care, but hearing everything. "I lost my job! Because some bitch falsely accused me of kissing her!"

Jason didn't know what to do. Should he drag him out of there? There were kids everywhere.

Lauren tugged Jason's sleeve and whispered in his ear, "I called Jen. She's on her way."

Then Sam took off, running at full speed toward the Great South Bay. He launched himself into the water like an excited kid at an amusement park, creating a large cannonball-like splash.

"Sam Weinstein jumped in the bay!" Jason heard someone scream, sending nearly the whole town of Salcombe racing to the bulkhead to get a glimpse of the village golden boy having a drunken breakdown. Sam was floating on his back, about ten feet out. His face looked calm, and his eyes were closed. Jason felt a hand on his arm and turned to see Jen, panicked. She was still in her bathing suit and cover-up; her hair was matted to her head, and she didn't have any makeup on.

"You have to get him out of there. Now. Get him out!" She was nearly crying.

Jason saw Rachel staring at him and Jen coldly, eyeing Jen's hand on Jason's arm.

Motherfucker, thought Jason. *Rachel knows.* But he didn't have time to think about it, not really, because he had to go rescue Sam. Once, when they were seventeen, a group of them had gone swimming in the ocean at night, stupidly, drunkenly. The waves weren't huge, but there was a strong pull that Jason hadn't anticipated. He'd suddenly found himself far away from the shoreline in the pitch-blackness, the water cold and gray. A surge plunged him under, and he didn't know if he was headed up or down. He'd finally sputtered up into the air, gasping and frightened. He couldn't see his friends, though he could hear their voices. He thought about how mad his mom and dad would be to get a call that he'd drowned after chugging eight beers and jumping in the freezing Atlantic. "Jason! Jason!" He'd heard Sam first and then felt his grip on his torso, strong for a kid. "Let's get you back. Come on, come on," Sam repeated, dragging him along as they went, reaching the sand and collapsing together.

Now it was his turn to help, though it didn't look like Sam was at risk of drowning. Just of making an even bigger fool of himself. He went to the bulkhead, teetering on the edge. "I'm coming to get you!"

Jason jumped into the bay. The shock of the water hit his clothed body. He dunked his head in the murky liquid before bobbing back up, almost directly next to his friend. Sam was still doing a back float. Jason doggy paddled over to him. Everyone was watching them.

"Let's go, get the fuck out of the water. You're making a scene and you're also scaring Jen."

"Oh, fuck Jen," said Sam, not opening his eyes.

"Come on, dude, that's your wife." The words got stuck in his throat as he said it. It was freezing in the water, and Jason was feeling weighed down by his clothes. He was circling his legs underneath him to stay afloat. He didn't want to do this for much longer.

"She's cheating on me. Rachel told me. I was going to speak to you about it, but you've been avoiding me. Why?"

"I told you, I've been slammed with work," said Jason. He couldn't think quickly in this situation — he needed to get out of the bay to get his story straight. He looked up to see revelers lining the shore, methodically sipping their wines.

"Who could it be?" asked Sam. "Max Leavitt? I saw them talking closely once at a party at the Grobels'. It couldn't be Paul, could it?! No, he's way too short for her. Plus, she hates him." Sam paused. "Do you think she's fucking that tennis pro? He's good-looking. But that would be such a cliché. That's not Jen's thing. Anyway, it seems like that guy only has eyes for Lauren."

"Oh, I don't think so," said Jason. Though maybe it was true. Lauren had been acting odd lately, hadn't she? His heart was beating in his ears and his shoes felt like rocks on his legs. "What happened at work?" Jason asked. "Is the investigation over?"

"I got a call from Henry this morning informing me that I'll no longer be working while they finish it. They're not firing me; I'm just 'on pause,' as that dickhead put it."

"And what about the girl? Any news of her?"

"No, no idea. I believe she's still at the firm on the corporate side. I haven't heard otherwise."

"What are you going to do?"

"Well, now everyone in town knows, including Jen, so I guess I'll just kill myself."

"Not funny," said Jason. "Listen, I'll help you. We can find the best lawyers to represent you. Even if you end up losing your job, the firm will have to pay you millions in reputational damage."

Sam was silent. They'd floated farther out, to the point that they were semi in danger of entering boat traffic. Jason saw Jen standing on the edge of the bulkhead. She looked young. She was shivering. Someone had given her a sweater, which was wrapped around her small shoulders.

Jason felt weird, like his whole life had led up to this uncomfortable moment. "Come on, let's go back. Lauren is going to cut my head off if we don't eat some of her fucking gourmet churros."

Sam laughed softly. He turned over, finally, and started doing the crawl stroke to the small ladder that led up to the beach. Jason followed in his wake, grateful the end was in sight. They climbed out one after the other, just like they used to when they were kids during swimming lessons at camp. First Sam, then Jason.

The crowd mercifully dispersed as they emerged, everyone too embarrassed to ask if they were okay, retreating to their own picnic areas to privately, gleefully discuss what had just happened.

Jen and Rachel handed them both towels, which they'd gotten from who knows where, and Lauren appeared in front of Jason, looking concerned for once. The group went back to their spread, everyone standing around awkwardly in front of the cold nachos and browned guacamole. Brian and Lisa had made their way to another area, perhaps ashamed to be associated with Sam's antics. The sun was hanging at the horizon, a gigantic red orb, about to set. Jason needed to get out of his soaked clothes, but he wasn't sure what the protocol was for a situation like this. It was Sam, Jason, Lauren, Jen, Rachel, and Robert, hands in his pockets, looking amused. Sam broke the ice.

"Well, everyone, you could say I had a bad day. I'm having an issue at work — someone accused me of something I didn't do — and so I'm now on leave from my job. It really set me off. I'm sorry to everyone here for my behavior. I'm sorry especially to Rachel's guacamole. I know I've let you down."

Everyone laughed. After all these years, Jason was still shocked at Sam's ability to disarm and charm people.

Jen walked over to Sam and locked arms with him. They looked at each other and smiled, and Jen whispered something into Sam's ear. Jason felt light-headed. What was happening here? He started to shake, maybe from the cold, maybe from nerves.

"Lauren, I have to go home and get out of these clothes," said Jason. "Are you okay with the kids?"

Lauren nodded. He didn't say goodbye to anyone. People stared as he passed, but he didn't give a shit. He wasn't the one who'd flown off the handle and humiliated himself in front of the entire town. He hurried home as the sky darkened, nearly running all the way along the boardwalk. Jason could hear the band playing as he went. "Hey Jude," then a weak version of "When I'm Sixty-Four." He wondered if he'd be with Lauren until then. That was over twenty more years.

When he got back, he went into his room, with its soothing blues and charming beachy décor, and closed the door. He grabbed his phone and opened Signal.

Jason Parker: Jen, what's happening? What's going on with Sam? Does he know anything?

He kept the app open to see if she was typing. No response.

Jason Parker: Jen, I love you.

Nothing.

16
LISA METZNER

Lisa Metzner's life had been changed by
mushrooms. Every three days, she swallowed a thumbnail-size amount of gray
powder, just the right dosage of crushed
psychedelics to make her feel alive. She'd
discovered microdosing last year, through a
mom friend from Horace Mann, a granola-
loving woman in the model of Gwyneth Pal-
trow. She'd sworn that microdosing would
cure Lisa of her headaches and her minor
depression and had passed along her deal-
er's info. Lisa, curious, in need of a jolt,
tried it immediately. She'd never looked
back.

Mushrooms made her feel alert. Happy.
She could focus on her life coach course-
work in a way she'd never imagined possible. She loved Brian more. She enjoyed
being a mom.

She was particularly grateful to be tripping when Brian had told her, a month ago,

that his fund had gone to shit. They'd made some bad bet, and now Brian was paying for it, to the point that Lisa was worried they'd have to sell their place in Salcombe. It hadn't come to that yet, but Brian, between his blustering lies to everyone else, was in total panic mode. Lisa was trying to keep it together, to stay upbeat for Maryloo and Myrna, but it had been tough. The mushrooms were getting her through.

So, when she'd seen Sam Weinstein jump into the bay, for a moment she'd thought she'd mistakenly taken too much. Was she hallucinating? But no, Sam was really in the water. Doing a back float while the rest of the village watched in surprise. Jason had gone in after him, their two heads bobbing up and down as the sun set. Maybe she and Brian weren't the only ones with things to hide.

Lisa was generally an open person. She'd risen in the celebrity PR world in her twenties and thirties, representing spoiled, demanding movie and TV stars. She was adept at handling difficult personalities, stroking people's egos, and allowing them to think they were in charge.

Brian liked that Lisa was fine with him being the center of attention, so long as she was steering the ship. She treated him like a client; hyping him up, turning the other way when he made a fool of himself, and ultimately making peace with the idea that he was providing her income.

She'd stopped working when the girls were small, but when Myrna went to school full-time, Lisa needed something else. It was too late to get back into the PR game, an industry for which the off-ramp was final. She'd heard of a friend of a friend becoming a life coach and, after some wine-drunk online research, had signed up for a course.

"Life coaches are the new real estate agents," she'd heard someone scoff at a cocktail party soon after. Lisa didn't care about the bored-housewife connotations. She liked talking to people and having something to focus on other than the kids and the gym.

Coming into the summer, Lisa had felt better than ever. The microdosing, the new career, plus she'd gotten a great refresh from Dr. Liotta, the most talented Park Avenue plastic surgeon, and now she looked younger than she had in years. And then Brian had told her about his fund.

A short that didn't pan out, he'd said. It wasn't his fault, he'd said. Lisa didn't really understand the details, but she knew it was bad. In the month since, Brian had pulled away from her. He was acting normal in public — doing his Brian thing, talking too much, amusing the crowd. But in private, he'd gone quiet, and Lisa couldn't break through, as much as she tried. She was worried about what it meant for them. Because she did love Brian. She made fun of him, sure, and rolled her eyes at his jokes. She cringed when he said something crass. But he was her big lunkhead, and he took care of her and the girls. Brian had always reminded her of her father, who died of a stroke when she was twenty-two, a first-generation Italian American who ran his own plumbing business in Fairfield, New Jersey, where Lisa grew up. They were both warm, generous, slightly ridiculous men.

Lisa thought about her dad as she watched Jason and Sam climb out of the bay, fully clothed, big babies, dripping wet. What would he make of these men? These rich guys with their soft hands and their therapists and their expensive linen shirts.

She and Brian had walked over to chat with Jessica and Max Leavitt, who'd separated from their picnic group. Everyone was rehashing the drama.

"What on earth was that?" said Jessica.

Lisa noticed that Jessica looked five years younger than she did last summer. She'd have to remember to ask who her doctor was.

"Oh, who knows. Boys being boys," said Brian diplomatically.

Brian had a soft spot for Sam and Jason. It made Lisa sad, because she could tell they didn't like him as much as he did them.

"Did you hear Sam ranting about being fired for sexual harassment?" said Max. "And about Jen cheating on him? It's all too good to be true. Turns out perfect Sam Weinstein isn't so perfect. Ha!" Max had a long neck and a prominent Adam's apple; when he got excited, it bobbed up and down like a bouncy ball.

Lisa thought about what it would be like when everyone heard about Brian's fund. The spiteful schadenfreude they'd all spew at dinner parties and the yacht club. She put on her best, barking PR voice. "You know what, Max? Everyone has stuff. I'm sure you and Jessica have stuff. Brian and I have stuff. Just have a little fucking sympathy for people."

Jessica's eyes nearly rocketed out of her head. Max looked down, embarrassed, his bird neck arching awkwardly.

Brian took Lisa's hand and squeezed it appreciatively. They walked away, back toward their real friends. Lisa couldn't wait to get home. Her mushrooms awaited.

17
ROBERT HEYWORTH

Robert Heyworth had already stolen $5,000 from the Salcombe Yacht Club. Not a lot — just about two months' rent for a no-frills studio apartment in Manhattan. But enough to make him feel like a criminal. Was he a criminal? He tried not to focus on it, distracting himself with work and sex.

Maybe too much sex. Lately, the thing with Lauren was getting out of control. They were acting reckless. Earlier in the day, they'd slept together in the maintenance closet of the yacht club, where the cleaning supplies were stored. It was late morning, and no one was inside the club, but it had been a risk. Someone could have come in to use the bathroom and seen one of them leaving, or Micah could have popped in to get some bleach to clean the bar.

The closet was tight, and it smelled like chlorine. Robert had pushed Lauren up against a shelfful of paper towels and toilet paper. She was in a black tennis skirt, which he'd lifted before realizing the built-in underwear meant he had to push it down to her knees.

Now it was 8:30 p.m., still a slight glow in the sky, and Robert was walking home, hands in pockets, looking down at the boardwalk's slanted wooden slats. The picnic had been a disaster. If Robert were rich, he'd stay far away from scenes like that. He'd liked how Julie and her family had been. Understated, private. They couldn't be bothered to compete with others, because they knew they were superior. Julie would have hated Salcombe — how everyone tallied each other's wins, how men measured themselves by their net worth and women by their tennis games.

He'd been surprised to hear that Sam thought Jen was cheating on him. Jen seemed so nice. Not that being nice meant you couldn't also be having an affair. Look at what Robert was up to. Lying and stealing and sleeping with someone else's wife.

Robert passed the tennis courts, empty, tidy from his early-evening brushing, ready for tomorrow's play. He was starting to loathe the sight of them.

"Robert! Robert!"

He heard a hoarse whisper from behind

249

him and turned to see Rachel Woolf approaching, hurrying toward him, her too-tight dress making a swishing noise as she ran. He'd left them all at the picnic about ten minutes ago, catching Lauren alone before he did and telling her, quietly, to try to come over after her kids were asleep. Jason had already left to go change his clothes, never to return. Sam and Jen had also gone home soon after "the incident," as the town was already referring to it, hand in hand, Sam still soaking wet. Rachel had been chatting with Emily and Lisa and their husbands when he'd said goodbye, always the odd woman out.

He stopped and waited, even though he really had no interest in speaking to her. She was out of breath and seemed a little drunk. She was still clutching a red plastic Solo cup, half filled with a margarita. They were nearly in front of her house when she got to him.

"Robert, can I speak with you? Can you come to my place? It'll only take a second."

"Okay, sure," he said warily, following her onto her screened-in porch.

She turned on the lights and offered him a seat on her white couch, plopping down beside him. He shifted so he was farther away from her. She noticed and gave him an annoyed look.

"I'm not going to try anything, don't worry," she said. "Can I get you a drink?"

"No, no, I'm good," said Robert. He wanted to get out of there as fast as possible. "What's up?"

"How wild was that picnic?" she said. She was taking small sips of her margarita. The lighting emphasized her wrinkles, and she looked old to him, her makeup caked in the creases. "I couldn't believe that Sam jumped in the bay. He's clearly going through something," she said.

"Yeah, seems that way." Robert didn't know where she was heading.

"And that stuff about Jen having an affair . . ."

He could tell she was looking to gauge his reaction. He willed his face to remain still. "Sounds messy," he said. "But I suppose marriages go through ups and downs. Not that I would know. You've never been married, right?"

She shook her head, then finished her drink in one swig. "That's what I wanted to talk to you about," she said.

Robert could hear the crickets outside. He suddenly felt very hot.

"You know Susan Steinhagen, right? Of course you do."

Robert nodded. Had Susan somehow found out that he was stealing? How could she have? Robert felt the blood pulsing through his wrists.

"I know she's a busybody, so take this with a grain of salt. She mentioned to me that she'd seen you, um, getting cozy with Lauren Parker. And, well, Lauren is my friend, and I like you a lot. And I just don't want people to start talking about you guys. You know this town by now — they will *definitely* start talking."

Robert took a deep breath. Thank fucking God it was only about Lauren and not about the money. He could handle this. No one had any proof.

"Oh, man, thanks for telling me. That's good for me to hear — I love this job and don't want to risk anything happening to it. For the record, there's absolutely nothing going on with me and Lauren. She's a valued client — like you! — but no more. If I'm giving off the wrong impression, that's on me, and I'll fix it." He said it as earnestly as possible, staring straight into Rachel's googly eyes. He shifted closer to her. She was such an easy mark. "You believe me, right?"

"I believe you!" she said. "I notice every-thing around here, and I never thought you two were sneaking around. I can't say the same for everyone else, however."

Oh, here she goes, thought Robert. Now was his chance to put her off the trail. "Oh yeah? Like who?" he asked.

Rachel's eyes glittered drunkenly. "You *heard* Sam speaking about Jen, right? Well, I know who she's having an affair with, and you'll never guess who it is."

Robert played along. "Hmmm," he said. "Paul Grobel?"

"Ha!" said Rachel. "Jen wouldn't even look at Paul."

"Okay, okay," said Robert. "Ummm. Theo Burch?" He was just grasping for names. How would he know who Jen Weinstein was fucking?

"No, no," said Rachel. "It's way more scandalous than that. And I'm only telling you because I know you'll keep it a secret, and I just *have* to share it with someone. I'll give you a hint. If Sam ever finds out, he might never recover."

Shit, thought Robert. *It's Jason.*

Lauren would die if this ever got out. Her husband sleeping with his best friend's wife? He'd known there was something rotten about Jason.

"I'm not sure, but maybe you should keep it to yourself. I don't want the burden of this information!" Robert said it lightly, but he meant it. She should shut up about it. No one needed to know.

"Okay, up to you!" she said, disappointed.

He could tell he'd hurt her feelings. He smiled charmingly and put his hand on her arm, her skin clammy to the touch. "I try to not learn too much about my clients, for obvious reasons," he said.

Now that he thought about it, it made perfect sense that Jason was with Jen. Jason, who seemed so threatened by Sam. Jason, who ignored his hot wife. Robert squeezed Rachel's arm and let his fingers linger for two seconds too long. Rachel's face turned pink.

"But I want to say thanks again for the heads-up about Susan. I'll stay far, far away from my female clients from now on." He gave her a little wink, stood up, and left her house.

It was completely dark by then, and the air felt chilled. Robert wished he had a real plan for his life. What was he doing messing around with a married woman? There was no future there and none in this job. He'd worked with a guy in Los Angeles named Rick, another former college player, who'd been saving up his money from teaching to put himself through law school. He was now an entertainment lawyer; Robert saw his updates on social media. Robert should have done that, too, but he'd just always assumed something good would come along. He looked and acted the part — it should have fallen into his lap.

He turned on Harbor, which cut through the middle of town, and continued on to Neptune, where he lived.

The lights were on in most of the houses, and he could see people going about their evening routines, watching TV and reading books. The picnic was done by now, and he assumed everyone was taking it easy for the rest of the night, given that they'd all started drinking heavily at 6:00 p.m. He considered texting Lauren to see if she could sneak out, but decided not to. Instead, he opened his Citibank app to check the balance of his "new" account — $5,200. That was twenty-six lessons that he'd charged to himself. Twenty-six times he'd chosen to do the wrong thing.

As he stared at the number, he was startled by a loud sound, causing him to nearly drop his phone. He looked up to see an enormous deer, a stag with antlers that belonged on a trophy wall, standing directly in front of him on the boardwalk, not moving. Robert knew it wasn't going to attack him — right? —

but he felt deep fear, anyway. Should he run? A second later, the stag was joined by another, smaller deer, which Robert assumed was a female.

Robert froze. He saw his phone light up with a text, but he didn't want to check it until these two deer got out of his way. The antlers on the stag were truly intimidating, and animals were volatile. He'd never heard of someone getting gored by a deer on Fire Island, but there was a first time for everything. And this summer was already unraveling in unpredictable ways.

After another moment, the two deer casually stepped back into the grass, one after the other. Robert continued to his house, just a few yards away. He was relieved for the evening to be over, even if it meant it was just him alone with the bugs.

He stepped inside, the screen door squeaking loudly, and faced his shitty little setup; raggedy love seat, crummy rattan rug that had probably seen three tennis pros before Robert. Before he could switch on the light, he felt arms around his waist and a hand sneaking its way into the top of his shorts. He turned around and playfully pushed Lauren up against the door.

"What if I thought you were an intruder? I might have killed you," he said, kissing her. She was still in her dress from the picnic, a sky-blue number, and he buried his face in her chest.

"You wouldn't kill me," she said. "At least not on purpose."

They had sex standing up, a position they both liked, and afterward, Lauren used his grungy bathroom and then sat on his couch. He was always embarrassed when she was here.

"What did you tell Jason?" Robert asked. He spotted an ant crawling on the floor near Lauren's foot, but he didn't do anything. He didn't want her to know.

"Just that I was going to get drinks with some of the girls. He didn't ask who or where. We're good. I think the whole Sam thing threw him for a loop. He was sitting on the deck like a zombie. How strange was that?"

Robert didn't like that he had information about Jason that Lauren didn't know. Should he tell her what Rachel had said? She seemed to hate Jason, but Robert couldn't predict how she'd react to the news. He'd keep it quiet for now.

"It was very odd," said Robert. "And you know I find a lot about this town strange, but that took it to another level."

"I think he's having a nervous breakdown

or something," said Lauren. "But Jen should be helping him — she's a psychologist! They're clearly in a bad place. I mean, Sam was accused of sexually harassing someone. He's saying she's cheating. It's such a mess."

"No, none of that seems good for a marriage," said Robert. He sat down next to Lauren and cupped his hand around her breast. "This probably isn't good for a marriage, either."

He kissed her stomach and pushed her dress up, going down on her until she climaxed. She pulled her dress back down and slumped attractively.

"What if someone finds out about us?" Lauren mused. They often came back to this topic, poking at it but never fully engaging. "Jen saw me coming out of your hut on July 4. At least, I think she did. Though she hasn't said anything about it."

"Then your husband will be pissed, and I'll lose my job." Robert shrugged. "Rachel made me come over to her house tonight." He'd been saving it until they were done fucking. He hadn't wanted to ruin the mood.

"Why? Was she hitting on you?" Lauren giggled.

"At first, I thought she was," said Robert.

"But then it turned out she was warning me."

"Warning you about what?"

"About us."

Lauren sat up straight. She pushed her hair out of her face. "What did she say?" she asked.

"She said that Susan Steinhagen had noticed that we were" — here Robert did air quotes — 'getting cozy.' Rachel was telling me to cool it, basically. She was trying to be nice, I think. I totally denied everything. She believed me. She's a dummy."

Lauren scrunched up her face unhappily. "That's not great," she said. "Susan can get you fired. Also, Rachel is going to tell other people. She can't help herself."

Robert knew Lauren was right. "So, what should we do? Should we stop?"

Lauren looked at him and frowned. "No, I don't want to stop," she said.

It sounded like she might have more to say on the matter, but she didn't go on. They sat in silence for a few seconds. She got up, smoothed out her blue dress, and tucked her hair behind her ears.

"I have to go. Silvia put the kids to bed, but Jason will eventually wonder where I am. Maybe." She left via the squeaky screen door.

"Watch out for the deer!" Robert called after her.

He crashed down on the couch and took out his phone. He checked the Citi app again. He'd add another $200 tomorrow. He'd booked a lesson with Seth Laurell for 2:00 p.m., which he hadn't added to the official ledger. As long as that account kept ticking up, he felt like he had some control over his stupid life. He closed his eyes. What a strange day it had been. He was worried about Susan Steinhagen. He and Lauren needed to be more careful. But it was hard to feel like there were real-life consequences for his actions in this place. It wasn't anything at all like real life.

18
MICAH HOLT

Micah Holt was in a foul mood. Ronan had been avoiding him since July 4, and after weeks of proudly resisting texting him, Micah had just sent him a pleading message. That was an hour ago, and Ronan still hadn't written back. Micah felt like such a fool.

Earlier, he'd attended the Bay Picnic with his friends, drinking lukewarm wine out of a plastic cup, enduring the lame old-dude Beatles cover band. Then Sam Weinstein had lost his shit. He'd loudly accused Jen of cheating on him (which Micah knew to be true) and revealed he'd been accused of sexual harassment. It was such a cliché. Handsome, slick Sam using his power to get younger women to fuck him? On the one hand, it was everything Micah had been taught to believe happened in the workplace. On the other: Really? *Sam?* He's the last person Micah would have guessed would do that sort of thing.

Micah had used the drama as an excuse to text Ronan, giving him a quippy recounting of the night, and then following up with a sad one-liner:

I miss you. Can I see you?

Micah knew it was a bad idea as he pressed Send, but he couldn't help himself. He did miss him. He didn't understand why Ronan was freezing him out. Desperate to connect, Micah had gone to the beach that afternoon. He'd worn his favorite Jacquemus trunks, the ones that hit right at the top of his thighs, and had lounged on his towel in the warm sun, rereading his vintage copy of *Giovanni's Room.* Every so often, he'd glanced up at the white lifeguard stand to see Ronan, muscular and focused in Ray-Bans and that signature red bathing suit. Ronan wouldn't acknowledge his gaze — he looked forward intently, searching for swimmers to save.

Micah looked at his phone again. No new messages. He was walking along Bay Promenade. The picnic had ended some time ago, and Micah had been alone since, pacing the boardwalks, headphones in, half listening to a podcast about the economy. Everyone else

262

had gone home, wiped and drunk and overstimulated from the Sam Weinstein show. (Micah had been surprised when Jason jumped into the bay after Sam; if only people knew the real story.)

He turned up Neptune, thinking maybe he'd go for a swing alone in the playground before heading back home. It seemed an appropriately morose thing to do, given his current state. His mom and dad would likely still be up watching TV, and Micah didn't feel like dealing with them. Though he was technically an adult, on Fire Island, he was eternally twelve. His mom did his laundry and made his meals; his dad forced him to go sailing with him every Sunday afternoon. They were fine, as parents went. Liberal, easy, proud of Micah. But it was still a little much to be around them all the time.

As Micah continued toward the playground, he heard the squeak of a screen door and the subsequent bang as it shut. He walked toward the edge of the boardwalk, shielding himself from view behind the long, overhanging reeds. He saw Lauren Parker, still in that light blue dress, come out from Robert's house. Lauren had always seemed so glamorous to Micah, with her perfect hair and expensive clothes. She checked to see that she was alone, and then scurried up Neptune, presumably toward her and Jason's house by the beach.

Micah nearly laughed out loud. At least now he knew for sure that Robert wasn't gay. Was this what happened when you got old? You destroyed your marriage and lost your mind? Or was that just a Salcombe thing? Micah checked his phone. One new message, a reply from Ronan. With a shaky hand, Micah opened it.

Funny about the picnic. Those people sound crazy.

Micah saw the three dots appear, then go away. He watched as the dots reappeared, followed by a second message.

I'm sorry, but this isn't the right time for me. I'm not even sure what I'm into. I hope you understand. I'll see you around.

Micah quickly closed the text and stuck his phone in his pocket. He felt tears wet his eyes, one of which spilled over onto his cheek. He wiped it away, annoyed by his own weakness. It was getting colder out, so he decided to skip the swings and go straight home. Maybe TV with his mom and dad wasn't such a bad idea, after all.

19
SUSAN STEINHAGEN

Susan Steinhagen was always discovering things she didn't want to discover. There was the time, twenty years ago, when she'd walked into Claire and Seth Laurell's house only to find them engaged in horrible sex acts with Nat and Carol Jacobs. She'd been dropping off a blender Claire had lent her; the lights were out — it was only 8:00 p.m.! — and Susan had figured the Laurells were out to dinner. She'd turned on the lamp to witness the nauseating scene. "Susan! Get out of here!" Claire had shrieked, naked and red-faced, tangled up with Nat, skinny and bent over. Susan had placed the blender on the kitchen table and slowly backed out, traumatized. They'd never spoken of it afterward. Susan hadn't even told her now-dead husband, Garry. She hadn't really known what she'd seen, to be honest.

There was also the Battles scandal in 2002. At the time, Jack Battles was one of the richest guys on Fire Island. It turned out he had two families, one he summered with in Salcombe, and one he kept hidden in Palm Beach. Susan had been sitting behind him on the beach when he'd taken a call from his secret wife, Eileen, and said, "I love you," to her. Susan had later seen Jack's other wife, Marlene Battles, on the boardwalk heading home. "Who's Eileen?" she'd asked innocently, setting off a storm that ended up, eventually, as a story in the *New York Post* ("Financier Jack Battles Battles Ex-Wife in Secret Family Lawsuit").

Last year, it was the saga of Dave the tennis pro. Susan had never liked him. He'd been too chummy with the guests, not to mention he'd once said to Susan that she must have been great at tennis "when you were younger." Hmph. But she'd also suspected something fishy was going on with the tennis finances. She didn't have proof; it was just a hunch — she often got these kinds of feelings. One day late in the summer, she'd been in the tennis hut hunting for some extra grip. Dave had been out on the court, giving Arlo Parker a lesson. The ledger was open to that day's lineup. She'd taken a quick glance — she was on the yacht club tennis committee, so it was fair game — but hadn't seen anything amiss. But she did find, underneath a pile of papers and strings and, yes, grip, which she pocketed, a small flask filled with vodka. He'd been drinking on the job. A fireable offense.

That weekend was the mixed doubles tournament, which, in the old days, had been Susan's favorite. She and Garry had always made a strong showing, winning twice, in 1988 and 1993. Susan was now in the seniors tournament, which she hated. (Garry died three years ago, and since then, she'd played with Richie Trimble, a jovial eighty-two-year-old with one shot, a slice backhand.) Dave was stumbling around the joint, trying to keep order, and Susan had lost it, yelling at him in front of a small crowd, accusing him of being a drunk. It hadn't been her finest moment, even she'd admit that. But she'd been upset about everything. Having to play with the other old people, Dave's behavior, Garry still being dead. In the end, she'd been right to get rid of him. After Dave left, she did a close audit of his bookkeeping. She learned he'd been charging certain clients twice and keeping the second round for himself. She hadn't publicly announced it, just told a few key members of the board, who'd then spread it around to the rest of the town.

This year, they'd deliberately gone with a

squeaky-clean hire, a Stanford grad who'd been home caring for his grieving mother for the last couple of years. Robert seemed like an ace. He was sweet, handsome, great with kids. Susan was getting nothing but rave reviews about him.

But she'd seen what others hadn't or wouldn't. Robert and Lauren Parker, all over each other, all the time. She just *knew* something was going on there. Earlier that day, she'd told Rachel Woolf, the reigning town gossip, to warn Lauren to back off Susan didn't want to have to fire another pro in the middle of the summer, particularly because this one was, otherwise, a star. Hopefully, Rachel's interference would help.

Susan saw some of herself in Rachel. Rachel was passionate about tennis, she cared about the town, and she was also all alone (Susan was thankful to have had Garry all those years; imagine going through life without anyone?). She knew how devastated Rachel had been by the early death of her father, who'd been a kind man. She knew Rachel had always been in love with Sam Weinstein. And she understood why. Sam was such a special boy growing up, so good-looking and sad. His parents were a terrible pair, a blight on Salcombe, and Susan had been happy when they'd gone their separate ways and left Sam that beautiful house.

Susan remembered one summer long ago, when Sam and Rachel were a happy young couple, hanging together on the beach and holding hands at the yacht club. People in this town really had so much history together. That's why she hadn't been surprised to see Sam in Rachel's house the other week when she'd stopped in to get help with the tournament. She'd not mentioned it to Rachel — nor to anyone, for that matter. Lots of baggage with those two. She felt Sam was committed to his wife, Jen, and his little brood of cute children. Jen, on the other hand, was a mystery to Susan. She was lovely and sweet and always said the right thing, but Susan felt there was maybe a darkness there that trusting Sam couldn't see.

Susan was now on her way to the Bay Picnic, lugging a bag filled with artisanal cheeses, where she always sat with her crew of old-timers. There were the Ponds and the Trimbles and the Todds. The Todds' daughter, Erica, and her husband, Theo, sat with them, as well. So did their two kids, the Todds' grandchildren.

Susan was the only one in the group without a spouse. Garry had died suddenly three years ago, a heart attack. They'd been eating dinner at Paola's on the Upper East Side, one of their favorite restaurants, when he'd clutched his chest and keeled over. The ambulance had come just a few minutes later, but by that point he was gone, Susan could tell. They'd taken him to Mount Sinai anyway, and Susan had cried the entire ride to Ninety-sixth Street. They'd been married for forty-one years, and they'd never had children. She'd been teaching at Columbia, and Garry had been so busy with his law career. By the time they'd started trying, when Susan was in her late thirties, it just didn't happen. And it wasn't like nowadays, with IVF and surrogacy and whatever else these kids do to have babies. Back then, if it didn't work, it didn't work. Susan always regretted not thinking about it earlier. Now here she was at seventy-three, dragging a bag of fontina from Murray's to the Salcombe picnic alone.

She and Garry had bought their home on Lighthouse and Neptune in 1985, always with the idea that eventually they'd fill it with babies. Instead, they'd both become very involved in the town, Susan running the tennis program at the club, and Garry part of the local government. He'd been mayor of Salcombe from 1994 to 2002, a fact he was so proud of he'd had T-shirts made for him and Susan that said THE MAYOR and THE MAYOR'S WIFE. Susan missed him. He used to make her laugh.

She knew it was her job to keep the tennis program humming, but she was worried she was becoming a grumpy old lady with all her surveillance. Why did she care if Robert, the cute young tennis pro, was sleeping with Lauren Parker, who was clearly unhappy in her marriage to that pill Jason? Susan had always been wary of Jason, whom she'd known since he was a boy, coming out to visit Sam. He was dark and glum and didn't say hi to her when he rode by on his bike.

The truth was, Susan wasn't nearly as scary or mean as everyone made her out to be. She was funny — she thought she was, at least — and she cared about people's welfare. Yes, she could be stern, and she didn't like when anyone broke the rules. That was the professor in her. She felt like the world was her classroom, and her role was to make sure things were in order. Since Garry had died, she'd become shriller, she knew that, and it was something she wanted to work on. A friend had suggested she see a therapist to talk about grief, and Susan had politely nodded at the advice with the intention of ignoring it. She didn't need a therapist. She just needed someone to help her carry all this cheese.

The picnic was in full swing by the time Susan arrived. Her group was set up toward the front, closer to the houses than the bay. There were two wagons filled with food, surrounded by her friends Bonnie and Richie Trimble, Marie and Steve Pond, and Betsy and Mike Todd. Susan greeted everyone hello and arranged her goods on a platter. Their gang always went with an artisanal cheese board theme, including aged prosciuttos, olives and pickles, crusty breads and crackers, fig spreads, grapes, the works. Susan loved how casually upscale the whole night was, barefoot on the sand while sipping a delightful French brut.

The Bay Picnic had been Garry's idea; the first one was in 1994, the summer Garry became mayor. One night while they were walking home from drinks at Marie and Steve's, the sun setting over the water, he'd had the inspiration for this evening of fun. It was now a solidified annual tradition, one that Susan treasured even more so for that reason.

"Susan! Have a champagne, have some food. Let's mingle," said Bonnie Trimble. She was about seven years older than Susan, nearing eighty, a real yenta, always up for a chat and a drink. She was wearing a flowing red caftan with large gold earrings, and she'd matched her lipstick to her dress. Bonnie had been trying to set Susan up on dates in the city with her widower friends, but Susan had resisted. What did she need a boyfriend for?

They clinked glasses with Marie and Steve Pond, both in their seventies. Marie was a workout queen; at seventy, she looked as good as the fifty-year-olds on the beach, with her flat stomach and toned arms. She led a yoga class in the town gazebo on Sunday mornings, which, to be supportive, Susan attended occasionally, even though she couldn't hold any of the poses. Steve was a smooth operator, a longtime retired finance guy who'd made it big in the 1990s. He was the current commodore of the yacht club, a position he both relished and lorded over people. They had three children scattered around the country and six grandchildren to show for it.

"Susan, you're doing a great job this year with the tennis program," said Marie. She was in a formfitting black-and-white dress, her hair slicked back into an elegant salt-and-pepper bun.

"Thanks," said Susan, self-conscious suddenly in her green chinos and white button-down. She was most comfortable in tennis clothes; the women out here dressed better than she knew how to. Garry used to tell her he preferred her in a tracksuit, and she'd taken that to heart.

"That pro, Robert, is such a doll," Marie continued. "He's really helped my doubles strategy — he's even gotten me to come up to the net after all these years," she said.

"Yes, he's a hit," said Susan.

"I saw him over there, hanging with the Parkers and Lisa and Brian Metzner," said Bonnie. "That's nice that they've all taken such a shine to him."

Susan looked over to see Robert sitting on a beach chair, Lauren Parker swanning about in a sexy dress. She wondered if Rachel had spoken to Lauren yet about it. Probably not.

Just then, there was a commotion over by the Beatles band (also a Garry idea, Susan thought proudly). Susan saw Sam Weinstein, still in his beach clothes, stumbling toward his friends. Everyone stopped talking and gawked as Sam passed by. He was not in a good way. He looked drunk and angry, and Susan was worried something bad was about to happen. Where was Jen? Wives shouldn't let their husbands get in this state.

Robert got up and gave Sam his chair, and for a moment, Susan thought all would be okay, that the picnic might not be disturbed. But Salcombe always had a trick up its sleeve. She and the others heard Sam raising his voice, yelling about Jen having an affair and something about possibly losing his job. Susan watched in horror as Sam ran toward the bay and launched himself into the water.

"Sam Weinstein jumped into the bay!" Susan heard someone shout, and then she was swept up in a moving crowd, rushing to get a glimpse of the fallen hero. She still had her champagne in hand as she lined the bulkhead with the rest of the spectators, feeling a little sick as she did.

Jason Parker jumped in after his friend, thank goodness. Sam was doing a back float, his eyes closed, as Jason paddled up to him. She wished Garry were here to see this. They'd discuss it afterward over a glass of good red wine, recounting all the little details — Jen Weinstein showing up in a bathing suit, frantic, Rachel Woolf acting like her house was on fire, Brian and Lisa Metzner slipping away, mortified.

After a few minutes of talking about who knows what, Sam and Jason swam to the ladder and climbed out of the water. Susan was relieved for the incident to be over. She and her friends retreated to their artisanal spread, Bonnie making eyes at her as they went.

"What *was* that?" Bonnie asked in a low voice. She picked up a piece of prosciutto, rolled it into a small log, and took a bite.

"Looked like a man scorned," said Steve Pond, his shirtsleeves rolled up to reveal a Rolex and very tan, hairy forearms. Mike Todd nodded. Susan wondered if he and Betsy had been disappointed that Erica had married a Black man. They'd always made a big deal of saying how happy they were to have such a diverse family, but Susan wasn't sure she bought it. They were so preppy — it must have been a surprise.

"I always knew there was something off about that Jen," said Marie. "She's too perfect to be real. Sam is such a sweetheart. He deserves better."

"Yes, poor Sam," said Bonnie. "He's the nicest man. I hope he's okay."

"I'm not necessarily the best one to weigh in on this, as I don't really know the guy," said Theo Burch, dressed to perfection in golf clothes, as always. "But why are we all feeling bad for Sam, when he's the one who caused a scene? Maybe Jen isn't to blame. Didn't Sam say he'd lost his job for harassing someone?"

"Oh, sure, but that can't be true. He wouldn't do that," said Marie. "I've known him since he was a boy."

"That doesn't really mean anything," said Theo. "There was a guy at our company who seemed great, but it turned out he'd been taking pictures of women in the ladies' restroom without them knowing."

There was a moment of awkward silence.

Susan took the opportunity to walk away. She spotted Rachel standing alone and went over to say hello. Sam and Jen had left together, as had Jason. Rachel was out of it. She was clutching a red plastic cup filled with some sort of tequila drink.

"Rachel, what happened there?" Susan asked. It came out more forcefully than she'd intended.

"I'm not sure," said Rachel. She couldn't make eye contact with Susan, which led Susan to believe Rachel knew exactly what had happened. "You saw Sam flip out, just like everyone else. I guess he's having a bad summer."

"Looked like a little more than that to me," said Susan. She could usually get Rachel to talk, and she figured that now was the time, given Rachel's boozy condition. "I don't want to pry . . ."

"Sure you don't," said Rachel under her breath.

"Rachel Woolf, I've known you since you were a little girl. Don't use that tone with me."

Rachel looked up at Susan. There were tears in her eyes. Oh, dear, had Susan gone too far again? Maybe a therapist wasn't such a bad idea. Rachel grabbed Susan's sensible shirtsleeve and pulled her toward the boardwalk, away from the gathering. Susan wasn't sure where Rachel was going with this. They walked a little way up Surf Walk, clear of people. The band was now playing "Blackbird," and Susan felt a twinge in her chest. It had been one of Garry's favorites.

"Susan, I need your help," said Rachel, a little breathlessly. She could certainly be dramatic, thought Susan.

"I saw Jen Weinstein together with Jason Parker," Rachel continued. "That's who Jen is having an affair with." Her eyes were watery in the low light.

This was not what Susan was expecting to hear — she'd thought maybe Rachel was in financial trouble, or had finally gotten Sam to relent. Not so. "Oh boy," said Susan. She meant it. "Are you sure?"

"I'm totally positive. I saw them kissing on the beach. I don't know if I should tell

278

Sam about it. I told him that Jen was being unfaithful, but I haven't given him specifics. He's already in such a delicate state about work, I'm worried this would put him over the edge."

"Why are you telling *me*?" said Susan. Couldn't she just get through one summer without a massive scandal landing in her lap?

"I don't have anyone else to tell!" said Rachel. "I'm not sure what to do."

"Rachel, I have a feeling you'd like everyone to find out the truth, just not from you," said Susan bluntly. "You've always loved Sam, and this would wreck his marriage and his friendship with Jason. Perhaps, then, you'd be the only one left for him to lean on." Rachel couldn't pull one over on her; she'd been around the block too many times. "Are you asking me to be the one to spread the info? Because I don't think I want to do that."

"No, I'm not asking you to do that. But . . ." Rachel paused and took a sip of her pink drink.

"But what?"

"But maybe you could discover them? By accident? And then Jen would be forced to tell Sam."

Susan shook her head. "Why would I want

to be part of this?"

Rachel started to cry, crocodile tears spilling down her face. Just then, Beth Ledbetter strolled past, perhaps on her way to go pee at her house. (That was the one part of the picnic Garry didn't live to solve; the lack of bathrooms sent people scattering home all night.) She sauntered over as Rachel quickly wiped her eyes.

"What's shaking, guys?" Beth asked. She was in her typical uniform, cutoffs and an old white T-shirt. "Sam just put on quite a show."

"Yes, indeed. Rachel and I were just discussing the seeding of the women's doubles tournament. Are you and Jessica playing this year?" Rachel looked at Susan gratefully.

"We sure are," Beth said. "And hopefully we'll make it past the first round. Our draw was impossible last year, playing against Claire Laurell and Erica Todd. That felt like an affront!"

"Oh, you know me," said Susan. "Fair and square, always."

Beth rolled her eyes. "I'm dying for the bathroom. I'll see you two later." She walked off.

Rachel let out a big sigh. Susan eyed her sympathetically. She felt bad for Rachel and did want to help her. Susan knew what it was like to be desperately lonely.

"I refuse to discover Jen and Jason in the act. But you know that you could leak the info elsewhere, right? The more people in town who know, the faster it will get out. But be smart about it. You don't want to look like you're trying too hard. Why don't you start with the tennis pro? Maybe he'll end up telling his girlfriend, Lauren, that her husband is sleeping with Jen." Susan snorted. It was all too absurd, these kids and their nasty affairs. Why was she allowing herself to get dragged into this nonsense? She must be bored. Now that Garry was gone, she needed a new hobby beyond tennis. Maybe she should get into bridge.

As if on cue, Susan and Rachel saw Robert walking away from the picnic, heading back toward his home. Rachel smiled at Susan and hurried after him, her dress swish-swashing as she went. *Good luck to that girl,* thought Susan.

She returned to her friends, still gathered around their wagons. There was an orange light in the sky, and the water looked particularly shiny and beautiful. The picnic had an electric energy; everyone was still buzzing from the earlier events, and Susan could hear whispers coming from every corner.

"Sam Weinstein has been #MeToo'd!"

"Sam and Jen are on the rocks."

"Jen Weinstein is a fake."

"Jason Parker is super shady."

And on and on. How this town loved to gossip. Garry used to find it so amusing, the ins and outs of other people's lives. Perhaps because they'd never had children and there wasn't much to discuss beyond their own problems at work. She wished he were waiting for her now at their house on Lighthouse Road, sitting in his Adirondack chair on their little back deck, sipping a vodka and soda with a twist, wearing his THE MAYOR T-shirt. They'd clink glasses, Susan with her chardonnay, and she'd sit down next to him and regale him with tales of tennis tournament drama. He'd laugh and hold her hand and she'd tell him all about how Sam Weinstein jumped into the bay at the picnic — Garry's picnic! — and about how Sam's wife, Jen, was sleeping with Jason Parker and how she suspected that Jason's wife, Lauren, was having an affair with Robert, the new tennis pro. And she'd tell him about lonely Rachel Woolf and how she, Susan Steinhagen, was so lucky to have Garry Steinhagen in her life.

■ ■ ■ ■

PART IV

■ ■ ■ ■

August 21

20
JEN WEINSTEIN

Jen Weinstein was on a roll. Not only had she managed to end her relationship with Jason — while getting back in Sam's good graces — she was also playing great tennis. Which was important, as this weekend was the women's doubles tournament. Jen and her partner, Lauren Parker, had already made it to the semifinals, shocking everyone, including themselves.

Yesterday, they'd eliminated three other teams. They'd first knocked out Laura June and Hailey Milotic, beating them 6–4 (the early rounds were only one-set matches). Then they'd killed Jenny Jamison and Paula Rudnick, 6–0. Jenny had hip replacement surgery over the winter and could barely move. It hadn't been nice, but Lauren and Jen had hit nearly every ball to her, short, and she couldn't get to any of them. That's what winners had to do.

Then, in the afternoon quarterfinals,

they'd had a tough match against Trisha Spencer and Jane Rosen, a strong team. Trisha had a great serve, spinny with a kick, and Jane got everything back. Rachel Woolf, who'd been helping with strategy, had huddled with them beforehand, and told them to hit down the line as much as possible. They went down 0–3 quickly (Jen's serve was broken, which she wasn't happy about). But then they'd managed to turn around the momentum, winning the next three games, breaking Trisha. Jen held her serve after a marathon game that went to deuce four times. They played a tiebreak at 6–6, and pulled it off, 7–5. A small crowd had gathered to watch the final games, and Jen thrilled at the cheering after she hit the winning shot down the line. Trisha and Jane were gracious afterward, but Jen could tell they were upset. Jen and Lauren weren't supposed to beat them.

The women's doubles tournament took place during a late August weekend each year. It was the culmination of that season's tennis program. The men's doubles tournament happened in July — this year, Theo Burch and Jerry Braun had taken it in a three-set stunner — and the mixed doubles took place in the beginning of August (the Mulders trounced the Romans in the final,

6–2, 6–1).

The women's, counterintuitively, had the most anticipation and drew the biggest crowds. Last year, around a hundred people sat packed around the stadium court, drinking beer and eating stale popcorn, to watch Rachel Woolf and Emily Grobel lose to Vicky Mulder and Janet Braun. Jen had been on the sidelines then, admiring the game. It felt good to be part of the action this summer.

The tournament lasted all weekend. Saturdays were for early rounds, and Sundays were the semifinals and finals. There were twenty-five pairs playing this year, a mix of old and new faces. Yesterday was a success. Susan Steinhagen had lorded over the courts like an empress, making sure matches started promptly — it annoyed Susan when warmups took too long; Jen heard her shout "Let's get on with it!" at numerous foursomes. The final four teams standing were Jen and Lauren, Rachel and Emily, Erica Todd and Claire Laurell, and Vicky Mulder and Janet Braun, last year's champions. (To Rachel's frustration, Vicky had sent her husband, Aaron, off to Maine to pick up their daughter from sleepaway camp, rather than miss the tournament.)

Jen was at the courts now, milling about

before her start time at 10:00 a.m. She and Lauren were set to play Emily and Rachel in the semis, and everyone was checking out the draw, laminated and hung up on the side of Robert's tennis hut. Women were chatting, saying hello, whispering about favorites and likely upsets. Jen was happy that she and Lauren were underdogs. She'd seen Rachel on her way in, standing away from it all, trying to maintain her composure. Jen had waved but not gone over. Fake friendliness was the mood of the day.

This weekend was like Rachel's Super Bowl, and she looked forward to it all summer. Last year, she'd been so close to winning. From her professional perspective, Jen knew it wasn't healthy for Rachel to be so focused on this small-town club competition. But she also knew Rachel didn't have much else going on. Plus, concentrating on tennis meant Rachel wasn't blabbing to everyone about Jen's private life.

Jen was truly thrilled to still be in it. She didn't generally have such genuine joy. She'd woken up feeling great. She'd had sex with Sam in the morning, which they never did, and had delighted in picking her clothes for the day (all Lacoste; she and Lauren had agreed to be in matching whites).

She felt a squeeze on her arm. Lauren was there, smiling, in her identical outfit, her blond hair pulled back in a neat pony. This experience had been good for them, Jen thought. It had brought them closer together in the way that joint physical activity can. She admired how Lauren ran for drop shots, and thought it was funny when Lauren said "Whoopsie!" when she missed a shot, as if she were a child instead of a grown woman.

"Beautiful day for tennis!" Lauren said. She was beaming.

Jen wasn't sure she'd ever seen her so happy. Lauren seemed changed this summer. She'd arrived as her typical snobby, Upper East Side self. Now Jen felt Lauren was nicer, less judgmental, more fun to be around. She'd barely heard a word lately about that scammer scandal at Lauren's kids' school, which was all Lauren could talk about in June. Jen wasn't sure what had happened — maybe that fight with Beth Ledbetter had set her free? Jen did know it didn't have to do with Jason, who was still off moping about Jen. What Jason didn't realize — had never realized — was that their affair wasn't about him at all. Never had been.

It was a gorgeous day. Clear, high seventies, a slight breeze off the ocean side of the island. The green flies had been bad for the past couple of weeks, but they seemed to have disappeared completely in honor of the tournament.

"I heard we might get a storm tonight, but it's supposed to hold off until late, so it looks like we'll get a full day in, including the finals. If we make it!" Jen laughed as she said it, but it was starting to feel like a real possibility.

"Here are the partners of the hour," said Brian Metzner, putting his arm around each of them. An acrid odor was wafting from his underarms. Jen had seen him playing earlier with his crew of hefty finance guys. She shook him off politely. They were standing in front of the stadium court, currently occupied by a game of eighty-year-olds, and Lisa came over to join them.

"Champions! How does it feel to make it to Sunday in the women's doubles tournament? You're two games away from having your name etched forever on a plaque in the vaunted Salcombe Yacht Club. I can't even imagine the pressure," Lisa said teasingly. "I'm rooting for you. Don't tell Rachel or Emily; they'd die."

"It'll be a tough match," said Lauren. "They're super steady and have been playing together forever."

"Come on. Rachel's got that weird serve, and Emily can't volley to save her life," chimed in Brian, apparently an expert on the women's draw. On this particular weekend, everyone magically knew the ins and outs of the ladies' games. "You can take them."

Jen saw Sam hop off his bike and pull it into the yacht club bike rack, already filled with other spectators' bikes. He'd told her he'd come to watch. It had been a long few weeks for them. That afternoon of the Bay Picnic, Sam had come back from the beach raging, screaming about how Jen was fucking someone else. She'd immediately had the kids go upstairs to watch TV and then tried to calm him down, but it was useless. He'd chugged a bottle of Grey Goose in front of her, silently. Then he'd revealed that Rachel Woolf had told him Jen was cheating on him. On top of that, he'd informed her he'd lost his job, maybe temporarily, maybe permanently, because a woman had accused him of forcefully kissing her. Jen was shaken by this news, but she stored it away for future examination — the more pressing issue was convincing Sam that Rachel wasn't telling the truth.

She'd told him Rachel was wrong, that

she wasn't sleeping with anyone else. "Rachel's just jealous; she's in love with you, she always has been," Jen had said over and over. "She's lying. She's a liar! That's her thing."

He'd raced out of the house and headed to the picnic before she could stop him. She wasn't sure what had happened in the water with Jason — she'd been absolutely terrified that Jason would tell him the truth — but Sam had emerged calmer. She'd seen an opening with him afterward and taken it, escorting him home and having sex with him immediately, the kids still watching whatever junk they wanted on TV.

They were in a good place now; they'd had many draining heart-to-hearts about the dangers of keeping things from each other. Sam had apologized for not telling her about his sexual harassment issue at work. She'd forgiven him — and she did believe he was telling the truth. But she also had to admit that she felt rattled. What if he ended up losing his job? What would people think then? Sam was her cover; everyone took her to be a good person, because they believed that's what squeaky-clean Sam deserved. But if Sam's façade crumbled, Jen worried that her misdeeds could also be exposed. Of course, she never fessed up to having affairs, let alone one with Jason, but she did tell Sam she'd been feeling unhappy lately. That was enough of a bone to get him off the scent. The issue was Rachel, who couldn't be trusted to keep her mouth shut.

She'd been avoiding Jason since that night, using Sam's meltdown as an excuse to cool things off. For the first week, he'd been relentless, texting her on Signal at all hours, obsessively riding by her house on his bike, to the point that Sam, sitting on their porch one evening, went outside and asked what he was doing ("I'm exercising, dude. You should try it," was Jason's answer).

He seemed to get the hint as time went on. He glowered at Jen at the beach and the yacht club and always seemed to be by the tennis courts when she was there. But at least he'd stopped contacting her. She was surprised to find that, after speaking to him every day for a year, she didn't miss him at all. But that was Jen's superpower.

Not being with Jason allowed her to think about other priorities, like tennis. It also let her partner with Lauren without feeling awkward. Sure, she *had* been sleeping with Lauren's husband, but she wasn't anymore. Not that Lauren cared much about Jason, based on the looks she exchanged with

Robert the pro. Jen had seen her on July 4 coming out of his hut, and she was almost positive she knew now what that meant. Good for Lauren. That guy was gorgeous.

Sam walked over and put his arm around her waist, giving it a little squeeze. He was looking particularly tan and attractive, wearing the orange linen button-down she'd bought for him a couple of years ago. Every now and then, her heart would seize at the idea that their marriage could come crashing down so easily, and it would all be her fault. But then she'd flick the thought away. Or put it in a box. Or lock it behind a door. She'd studied cognitive therapy at school, and it came in handy when managing her own mind.

"Lauren, is Jason coming to watch this round?" Sam asked. He was still waiting to hear about the future of his job, and other than jumping into the bay in front of the entire town, Jen thought he was doing an admirable job of managing his stress.

"I'm not sure," said Lauren. "Silvia's watching the kids, so unless he's busy with work, he should." She didn't seem too bothered about it, as far as Jen could tell.

Susan Steinhagen broke up the chat, appearing over Lisa's shoulder with a serious look. She was all business in a white pleated tennis skirt and an Adidas tracksuit jacket. "Parker and Weinstein, let's get on the court now!" she directed, sharp as an army sergeant.

Brian raised his eyebrows in horror, and Lisa giggled at him.

Rachel and Emily were already out warming up, doing stretches and little jumps on their side of the court. Lauren and Jen put their heads together toward the back.

"We've got this," whispered Lauren. Her cheeks were rosy, and her lips looked plump. For a second, Jen could picture what she looked like during sex. "Hit to Emily's backhand — it always goes long. And make Rachel run her saggy butt off."

Jen laughed and nodded. Lauren was such a snot. They high-fived and went to their positions. Jen began to hit back and forth with Emily down the line to warm up. She was feeling nervous and stiff. She'd had a tennis pro in Scarsdale, Chuck. She tried to hear his voice in her ear as she hit. "Follow through, Jenny," he'd say. He'd started calling her *Jenny* during their first lesson, and she hadn't corrected him. Now she thought of tennis Jen as "Jenny." "Bend your knees, girl!" he'd shout at her.

Jen hit a ball long, which sent Emily scurrying off court to retrieve it. They hadn't even started, and already she was messing up. *Concentrate, Jenny,* she thought. *You've got this, Jenny.*

"Time to play!" called Susan sharply from behind the green fencing that bordered the court. The benches lining the area were full. Jen saw Sam sitting with Emily's husband, Paul Grobel, mock-strangling him (Paul was wearing a black T-shirt that read CANCEL CANCEL CULTURE). She didn't spot Jason in the mix and was happier for it. She didn't need him leering darkly at her as she played.

The match got underway. Jen and Lauren had won the toss, and so Lauren served first, making a strong showing and winning the game in four quick points. People were clapping after good shots, which threw Jen. She smashed an overhead right into Emily and then heard cheers. It was brutal.

The partners were evenly matched. Everyone held their own serve, until the first set was tied 6–6, sending them to a tiebreak. Jen had never been so focused. She could hear her heart beating in her ears. "You!" screamed Lauren at her from the net. Rachel had sent a lob over Lauren's head, and Jen raced to the other side of the court to lob it back. Emily backed up to take it as an overhead, swung, and ended up hitting it into the net. The crowd screamed. Lauren and Jen had won the first set.

They all took a break at the middle of the court, sipping from paper cups that stacked into the watercooler. Rachel, in her favorite black tennis skirt from Nike, looked pale. She didn't say anything as she drank, just stared off into space.

"Great set, guys," said Emily politely. Her blond hair was pulled into a swishy pony. Jen admired her upper chest bones, which stuck out prominently. There was something about Emily's voice — weak, soft — that imbued Jen with confidence. They were going to win. She knew it now. She looked at Lauren, who clearly felt the same way. Lauren winked at her. They would do it together.

The next set was over in a flash, and the upset was solidified. Parker/Weinstein had beaten Woolf/Grobel 6–6 (7–3), 6–2.

"Yes!" screamed Lauren after match point, a long rally that ended when she'd hit a forehand winner down the line. *"Yes!"* It was a guttural, animalistic shout, and very unlike Lauren. She raced over to Jen and gave her a big hug, their rackets clanking, and whispered in Jen's ear, "Fuck yes." Jen couldn't stop smiling. Her mouth started to hurt.

They walked to the center of the net to

shake Rachel's and Emily's hands, both limp. Rachel was biting her bottom lip, and Jen was worried she was going to cry. She looked shaken, her eyes shifting to the left when Jen offered her thanks for playing. Rachel shuffled behind the trio as they walked off the dusty clay court together. Sam was standing in front of the gate and wrapped Jen in a bear hug as soon as she stepped out, lifting her off the ground.

Paul Grobel was there, looking appropriately somber. He patted Emily's back when she emerged. "Sorry, honey," he said to her. She shrugged.

"I can't believe it!" Sam beamed. "You played great! My Jen, tennis champ of Salcombe."

Lauren was there, too, receiving congratulations from various friends. Jason was nowhere to be seen.

It did feel good to have won. She was used to only getting this high from having sex with someone other than Sam. They'd beaten Rachel, of all people. Rachel! Tennis was Rachel's life! Jen saw Rachel sitting on a bench alone, slumped, her tennis top sagging around her chest. She almost felt bad for her — a sad, lonely forty-two-year-old — before remembering yet again that Rachel had tried to torpedo her marriage.

Susan Steinhagen came over to Jen and shook Jen's hand with her bony, cool fingers. It was Salcombe's highest honor. "Jen Weinstein, I didn't know you had it in you," said Susan. "I'm impressed."

Jen felt herself blush. She put her hand on her hot, damp cheek. "Thanks to you, Susan, for putting on such a great tournament," she said. "I can't wait for the final this afternoon. How's the other match going?"

"Vicky and Janet are running away with it. You and Lauren have your work cut out for you."

"They can pull it off," said Sam.

Susan smiled at him gently. The town had been treating Sam with kid gloves since the picnic. Yes, there had been the occasional whisper, some stares at the beach, the raised eyebrows when Jen and Sam had dinner alone at the yacht club. But mostly, people had rallied around him, checking in to see how he was holding up, sending notes of support via email and text. Jen welcomed the care. She was semi-shocked at how little enjoyment everyone was taking in their embarrassment. Things would be different, she thought, if Sam were a woman. But he was a beloved man in a small town. No one wanted to see him brought low.

Lisa approached and gave Jen a celebratory hug. Sam went over to chat with Paul, towering over him, nearly different species.

"You played amazingly," said Lisa, her eyes crinkling with mischief. As the summer went on, the women's fillers and injectables wore off; by Labor Day, they all looked like an approximation of their real selves. Older, tanner, their bodies more lived-in. Jen preferred this Lisa to the one who'd arrived in June, frozen and plumped.

"Look at Rachel," she whispered, stepping closer to Jen. "This is the worst moment of her life." She smirked as she said it.

Rachel glared at them as if she'd heard her.

"Be kind," said Jen, even though she didn't really mean it. "You should go offer your services as a life coach. She's clearly in need."

Lisa giggled conspiratorially. "What's gotten into you! You're supposed to be the nice one."

They watched as Rachel got up and went over to Sam and Paul, who both offered their condolences. Lisa set off to congratulate Lauren, who was still making the rounds, leaving Jen alone. She felt great. Invigorated. Proud.

She saw Rachel tug on Sam's sleeve and

pull him away from Paul. Then Rachel disappeared with Sam into Robert's tennis hut, closing the door behind them. What was she doing? Jen felt her heart quicken, and she followed them, pulling to open the door, but it was jammed. Rachel must have locked it. She knocked on it, trying to remain quiet so as not to attract anyone's attention. She smiled at Brian Metzner as he walked by, and then stood there helplessly for at least a minute. "Sam," she hoarsely whispered into the door. *"Sam!"*

The door opened, and there they were. Sam standing near the stringing machine and Rachel leaning against Robert's desk, next to his open lesson ledger. Sam looked strange, white and drawn, his lips parted oddly over his teeth. Rachel guiltily looked down at the floor instead of at Jen, then walked out, pushing past her.

"Sam," said Jen.

He was staring at her as if he didn't recognize her.

"What did she say to you? She's a liar. Remember that. And she's upset she lost to me."

Sam shook his head, his curls flopping. Then he silently walked out of the hut. Jen tried to grab his arm as he passed, but he shook it off, his head down. He continued

out of there, not looking where he was going, and then violently bumped into poor
Micah Holt, standing next to Lauren near
the bike rack. Surprised, Micah fell to the
boardwalk. Sam went over and lifted him
up like a little boy, placing him gently on
his feet. Then Sam took Lauren's head in
his hands and whispered something into her
ear. Lauren turned to face Jen, shock
spreading over her pretty face like water filling a bathtub.

Sam grabbed his bike, freeing it from the
surrounding ones with a strong shake, and
took off, riding up Marine, away from the
courts, away from Jen. She stood there and
watched him go, not sure of her next move.
Fuck Rachel Woolf, thought Jen. She was
going to kill her. Jen went over to her own
bike and took her phone out of her tennis
bag in the basket. Lauren was still standing
there, not having moved at all. Jen opened
Signal and typed a message.

Jen Weinstein: I think he knows. Watch
out.

21
ROBERT HEYWORTH

Robert Heyworth was about to have a fantastic fall. But first, he couldn't believe how seriously people were taking this tennis tournament. It was a joke. A bunch of middle-aged women, not one of them above a 3.5 USTA tennis ranking, playing each other as if they were at Roland Garros. He'd been a pro long enough to know that wealthy people loved to exaggerate their athletic abilities, but this was a new level. You'd have thought Rachel Woolf was the next Serena Williams by how hard she took her loss in the semifinals to Lauren and Jen.

Robert had watched the entire match, admiring Lauren's legs in her white skirt. He'd coached her beforehand, last night at his place after they'd had sex. She'd been lying on his bed, naked.

"You have to keep your eyes on Rachel. If she drifts to the middle, hit winners down the line," he'd said, tracing a line down from her breasts to her stomach with his finger.

She'd listened and executed, and Robert was proud of her. As dumb as this thing was, he wanted Lauren to win it. They were now in the limbo period between the semis and the finals, which started at 4:00 p.m. It was his job to organize the courts so more people could watch; dragging extra seats outside from the yacht club, angling benches so everyone could have a view. Willa Thomas and Micah Holt were helping with it all, bouncing around cheerfully, carefully carrying out plastic pitchers of Stella and tubs of freshly popped popcorn. The yacht club staff was a mix of locals, like Willa and Micah, and working-class kids from across the bay in Long Island, who took the ferry back and forth and actually needed the money.

"Hey, Micah," said Robert, sitting down for a quick break. He patted the seat next to him.

Micah, dressed in tennis whites for the occasion, came over, perching on the other side of the bench.

"Who are you rooting for?" Robert asked, grasping for conversation. Micah had been a bit standoffish lately, though Robert couldn't say why. It's not like they interacted beyond tasks like this.

"I guess I'm rooting for Lauren and Jen," said Micah, eyeing him warily. "I like an underdog, and I feel that Lauren deserves this." He quickly followed with, "She's been working so hard. I've seen her out on the court with you almost every day."

Robert was struck with the sudden feeling that Micah knew more than he should.

"What about you?" Micah asked innocently.

"Oh, I'm a neutral party," said Robert, shaking it off. He was probably just imagining things. Robert was in high spirits. After the morning match, he'd had a few lessons, including one with Larry Higgins. Afterward, they'd sat together drinking water and discussing life, which was Larry's favorite thing to do.

"So, kid, the summer's almost over. What are your plans for the fall?" Larry had taken a fatherly interest in Robert, which Robert appreciated. There was always one kind older guy at the club who wanted to see Robert succeed.

"I'm honestly not sure," said Robert. "I want to stay in the city for the year and look for work, real work," he added. "But beyond that, I've got nothing."

Larry took a long sip of water from his purple Contigo. Robert realized he knew

305

very little about Larry, other than that his wife, Henrietta, didn't play tennis and that he had two grown sons. Where did they live? Why weren't they out here spending time with their dad while he was still alive?

"I have an idea for you," said Larry, looking at him seriously, his thick white eyebrows drawn together. "I want you to come work for me."

"But I thought you were retired," said Robert.

"I'm semiretired," said Larry. "I still dabble. And I need someone to source investment ideas for me and help me keep my books. I know you're not trained in any of this, but you're a smart guy, a lot smarter than most of the people I've worked with during my career, and I think I could teach you. I could set you up to get hired by a real firm in a couple of years' time."

This was exactly, word for word, what Robert had always hoped someone would say to him. A benefactor, at last.

"I'd love that. I'd work so hard; you know that about me. And I could scrape by on my savings from the summer," said Robert, thinking of the tax-free $16,000 he'd squirreled away by stealing from the club.

"Oh, I'll pay you, son," said Larry. "I'd never hire someone without paying them;

that's called slavery. I'll start you at a hundred and fifty thousand for the year. How does that sound?"

Robert nearly fell from the bench.

"That's too much. How do you even know that it'll work? I was thinking it would be more of an internship opportunity, and that would be fine by me."

"Oh, kid, just take a good offer when you hear one. That's lesson number one," said Larry. "My sons are off in Europe, partying away their inheritance. It'll be nice to have a young man around who wants to learn the ropes. The one catch is that you'll have to give me free tennis lessons."

"Yes, I will! That sounds perfect. Thank you so much," said Robert, nearly vibrating with happiness.

"Let's start the week after Labor Day," said Larry. "You'll have to find yourself an apartment, but I trust you can take care of that."

"Certainly, yes," said Robert. Larry stuck out his hand, and Robert shook it vigorously. "I won't let you down," he said to Larry as they walked off the court.

"You'd better not," Larry said, laughing.

That was a couple of hours ago, and Robert was still high on the idea that he'd get to stay in the city for the year and work for Larry, even if it was just charity. Either way, Robert was committed to working his ass off in any capacity Larry needed.

Micah had gone back inside, so Robert went out to the stadium court, brushing it back and forth with the large broom, making it perfect for the finals. He hadn't seen Lauren since she'd left after the semis, and he was looking forward to watching her play again.

People were starting to arrive for the match, which was Robert's cue to shut himself in his hut and chill at his desk for the time being. He didn't like to hang out with the members during tournaments, as one by one they'd approach him for his thoughts on the matchup. He couldn't bring himself to seriously opine as if they were at Wimbledon. Vicky Mulder was in her fifties.

He paged through his lesson ledger, noting the empty hours during which he'd really been teaching. He'd been getting a little bold, hiding two lessons a day for the past couple of weeks, but now that he had a job lined up, he'd pull back. Maybe he'd stop entirely. He'd used his weekly salary to pay off his credit card bills, and he had that $16,000. Plus, he'd still get 20 percent of the lesson pool from the club — hopefully that would at least be another $10,000. That should be more than enough to secure him a small place and pay the security deposit. If he got caught now, it'd all be for nothing.

There was a loud knock on the door, which swung open before Robert could get up to answer. Susan Steinhagen was there, all dolled up in her favorite tennis skirt, like a kid at her own birthday party. This was Susan's moment. Robert couldn't even imagine back in the day when Susan used to both run *and* win the tournament. She played with the other seniors now, begrudgingly. Every time she used the word *senior,* she scrunched up her nose like she was smelling something rotten.

"The time has come," she said ominously. He knew she was just referring to the finals, but it still sounded like a threat. She glanced down at his ledger, still open to today's date. "You working on bookkeeping?"

Robert shut the ledger with a thud, harder than he'd meant to.

"Just dotting my i's and crossing my t's," he said with a forced smile. His charm was powerless against Susan Steinhagen; she was the one person in town who wasn't half in love with him.

"Shall we get to it, then," he said, ushering her out of the doorway.

The viewing area was packed. There were

probably fifty people lining the benches all the way around the court, plus an additional forty or so standing up behind them. It had the feel of a carnival. The smell of popcorn mixed with beer, a buzzy chat ringing through the late-summer air. The two teams were already out on the court warming up, hitting ground strokes back and forth down the line.

Lauren looked great, freshly outfitted in a blue Adidas dress, her hair shining in the afternoon sun. Jen was less radiant than usual, but Robert couldn't put his finger on why. She was in all blue as well, a skirt and tank combo, but her face was pinched. *She must just be nervous,* thought Robert. She had the least tournament experience of them all.

Robert surveyed the crowd. He didn't see Sam or Jason, which was strange. Lauren and Jen's friends were huddled in a little group. Lisa, Emily, Brian, Paul — where was Rachel? Robert couldn't believe she'd miss this, even after her heartbreaker earlier this morning. On the opposite end of the court was the rival gang — Beth Ledbetter, Jessica Leavitt, Jeanette Oberman. They were all wearing red in solidarity (Vicky and Janet wore matching red tennis skirts every year) and drinking vodka sodas out of plastic cups. The town's allegiances were divided evenly.

Robert, in his official Salcombe Yacht Club tennis polo, took a seat close to the court. He was the nominal linesman, though his role was only to make sure there weren't any egregious errors; he didn't call balls in or out. He also kept track of the score so that no one could steal points. He'd found in his career that women were, as a whole, huge cheaters. It surprised Robert that women were worse than men in this regard, but perhaps men just saved it for their lives outside tennis. Salcombe was the same.

The game started, and the crowd hushed, sort of. He could still hear Beth Ledbetter cackling about something. "Quiet, please!" Susan boomed from her seat, cupping her hands around her mouth for dramatic effect. Jason and Sam were still absentee. Robert knew people would notice and start whispering about it. The entire village was here, but not the two husbands of the underdogs? Robert was worried something was wrong. Rachel hadn't shown, either.

Jen and Lauren started off shakily. They were both stiff and not hitting with their normal pace. Jen was stopping her shots midway without following through, and Lauren was dinking it over instead of step-

311

ping into the ball. Vicky and Janet pounced, going up a quick 3–0, breaking Lauren's serve. At the changeover, Robert saw both Jen and Lauren searching the spectators, possibly looking for their husbands. He locked eyes with Lauren, but she didn't smile at him, instead averting her gaze and whispering something to Jen before they headed back out to the court.

As the game resumed, Lauren and Jen loosened up. Lauren began hitting with her normal power, and Jen was finding angles, getting the ball behind Janet when she ran to the net. They tied it up at 3–3 and then jumped ahead to 5–4. Robert hadn't had to interject about the score or calls, and he was hoping they'd close out the set before he did.

No such luck. Vicky was serving at 40–30; if she won the game, they'd be tied at 5–5 and likely headed toward a tiebreak. If they lost, Jen and Lauren would take the set, and the upset would be well underway. Her first serve to Jen was out, wide. Her second serve, a spinny, slice-y, confusing number, skidded at the back of the box.

"Out," said Jen, holding up her finger to indicate.

There was a low murmur from the onlookers.

"That was in," Robert heard Beth say loudly.

Lauren's face reddened — she knew her partner was lying.

"Are you sure?" asked Vicky from the back of the court.

"Jen's cheating," Robert heard someone sitting behind him say.

"I'm *sure*. It was out," said Jen defensively. "It's deuce now."

Vicky and Janet stood there dumbly, not switching sides. Vicky's hands were on her hips. Even though she was older, Vicky was tough. Robert had heard she'd grown up on the Jersey Shore and had distant relatives in the Mafia.

"Check the mark, please," said Vicky flatly.

"It's their game! The ball was in!" Jerry Braun, Janet's husband, dressed in a green floral Tommy Bahama shirt, shouted.

Everyone erupted. Men started yelling at each other ("In!" "Out!"), popcorn fell, beer spilled. The players stood frozen on the court, watching the chaos along with Robert, who wasn't sure what to do.

Someone approached him from behind. "It's time to intervene!" Susan said into his ear, her breath tickling his neck. She nearly pushed him out of his seat.

"Susan, if they called it out, it's out.

313

There's no Hawk-Eye in Salcombe. This is ridiculous." He looked at Susan pleadingly, but she gave him nothing, just a forceful tug of his short sleeve.

He opened the green gate and stepped out onto the court, walking toward the back where the serve landed. Lauren and Jen jogged over to him as he did.

"Robert, it was out, I'm sure of it," said Jen softly. He saw the mark, clear as day, right on the back of the white line. Lauren looked down at the clay and then up at Jen. She shrugged.

"Okay, let's just give it to those bitches," Lauren said to Jen, patting her on the back.

Jen nodded, embarrassed. Robert walked back out of the gate to his seat and pulled his cap low over his head. Larry waved to him from a neighboring bench, mouthing, *Can you believe this shit?*

"It was in. I'm sorry about that," said Jen, loudly enough for everyone to hear.

A cheer went up from the Beth Ledbetter group.

It was now tied 5–5, and the rest of the match was a goner. Vicky and Janet took the set in a tiebreak and then won the second set 6–3. It wasn't even close. Robert watched through his fingers. After the final point, Vicky and Janet threw their rackets in the air and screeched. The champions had won again. Robert wanted to die; it was all so embarrassing.

The pairs shook hands, everyone exchanging their phony niceties. Lauren and Jen came off the court first, to the hugs of Lisa and Emily. The mystery of Sam's, Jason's, and Rachel's whereabouts still hadn't been solved.

Robert approached Vicky and Janet to say congratulations. The crowd had thinned by that point, with only family and very close friends still hanging out, talking to the players.

"You did great, ladies. Really well played," said Robert, flashing his shiniest smile.

"Thanks, Robert," said Vicky. Her voice was husky, with a sharp New Jersey accent. She had impressively defined musculature; her lats bulged above her neck like small mountains.

"I just couldn't believe that call, though," said Janet, the less forceful of the pair.

"I've played with Jen before," said Vicky. "And she cheats. I've seen it."

Robert didn't doubt it, given what he knew about her personal life. He just wished she hadn't done it during the finals of the women's doubles tournament.

"It's always tough to make a call in the

heat of the moment," said Robert diplomatically. "The important part was that you two didn't let it throw you. You kept your cool" — here, Robert was lying, as Vicky certainly hadn't — "and soldiered on, taking the win."

The women looked pleased with themselves. Robert went off in search of the losers, who were huddled together off to the side. They glanced up as Robert came over, and he got the sense that they didn't want to speak to him, which was odd. He hesitated, but then felt like it'd be even awkwarder to turn around.

"Great match, guys. You gave it your all," he said. He tried to catch Lauren's eye, but she was staring at the bike rack, as if waiting for someone to arrive.

"Thanks," said Jen after an unusually long pause. "Sorry about that flubbed call. I really thought it was out. Maybe I need to get a new contacts prescription." She laughed lightly.

"It happens to the best of us," said Robert. "I've definitely done it myself." Except he hadn't. At least not knowingly. He didn't cheat at tennis. He thought about his lesson ledger. Had he put it back in the drawer when he'd left the hut to watch the match?

No one said anything.

"Were your husbands too nervous to attend?" he asked.

Lauren and Jen looked at each other.

"Yes," Lauren said. "Jason and Sam couldn't bear it. It was all too much for them."

Robert felt nauseated. Did any of this have to do with him? If Jen would leave, he could ask Lauren directly, but she wasn't moving.

"I'm proud of you both for making it to the finals," said Robert finally. "You've really improved so much this summer. It's been fun to teach you."

Just then, he saw Rachel emerge from her front porch, still in her tennis clothes from the morning, her head turning left and right as if she were a lookout. Jen and Lauren clocked her and nearly broke out in a full run in her direction. Rachel spotted them coming. For a second, Robert thought she might jump off the boardwalk into the tick grass and take off into the woods. Instead, she got on her bike and pedaled away, fast, leaving Lauren and Jen standing about fifteen feet from her house. Robert had been having such a great day — a new job, a clearer future. Now all he felt was uneasiness.

Lauren and Jen jogged to their own bikes, parked side by side in the bike rack, and, to

Robert's shock, went racing off together without saying goodbye. They'd left their rackets together on a bench near where Robert was standing. He picked them up — he'd put them in his hut until they came back. He hoped Lauren would have an explanation for him later.

There was barely anyone left at the courts. It was nearing 6:00, and there was a slight freshness to the air, an end-of-summer reminder that none of this would last forever. Robert was planning on having an early night. He was exhausted. The idea that he'd be wiped out by a ladies' doubles tournament would have been ludicrous two months ago. But here he was.

The Lauren situation was bothering him. He took her and Jen's rackets into his hut and was surprised to see Susan sitting at his desk, her distinct profile in full view. Had she been there the whole time?

She turned when she heard him come in. Robert recognized her look. He was caught.

"Robert Heyworth, I have a question for you," she said, her deep voice gone trembly.

Robert felt a green fly latch onto his leg and bite, taking its time. Pain shot up from his thigh into his torso.

Susan stood up, and Robert could see she was holding his lesson ledger, her arthritic hands curled tightly around the book. She didn't have any proof, he thought. She was smart, but so was he.

"Sure, Susan," he said, casually. He propped the rackets against the wooden wall. "What can I do for you?" He stared at her, trying to make her uncomfortable.

"It seems some lessons are missing from your daily schedule," she said. She opened his ledger and flipped through to yesterday's lineup. He could clearly read his writing:

August 22 — Lesson Schedule
Larry Higgins — 9:00 a.m.–10:00a.m.
Jerry Braun — 10:00 a.m.–11:00 a.m.
Kids clinic — 11:30 a.m.–1:00 p.m.
Lunch
Beth Ledbetter — 2:00–3:00 p.m.
Lisa and Brian Metzner, doubles — 3:30–4:30 p.m.

She pointed a long finger at the page. "Here, where it says, 'Lunch,' at 1:00 p.m. I saw you giving Claire Laurell a lesson. I was playing on the stadium court with my normal game. Why isn't that written down?"

Robert shrugged. "Must have been an oversight. I'll double-check with Claire." He smiled at her, purposefully showing all his perfect white teeth. "I'm not even sure if you're right."

"Oh, I'm right," Susan shot back quickly. She narrowed her eyes. "If I inspect this book . . . ," she said, paging through it. "What will I find?"

"I think you'll find that I'm a good book-keeper," said Robert. He laughed. He could feel the sweat gathering in his armpits, threatening to reveal itself.

"I'm not so sure," said Susan. She moved to leave the hut, but Robert stood in front of the door to block her. It was more menacing than he'd planned, but he needed that ledger back. Susan, eyes wide like a cornered animal, picked up Lauren's racket and, with a dramatic arc, whacked Robert's head, sending him careening forward toward his desk. She'd always had a great overhead; Robert had seen it himself.

Susan scooted out the door with his ledger before he'd recovered. By the time he got outside, she was gone. The courts were empty. It was dinnertime. Robert could hear the clatter on the deck as people ate and drank at the yacht club. He was now alone, in a panic. Should he follow her? If she exposed him, he'd lose everything. This job, his position with Larry, his reputation.

He'd find Susan. He'd get the ledger back. He walked to get his bike. Heavy raindrops hit his head, and a strong gust of wind came off the bay, rustling the trees and lifting his hair. The sky was gray and darkening. He spotted a deer up ahead on Marine, just past the courts, staring at him. He took off, headed out into the storm to search for Susan.

22
LARRY HIGGINS

Larry Higgins knew a thief when he saw one. And he knew young, handsome Robert Heyworth was a thief. Did Robert really think Larry, who oversaw the tennis finances, wouldn't notice lessons charges missing from the bank? *Larry Higgins?* He'd run a successful investment firm for forty-five years. He'd dealt with swindlers and frauds. He'd palled around with Bernie Madoff, for God's sake.

It was his fault, really. He was the one who'd told Robert about Dave, planted the seed in Robert's greedy, broke brain that it was possible — easy, even — to skim off the top. Robert was ripe for corruption; Larry should have known better. He was a kid batting below his level. He was smarter and more talented than the fuckers he was a slave to, and that must have made him insane.

Larry didn't care. But he did want him to

stop. Because it wouldn't be long before that witch Susan Steinhagen caught wind of it, and after that, it'd be all over for charming Robert Heyworth. So, he'd decided to offer him that job. Larry did need the help, and he knew Robert could do it. Robert wouldn't mess with such a good offer. He'd right his ways, and they could all go on with their lives, none the wiser. Historically, some of Larry's best employees were also the most dishonest. So long as it wasn't directed at Larry, which it wouldn't be. He'd make sure of that.

Larry was having a drink at the yacht club after the women's finals. Vicky and Janet had crushed Lauren and Jen, much to Larry's disappointment. He loved an underdog. He'd always thought of himself that way. He came from nothing. He'd grown up in Brooklyn; his dad was a garmento, working in women's wholesale clothing, and Larry had been the first in his family to go to college. He was bright and scrappy and had gotten into investment banking when the going was good. He and Henrietta had two sons, Peter and Lee, who were both disappointments. Peter lived in Paris, "working" freelance for some ad agency, and Lee was in London, not even pretending to hold down a job. They were both in their late thirties, neither married, and the thought of them made Larry want to both scream and cry. What had he done wrong? He'd given them everything.

He waved over Micah Holt to refill his whiskey.

Micah bopped over. "Here you go, Larry," Micah said, giving him a generous pour.

"Thanks, kid," said Larry with a sigh. Now that was a good boy. A hard worker. Gay, sure, but weren't all the kids gay nowadays? His parents must be proud.

Larry took his drink and walked through the back room out to the courts. The air felt damp and heavy, and Larry's leg, which he'd busted up in his forties, skiing in Zermatt, was aching. That meant a storm was coming. He'd have to bike home soon; Henrietta was making dinner, and he didn't want to be late, delayed by the rain. The courts were empty. He wondered where Robert had gone. Probably out to celebrate his new gig as Larry's apprentice. Larry sat down on a bench and rested his eyes. He was getting unusually tired lately, his age finally catching up to him. He'd be seventy-two in the spring. It was so strange. He still felt like he was thirty-five.

His silence was punctured by a dramatic crash from inside Robert's tennis hut. Larry opened his eyes to see Susan exit, her tennis skirt flapping wildly, holding Robert's lesson ledger. She ran the opposite way, toward her bike, not noticing Larry in her insane rush. Larry was sure he knew what had happened. He got up and immediately crept back to the club, hoping Robert didn't emerge in time to see him.

He slipped in through the back door just as the rain began to fall. Poor Robert. He was screwed. Susan would never let this go unpunished. Larry supposed he'd have to rescind his job offer when this got out. What a shame.

He sat back at the bar and motioned to Micah for another. He was happy to settle in for a while and chat with whomever else was waiting out the storm. A loud crack of thunder rattled him on his red stool. It was going to be a long night.

23
THE STORM

Jason Parker had always thought, maybe, accidentally, he'd kill his best friend, Sam Weinstein. When he was a kid, he'd have fantasies of Sam tripping over Jason's foot and careening off his eighth-floor balcony onto Ninety-third Street. Or a sailing accident: Jason would capsize the boat in rough waters, and Sam would drown. Everyone would be sad, so sad, but mostly they'd feel terrible for Jason. Poor Jason, now best friend–less, having to deal with that guilt at such a young age. He'd become an object of fascination in school; girls would give him sympathetic attention, and guys would welcome him into their groups.

As they grew into adults, Jason's thoughts turned from accidental death to ruin. Sam would lose all his money on a bad investment and turn to Jason to keep his family off the street. Or Sam would become addicted to painkillers, and Jason would have to wrestle him into rehab, selling Sam's Fire Island house, Sam's most beloved possession, to pay for it.

Jason knew this wasn't healthy. He knew that most people didn't want to murder their best friends. He couldn't help it. Sam had everything. Jason had always had to work twice as hard to find success, women, and respect. Why couldn't he ever be the star?

Now, in a twist, Sam might be the one to end up killing *him*. Jason thought about the dark humor of this turn. He was soaking wet, freezing, hiding underneath the rusty slide in the playground across from the field. The sun had set an hour ago, and it was storming, harder than Jason had expected. When he'd left his house this afternoon, after that cryptic text from Jen, it had been hot and sunny. He was wearing shorts and a T-shirt that read SALCOMBE GOLF OUTING 2017. Hiding from Sam! Gentle Sam, who'd never been in a fight in his life. Once, when they were nine or ten, Keith Longeran, the nasty, redheaded bully, had sucker punched Sam in the back after a kickball game at camp. Jason remembered Sam standing on the dusty baseline, hunched over in pain, confused as to how to handle the situation. Instead of retaliating, Sam had shrugged and walked off, to the other boys' disappointment. "Pussy!" Keith had shouted after him. Jason then walked up to Keith and punched him in the face, sending a trickle of blood from his nose down to his chin.

Would Sam really do anything to Jason, even if he found him? His longtime defender? A flash of lightning lit up the sky, followed by a crash of thunder. Jason was uncomfortable. Soggy, shivery, and starving. He wanted to go home, but Lauren kept texting him to stay away, and Jen kept sending him desperate Signal messages, saying that Sam was "dangerous" and that Jason should lie low.

Everyone knew everything. After the tennis match, Rachel had told Sam that he and Jen were having an affair, and then Sam had told Lauren. For a long time, Jason had been hoping for it all to come out, but the moment had passed. Now it felt more like a crisis than an opportunity to start a new life. Rachel must have seen him and Jen together earlier in the summer, that sneaky bitch. He was honestly amazed that she'd kept it to herself for this long.

If this was the drama he had to endure — Lauren sending angry texts, Sam "hunting" for him — for his affair with Jen, he'd take it. The worst had come to pass; the cat was out of the bag, and they'd still never be together. Jen was a psychologist — wasn't that something they'd talked about? The catastrophe had happened, and now they could all move on.

This would blow over, and Sam would relax. They wouldn't be friends, but they'd have to come to a truce for their children's sakes. Lauren would be pissed for life, but he'd pay her a great alimony, and she could continue to rule the Upper East Side. Half of her friends were divorced; it wasn't a big deal. Maybe he'd move to Miami alone. Jason chuckled thinking about how angry that would make Lauren, who'd been wanting to settle there for years.

Another streak of light, another groan of thunder. The wind was really picking up now. The playground sand was lightly pelting Jason in the face. This was ridiculous. He was going home. He didn't even really know what he was avoiding. Couldn't he hide in his own house? Sam wasn't going to hurt him in front of his kids. The thought was too absurd. He was more worried that Lauren might murder him for cheating on her.

He got on his stomach to crawl out from

under the slide and was immediately pelted by rain. This hadn't been in the forecast. Fire Island occasionally got rogue storms that entirely missed the mainland, ones that gathered speed over the bay before crushing into the narrow barrier island. The wind pushed Jason back as he made his way from the playground to Neptune Walk. He didn't have his bike. He'd have to walk all the way home in this nightmare, hopefully not running into Sam on the way there.

SAM WEINSTEIN

Sam Weinstein had never considered himself a murderer. In fact, he'd always been a peace-and-love kind of guy. He barely even yelled at his own kids, let alone ever hit them, leaving Jen to do the dirty work of being the house disciplinarian. But here he was, out in a storm, carrying a large kitchen knife, of all things, looking everywhere for his former best friend, Jason Parker.

Fucking Jason, who was fucking Jen. He couldn't fucking believe it. Actually, scratch that: when Rachel whispered it to him at the courts, the moment after she'd said, "It's Jason," her breath moist in his ear, it clicked. Who else could it have been *but* Jason? That's why Jason had been avoiding him. But how could he have done this to

330

him? How could Jen?

When he thought about it, and he'd been thinking about it every second since he'd found out, it made him want to throw up. It made him want to die. It made him want to kill someone. It wasn't a feeling Sam had ever experienced. Red-hot fury. It was almost fun. Before this summer, Sam had spent his life being the easiest, coolest guy. Not stalking people with a Japanese knife, a Shun Premier that he'd bought on sale years ago at Williams-Sonoma on Madison and Eighty-sixth for $150.

It was cold and wet and dark out, and he was still in his clothes from the day, his favorite orange linen shirt. It was clinging to his chest, and he thought about how silly he must look. The world's most bougie killer. He'd been walking around town for hours at this point, looking everywhere for Jason.

At first, after he'd found out, he'd raced up to Jason's house to confront him. Jason's black cruiser bike was out front, and Sam thought he'd caught him. He quickly tore through the rooms, from Lauren and Jason's downstairs bedroom to their pristine kitchen up top, with those fantastic ocean views. But it was empty. Jason must have run out without his bike. So, Sam rode back down to the bay to his house, walked in casually, saying hi to his nanny and children, grabbed the Shun Premier from the kitchen island, tucked it under his shirt, and left. He hadn't been back since.

He'd initially gone to the beach and had walked about a mile west before plopping down on the sand, nearly directly in front of the Fire Island Lighthouse. He'd sat there for a while — hours, maybe, he didn't know how long — just staring at the ocean, which was growing wilder by the minute. The waves were around five feet high, whipping back and forth. He'd imagined punching Jason in his stupid face. He'd imagined Jason and Jen having sex. He'd imagined slowly sticking the knife into Jason's back, just like Jason had done to him.

The clouds had rolled in from the bay side, quickly passing over Sam's head and spreading out into the sky above the water. The rain had followed soon after, a hard, driving kind, and Sam had reluctantly gotten up and walked back, completely uncovered, the wind throwing wet sand into his face and eyes. He was the only person on the beach. He wondered if anyone could see him from their oceanfront homes. Damaged Sam, who'd recently jumped into the bay in front of everyone in Salcombe, stomping through a squall. If only people could see the knife tucked into his pants.

He hadn't really known where to go after, so he headed down the Broadway boardwalk toward the store. The wood was wet and slippery underneath his flip-flops, and he had a sudden fear that he'd fall and stick himself with the knife by accident.

He'd spent the next hour going up and down each walk, with no plan other than to find Jason, and then . . . he didn't know. The town was deserted; everyone was taking refuge from the violent storm. Sam could barely see a few feet in front of him, and time was passing oddly. He felt nearly delirious. Were the trees lining the board- walks closing in on him? He missed his kids. He missed Jen. He hated Jen.

He was near the playground by that point, across from the field, and he walked up to the porch of the camp art shack, the one in which his children made papier-mâché fish and wove friendship bracelets. The lights were off, and the sliding doors were locked, but the roof provided some cover. He took his phone out of his shorts' pocket, sur- prised it hadn't been completely water- logged. He had twenty-seven text messages, mostly from Jen, asking where he was, tell- ing him it wasn't true. *Not this time, Jen.* He couldn't be fooled forever. A few of the messages were from Rachel, desperate pleas for him to come to meet her in Kismet. Why was she in Kismet? Lauren had even texted him asking him to "fucking kill" Jason if he saw him. There was also a voice mail from a New York City number. He put the phone as close to his ear as possible and played it, struggling to hear the message over the wind and rain.

"Sam, hi. It's Mary" — Mary Martin, his firm's head of HR.

Sam's stomach tightened. It was the call he'd been waiting all summer for.

"I've got some news for you."

Sam paused the message and pressed the phone harder into his ear. Lightning flashed and thunder followed. He unpaused it.

"The committee has wrapped up its investigation. You'll be happy to know, we found no wrongdoing on your part. This might come as a surprise, but after months of digging, we found a pattern of covered-up abuse coming from the top — Henry Boro, in fact, had been harassing young associates and then pressuring them to make false accusations against others. Lydia will remain at the firm, but won't be in your department. We're going to be very tight-lipped about this — say Henry's retiring, dole out settlements where need be. We're sorry for how long this has taken to clear up and the impact it's had on you and your family, but we're happy to welcome you back to Sullivan & Cromwell immediately. Please call me tomorrow to discuss, but I wanted to let you know as soon as I'd heard. Have a good night, Sam."

Sam played it again to make sure he'd heard it right. He leaned against the side of the shack and slid down the wood, not remembering the knife, which nicked his thigh as he did. "Ow! Fuck!" he shouted to no one, taking the Shun out and holding it in both of his water-wrinkled hands. Henry Boro! Was everyone in his life — his best friend, his wife, his boss — a lying asshole? He was starting to think that no one was who they said they were. Lightning sizzled, and thunder banged down from the sky. In the millisecond of illumination, Sam saw a shadow move from underneath the playground slide. He burrowed down where he was, lowering his body to the porch, staying flat and still. He saw Jason emerge from under the slide, a six-foot-tall wet rat. Jason looked left and right, checking to see if Sam was lurking, and then headed up Neptune toward his house. Ten seconds after he passed, Sam slithered up, still clutching the knife, and set off behind him.

LAUREN PARKER AND JEN WEINSTEIN

Lauren Parker and Jen Weinstein had never been close. It was a relationship forged by proximity, like friends from a freshman-year dorm. They could have a nice chat at a dinner or a party or even tolerate each other on a weeklong vacation with their families — they'd gone skiing together with the kids in Snowmass, rented a big home in Maine before they all got married, and spent long weekends in upstate New York in luxurious converted barns during endless frigid winters. But it was all surface level. How are the kids doing, how are your in-laws, how much tennis are you playing / Pilates are you getting in? They just didn't click. Sometimes women don't, much to men's confusion. But something this summer had shifted between Lauren and Jen, starting with their unlikely success on the tennis courts.

It was horrible out; the wind was howling, the rain was incessant, and the boardwalk was barely visible. Lauren and Jen were walking up Broadway, alone in the Salcombe darkness, searching for their husbands. The kids were all together at Jen and Sam's house, watching a movie and eating microwave popcorn, unaware that their parents' marriages were both on the verge of imploding.

An hour ago, it became clear that Sam and Jason were missing, neither answering the panicked texts their wives were shooting off into the night. So, Silvia had bundled Lauren's kids in rain gear, and she and Lauren carried Amelie the entire way down to the bay, switching off, with Arlo holding the flashlight up front as they walked through the storm. Was Lauren's marriage over? Would she now be a single mom? She wasn't sure she could take the faux concern from her city friends; Mimi and company pointedly asking, "How *are* you?" while they gossiped behind her back. She'd get the apartment, surely. But what about Fire Island? At least she'd have all the leverage. Robert was still a secret, and she'd make sure to keep it that way.

When they arrived, Jen was ready to go, wearing an oversize yellow raincoat adorned by the Salcombe Yacht Club logo, her big hazel eyes peeking out from under the hood. Lauren nearly laughed when she saw her. Jen grabbed another flashlight from the vintage jelly cabinet in her kitchen. As she passed her center island, she paused in front of her knife set. The Shun Premier was missing. She opened her utensil drawer — maybe Luana had put it there by mistake? But it was gone.

"Lauren, I think Sam has a knife."

Lauren stared at her. "What the hell does he think he's going to do with that?" she said.

Jen shrugged. "I don't know. We have to find these idiots."

They didn't say much as they left Jen's house, heading east on Bay Promenade. The water was swirling with whitecaps, and there were no boats on the horizon. The only light was the constant spin of the lighthouse beam, flashing on cue every few seconds.

Jen truly felt terrible. She'd always thought of her affairs as *hers,* private matters meant to sate her own needs. She should have known better than to get involved with Jason. It had been a mistake. Though, as a therapist, she knew "mistake" was a misnomer — something subconscious must have been driving her toward self-destruction. What kind of damaged soul sleeps with her husband's best friend? Now everything had unraveled, and her actions had triggered a cascade of hurt. Jason, Sam, Lauren, possibly all their children.

They turned up Marine Walk, passing the yacht club, which was open but, based on what they could see, empty save Micah Holt, Willa Thomas, and Larry Higgins. No one was out in this.

"Let's check out the courts," said Lauren.

They walked over, sweeping the green clay with their flashlights. Everything was still, no sound other than raindrops falling in the puddles lining the baselines. The lights in the yacht club suddenly went out, plunging the night into blackness.

"Must be a power outage," said Jen, continuing to shine her light this way and that.

It was just this morning they'd won the semifinal against Emily and Rachel. It felt like a year ago. "I still can't believe we got to the finals," said Lauren.

"I know," said Jen. "Quite an upset. I'm not sure if Rachel will ever recover. Or if we ever will." She laughed darkly.

Lauren went over to Robert's tennis hut and pulled on the door, but it was locked. She hadn't heard from him since after the match, when she and Jen had gone racing after Rachel. They'd never found her.

"I saw you come out of there on July 4. Remember?" Jen said pointedly. She walked closer to Lauren. The wind was making it hard to hear.

"I do," said Lauren. Neither had broached

the fact that Jen had been sleeping with Jason, and neither wanted to.

"Let's walk over to Broadway," said Lauren at last. They started up Marine and passed Rachel's house. The porch light was off, and her bike wasn't outside.

"Where do you think she went?" said Jen. "We weren't going to hurt her or anything," she said.

Lauren giggled. "I mean, I'd like to," she said. "She's basically ruined all our lives."

They turned onto Harbor, ducking under sagging, waterlogged reeds. There was another crackling of thunder.

"I'm the one who ruined our lives," said Jen. She shivered underneath her oversize raincoat. Water was dripping from her hood into her eyes.

"Honestly, Jen, I couldn't give a shit," said Lauren, relieved to say it out loud. "I've been sleeping with Robert for months," she continued.

"I figured," said Jen.

"The only reason I care about you and Jason is that it's going to make *me* look bad. I'll be the sad woman whose husband left her for his best friend's wife. It's so embarrassing. I'll be the talk of Braeburn."

"Oh, we're being honest now, are we?" said Jen, smiling. "I think it's great that

340

you're fucking Robert. He's amazing-looking."

"He is so hot," said Lauren. "I think he's in love with me. Too bad he's just a tennis pro." Lauren snorted. She paused. "Are you and Jason going to run off together? I don't care, I just want to know."

Now it was Jen's turn to snort. "No. I ended it with him. He's all yours."

"I don't want him, either. He's an asshole."

They both laughed. A large gust pushed the women back on their heels. They turned left on Broadway, headed back toward the bay, nearing the field.

"I'll tell you the truth," said Jen, pulling her hood tighter around her head. "I've been cheating on Sam since we met. I'm always with someone else; this year, it was Jason. He doesn't mean anything to me. But I'm sorry that I did that to you. You didn't deserve it."

"That's crazy," said Lauren, genuinely interested. "I honestly never would have suspected. You seem so . . . *good.*"

"What I'm good at is living a double life," said Jen. "I do love Sam — how can you not love Sam? — but he doesn't know me at all."

"Men are truly clueless," said Lauren.

"I've always known deep down that Jason was in love with you. I just didn't care. Why would I care? I have my life, we have the kids, we have nice things. What else could I want?"

"Happiness isn't always what you think it will be," said Jen. "At least that's what I tell my clients."

"I know I should hate you," said Lauren. "But I don't. I feel bad for you — you're going to have to deal with Sam. What are you going to do?"

"Don't worry. Sam and I will be fine," said Jen. "He needs me. He'll never want to be like his parents. Never. He'll forgive me, I know he will."

They were in front of the field now, shining their flashlights through the tall green fence. The light passed over the baseball diamond and bleachers, all empty. Lightning shocked the sky.

"Lauren, Lauren," whispered Jen, pulling Lauren closer to her and linking her arm in hers. "I saw something moving in the playground."

The playground was just on the other side of Neptune, visible at the far end of the field.

They crouched down together at the edge of the boardwalk, careful not to fall off the side into the brush. Through the fence, across the field, they could see Jason shimmy out from under the slide and continue to walk up toward the beach. Less than a minute later, they saw another man, in an orange shirt, leave the porch of the art shack and follow Jason.

"It's Sam," Jen whispered.

"Holy fuck," said Lauren. "Let's follow them."

MICAH HOLT

Micah Holt was bored. He'd been waiting out the storm for what felt like forever, and he wanted to leave the club and sink into his bed. But it was still too wild out — his parents had texted him to stay put for now, worried about falling branches or downed wires. He and Willa were sitting at the bar, nursing vodkas quietly, having run out of conversation long ago. The only other person there was Larry Higgins, slumped at a small table, staring off into space, drunk, drunk, drunk. Micah had poured him about eight large whiskeys as the night went on (and on), and Larry was a goner. When the rain and wind eventually stopped, Micah and Willa would make sure Larry got back to his house in one piece. They were just bartenders, sure, but they also occasionally

343

had to escort particularly sauced grown-ups home.

Willa, in her uniform of a Salcombe Yacht Club polo and jean shorts, put her head down at the bar. She and Micah had been best friends since they were babies; they'd both spent every summer of their young lives in Salcombe. Willa went to Michigan now. She was a party girl. Cute in a bubbly way; men liked her energy and laugh. Micah had told her he was gay when they were twelve, a big deal for him at the time, and she'd giggled and said, "Duh." Would Micah be close to Willa had he met her in the outside world? Probably not. Her friends from college were straight, and they liked to chug beers and dress up for football games. But he loved Willa nonetheless. Salcombe did that to you.

"Micaahhhhh," she said, lifting her head. "Can we just leave now? I'm sure we won't get killed by a flying cow. We're not in *The Wizard of Oz.*"

"Let's just wait a few more minutes," said Micah.

Willa stuck out her tongue. The lights flickered on and off for a few seconds, settling off.

"The power is out," said Willa. He couldn't see her face in the darkness.

"Yes, I'm aware," said Micah. He turned on his phone flashlight and navigated to the fuse box, right near where Larry Higgins was drunkenly parked. Larry was half-asleep, half–passed out. He was muttering to himself, nonsense that Micah couldn't understand. Micah banged on the rusty box, which opened with a clang (he must remember to speak to Steve Pond, the yacht club commodore, about fixing the electrical for next summer). He flipped a few switches back and forth, but nothing happened.

"It's not working," he called to Willa.

"I can see that!" she called back, laughing.

"I'll go into the other room and look for some candles," Micah said. He walked toward the back of the club, careful not to bump into any tables or chairs, and made his way to the supply closet near the doors. He looked up at the big windows that faced the tennis courts, and noticed two beams of light sweeping over the green clay.

He went closer, hidden by the darkness, nearly pressing up against the glass to get a better look. He saw Jen Weinstein and Lauren Parker, both wearing ridiculously large yellow raincoats, hoods pulled up over their heads. They had flashlights in their hands and were looking for . . . something.

345

Or someone. On the tennis courts? He stepped back into the black, making sure they didn't spot him through the window. And good thing he did, because not a second later, the lights went back on in the club, illuminating the scuffed wooden walls and floor, the bright green felt of the pool table assaulting Micah's eyes. He quickly turned and ran back to the bar area. What were Lauren and Jen doing out in the storm together? And what were they searching for?

Willa was still in her seat, scrolling through her phone.

"Can we get out of here now? *Please?*" she said, not looking up.

"Yeah, yeah, okay," said Micah, frazzled and a bit freaked out. "But you need to help me with Mr. Higgins here."

Willa sighed and nodded, and the two friends went to work, rousing Larry. Micah put his arm around him and lifted him to his feet. They had a long, wet walk ahead of them.

RACHEL WOOLF

Rachel Woolf had been drinking at the Anchor Inn, the dive bar in Kismet, the next town over from Salcombe, since earlier that afternoon. When she saw Lauren and Jen heading over to confront her, she'd fled without a destination, turning right on Lighthouse and riding the fifteen minutes over to Kismet on the sandy road that connected the two towns.

She'd now been at the Anchor Inn for hours, who knew how long, and it was dark out and pouring, and she didn't know where to go or who to call. She was drunk. She didn't have an umbrella. The bartender, a grizzled Fire Island lifer with a weathered sailor's face, kept giving her the "get the fuck out of here" look. But Rachel wasn't budging. She looked at her phone — 8:38. No calls or texts. She was the only one left in the bar.

The door crashed open, and Rachel turned fearfully. She hoped it wasn't Lauren or Jen or Sam or Jason — she'd thrown a bomb, and she didn't want anything to do with the consequences. She exhaled when she saw it was Robert, soaked through, still in his tennis clothes. He spotted her immediately and collapsed onto the stool next to her. The bartender came over and silently handed him a dish towel, which Robert used to dry his face and hair.

"Whiskey on the rocks, please," Robert said as he handed it back.

"There he is, the man of the moment," said Rachel, patting his back in what she felt was a sisterly manner. "What are you doing in Kismet? Lauren not answering her phone?" Rachel could feel the words slur out of her mouth. She hadn't meant to be aggressive with him. She was just in a state.

"Very funny," said Robert. "I told you nothing was happening between us." He sounded stressed, and his tan forehead looked pinched. "Why are *you* here? Where have you been all day?"

Rachel figured she might as well tell him. Who was he in the scheme of things, anyway? He wouldn't be back next year. Also, she felt very, very drunk.

"Remember when I mentioned that I knew who Jen was having an affair with?" Robert nodded warily. "Well, it was Jason. As in, Sam's best friend, Jason. Can you believe it? I saw them together at the beach in the beginning of the summer, and I'd been keeping it to myself this whole time. The entire summer! I still can't believe she'd do that to Sam. It's *Sam.*"

Rachel felt like she deserved some praise for this. Robert nodded but didn't say anything. Rachel went on.

"So, then, when I lost to Jen this morning . . ." She trailed off, knowing how the rest would sound.

"You mean to tell me that because you

348

were so upset about losing to Jen and Lauren, you *told* Sam about Jen and Jason!" Robert let out a big, loud laugh. "You people are all insane," he said, taking a big sip of his drink. "Fucking lunatics. All of you."

Rachel looked down at her hands. They looked like her mom's hands. How had she gotten so old with nothing to show for it? She motioned for the bartender to bring her another vodka soda, but he shook his shaggy head. Fuck him.

"You haven't told me why you're here," said Rachel. "Out in the storm alone. It's odd, Robert, I have to say."

"Oh, I was just looking for someone, that's all," he said.

Rachel assumed he meant Lauren. She wondered where Lauren and Jen were now. And Sam and Jason, for that matter. She worried that Sam was going to do something dramatic. He was unpredictable lately. What would he do to Jason? Robert swigged the rest of his whiskey and put a twenty down on the bar.

"Let's go. You have to go home, and so do I. You think you can hide from your friends forever?"

She did, in fact, want to stay hidden for good. It hadn't been her mess, but she'd made it even bigger. What would happen to them after the summer was over? Would Salcombe ever be the same for her? The thought of heading back to the city gave her a stomachache. Back to her normal, sad life.

She slid off the stool, and the two of them walked out into the gale. It was so windy and rainy she could barely pedal her bike — Robert led the way on his, down a narrow, unkempt boardwalk that opened to the dirt road back home.

Rachel was wobbly; drunk-riding through a huge storm was a difficult task. Twice, she ran into the bushes off the side of the walk, one time scraping her wet face on a branch, yelling for Robert to come help her. She could hardly see a foot in front of her. After nearly thirty minutes of struggling, they spotted the streetlamp on West Walk, which marked the beginning of Salcombe.

Robert continued ahead of her, the outline of his strong back showing through his T-shirt. She followed him on Lighthouse. At Marine, her walk, he stopped. She did, too, and he pointed her down the walk in the right direction, waving goodbye. Then he took off again. She knew she should go straight home, but she wasn't ready. Where was he going? She waited a few seconds and then followed him past Broadway, and continued toward Neptune. She passed the Mulders' house and, closely after, the Brauns'. She'd been on a few group texts congratulating Vicky and Janet on their win, including some snide remarks about Jen's terrible line calls. Rachel *almost* wished she hadn't skipped the finals. Almost. Because she knew seeing Jen and Lauren lose would have been sweet. She wondered how Vicky and Janet were celebrating their victory.

Robert stopped at Neptune, right in front of Susan Steinhagen's house. He got off his bike and went around to the side entrance. He hadn't seen that Rachel was trailing him. She stepped off her bike, put her kickstand down (though it seemed a useless endeavor against the wind), and followed him. The lights in Susan's house were off — maybe she was sleeping already? She couldn't be anywhere but home in this storm.

"Robert!" she called after him. He was at the door, shaking it. "Robert! What are you doing? Why are you at Susan's house?"

He didn't hear her; the wind was too loud. She saw him kick the door violently, once, then twice, his tennis sneaker cracking against the damp wood. Nothing happened. Rachel was shocked. For the first time all night, she felt as though she might be in danger. Just then, a figure whirred past her

351

on a bike — an older woman in an Adidas tracksuit riding away down the boardwalk toward the bay, with what looked to be a notebook in her basket. Susan. She must have gone out the front door. Robert saw her, too, and then ran past Rachel, finally noticing her, his face set in a grim scowl.

"Robert, what's happening?" Rachel shouted at him as he rode down Neptune after Susan. She quickly got her bike, which was miraculously still standing, and pedaled off behind him.

He was nearly fifty yards in front of her at this point. She couldn't see Susan ahead of him; she'd disappeared in the fog. There were no lights on Neptune, and the rain was blinding. Rachel, drunk, was riding in an S formation, trying hard to stay steady. The boardwalk was more than three feet off the ground. If you landed at the wrong angle, you could easily break your neck.

"Stay straight, stay straight, stay straight," Rachel mumbled to herself as she followed Robert toward the bay. She was halfway between Lighthouse and Harbor on Neptune when she saw something that stopped her. A pair of men and a pair of women, standing in what looked to be a face-off.

She watched as Robert pulled up behind them, pausing on his bike. Where had Susan gone? She heard shouting, but because of the wind, she couldn't make out who was saying what. She rode closer before stopping. She could see a bright orange shirt. Sam. And a tall figure standing close to him. Jason. The other two were smaller, with large hoods covering their heads. "Jason!" she heard one of them shout. It was Lauren. Lauren and Jen.

Rachel was drunk, sure, but not drunk enough to want to be part of this scene. She inched her bike around in a circle and took off toward the ocean. Riding was difficult; the wind was pushing her back into the commotion. She stood up on her pedals like she used to do as a kid, trying to get more leverage as she circled them around. She thought about how her dad had taught her to ride a two-wheeler on these same boardwalks. He'd hold the back of the bike and run with her as she pedaled, pedaled, pedaled. "I've got you!" he'd shout as she went, letting go as she skidded away. "I've got you!"

There was another hard gust, and she felt a strong smack against her face — she'd been hit by a flying branch. She careened to the side of the boardwalk, surprised and off balance, her bike teetering on the edge. From a distance, she heard a loud shriek.

Then she went over, headfirst into the brush, her bike landing on top of her with a thud.

■ ■ ■ ■ ■

PART V
LABOR DAY
WEEKEND

■ ■ ■ ■ ■

Part V
Labor Day Weekend

24
LAUREN PARKER

Lauren Parker was exhausted. She'd been packing up the house for the last two days, throwing out junk that had accumulated over the summer, sorting clothes and bathing suits and flip-flops and tennis gear, separating Salcombe things from New York City things. As usual, Jason was no help at all. Thank goodness for Silvia.

Lauren hated Labor Day. She hated the organizing and the end-of-summer-ness, and the feeling that the party was finally over. The kids started Braeburn next week, and they would leave the island for good tomorrow. They weren't planning on coming back for any weekends this fall. That they'd stayed this long after the accident was a small miracle, and they'd only done it because Arlo and Amelie had epic meltdowns at the idea of missing out on the end-of-season fun.

Lauren was sitting in the audience at the

annual Labor Day Extravaganza, a talent show for kids that was held in the big back room of the yacht club. Both Arlo and Amelie were set to perform — Arlo and his friend Rhenn, Mollie Davidson's son, were going to do a magic trick routine (which Lauren had ordered to the tune of a hundred dollars from Amazon), and Amelie and Myrna Metzner were singing "Let It Go." It was a sweet Salcombe tradition, but this year, the whole thing felt off. Lauren was sitting in a plastic chair, shifting uncomfortably, waiting for Jason to bring her a cold glass of chardonnay. The camp counselors had set up the small stage for the show, rigging a makeshift curtain out of two Sunfish sails. Lauren's peers were scattered among the audience. Lisa and Emily were sitting toward the front of the room, heads bent together, in matching tan sack dresses. Beth and Jeanette were close to the door, Beth in a black V neck and ripped jeans, and Jeanette inappropriately attired in a blue skintight top, her cleavage out for all the dads to notice. Absent from the usual trio was Jessica Leavitt. The Leavitts had left for the city immediately after Danny was interviewed by the police, not even bothering to pack up their house. Lauren had seen them dragging their wagon down to the ferry on

Broadway that afternoon, Danny and Rose glumly following behind, upset to miss the last weeks of camp.

Jason slid into the chair next to Lauren, handing her the oaky chardonnay from the yacht club bar. She wouldn't miss the lackluster wine selection here, that was for sure. Jason had a deep late-summer tan, and he smelled like aftershave. Lauren gave him a once-over and wasn't repulsed. Progress.

Lauren saw Jen and Sam walk in through the back entrance. They were holding hands. Jen was in her favorite white shirtdress, her red lipstick striking, and Sam was in a white linen button-down. They were a good-looking pair. Lauren waved them over, and they navigated the chairs, sitting directly in front of them. Jason and Sam nodded at each other cordially.

Jen reached over to Lauren and squeezed her shoulder as the lights flashed on and off, signaling the start of the show. Normally, it kicked off with a group song, the town anthem, but today, there was a screech of feedback before Steve Pond, the yacht club's commodore, got up on the stage, microphone in hand. Jen glanced back at Lauren quickly, frowning.

"Welcome, folks, welcome," said Steve. His pearly veneers looked neon in the stage lights. "I wanted to thank everyone for coming. The children are backstage and are so excited to perform for you tonight. They've been working hard on their adorable acts." Someone in the audience sneezed loudly. "We're always sad to see summer end," Steve continued. His voice was scratchy; Lauren thought someone should hand him a glass of water. "This year, though, it's particularly bittersweet."

Lauren's ears got hot. She placed a frozen smile on her face in case anyone was looking at her.

"That's because we've lost one of our own, someone near and dear to us who was a big part of the Salcombe community and yacht club family."

Lauren noticed Rachel slip in through the side door. She was in jeans and a ruffled white top, with dangly earrings that Lauren thought looked cheap.

"We will all miss Susan Steinhagen enormously," said Steve. The microphone screeched with more feedback, causing many in the crowd to cover their ears. "She dedicated her life to making the tennis program in Salcombe a resounding success, and she and her late husband, Garry, were such a delight to have in our orbit. Susan's passing has hit us all very hard — she was a personal friend of mine and Marie's, and we still are in shock over it."

People nodded. Lauren saw some of the older women in Susan's friendship group wiping away tears. Rachel had made her way over to Beth and Jeanette, claiming a seat next to them.

"Now, I'd love to do a special rendition of the Salcombe song, dedicated to Susan. I expect you all to cheer as loudly as possible! We've had the children practice. Here they come," said Steve, motioning to the teenage counselors to bring out the little ones.

About forty kids, aged three to twelve, walked out onto the stage, dressed in various costumes. Lauren saw Arlo next to Rhenn, both in tuxes and black top hats, clutching the magician's wands and scarves. Amelie was holding hands with Myrna, the two of them in matching blue *Frozen* dresses.

"One, two, three!" shouted the head counselor, Jessie Longeran, a sixteen-year-old with a streak of pink running through her curly red hair.

"S-A-L-C-O-M-B-E, that's the place we love to be-eee," they all sang in unison.

Lauren looked over at Jason, who was singing along. So was Sam. This stupid place.

"S-A-L-C-O-M-B-E, season's over, now we're sorry, that we have to say goodbye, pack our bags and heave a sigh, leave old Salcombe with a cheer —"

Here the crowd roared all together, screaming and yelling and applauding. Lauren stood but didn't join in.

The song then ended with a rousing "We'll all be back next year!"

Everyone sat back down, ready for the show to kick off. Lauren realized she already needed a refill of her wine. She shimmied out of her row and walked through the back door into the restaurant area, populated by a few childless stragglers who didn't feel like watching a bunch of kids sing off-key. Through the door, Lauren could see which acts were performing, so she decided to sit there until she heard Arlo's or Amelie's name announced. Hell was watching other people's talentless children. Micah Holt was behind the bar. He was the kind of stylish gay guy she'd always been friends with, and she felt a fondness toward him.

"Another chardonnay, please, Micah," said Lauren. He brought over the bottle and poured her a large glass. "Shouldn't you be back at Yale?" she asked.

"Yes, I started already. I'm just here for the long weekend, helping my parents close the house," he said, running his hand through his impressive hair.

Lauren hoped Arlo grew up to be as polite and thoughtful as Micah. So far, Arlo was taking after Jason, waking up in dark moods, no matter how much *Minecraft* Lauren allowed. She was looking forward to getting the kids back into a school routine and filling their days with things other than the ocean, tennis, and camp. Salcombe fried their brains. College applications weren't *that* far off, and there was only so much money could buy.

The Braeburn drama seemed so long ago. She couldn't believe she'd been so obsessed with a school scandal about a fraudulent headmaster. How innocent she'd been. A woman was dead! And she'd been involved! Sort of. She tried not to think about it. But that was impossible, because in walked Robert, looking sexy in fitted jeans and a light gray sweater. He immediately noticed Lauren at the bar, froze for a second, and then continued toward her. She was caught. She hadn't spoken to him since that night, and she'd been planning on avoiding him until she left the island for good. No such luck.

She sat up straighter and pushed out her breasts. She was wearing a simple white tank and her favorite Frame jeans, cropped with a slight flare. Robert sat down on the stool next to her, his legs turned toward hers, his knees nearly touching her own.

"So," he said, locking his blue eyes with hers. "How are you?"

"I'm fine, thanks," she said, trying to sound breezy. "We're packing up the house and are taking off tomorrow for good. How are you?"

She motioned for Micah to come over and take Robert's order. He hesitated, oddly, with a slight frown. Why didn't Micah like Robert?

"Hey, Robert, would you like a pilsner?" he finally asked.

Robert nodded genially.

Micah brought one over and then disappeared.

"I'm doing well," said Robert, sipping his beer. "I finish up here next week, and then I'll be heading to the city. I rented an apartment in Chelsea, on Twenty-first and Seventh. I start my new job next week."

Lauren was surprised by this news, but she tried not to show it. "Oh, that's so great for you. What will you be doing?"

"I'm working for Larry Higgins, learning his business and helping out however I can."

"That sounds perfect," she said. She

pushed her knees closer, so they were in full contact. He smelled so good.

"If you ever need lessons during the winter, let me know," he said. His hand brushed her arm as he went to grab his beer.

Lauren felt her body warm at his touch.

"I'll be busy during the week but could find some time during the weekends to hit with you."

She nodded.

She felt a hand on her back and turned to see Brian Metzner standing behind them. She couldn't tell for sure, but she thought he might have glanced down at her and Robert's legs. She quickly shifted away.

"Hi to you both," said Brian. He'd gained weight over the course of the summer, and he was nearly vibrating with stress. "I see you also wanted to escape the screeching."

"I'll go in when Myrna and Amelie are up — I think Arlo and Rhenn are the show's closer," said Lauren. She wished he'd leave.

Robert didn't say anything. Brian didn't get the hint. Micah handed him a vodka on the rocks.

"I still can't get over Susan Steinhagen," said Brian, breaking the silence.

Lauren and Robert looked down at the bar at the same moment.

"I never would have shorted that stock. I

thought that woman would live forever. She'd be a hundred, screaming at all of us on the tennis courts," he said.

Lauren nodded sympathetically. The good news about Brian was that he was so self-centered, he'd never notice if someone was acting off.

"What the hell was she doing out of her house?" said Brian. "She'd know better than to ride her bike in that wild storm — she's lived here for forty years. I heard the police barely looked into it. Some jokers from Suffolk County. They spoke to Danny Leavitt and the Cahulls, who'd found her, but that's it." Brian drained his vodka. "I just hope it doesn't affect property values," he continued. "A mysterious death, accidental or not, isn't a great sell for real estate agents. The town should never have raised the boardwalks so high."

"It's a real shame," said Robert. "I loved working with her at the courts." He got off the stool, leaving his beer half-full on the bar. "Well, I'm off. Going to have an early night in front of the TV. Brian, Lauren, enjoy the rest of the show." He went out into the evening, leaving the other pair awkwardly hovering together.

Lauren wasn't quite sure what else to say. She couldn't comprehend how she'd gotten into this situation. She was an upstanding, law-abiding Upper East Side mom. She was a class parent at Braeburn Academy! She thought back to that night, the chaos and confusion. She still didn't know exactly what had happened or why Susan had been there in the first place.

Here's what she did know: She and Jen had followed Jason and Sam up Neptune after they'd spotted them in the playground. They'd reached them right above Harbor. Sam was shouting at Jason, waving a knife at him in an almost comically menacing way. Both men were soaked through. Lauren understood Sam's anger — Jason had betrayed Sam in the most hurtful of ways. Jen's actions could also be explained. Jen was bored and unhappy. Those were feelings Lauren could relate to. But Jason, ugh, what the *fuck* was wrong with him? Lauren had suddenly been super pissed. Sure, she was also having an affair, but at least she went out of their friend circle to do it! What Jason had done was inexcusable. How could they ever come to Salcombe again if anyone found out? Jason was such a selfish prick. She'd felt something come over her, the same something she'd felt during her fight with Beth Ledbetter. Rage.

"Jason!" she'd screamed. Both men turned

to look at her. She ran toward her husband blindly, pushing him with all her strength, tightening her Pilates-toned core as she did. He'd stumbled backward, caught by surprise by his 110-pound wife. At that unlucky moment, a bike had come flying into the scene. Jason had crashed into it, breaking his fall, sending the rider sailing off the boardwalk, three feet down onto the wet, hard ground. Lauren heard a crunch as it landed. Jen shrieked.

Lauren ran to the edge of the boardwalk and saw an old woman lying at an impossible angle, her bike on top of her. She wasn't moving. Sam was the first to reach Lauren's side; she'd felt the heat of his body next to her, his heaving breaths.

"It's Susan. Susan Steinhagen," he'd said. "It's her tracksuit."

Lauren couldn't look. She wouldn't. Instead, she'd glanced up the boardwalk. About twenty feet north, she'd seen a man paused on his bike, feet on the ground, still as stone. Robert. What was he doing there? No more than a second passed before he'd turned his bike around and rode back toward Lighthouse. She'd lost sight of him in the night. She didn't think anyone else had spotted him.

"We have to get out of here," Jen said,

pulling Lauren's raincoat sleeve.

"I think she's dead," said Jason.

Sam climbed down and felt for a pulse, taking care not to touch the bike as he did. "Nothing," Sam said softly, scrambling back up to the boardwalk.

"Let's separate and meet back at our house," Jen said firmly. Lauren assumed this was the voice she used with her therapy patients. "This can't get out. We'd all be ruined. Our children's lives would be ruined. Let's go down the darkest walks. Sam, you take West, Jason, you take Surf, Lauren, you take Atlantic, and I'll head down Neptune. No one go near Broadway; it has streetlamps. Walk quickly, but don't run. Stay in the shadows. No one else will be out, but we don't want anyone to see us from a window. The story, if anyone asks, is that we were having a family movie night at our house with the kids. The only people who know that's not true are Luana and Silvia, and they won't say anything. This never happened. It was a horrible accident."

Jason and Sam nodded.

"Jason, you and I are finished," Jen said. Lauren felt Jason flinch in the darkness. "Sam, I love you. I'll see you at home."

At that, Jen had turned and stalked off down the walk, leaving Lauren, Sam, and

Jason reeling. They'd all met back at the house as instructed, changed into dry clothes, and watched the end of *Toy Story 2* with their children.

The next day, Lauren walked around concealed by lipstick and sunglasses, thinking every moment that the police would barge through the door to their $2.3 million beach home and arrest her. But no one came. And no one came the day after. The town was humming with the tragic news of Susan Steinhagen's death. The tennis courts felt odd, like no one should be playing (everyone was still playing). There were whispers it was depression; she was still so devastated by Garry's death that she'd ridden off the walk on purpose. What else could she have been doing out in that storm? Her friends set up a makeshift memorial; a group of them held candles one evening and walked from the tennis courts to the ferry dock, gathering on the bay beach, reading tributes into the night. Lauren had a macabre interest in attending, but Jason, smartly, forbade her from going. "It's not for people our age. It will look strange," he'd said. "Like when the serial killer hangs out at the scene of the crime."

Lauren was hardly a serial killer! But she realized Jason was right. Things between them had thawed since that night. He'd seemed more interested in her than he had in years, asking her about her day, inquiring about the kids' school preparations. Lauren wasn't sure if it was because he knew for certain he'd never end up with Jen or that now they were bonded by an accidental death. Or maybe he'd been scared shitless by her anger. Either way, it was nice to not feel completely ignored. And there *was* something exciting about sharing a major secret. They'd had sex twice that week. That hadn't happened in years.

"Introducing Amelie Parker and Myrna Metzner!" Lauren heard the emcee announce into the microphone. She waved bye to Brian and headed back into the big room, sitting next to Jason. The girls, cute as buttons, went onstage and launched into an impossibly loud version of "Let It Go." Amelie twirled around as Myrna, tired, sat down. Everyone in the audience laughed and applauded when it was over.

Jason slipped his smooth, cool hand into Lauren's. It felt like a stranger's. She hadn't told any of them about Robert being at the scene of Susan's death; she never would. What would be the point?

She decided then that she wouldn't see Robert in the city. That feeling she'd had tonight was just her body reacting to him, not her mind. Lauren Parker was nothing if not practical. This summer had been out of character for her, but she vowed to return to her normal ways. The sex with Robert was good, but she loved her life more. Anyway, she'd be too busy with her mom groups and her SoulCycle classes. She'd also decided to renovate their kitchen — it had been needing an update for years, and that was a project she could dive into.

Arlo and Rhenn took the stage, waving their wands, Arlo pulling out a twenty-foot handkerchief from his sleeve.

"They're so sweet," Jen whispered over her shoulder to Lauren.

Lauren wondered if she and Jen would remain as close as they'd become in the past month. Her other mom friendships felt thin, comparatively. Perhaps she'd have to commit murder with them, too. Lauren chuckled at her own twisted thoughts.

A few rows away, she saw Rachel get up and duck out of the side door. Lauren hadn't spoken to her since that day, either. She didn't know where Rachel had gone after she'd run from her and Jen, nor did she want to ask. They'd all kept their distance. Rachel could stew on her actions all she liked for all Lauren cared. It served her right to be friendless after what she'd done. Imagine purposefully trying to blow up someone's marriage.

Was Rachel limping? Lauren watched as she opened the door and stepped out, clearly favoring her right foot. Now that she thought about it, she hadn't seen Rachel on the tennis courts at all these past two weeks. Not that Lauren would have played with her. She wondered if she'd gotten injured somehow. Or, more likely, toppled over drunk and alone in her home. Oh well. Rachel was dead to her. No more supportive chats about how she'd eventually find a husband. No more pity invites. She could join Beth and Jeanette and the other Salcombe rejects from now on.

"It's all an illusion!" Arlo shouted.

Rhenn threw a deck of cards in the air, scattering them over the stage. She gave Jason's hand a squeeze and smiled at him. Another Salcombe summer in the books. Time to head home.

25

LISA METZNER AND
EMILY GROBEL

Lisa Metzner and Emily Grobel were on the same wavelength. They'd met years ago at the town library during an arts and crafts program for kids who were too small for day camp. Emily and Paul had finally finished building their new house that year, and Lisa and Brian had bought theirs that winter on the urging of one of Brian's finance friends, Matt Hanon, who'd been coming out to Salcombe his whole life.

Neither woman quite knew what she was getting into, and on arrival, both felt overwhelmed by the town dynamics. They bonded that day over their confusion about how to book a tennis court. The system was complicated and involved little round tags, referred to as "chits," with members' last names printed on them. Every night at 7:00 p.m., the entire community arrived at the yacht club for "sign-up" for the next day's courts, run by an intimidating woman named Susan Steinhagen. It entailed putting your family chit into a bowl and waiting until Susan pulled it out, bingo-style, and then shouted your last name. (Even if you were called dead last, you could usually get a court at noon, the hottest, worst time to play. But desperate times called for sweltering tennis games.)

That day, Lisa and Emily made a pact to figure it all out together, relieved to find another woman who A) hadn't been in Salcombe forever and B) whose style she admired. They became an inseparable summer pair, to the point that people started to joke that they couldn't tell them apart, even though Emily was a blonde and Lisa was a brunette. They did have a similar fashion sense and often ended up in variations of the same outfit — oversize dresses that accentuated their slenderness, cozy linen pants with silk tanks — which brought an elementary-school-best-friend comfort to them both. They joined forces with Lauren Parker and Rachel Woolf soon after, happy to have a little group with whom to get drinks and to sit on the beach and trash-talk others.

They were trash-talking now, on Emily's beautiful back deck, having last-night-of-summer negronis. The kids were all in bed post–Labor Day Extravaganza, and Lisa had ridden over in the darkness, enjoying the cool air as she pedaled her bike. She was worried about Brian and his fund. She felt like he wasn't telling her everything.

"Did you see Rachel there?" Emily asked. Emily was the kinder of the two; Lisa wasn't mean, but she could be startlingly direct. "I hadn't seen her since we lost in the doubles tournament. Has she been sick or something?"

"I'm not sure," said Lisa. "I spoke with her when Susan died, but not really since then. I figured she had to go off island for something, like a wedding maybe."

"And then tonight she sat with Beth and Jeanette, which is weird," added Emily. "I wonder if she's embarrassed about tennis. Listen, I wanted to win, too, but they beat us! It happens. They played well."

"Speaking of Jen and Lauren, have you noticed how close they seem lately? I never thought they were *really* friends," said Lisa.

"Who knows what's going on with them," said Emily. "At least Sam seems like he's doing better. I saw him and Jen holding hands."

Paul wandered out onto the deck holding a glass of wine. Lisa had never understood Emily and Paul's relationship — he'd always struck her as a bit of a blowhard, and Emily was so sweet. But you never knew what went on in other people's marriages, Lisa supposed.

"Honey, can you get us some cheese and fruit?" asked Emily, smiling at him.

He was in a black Vetements hoodie, which Lisa knew was sold out everywhere. He dutifully nodded and went inside to fetch them a spread. The moon was high, and the Great South Bay was black and still. The sound of crickets surrounded the women, who sat together calmly, not speaking. Paul's motorboat, which he'd named *Depth* — a mix of his family's names (**D**ash, **E**mily, **P**aul, **H**ayden), but also because he thought he was deep — was knocking lightly against their private dock.

"Over the winter, I try not to forget how special this place is," said Lisa. She felt stressed. Maybe she'd up her mushroom dose a bit tonight. "To another great summer," she said, holding her orangey-red negroni for Emily to toast.

"I'm glad we have each other," said Emily with a wink. "Everyone else is nuts."

26
RACHEL WOOLF

Rachel Woolf's left ankle was killing her. It was swollen and bruised and ugly, and she could barely put any weight on it. She hadn't gone to the doctor for obvious reasons, but she was almost certain it was sprained, which was highly inconvenient, not to mention embarrassing. Nothing worse than a gimpy lady, hobbling around, showing her age. For the past two weeks, she'd been holed up in her house, watching Netflix and working, avoiding everyone. She was almost certain no one had even noticed. After the first couple of days, refusing tennis matches via text, claiming her tennis elbow was acting up, she hadn't been invited anywhere. It was the end of the summer, and so events — parties, drinks, dinners — were happening. But no one thought to include her.

Rachel felt like such a reject. She never should have told Sam about Jen and Jason.

She thought about it every few minutes, continually feeling the physical pain of regret. Ugh. Ugh ugh ugh. She'd just been *so* upset with Jen and Lauren for beating her, and the only thing at her disposal had been that weapon. But now she was friendless. What an idiot she'd been.

The worst part was that both couples appeared to be doing better than ever. She'd seen them all over each other at the Labor Day Extravaganza, shoving their happiness in her face. She hadn't stayed through the end of the show — the spectacle had made her sick. She'd left without telling anyone, hiding her limp as best as she could.

She was home now, sipping a glass of cabernet on her screened-in porch. Her house felt very empty lately. It made her miss her family. Should she move closer to her sisters? Nothing was tethering her to New York; she could work remotely from anywhere. She'd met every available man in NYC, none of whom had stuck.

A chilled breeze came in through the open window. Fall was almost here. Rachel wrapped herself in her cashmere throw. If only she had someone to sit with on cold nights. She was leaving Salcombe tomorrow for the city and would be back some weekends in September and October. Then she'd close the house by Halloween. She had a vague unease about, well, everything. She was missing key moments that only Jason, Sam, Jen, Lauren, and Robert could fill in. (Robert knew she'd been there, but the others did not, and she intended to keep it that way.) And she wasn't speaking to any of them.

She looked down at her phone. No texts. Nothing. Maybe she should reach out to Lauren. Lauren was right to be mad — all summer, Rachel had withheld the fact that Jason was cheating on her. She'd been busy dangling nuggets to Sam, and Lauren hadn't much crossed her mind. But had it really been Rachel's place to tell her? She pressed Lauren's name in her contacts to compose a text:

Hi!

The exclamation point was too chipper. She started again.

Hi, Lauren. I hope you're well!

Nope, too formal. It sounded like a work email.

Hey, I hope you're well. I'm sorry for what happened. I should have told you, but I didn't know how. I hope you'll forgive me! I'd love to see you in the city this fall.

She pressed Send before she could stop herself.

She thought back to that night. Would she ever know what really happened? After she'd fallen off the boardwalk, she'd stayed still for a minute, trying to assess her injuries, not wanting to bring attention to herself. She'd eventually moved the bike from on top of her and attempted to stand, pain shooting through her ankle as she did. She'd then felt two strong arms under hers, lifting her up onto the boardwalk. It was Robert. He jumped off the side and wrestled her bike out of the shrubs, climbing back up with it.

"What are you doing here? Are you okay?"

"Just my ankle. I think it's sprained."

"Okay, let's get you home. I'll walk you and then come back and get your bike."

Rachel was wary — she still didn't know why he'd been looking for Susan or where Susan was now. But she didn't have a choice. She couldn't move easily, and the boardwalks were treacherously slippery.

They'd walked in silence, Robert with his arm firmly around her waist, supporting her as she'd stepped gingerly. In another situation, she'd have thrilled at his touch, but nothing felt right about that night. They were nearly back to her home on Marine before she'd said anything.

"What happened? Who screamed?"

"I don't know," he said. "I couldn't see."

Rachel thought back to the beginning of the summer, when she and Lauren had spotted Robert on the ferry, and later that night when they'd all had drinks. It felt like a lifetime ago.

"Why did you go to Susan's?" Rachel asked.

Robert didn't answer. They were approaching her house. The lights were off. Robert managed to get her, hopping, inside onto her porch. She'd collapsed on her white couch, too tired to care that it was getting wet and muddy.

She was sitting on the same couch now. She'd scrubbed it with fabric cleaner, over and over, but there were still faint brown stains near where she'd slept that night. She'd woken up to see her bike back in its place on her entry walk as if nothing had happened. Her hangover, her ankle, and the bruise on her cheek the only reminders.

Rachel hadn't known what to expect that next day, but she'd had a sinking feeling that the news would be bad. Had Jason or

Sam hurt Lauren or Jen? Had someone been injured? At 8:00 a.m., she'd heard the emergency siren, a loud, unsettling sound that reverberated across town. It was Salcombe's Bat-Signal, alerting firefighters and EMTs to hurry and ride down to the firehouse: a person needed saving. The siren went off when someone was hurt or having a heart attack, or a kid had fallen off his bike and broken his arm. It went on for a full minute, sending dread through townspeople's stomachs, everyone hoping that it wasn't their child, their husband or wife, their friend, who had to be taken off island to the nearest hospital in Long Island.

Rachel sat on her porch and watched as the ragtag volunteers rode by, avoiding the storm debris — leaves, small branches, a random shoe and sand toy that someone had left on their deck. Brian Metzner, Theo Burch, Jerry Braun, Seth Laurell, all heading toward the firehouse on Broadway, awaiting instructions. It didn't instill confidence. She hadn't known what to do with herself other than ice her ankle and wait. She'd scrolled anxiously on her phone, resisting texting anyone. She read an article about the freak storm that had hit last night — a *microburst* it was called — that had brought whipping rain and winds up to fifty miles per hour. She knew she'd hear from someone soon; nothing in this town stayed a mystery for long. At 8:30, her phone buzzed. Lisa Metzner. Rachel, hand shaking, answered.

"Have you heard?"

"No, what happened?" Rachel tried to sound as normal as possible.

"Susan Steinhagen died."

"She *died*? Oh my God. How?" Rachel nearly dropped the phone.

"She rode off the boardwalk last night and broke her neck. Brian's there with the ambulance now. Danny Leavitt found her."

"That's awful. I can't believe it! Poor Susan."

"It's truly bizarre. I mean, what the hell was she doing riding around in that storm? In that wind and rain? Had she lost her mind?"

"It's very strange. I assume they'll speak to people around town to see if anyone saw anything." Rachel said it carefully.

"I don't know," Lisa said. "Right now, it's just our guys there, but I'm sure Suffolk County police will arrive soon."

A buzz of pain ran through Rachel's ankle. She couldn't let anyone see her like this, all bruised.

"It's so sad," Lisa continued. "I liked

Susan, even though she could be tough. And to die on the night of the women's doubles tournament! That was the highlight of her summer. Someone needs to tell Robert. Should I have Lauren do that? Ha."

Rachel gamely chuckled along, but her mind was racing. Would the police come for her? Would she tell them about Robert if they did? Should she give Sam a heads-up?

But none of that had happened. She hung up with Lisa and had just . . . sat. For days. No one had come to speak with her, not police, not Robert or anyone else. Tonight had been the first time she'd ventured out. She'd thought it would be weirder if she *didn't* show up at the Labor Day Extravaganza. She'd sat with Beth Ledbetter and Jeanette Oberman and had made polite conversation with them about their plans for the fall. Steve Pond's memorial speech for Susan had been a gut punch. She felt queasy as he spoke about what a wonderful person she'd been.

"It's such a shame," Beth whispered in her ear during the S-A-L-C-O-M-B-E song. "I heard that after Garry died, she'd been despondent. I wonder if she went out in the storm *hoping* to fall." Beth said it with evil glee.

Rachel took the bait. Anything to deflect

385

blame and confuse the story. Now was her chance. "I haven't told anyone this yet, but we'd been working together on the tournament draws, and she'd mentioned how depressed she'd been feeling lately. Like everything was hopeless" — Rachel leaned in closer for emphasis, lowering her voice — "like she wasn't sure life was worth living. Riding off the boardwalk isn't like hanging yourself, but maybe she was just being purposefully reckless."

Beth received this info like a precious gift, slowly curling her lips into a smile.

"Oh, how interesting," she said. The song was coming to its rowdy climax — "Leave old Salcombe with a cheer" — everyone around them erupted in whoops, but Beth and Rachel were still.

The song ended with a bang: "We'll all be back next year!"

"Not Susan," Beth said.

Rachel gave her a half smile.

Hours later, Rachel, lonely, curled up in her blanket, hoped her words were enough to end any suspicion for good. She wanted everything to return to normal. She didn't care how Susan had died. What did it even matter? She didn't care why Robert had been looking for her. He must have had his reasons. Susan was a snoop and a troublemaker; she'd probably been asking for it.

But Rachel feared it was too late to return to the old days. They'd all been irreparably changed. She wished her dad were alive. She needed a man on earth who loved her. She really should move to the West Coast. But what about Fire Island? Could she leave this place forever?

Her phone buzzed. Maybe Lauren had written her back. Sam's name popped up. Rachel sucked in her breath and opened the message.

Hey, I'm on my way. We need to talk.

She got up in a panic, limping to the bathroom to check her makeup. She quickly applied blush, curled her eyelashes, and swiped a gloss over her lips. She looked old. There were lines on her forehead and dark circles under her eyes.

She sat back down on her couch and tried to remain calm. What did Sam want? He didn't know she'd seen him that night. Maybe he just missed her? Maybe he wanted to thank her for telling him the truth about Jen?

A few minutes passed, and Sam knocked lightly, letting himself in. He looked tired, more ragged than normal, in worn jeans and a light blue button-down. His glasses were perched on his nose and his deep tan looked painted on. Even with all the weirdness this summer — how uncharacteristically mean he'd been, the threats — she was still in love with him. How pathetic was that?

He sat down next to her. His Salcombe scent, a mix of cologne and bug spray, wafted over.

"How are you? I feel like I haven't seen you in a while," he said.

"I'm fine. Nothing new to report. I went to the Labor Day show earlier. The kids were all so cute," she said. There was an awkward silence. "Would you like a drink?"

"Sure," he said. Halfway through getting up, Rachel realized that Sam would notice her limp. He noticed everything. It took all her power to walk normally to the kitchen — she poured him a large vodka soda and refilled her glass of cabernet. She made it back, gritting her teeth, settled into the couch, and took a large sip. Her ankle was throbbing from the weight she'd put on it. Sam wasn't talking. She couldn't take this.

"What's going on? Why are you here?"

"I've come because I missed you, Rachel. You've been my friend for a long time, and I feel like I can trust you."

"I appreciate that."

"Even though you totally fucked me over this summer."

Rachel looked into her glass, avoiding his gaze.

"You knew about Jason — Jason! — and you kept it from me to play some little game for my attention. It's really kind of sick when you think about it."

"I just didn't know what to do," said Rachel. "I did eventually tell you."

"Yeah, as revenge for some stupid tennis match. Well done, very mature. As always."

Tears filled her eyes, making it hard to see. Did he come here to torture her?

"It seems like it's all fine," spat Rachel at last. "I saw you two tonight holding hands. And Lauren and Jason looked happy, too. So, it worked out for everyone but me. As usual, as you would say."

"Oh, stop feeling sorry for yourself," said Sam. "You're a shit stirrer from way back. You've always been like this."

Rachel felt shaky. "All right, then. Either tell me why you're here, or get the fuck out of my house."

Sam's face softened. He resembled the old Sam. The good Sam.

"First, I wanted to tell you that I'm going back to work. The woman's story was bullshit — she'd been pressured to lie about it by my managing partner, who was behind the whole thing. Starting in September, everything will be normal for me. You were the only person I could speak to about the situation this summer, and I appreciate that." Sam took her hand and gave it a light pat. "I guess you can't always believe women. Or men." He laughed softly.

"That's good. I'm happy for you."

"One more thing: you speak to everyone in this town, and I wanted to know if you'd heard anything about Susan. Does anyone have any idea how she died?"

"Why do you care?" she asked. She knew why he cared.

He moved his body closer on the couch, still holding her hand. Rachel wasn't sure what to reveal. Should she tell him she'd seen him there? Should she tell him about Robert?

On impulse, she stood, pulling him up alongside her, and led him into her bedroom. The last time they'd been there, Susan Steinhagen had walked in on them. Now Susan was dead. Rachel sat down on the bed, and Sam sat next to her. He reached over and pulled her shirt over her head, pushing her back so just her legs were dangling off the side. Then he knelt over her, his glasses falling off as he did, and sucked her nipples until she came, like he used to do when they were young. He undressed himself as she lay there, writhing, and pulled off her Gap jeans. Then he lifted her up and turned her over, fucking her from behind, lightly slapping her bottom, grunting. He collapsed on top of her after he finished.

The weight of his body nearly made Rachel cry from joy; there was no more pleasurable sensation on earth. She allowed him to crush her with his chest and legs, his face buried in her hair. They didn't move for a few minutes.

Sam finally rolled off her, settling in next to her side. He looked the same as when they were teens, sleeping together in his parents' bedroom, Jason down the hall.

"I'll tell you what I know," said Rachel, stroking Sam's lovely cheeks. If only she could convince him to stay there forever.

"I was out that night at the Anchor Inn. I'd gone there alone to get away from all of you. I couldn't face anyone. I was too ashamed."

Sam nodded. He put his hand on her back and began tracing letters, something he'd done to her the summer they were together.

"I was drunk. It was terrible out, and I didn't want to go home in the storm. Robert walked into the bar at some point and was acting weird. He told me he'd been looking for someone, but not who it was. Then he dragged me out of there. We rode back to Salcombe, which took forever, but instead of turning on Marine, he kept going on Lighthouse, and I followed him. He stopped right in front of Susan's house and started banging on her side door."

Sam's eyes widened. "You went to Susan's house?" he asked incredulously.

Rachel nodded. "Well, I didn't go. I just followed Robert, and he didn't know I was trailing him. He was in a state."

"Did he go inside?"

"No, he couldn't get in. And then Susan ran out through the front door, got on her bike, and took off."

Sam sat up and reached for his boxers. Rachel suddenly felt very exposed. She grabbed her robe off her side chair and put it on, walking back to the bed. Sam watched her closely.

"Did you hurt your ankle?"

Rachel hesitated. Should she tell him everything? "Well, I was drunk. I told you. And it was windy."

"Did you fall off the boardwalk that night?"

"I did. And Robert helped me home."

"What else happened?"

Sam was standing now, naked except for his underwear. His curly hair was sticking up straight from his head. He'd put his glasses back on. He seemed jumpy.

"Nothing happened. I didn't see anything else," said Rachel.

"And Robert gave no indication as to *why* he was looking for Susan?"

Rachel remembered that Sam was a lawyer. He was looking for holes in her story.

"No, none." She wasn't lying. "He rode after her down Neptune, and I fell off the boardwalk. The next thing I knew, he was lifting me up and walking me home. I don't know what happened in between."

"You didn't see anyone else that night?" He left the question dangling in the air. She shook her head. She didn't want to be involved. She didn't care what had happened! Susan was dead, end of story. She wanted everything to return to the way it had been.

He sat close to her on her fluffy white comforter, rumpled from their recent sex. He grabbed the tie of her robe, gently unknotting it, opening the garment in the same way a doctor might. Rachel was very still. He moved his hands to her thighs, caressing them, inserting his fingers inside of her. She closed her eyes. He continued to touch her, slowly, than faster, faster, until she came, violently, shaking. She kept her eyes shut.

"You," she said to him after a moment.

"Me?"

"Yes, I saw you. I saw you and Jen and Jason and Lauren, standing on Neptune, arguing. And I heard someone scream. But I didn't see what happened. Did you kill her?"

Sam didn't say anything. She opened her eyes. He was buttoning his shirt.

"I love you," she said. She felt herself starting to cry. She missed her dad.

"Never tell anyone about this. Never. About us, but also about what you saw. It'll just be our secret, forever. And we can do this" — he gestured at her bed — "whenever you'd like. Jen's not the only one who can cheat."

Rachel felt a flood of happiness. He was hers.

"I won't tell. Don't worry. And so you know, I told Beth Ledbetter that Susan had been depressed and that it might have been suicide."

"Good girl." He kissed her on the head, put his jeans on, and was off. She lay down, exhausted. She smelled the spot next to her, inhaling Sam's cologne.

27
JEN WEINSTEIN

Jen Weinstein couldn't wait to get back to Scarsdale. She'd had it with Salcombe. With the people, with the drama, with the way Sam had been acting. He needed to calm down. He needed to just let it go. But he'd been in her face, every day and night, acting like a madman — "We *have* to find out why she was out there," he kept saying. "This won't end until we know." Jen was ready to punch him. The police had ruled the death an accident. No one was asking questions. No one even suspected anything other than the story of a lonely lady who died in a storm. Why was he pressing the issue? He was going to make it worse.

For a week after Susan died, there'd been an uproar; a memorial service held in her honor, a rowdy town meeting with the mayor, Don O'Connell, to discuss the issue of boardwalk safety. Nearly the entire village attended, everyone packed into the village hall on a rainy Thursday afternoon, piling their wet umbrellas in a soggy corner. There were more than 150 people there, everyone shouting over each other, and Mayor O'Connell, a seventy-year-old with a swoop of silver hair, attempting to keep order. "A child could *die!*" Beth Ledbetter kept yelling maniacally.

"We need to lower the boardwalks! We've raised them too high!"

"My son found a *dead woman!*" screamed Max Leavitt, who'd come back to the island for the day specifically to attend the meeting. Jen and Sam had gone, for appearances' sake, and Jen left even more convinced that they were going to get off scot-free.

Now she just wanted to go to the suburbs, get back to her practice, get the kids in school, and forget about this entire summer. What a disaster these past months had been. The only highlight had been tennis — playing it, getting to know Lauren as a partner, making it to the finals of the women's doubles tournament. Otherwise, the whole thing had been a total bust. When they got home, Sam would go to the office — thank God — and Jen could once again do her own thing.

They were on good terms now, at least. That was one silver lining. Sam had been forced to forgive Jen for Jason and to work with her to move on. He would have eventually, she was sure of it, but this expedited the process. She'd been speaking to him about remorse, honesty, and care, using all her therapy buzzwords to ease him into the idea that he'd just have to get over it. There was no other choice.

She'd have to be very careful going forward. He could never catch her again. No more family friends, dads he knew, former coworkers of his. Jason had been her last mistake.

She heard Sam coming in the side door, walking through the kitchen and up the creaky stairs. She was in the bedroom, reading her Kindle — *Think Again: The Power of Knowing What You Don't Know,* an Adam Grant book about how to stay curious that was putting her to sleep. She was in her purple pajama set, with the quilt pulled up over her.

They'd had a long day. Jen had organized the house for their departure — they were leaving the island tomorrow, back to Westchester. She did laundry, stuck clothes in suitcases, threw away food that would go bad (the cleaners would close the house for good next week, but she didn't want anything to rot in the meantime). The kids had then performed in the Labor Day Extrava-ganza — they'd sung "Do-Re-Mi" as a trio, changing the words to be about Fire Island.

"Do, a deer, a million deers. Ray, a drop of Salcombe sun . . ." And on. It was ador-able, and the Weinstein Family Singers got a standing ovation.

Usually, the day before Labor Day made her sad, but this year it felt invigorating. No one had come to take them away in the middle of the night. No one thought they were guilty of anything. The Jason thing was out and over. Jen was free.

Sam entered the bedroom. He looked strange. His hair was disheveled, and his eyes were glazed. She put down her Kindle. He'd told her he was going out for a walk. What had he been up to? She watched as he undressed and put on his sweats and a white T-shirt. She didn't say anything, wait-ing for him to speak.

"I need you to do something," he finally said. His voice sounded strained, like he was on the verge of a cold. He sat perched on their cream linen duvet from the White Company.

"Spit it out," said Jen.

"I need you to ask Robert to get a drink with you tonight. Right now."

"Excuse me? What are you even talking about?"

"I need to break into his house and look for something. I'm not quite sure what, but I'll know it when I see it."

"Uh, I need more info than that," said Jen. "Stop withholding, please. We've spoken about this. You need to be open with me." Her psychology tricks always worked.

Sam sighed. "I saw Rachel."

"What?!" Jen leaped out of bed and stood in front of him, hands on her hips.

"I went to ask if she'd heard any gossip about Susan, anything that might point to us."

"We agreed you wouldn't see her!"

"Well, we agreed on a lot of things during our marriage, some of which you've ignored, as well."

Jen frowned. "What did she say?"

"She said she was with Robert that night. And that he'd been looking for Susan. Susan was riding to get away from *him.*"

Jen was only mildly surprised. She'd recognized Robert as a kindred spirit — a shape-shifter like she was, able to fit in as need be. But what did he want with Susan?

"Does Rachel know we were there? Did she see what happened?"

"She saw us, but she didn't see how Susan

fell. And I didn't tell her anything."

Jen, who'd been so calm a few minutes ago, felt anxiety spike in her chest. If Rachel had seen them, if Robert had, too . . . well, there was a chance this whole thing wasn't over at all. Rachel was the world's biggest talker. And Robert was an unpredictable twist.

"So, the plan is that I get a drink with Robert, and you break into his house while he's out to look for, what, exactly?"

"I don't know," said Sam with a shrug.

"You're a corporate lawyer, not a burglar. This is ridiculous. You're wearing a button-down that cost four hundred dollars," said Jen. But she got her phone out and pulled up Robert's number.

> Hi! Random, but I was wondering if you were around to meet at the yacht club for a drink? Just want to catch up and say goodbye before the summer ends!

She pressed Send.

"He's going to know something is up," she said.

"Make up an excuse. You're good at lying."

She rolled her eyes and then got up to get

dressed, waiting for her phone to buzz. A minute later, she heard it.

Sure, meet you there in ten.

She slipped on a long white skirt and a striped cashmere sweater.

"How do you think you're going to get into his house?" she asked.

Sam was hovering, biting his already-raggedy nails. "The front door, if it's open. Or I can get in the side window. The lifeguards used to stay in that house when we were kids — they'd throw parties. I've been there a million times. Just keep him out for thirty minutes. And no fucking him."

"Very funny. I think Lauren has that last part taken care of."

Sam raised an eyebrow. Jen smeared on some red lipstick, and she and Sam crept out, passing Luana, who was sitting on the couch watching Bravo.

"We're heading out for a drink," Jen called to her as they left.

Jen walked on Bay Prom, and Sam disappeared up Surf. The plan was for Sam to go around the long way to Robert's house, waiting until Jen texted him that Robert was at the yacht club.

It was past 9:00, dark and cold. Jen saw

401

an unlucky crushed frog on the boardwalk. She hugged herself as she walked, shivering from the bay breeze. The club was relatively empty when she arrived, a few twentysomethings playing pool in the back, an older couple, the Longerans, having a nightcap in the front room, Micah Holt at his normal spot at the bar. Everyone was preparing for the trip home tomorrow. She was glad — she didn't want too many people to see her with Robert. He was already sitting and waiting for her, in a gray sweater and jeans, sipping a whiskey. She took out her phone and sent a quick text to Sam:

He's here.

She remembered the last time she and Robert were at the bar together, at the July 4 party, when Jason had interrupted them. She was so happy to be done with him.

"Hi, Robert. How are you? Thanks for meeting me," she said, sitting next to him.

"Happy to," he said. "I wasn't doing anything. It feels kind of weird, the summer ending and all."

This was a thing that Salcombe did. Seduced people until they had no memory of the bad moments.

"Yes, the end of summer is always like a

death," she said, not catching herself until after she'd spoken. "I don't mean a *real* death. Though this summer . . ." She trailed off.

Robert took a sip of his drink.

"I've been meaning to ask — what will you do this year? Are you going back to Florida to teach tennis?"

Robert smiled. "No, thankfully. I've taken a job with Larry Higgins. I'll be working with him in the city. And I've rented a place in Chelsea."

"That's so wonderful, Robert," Jen said. She briefly wondered if Lauren would continue to see him. No. Lauren was too smart for that. "I'm sure you'll do great with Larry. He's a savvy, successful guy."

"Yeah, I'm excited," he said. Poor Robert was just trying to get ahead. Whatever had happened with Susan, it wasn't Robert who'd sent her flying off that edge.

"The reason I wanted to see you was to thank you for encouraging me — I really feel like you upped my game enormously. I appreciate it so much. It was the highlight of my summer, playing tennis. I know that Salcombe can be difficult, and you did a wonderful job navigating it all."

Robert reddened a bit. "Thanks, Jen. You've always been kind to me. I'm glad I could help with your ground strokes, but really I'm just happy you were around to be a normal, nice person."

She smiled and raised her glass. "To your future, Robert. It's just the beginning for you."

They clinked.

"And it's really too bad about Susan," Jen continued, watching his reaction closely.

"Horrible thing," said Robert. "I'd been with her all day at the tournament. I was so shocked to wake up to the news. She was a wonderful woman. Stubborn, but good-hearted."

She glanced down at her phone. Twenty minutes had passed since she'd left with Sam. Another twenty before she could go home.

Marie and Steve Pond walked into the club, Marie in a formfitting black top and sparkly capris, Steve in a yellow sweater, his Rolex glinting in the overhead lights. They surveyed the empty scene and made their way to Jen and Robert, the only targets. Jen was relieved for the distraction.

"Well, hello, you two," said Steve. Jen couldn't look directly at his mouth; his teeth were blindingly white.

"Hi, Steve. Hi, Marie," said Jen. She'd always gotten the sense that Marie didn't like her. She was one of the older women in town who fawned over Sam, treating him like the adorable little boy they'd all loved. Jen hated it. None of them thought she was good enough for him.

"Hello, Jen. Hello, Robert," said Marie, sidling up to Robert, pressing her chest against the edge of the bar, squeezing her cleavage.

"How's your night going?" Steve asked.

"Oh, fine, we're just talking tennis," said Jen.

Robert nodded. "I'm giving Jen some last-minute pointers before the fall. She needs to take everything she's learned this summer and apply it to her women's league in Scarsdale."

"What a sweetheart you are," said Marie. "Susan, poor Susan, really liked working with you. I told her how much you were beloved by members."

"Thanks, Marie. That means a lot."

"Still can't believe she's gone," said Steve, shaking his head, his impressive white coif moving left and right, tears wetting the corners of his eyes. "Micah!" Steve bellowed out of nowhere, startling them all.

Jen realized she'd never even ordered a drink. Micah brought Steve over his usual gin and tonic and then silently backed away, which was unlike him.

"The boardwalks are death traps," Steve continued. "I've ridden home after a few too many cocktails and nearly killed myself in the process. I have a feeling that someone's going to sue the pants off Mayor O'Connell. Susan doesn't have family left so that's the only thing that could save him. No one really to file a wrongful death suit. Another reason to have children!" He chuckled grimly. "You were working with her that weekend," he continued, directing his attention to Robert. "Did you notice anything about her that was off?"

"No," said Robert, too quickly. "She seemed her normal self. She was always a little prickly, but that was her way."

Marie put her hand on Robert's shoulder, rubbing it aggressively. "That was definitely her way," she said. "You'd heard what happened with the pro last year, Dave, I assume?"

"Oh, that guy, what a disaster," Steve chimed in. "First of all, he was a drunk. Chugging vodka instead of water during lessons. I'm not sure how he did it. I have one Bloody Mary during brunch, and I'm ready to pass out."

"That's true," said Marie affectionately.

"Secondly, he was a thief," said Steve. "It

was never officially investigated, but we all knew. He was double charging some lessons. Susan was onto him from the start. She had a good nose for stuff like that."

Jen felt Robert tense, though it wasn't apparent to the older couple.

"If Dave were still on the island, I'd have the police look into *him* for foul play!"

Jen was amused that everyone in town, most of whom knew nothing of the criminal justice system, were now all throwing around terms like *foul play* and *wrongful death.*

"But he's not here," said Marie. "Last I heard, he was teaching at a local club in South Carolina."

"I suppose," said Steve. "But he definitely had a motive! Susan was the only one who knew for sure that he was stealing."

Jen had a sudden realization. She looked over at Robert, listening politely, his handsome face frozen in an inquisitive tilt. She was sure she knew what Sam would find at Robert's house. Or at least what he should be looking for.

"Okay, Columbo, whatever you say. Susan died by accident, falling off our dangerously high boardwalks. That's what must be addressed. Don and the town trustees have their work cut out for them," said Marie.

"I don't trust the Suffolk County police, is all I'm saying," said Steve. "They investigated for less than a week and barely asked any questions. I just think for Garry's sake, for Susan's sake, the police should have tried a little harder. I'm thinking about hiring my own private investigator. The idea that Susan committed suicide? That's bullshit. That woman wouldn't have killed herself. She'd sooner have killed someone else."

Marie finally took her hand off Robert's shoulder, slipping her arm through Steve's. "All right, folks, we're going to sit and have a piece of the yacht club's famous key lime pie, our last of the summer. I need to get Steve off his conspiracy theories. Enjoy the rest of your drink!"

"Lovely to see you," said Jen.

"Yes, thanks for the chat," said Robert. He looked a little pale.

Robert and Jen turned back toward their drinks, silent. Jen couldn't blame him for stealing from these people. Didn't they deserve it? Steve jangling his Rolex in Robert's face. Brian Metzner going on about his investment portfolios. Jeanette Oberman bragging about how she was going to take Greg for millions. How much money could Robert have even taken? Ten thousand? Twenty? That was nothing to anyone here, including Jen.

"I need you to come with me," Jen said to him quietly. He looked at her, alarmed. "I'm going to leave now and go to your house. You follow me five minutes later. You can trust me, Robert."

He nodded. Jen looked around to see if anyone was watching (no one but Micah; she was safe). Then she went out the side door, past the tennis courts, and doubled back to Bay Prom. She walked past Broadway and turned on Neptune, up past the gazebo, empty and foreboding. She shivered and looked at her phone. Sam would still be at Robert's house; she was ten minutes early.

She arrived at the little shack, which desperately needed a coat of paint. She saw that the side window was open, the one Sam had said he'd use to enter. She stepped through the overgrown tick grass and then lifted herself, with a soft grunt, up to the window, sliding her legs through first and hitting the floor with a bump.

"Jen?" It was Sam, standing in the kitchen area, holding a knife, not very convincingly.

"Sam, Robert's coming here in a minute. Have you found anything?"

He held up a ledger, the one Robert used

to record lessons. Jen nodded, unsurprised.

"I always knew I loved you," said Sam. He leaned against the kitchen counter, cluttered with Robert's stuff — a box of Cheerios, protein shake mix, a bag of Tostitos, half-eaten. The scene reminded Jen of when they were young, living in New York when Sam was still an associate, doing well but not making real money yet. The promise of their life still there. "From the first moment I saw you, I knew I'd marry you," he said.

"I've heard this story before."

"You were just so beautiful, and then you spoke, and your voice was so deep and soothing. And you were so smart and loving and kind."

Jen knew what was coming.

"I just can't believe you'd cheat on me with Jason. I'm not sure I'll ever get over it. I don't know how I can."

Jen didn't say anything. There was nothing to say. He didn't know her, not really.

"I think you will get over it," she finally whispered. Sam was simpler than she was. She went over to him and kissed him gently on the lips. It felt funny — they hadn't kissed in so long, even during sex. She couldn't tell if she liked it or not. Then she took the ledger. She ripped out page by page, crumpling each one, tearing them into jagged pieces, leaving them in a pile on the counter.

The door unlocked and opened, and in walked Robert, one hand shoved in his pocket, hunched from the chill. He turned on the light and took in Sam and Jen in the kitchen, and the ledger, his ledger, in an unrecognizable state. He collapsed on the couch.

"I didn't do it, you know," he said. Jen wasn't sure if he was speaking to them or to himself. "I saw you all there. She was running from me, but you're the ones who killed her."

"No one killed her," Jen said. "It was an accident. A terrible, unlucky accident." She realized that she felt absolutely no guilt at all. How funny. "But if Steve Pond hires an investigator, I worry that signs will point to you, not us," she said.

"Oh, don't I know it," said Robert. "It's always the poor guy who gets blamed. You lot will be back here next year, partying it up at the yacht club, torturing the next pro. I *was* stealing, but I'm not a murderer."

"I know," said Jen. She went over and sat down next to him, the couch crunching uncomfortably under her, taking his hand in hers.

Sam watched his unpredictable wife. "Don't worry. I have a plan," said Jen.

28
BRIAN METZNER

If Brian Metzner wasn't in such deep shit, he'd take them down himself. But he couldn't risk sticking his neck out, not now. He'd been out that night, in the storm. He'd left his house so Lisa wouldn't hear him on the phone with his lawyer, Simon Ketchum, discussing his admittedly limited options. He could barely make out Simon over the wind, but he needed privacy, and Lisa had been all over him lately, asking question after question, hovering until he'd shut down.

He couldn't tell Lisa what was really happening — she wouldn't understand. (And if she did, it would just be worse.) His top lieutenant, Michael Nerrot, had gotten a *teeny* amount of insider info about a drug company clinical trial that was about to fail. Nerrot then sold off a bunch of the company's shares. Unethical? Sure. Illegal? Brian hadn't known about the trade until after the

413

fact, but the SEC didn't really care about those specifics. Nerrot might end up in jail, and Brian's firm would go bust from any settlement with the drug company's investors. He'd also be banned from trading ever again. What would he do then? Become a chimney sweep?

That's what he was discussing with Simon the night of August 22, the night that Susan died, the night he saw her die.

The kids were asleep, and Lisa was up in bed, watching her iPad with her headphones on, when Brian snuck out in his Salcombe volunteer fire department slicker. The jacket was tight; he'd gained weight over the summer. He'd been stress eating constantly, never without a hot dog or a beer in his hand. His body felt heavy and hot. He hated himself.

"Brian, there's nothing you can do for the moment. The SEC will come back with their findings shortly. But you should be prepared; Nerrot is going down. The question remains as to what they'll do to you. Steve Cohen survived this, and now he's living it up as owner of the Mets. Don't get too upset. You're not out yet," said Simon.

Brian had walked across Bay Promenade, ducking for cover in the gazebo that overlooked the swirling, thrashing bay. He struggled to keep the slippery phone in his hand.

"Thanks, Simon. I'll just sit tight for now. Keep me posted. What do you think I should tell Lisa? How bad is this going to get?"

"Just stick with your story about a trade gone sour for now. You can tell her the truth when we hear back from the SEC."

"Okay," sighed Brian. Lightning flashed.

"Where are you, anyway? The middle of a hurricane?"

"Basically," said Brian. "I have to go. I'll call you again tomorrow." He hurried out of the gazebo, the rain hitting him in the face, then turned up Neptune, passing the playground and field. He could see a few people up ahead, but the darkness hid their faces. Who would be out in this storm?

He heard yelling and walked a few yards, close enough to see the crowd of Jen, Lauren, Sam, and Jason. Lauren shouted — "Jason!" — and Brian watched her ram into her husband at full speed. What the hell? At the same time, a bike went whizzing by. Jason fell back into it, sending the rider off the boardwalk with a sickening crunch. Jen shrieked, and Brian gasped. He should help them, he knew. He was an EMT. Instead, he turned and hurried across Harbor back

415

to Atlantic, where he and Lisa lived.

He slipped inside his house and sat down at his white kitchen table. He couldn't sleep at all that night. He lay next to Lisa, in her eye mask, snoring softly. She'd been so relaxed lately, given everything. Maybe she was on some new prescription she hadn't told him about. His chest felt tight. He hoped he wasn't about to die.

It served him right that he was the first to arrive at the scene. The siren went off early in the morning, after Danny Leavitt found the body. The sound cut through his head like a knife. He knew exactly where to go.

Susan's body was nestled underneath her bike, her neck at a weird angle. Her face was yellowish, her mouth in a now permanent grimace. Brian thought he might vomit, but he swallowed it, waiting around with the other guys for the ambulance to take her away.

Everyone was already talking about it as an accident, but Brian knew better. He'd thought maybe Sam or Jason would step up, but clearly, that wasn't going to happen; they'd have called the police right away. Brian wasn't going to tell. He hadn't done it, but he didn't want to get involved. His life was such a mess already, he couldn't add this.

Earlier tonight, he'd prodded Lauren a bit at the club, trying to get a rise, but she'd remained neutral, more interested in that Robert guy than Brian's conversation about the woman she'd murdered. Murder, manslaughter, fleeing a crime, whatever, Brian had no idea. He couldn't wait to get home tomorrow. Being in the city would make him feel more in control. He was going to be fine. Everyone in finance got a second chance.

29
SAM WEINSTEIN AND JASON PARKER

Sam Weinstein thought he might be going crazy. Did no one else care they'd left a woman for dead? Sure, he'd checked her pulse, but Sam wasn't a doctor — he could barely put a Band-Aid on his kids' knees. He hadn't felt anything, no heartbeat pumping through her neck or wrist, but maybe she could have been saved. Maybe if Jen hadn't forced them to leave the scene of a crime, maybe if Sam had suggested they all just wait a minute, that it was an accident, that they should call the ambulance . . .

Yes, it wouldn't have looked great, Sam knew that. What were they all doing out there, Sam with his stupid Japanese knife, no less? But they shouldn't have just *left* She might be alive now. It was insane that they were all just living their lives, packing up their summer homes, playing tennis as if nothing had happened. It was their fault! Mostly, it was Sam's fault, he thought, for stalking Jason in the first place. Even though Jason deserved it. That fucking asshole.

He'd mentioned this to Jen, over and over, to the point that every time he started to talk, she walked out of the room. And instead of investigating his marriage, trying to figure out why his wife had cheated on him *with his best friend,* he was stuck investigating a death. He had to know, even if it seemed like no one else gave a shit.

He wasn't speaking to Jason. He wasn't sure he'd ever speak to him again. Jen was Jen. She was the mother of his children. She lived in his house. She slept in his bed. But Jason he owed nothing. He had to hurt him. He had to get revenge. But what could he do? He'd tried and failed to kill him with a knife. That had been a joke. He'd bungled it so badly that an old lady had died instead. Could he somehow get him fired from his job? Concoct a story like the one Lydia-tits-a-lot made up about him?

Sam contemplated this as he walked to Robert's house, after convincing Jen to take Robert out for a drink. He was glad he'd visited Rachel, sucking info out of her like a straw. Rachel was probably still lying on her bed, dreaming of him coming back and asking her to marry him. He'd become such a terrible person this summer, he thought, ashamed. What had happened to him? Rachel was his friend.

Sam was sure he'd find something incriminating in Robert's house. Or at least something to point him in the right direction. Why would Susan run away from Robert? He must have threatened her, or she must have had something on him that he didn't want anyone to know.

Sam arrived at the house, the itty-bitty place where he used to attend lifeguard parties when he was a teenager. The door was locked, but he knew exactly how to get in — the side window opened easily; they used to prop it up to let out the copious marijuana smoke. He lodged a stick in the small gap at the bottom, jiggling it hard. The window crept up steadily. Sam then lifted himself up and inside Robert's house, careful to land as softly as possible. He'd never been inside a stranger's house, alone. He wasn't even sure what he was looking for.

First, he went into the bedroom, a little nook off the main living area. The whole place was less than a thousand square feet; it reminded Sam of his college frat house suite. The bed was unmade, and there were tennis clothes on top of the dresser. How old was Robert again? Thirty-two? It was time to grow up.

Sam opened each dresser drawer, shuddering when he reached the underwear. He sifted through the clothes. Then he moved into the kitchen, going through shelves and cabinets, finding only silverware, plates, cups, and the odd mug. The refrigerator was filled with bits and pieces — lettuce, a few beers, raw ground beef, carrots, cucumbers. But nothing looked out of place.

Sam wasn't sure where to search next. He sat down on the ratty couch, peeking under the pillows, but all he found was dust and old pennies. He leaned back and looked up. Something caught his eye on the old beams, a notebook or something tucked into the corner, where the triangle of the ceiling closed. He dragged a chair over and reached up on his tiptoes, feeling blindly for the object, grabbing it before nearly falling off the chair. He stumbled down. He was holding Robert's lesson ledger. He'd seen him scribbling in it, filling hours with people's names. Sam had been charged by Robert, many times, for Jen's lessons this summer. She'd been quite liberal with them, at $200 a pop, but Sam had indulged her. Tennis was the only thing that made her happy lately.

He flipped through, noting Robert's tight, neat handwriting. There was Jen's name.

There was her name again. There was Lauren. There was Lisa. And Beth. And Larry. And Brian. And Myrna. And Sam's kids. And on and on. Sam was relatively sure he'd hit on the incriminating evidence, though he didn't know exactly what it meant. He assumed Susan had discovered it. Had she taken the ledger? Is that what Robert was looking for at her house?

It was pretty cheeky of Robert to have pulled the same move as that guy from last year, Dave. Sam took the ledger to the kitchen, continuing to study it. He wasn't sure what to do now. If he gave it to the police, Robert might get in trouble for stealing, but would immediately give up the others. At least now Sam knew what had happened.

He heard a bump, then a crash. He grabbed a dull butter knife, not knowing what he'd do if he had to use it. And then his wife of ten years stood up. She was still so beautiful, so slim, even after three kids. She'd lied and manipulated him this entire time. Now she had a plan.

Jason Parker felt better than he had in years. He wasn't sure if it was the clean break with Jen — the idea that he didn't have to torture himself anymore — or the fact that, knock on wood, he'd gotten away with literal murder. He knew he shouldn't be happy about a woman's *death,* he got that. But there was something darkly satisfying about it that pleased him.

He and Lauren had barely spoken about it at all. His wife had an uncanny ability to compartmentalize. He was beginning to think she was slightly psychotic, with the violent outbursts and unpredictability. But maybe they all were. He'd been sleeping with his best friend's wife. His best friend had gone after him with a knife. He wasn't sure that normal people did stuff like that. There was something about Salcombe that teased it out — the intensity, the physical closeness, the fact that they were all competing against each other in sports. Sports! Ridiculous, when you thought about it.

More than Lauren, more than Susan, more than even Jen, Jason had been thinking about Sam. They hadn't spoken since that night, though they'd nodded and been friendly in social situations: the Labor Day Extravaganza, a cocktail party at the Metzners', a boys' ride on Paul Grobel's motorboat (Paul had worn a Bob Marley T-shirt that Jason desperately wanted to mock, but without Sam, the joke didn't work). They couldn't let anyone else know about their rift; they were all pretending nothing had happened.

The funny thing was, now that Sam hated *him,* he felt fonder toward his friend. Sam, golden Sam, was in a rut, just like the rest of them. It made Jason feel closer to him than he had before.

It wasn't like Jason to get sentimental. He was cold, he knew, even when it came to his wife and kids. He'd loved Jen, at least he thought he did, but perhaps what he'd loved the most about her was that she was Sam's. Even when they'd first slept together, that summer long ago, he'd been thinking about Sam, about taking something that was his.

Jason felt like it was time for a new start. He was forty years old. He'd just avoided something that could have been very bad. His marriage was intact, even though it probably shouldn't be. His kids were fine, as kids go. His job was lucrative. For the past year, he'd focused on Jen, Jen, Jen, but now it was time for something else. He wasn't quite sure what. Maybe he should train for a marathon. Or get back into tennis in a big way. Lauren had been happiest this summer playing tennis, taking lessons from Robert, nearly winning that silly tournament with Jen. Their newfound friendship confounded him. But he couldn't say anything about it to Lauren. She'd rip his head off.

Yes, it was time for a change. Clean slate. By the time he got back to Salcombe next year, he'd be a new man. The Susan stuff would have faded, a tragic memory in another Fire Island summer. It was part of the town's life cycle — the oldies, huddled in a circle at the back of the beach, bragging about their grandchildren, died off one by one. Jason had seen it all before. The eighty-year-olds from when he was a kid were all gone now. The sixty-year-olds had turned into the eighty-year-olds. Sam and his cohort were now the vibrant forty-year-olds with kids, soon, though, to become the sixty-year-olds. And on and on. Susan would have gone in the next wave, anyway, along with Marie and Steve Pond, Betsy and Mike Todd, Bonnie and Richie Trimble. In ten years, they'd all be dead or in nursing homes, their lovely Salcombe homes occupied by their children, or their children's children, or lucky buyers, new to town.

Jason was schlepping the large wooden wagon — PARKER in raised red letters along the back edge — to the dock. It was his second trip; they had so much shit they were taking back to the city, Jason wasn't sure how they'd accumulated anything in a town without stores. They were to take the 1:00 p.m. ferry, the most crowded boat of the year. Nearly the entire town was leaving today. Goodbye, Salcombe. We'll all be back next year! Jason would likely have to sit shoulder to shoulder with some annoying person and make small talk the whole ride back to Bay Shore ("How was your summer?" "Great! How was yours?" "Fabulous! So sad about Susan, though . . ."). Jason had wanted to take the 9:00 a.m. instead — "Let's just get up and go, avoid the crowd" — but Lauren insisted on getting the later boat.

"I still have stuff I need to do to get out of here," she whined to him. "Jen wants me to stay and take the 1:00 p.m. with them. And it's not like you've been any help." Well, she was right about that. There wasn't anything Jason hated more than packing up the house at the end of the summer. It was both laborious and depressing, and so he'd spent the past couple of days doing anything to get out of Lauren's way.

This was the last load. The rest of his family was already waiting at the dock, socializing, the kids playing with each other inside the little dock house, finally in sneakers instead of barefoot. Lauren was likely gossiping in a group with Lisa and Emily, getting in their last-minute digs before separating for the fall, winter, and spring. Jason turned down Bay Promenade toward the dock, sweat pouring, dampening the front of his checked button-down. It was hot for Labor Day; it felt like July, not September.

He looked up to see Sam coming toward him, also dragging his wagon, clearly on the same mission as Jason. Sam was in his "travel" clothing, which meant sleek athleisure — black fitted sweats and a kelly-green T-shirt, probably from A.P.C. or some trendy place like that. Sam had always been more fashionable than Jason. He'd always been more everything than Jason.

The men paused when they reached each other, directly in front of the yacht club entrance, sailboats lining the bay beach on the other side. Jason couldn't help but imagine it as a standoff. They'd not been alone together since that night. Sam made a move to keep going, but Jason, on instinct, blocked him. He was sad. He was sorry. He wasn't feeling himself.

"Sam, I need to say something," said Jason.

Sam blinked behind his glasses. "What?" he finally said.

"It wasn't about you. It was about Jen. I'm sorry," said Jason. He was lying. Sort of. But it felt good to say.

"You're an asshole. You're such an ass-hole," said Sam. His voice was low and shaky.

There were other people heading toward them. No one could overhear this.

"I know," said Jason. "You've always known that! You *know* me. It's just who I am."

Sam sighed. "Nothing will ever be the same. You totally fucked it all up. This place will never be the same. You and I won't, either."

The sun beat down on Jason's head. His hair was hot.

"Sam, do you remember when we were kids and we used to ride our bikes together on the boardwalks? I'd close my eyes, and you'd direct me — left, right, left, right — making sure I didn't fall off the side."

Sam nodded.

"I think that's the closest I've ever felt to someone in my life."

Just then, Brian came barreling through, walking alone. He was in khakis and a navy Lacoste shirt, his go-to ferry outfit.

"Hey-a, boys, am I interrupting something meaningful? Did someone's portfolio take a hit?" He guffawed.

"Nope. Just bringing the last load to the

dock," said Jason, collecting himself. "See you, guys," he said, not looking back.

He wheeled the wagon the length of the dock, navigating the pockets of people waiting for the ferry, and unloaded the suitcases in the pile in front of the boat's freight area. When the ferry arrived, he'd make sure all the bags got on; more than once, they'd landed at Bay Shore to find that a suitcase hadn't made it on the boat, much to Lauren's annoyance (somehow it was always the bag with all her clothes).

Lauren was exactly where Jason had expected — huddled with her friends on a bench, all of them in identical oversize sunglasses, a row of attractive bug ladies. He saw Brian Metzner, chatting with Paul Grobel. Paul was in what looked to be men's capri pants, his little hairy ankles on display. Beth Ledbetter was there with her husband, Kevin, loudly directing him to dump their bags and lock the wagon up, "Now!" Erica Todd and Theo Burch were sitting together on another bench, their children plopped down in front of them on a suitcase. There were the Ponds and the Trimbles and Jeanette Oberman, on speakerphone with an Uber driver. "Yes, meet us at the Salcombe terminal. S-A-L-C-O-M-B-E. You don't pronounce the *B*." Greg had always been the one who drove. Micah Holt was standing with his parents, checking his phone. Claire Laurell was with her daughters, the three of them roasting in the sun. And there was Rachel, standing off to the side, looking lost. She nodded at Jason as he passed. Where had she been hiding?

Jason went over to look for Arlo and Amelie in the dock house. He found them playing with Lilly, Ross, and Dara, some game where they each took a turn hitting the others on the back. *Whatever. Let them amuse themselves,* Jason thought. He went back to stand near his suitcases, taking out his phone, trying to focus on the news. But it was too bright to read anything. He glanced over to see Jen and Sam nearby, Jen in her black-and-white-striped T-shirt dress, the one that Jason joked made her look like a French sailor. They were discussing something, Sam speaking into Jen's ear. Jen looked agitated. She pulled on Sam's sleeve, her one forehead wrinkle flexed. Jason wondered what they were fighting about. Sam broke away from her and walked toward Jason, a few paces and he was there. He grabbed Jason's arm and pulled him to the side, away from the crowd.

"Get out of here," Sam said urgently.

Jason was confused. Get out of where?

"Leave the dock. Go home. Something's going to happen, but I don't want it to happen here."

Jason didn't understand. "What's going to happen?"

"Just go now."

"I can't. The ferry is coming. We're going back to the city."

"Go!" Sam pushed him, but Jason didn't budge. What the fuck was happening? Sam's sunglasses were off, and it looked like he had tears in his eyes. "Don't say anything," said Sam. "Just deny it all. Nothing's going to happen to you. That's not the point."

Jason heard a commotion. Everyone on the dock was talking at once, all of Salcombe shouting. There were three Suffolk County police officers approaching the group, parting people like the Red Sea. Jason stood still, his feet like weights. He was so hot he thought he might faint. "It's about Susan!" he heard someone shout. A few people gasped. Bonnie Trimble fell into Richie's arms, and Marie Pond started fanning her with a tissue.

He saw Lauren stand up and look for him. Arlo and Amelie were by her side.

One of the police officers, a young, freckled guy with a thick mustache, approached him. The other two stood next to him, hands behind their backs.

"Jason Parker?"

Jason nodded. This couldn't be happening. The entire village was watching. His children were watching.

"We need you to come with us. Now."

Jason didn't want to ask, but he knew he had to. "About what?"

Then Sam was there, standing next to him.

"Sam! No!" Jason heard Jen scream.

"I'm his lawyer," said Sam. "I'm coming with him."

The policeman shrugged. "Suit yourself. Let's go. We can drive you across the bridge to our station."

The group turned and walked through the townspeople, lined up as if to play a game of red rover, everyone gaping, everyone silent. Shocked. Amazed. Titillated. Jason Parker being questioned about Susan Steinhagen's death? It was all too much. Lauren stood there, ashen, with the kids. Her life was over. The queen bee felled. Beth Ledbetter smirked. "Oh my God!" said Jeanette Oberman. Theo Burch was rattled. Rachel Woolf put her hand over her mouth, nearly toppling over before Brian Metzner steadied her. Mayor O'Connell looked relieved; at least people could stop blaming him.

Jason and Sam walked side by side down the dock, behind the police, as if heading toward the altar. Or the plank.

30
MICAH HOLT

Micah Holt felt sick. He was sitting in the back seat of his parents' Lexus SUV — they were driving him from the ferry terminal in Bay Shore to school in New Haven, about a two-hour journey. More than enough time for Micah to confess everything and set off a chain that would, in all likelihood, end in the ruin of Salcombe.

"I still can't believe that Jason Parker got arrested for murdering Susan Steinhagen," said Micah's mom, Judy, shaking her head emphatically in the front passenger seat. Judy was fifty-three, and this summer, for the first time, Micah had noticed her age. The lines in her chest had deepened, and there was a new softness to the area below her chin. It made him depressed.

"Mom, he wasn't 'arrested,' he was taken for questioning about Susan's death, which no one has said was a murder," said Micah. Was she also getting stupider?

Micah turned the facts over in his mind, trying to find the best way to present them to his parents.

He thought back to the night that Susan died. First, seeing Lauren Parker and Jen Weinstein with their flashlights, looking for something on the tennis courts. Later, he and Willa had walked Larry Higgins back to Lighthouse Road, acting as guardrails so that Larry didn't go toppling off the boardwalk. Larry was chatting to himself, saying things about his sons, Peter and Lee, who were about fifteen years older than Micah.

"My Peter, my Lee, my disappointments," slurred Larry, likely unaware that Micah and Willa were still with him in the dark. Larry went on, "Funny that Robert had the same idea as Dave."

Willa pinched Micah's side.

"And that Susan was onto both of them." Larry then fell into silence, and the pair was able to get him inside his house with a light shove (very few people locked their doors in Salcombe, even at night).

The next morning, Micah woke to the town siren, queasy and exhausted. And then Susan was dead. "An accident." Such an unfortunate tragedy, people said, a mix of an elderly woman's poor judgment and shoddy town planning. Micah knew better.

Maybe Susan had somehow gotten mixed up in all those marital affairs. Maybe Robert had offed her when she found out he was stealing.

Micah went back to Yale the week after Susan died, moving into his off-campus house in the late-summer heat, registering for his classes, starting to plan for next semester in Madrid. He floated through it in a daze. Had a woman been killed? By people he'd known his whole life? He felt like an entirely different person than when he'd left school last June. Older, embittered. He missed being a kid, missed thinking that adults were there to protect him.

On the surface, he'd come back to Salcombe to help his parents close the house, but it was more than that. He couldn't stop thinking about Susan. He couldn't stop obsessing about what someone had done to her. He'd spent this weekend observing them all — Robert and Lauren flirting at the bar during the Labor Day Extravaganza, Jen and Sam seemingly happy again, Jen and Robert hatching some sort of plan, just out of Micah's earshot. Everyone was complicit, it seemed. Perhaps even Micah.

On the dock today, during all the commotion, Micah had locked eyes with Silvia, the Parkers' nanny. She was standing behind

Arlo and Amelie, her hands on their shoulders protectively as they watched their father being led away by the police. (Micah felt for the kids, privileged as they were; Salcombe was ruined for them, too, thanks to their parents' misbehavior.) Micah had never spoken to Silvia, but he'd seen her around town for the past few summers, looking miserable on an adult tricycle. He wondered what it must be like for her here. She'd raised an eyebrow at Micah as Jason passed them by; Micah clearly wasn't the only one who knew more than he should.

They were cruising up I-95, and his dad had Paul Simon on the speaker. It reminded Micah of summers when he was a kid, "Diamonds on the Soles of Her Shoes" playing as his parents danced together on the back deck of their Salcombe home. Micah's eyes stung with tears. He studied the back of his parents' heads, so familiar, his mom's curls, his dad's bald patch. He loved them so much. He looked at his phone and saw there was one unread message from Ronan. He hadn't heard from him in ages. He opened it.

Hi, sorry about the way everything ended this summer — I'm at school already. I have some figuring out to do, but I'd love to hang next summer on Fire Island. We'll all be back next year, right? x

Micah reread it. And reread it again. Right then, he decided to let it all go. He wouldn't tell anyone anything. He couldn't do that to the town. *His* town. To his parents. To himself. He'd have to live with the knowledge, which would be his punishment. But he'd figure out a way to atone. He knew the Yale School of Management had a focus on social impact — perhaps he could audit some classes this fall, figure out how to use his degree for good rather than as an entry to Goldman. And he'd been excited about Madrid, but it wasn't too late to switch locations — he'd heard of a program in Jordan, studying human rights and helping to fight against oppression. He was young, he had time.

Yes, Micah could choose another way. He took a deep breath as Paul Simon faded out, "Well, that's one way to lose these walking blues, diamonds on the soles of her shoes." He typed his reply to Ronan.

That's okay, I get it. I won't be in Salcombe next summer — I think we both have some sorting out to do. Hopefully we can meet again in another life. x M.

438

EPILOGUE

Robert Heyworth was on top of the world. He'd been living in his new apartment in Chelsea for two months, commuting back and forth to Larry's office on the Upper East Side. He loved his new place, a modern one-bedroom with a Poggenpohl kitchen on Twenty-first Street. He loved being in the city, the gritty speed of it all, the fact that every bar was teeming with hot women who paid attention to him. But what he loved most of all was *not* playing tennis for a living. He hadn't realized how burned out he'd been until he'd stopped. Now he knew he'd never go back. Never go back to coaching people through their shitty serves, encouraging them to stop swinging at their volleys, saying, "Low to high!" If he never heard those words again, it'd be too soon.

And he was enjoying the work with Larry, that lovable grump, who was teaching him to manage his family investment fund. It wasn't rocket science. Robert had gone to Stanford, something he'd nearly forgotten by summer's end.

He didn't like to think about Salcombe, but Larry always found some way to bring it up. He'd never go back to that town. Never go back to that run-down little house, to that hellish yacht club, to those bad, bad people. His job had served its purpose — he was headed toward a real career now, and he had enough money in the bank to float rent through the entire year. That extra $16,000 had certainly helped, though it hadn't come without consequences.

It was the middle of the day, and he was headed out to grab lunch for him and Larry — maybe pick up something at Dig Inn on Lexington. It felt nicely fall-ish outside; Robert was wearing a light cotton sweater and crisp dark jeans. He knew he looked good by the way all the Upper East Side women were staring at him. He turned onto Eighty-ninth Street, bumping into someone who'd been rushing.

"Hey!" she said, annoyed, looking up. It was Lauren.

Robert's stomach lurched.

"Robert!" Lauren said. She smiled, but then remembered herself.

"How are you?" he asked.

Her hair was sleek and shiny, and she had on an oversize sweater, one delicate shoulder exposed. He felt his usual pull toward her.

"I'm fine, you know . . ." She trailed off.

He'd heard from Larry that she and Jason had sold their house on Fire Island and had bought something in the Hamptons. Jason had been cleared in Susan's death — with Sam's help, he hadn't said a word, and they'd had no evidence. But the Parkers could never recover from the arrest at the boat that day. ("I knew that Jason Parker was a bad egg," said Marie Pond at the time, now an oft-repeated line.) That's what Jen had been banking on all along. She'd tipped off the police anonymously, saying she'd seen Jason walking on Neptune that night. She'd told them he'd be on the 1:00 p.m. boat back to the mainland, and they could find him there. Then she'd asked Lauren to wait for her to leave that day, saying she needed her emotional support. At the last minute, Sam had tried to ruin the plan, but it'd been too late. The police had arrived on time, and Jason had to do a perp walk in front of the entire town.

"How are you?" Lauren asked. "Job working out okay? You like your apartment?"

"Yes, it's all great," said Robert. It was strange talking to her this way. It made him

441

feel somewhat ill.

"That's good," she said. "Did you know Jason and I sold our house?"

"I did."

"We bought in East Hampton. It'll be better for me there. It's more my scene," she said unconvincingly. She was forgetting that Robert knew her very well.

"I'm happy for you," said Robert.

"I'm happy for you, too," she said. There was an uncomfortable pause. Lauren glimpsed her phone, which she'd been gripping tightly. "Did you hear about Sam and Jen?"

Robert nodded. Sam and Jen were getting a divorce. Sam's doing. A total shock to everyone. Apparently, Jen was getting the house in Salcombe. She'd be the only one of all of them to return next summer. Robert had also heard that Rachel Woolf had taken all the changes as her cue to move to California, to be closer to her sisters. End of an era.

They stood there for a moment, neither knowing how to end the conversation.

"Well, I have to pick up Arlo and Amelie at school. Braeburn's a few blocks away, and I don't want to be late. It was good to see you, though," Lauren said.

"Yes, good to see you, too," said Robert.

The thought that he'd wanted to continue their affair in the city was laughable now. She seemed much older to him here. She gave him a quick, awkward hug, her perfume washing over him, that intoxicating smell. Then she walked off heading west, toward her life.

Robert felt a little dizzy from the interaction. He thought back to that boat ride in early summer, seeing her sitting with Rachel, how she'd reminded him of Julie. And then speaking to her later that night, the excitement he'd felt touching her for the first time.

Disoriented, he followed the line of busy workers marching into Dig Inn. He wondered what would be different if he'd not seen Lauren that day. If he'd dutifully performed his job in Salcombe without getting involved in any of the town drama.

He paid for lunch and went out in the bright midday sun, walking up to Park Avenue toward Larry's, passing the latte-sipping stay-at-home moms pushing their UPPAbaby strollers, the old geezers sitting on benches and reading *The New York Times,* the nannies dragging screaming toddlers. The air was fresh, and he felt free.

Well, free-ish. Because like a Salcombe mosquito, hiding in the corner of the room, he couldn't seem to rid himself of that night. When he closed his eyes, he saw it. When he was in the shower, he saw it. He saw it right now, on this beautiful New York City day.

After he'd gotten Rachel home, hobbling and scared, and doubled back with her bike, he'd returned to Neptune to find the ledger. He'd seen Susan fall, and he'd heard Sam say she was dead, so he was hoping for an easy operation. He couldn't believe his luck. He ran back, through the wind and rain, to where Susan had gone off the boardwalk. There she was. Her bike was on top of her, and she wasn't moving. Robert jumped down from the boardwalk and landed next to her, turning on his phone flashlight to look for the evidence. There, underneath the walk, less than a foot away from Susan, was the ledger, soggy but intact. Robert grabbed it quickly and began to climb back up, but he heard a rustle. He turned to see Susan, still under the bike, moving her arm with effort. He froze. Her eyes were open, and she was looking at him, her face half-covered by the wheel.

He didn't know what to do. Should he help her? She'd expose him. His life would be over. He was so close to winning.

He bent down, kneeling next to her. She

was trying to say something. Robert thought of his dead father, a policeman. He thought of his mother, missing him from Florida. Then he stood and took off his soggy Salcombe Yacht Club tennis polo. Careful not to touch the rest of Susan's body, he placed the shirt over her nose and mouth, holding it there gently. Her eyes went wide with fear; for a moment, Robert thought she might put up a fight. But instead, she gently closed them, as if settling in for a nap on the beach. The wind and rain provided cover, and no one walked by. After only a few minutes, he felt her body relax. He was doing her a favor. Like killing an injured deer.

He put his shirt back on, pulled himself up onto the boardwalk, and got on his bike, which he'd parked where Rachel had fallen. He hid the ledger up near the rafters in his ceiling. He was going to destroy it, but figured he'd keep it in case the tennis committee asked him for it at the end of the summer. To *not* have it would be more suspicious than anything, and none of them knew what Susan had discovered. Then he cut his tennis polo into tiny pieces and threw them out with the rest of his trash.

The next couple of weeks were torture. He'd been convinced the police would arrest him at any moment. But as each day passed, he felt lighter and more hopeful. He acted appropriately sad about Susan, continued with his lessons, and solidified his job with Larry for the fall. Then Sam and Jen had arrived with their plan to implicate Jason, and that's when Robert knew he was going to get away with everything.

He passed the doorman of Larry's building with a wave, heading up in the elevator to the penthouse where Larry lived and worked. The views from the apartment were amazing. You could almost see Salcombe, Larry had joked when he'd first arrived. Almost, but not quite.

ACKNOWLEDGMENTS

I would like to extend my deepest thanks to . . .

My husband, Charles, for believing in me and the book, and for watching the kids while I worked on it, before "it" was anything other than a Word document at which I kept giggling. You are the most brilliant partner and dad. And, yes, you did come up with the storm, but everything else was my idea!

My mom, Barbara, for her lifelong, unwavering love and support, and for generously sharing her "blue-shingled stunner" with us every summer. I'm sorry that I'm so messy. To my readers: please order ten more copies, so we can afford to get out of my mom's (very neat) hair.

My dad, Scott, "The Mayor," who has always been my biggest fan, and who has been telling me for years that I "gotta write a book." So, I finally did, just to shut him

447

up. (I didn't let you read an early draft because I knew that after a martini, you'd spoil the ending for anyone who asked.)

My sister, Casey, my best friend and best tennis partner, who read the earliest version and enthusiastically said, "It's not only *not* bad, it's awesome!" I don't know what I'd do without you. And to Jared and Jude, Olive, and Sully. You guys, too.

My brother, Ari, who has always had my back, and who noted that it was good that I put some sex in the book, because "women will like that." I hope you're right. You usually are. And to Julie and baby Kai, who I can't wait to meet.

My family in England — Linda, Marcus, Alice, Lee, Daisy, and Olive — for always rooting me on from afar in the kindest possible ways.

My amazing agent, Alexandra Machinist, who sent me a life-changing email on April 1, in which she called my draft "the perfect summer read." By April 20, she'd sold the book. You are a genius, and I'm so lucky to have you on my side. I'm saving that email forever.

My book-to-TV agent, Josie Freedman, who knows everything and everyone in Hollywood, and whose patience I was so grateful for as we navigated the rights process.

I'm excited to keep going and going.

My top-notch UK agent, Cathryn Summerhayes, who, upon introduction, called me "an exceptionally clever writer," and who I will love forevermore for that line.

My editor, Megan Lynch, who, from our first conversation, I knew was *the* best person to bring this book to life. The dream is to have an editor who's smarter, kinder, and calmer than you are, and that's what I've found in Megan. Thank you for your sharp insights and continual encouragement. You make everything better.

The rest of the wonderful team at Flatiron Books: Kukuwa Ashun, Malati Chavali, Bob Miller, Nancy Trypuc, Marlena Bittner, Keith Hayes, Emily Walters, Claire McLaughlin, Katherine Turro, Jeremy Pink, and Jason Reigal. I'm thrilled to have landed at the best possible imprint and am amazed and grateful for all the hard work you've put into *Bad Summer People.*

Jessica Leeke, my talented editor at Penguin Michael Joseph, for her keen edits and infectious excitement, and to the rest of the lovely, hardworking PMJ crew, including Maxine Hitchcock, Emma Plater, Gaby Young, Sophie Shaw, and Louise Moore.

My supportive, hilarious boss, Bryan Goldberg, whose pride for me is only outweighed by his jealousy that he didn't write a novel first (you will, Bryan, I know it).

The rest of the team at BDG — Jason Wagenheim, Kimberly Bernhardt, Trisha Dearborn, Tyler Love, Kathy Kaplan, and everyone else, for cheering me on and for looking the other way when I definitely, didn't ever, not even once, use my work computer for this project. And Lindsay Leaf, whose children have the best names.

Amanda Schweitzer, my best reader-friend since kindergarten and the first person I gave a draft to. Your positive reaction gave me the confidence I needed, and your magical email set this whole thing in motion. For that I am eternally grateful.

Carole Sirovich, who I've known and admired for my entire life, and who I would never, ever run off the boardwalk in a million years.

The residents of Saltaire, for your tolerance and sense of humor. We'll all be back next year!

ABOUT THE AUTHOR

Emma Rosenblum is chief content officer at Bustle Digital Group, overseeing content and strategy for BDG's lifestyle, parenting, and culture & innovation portfolios, including *Bustle, Elite Daily, Romper, Nylon, The Zoe Report, Scary Mommy, Fatherly, The Dad, Gawker, Inverse,* and *Mic.* Prior to BDG, Emma served as the executive editor of *Elle.* Previously Rosenblum was a senior editor at *Bloomberg Businessweek* and before that, a senior editor at *Glamour.* She began her career at *New York* magazine. She lives in New York City with her husband and two sons.

The employees of Thorndike Press hope you have enjoyed this Large Print book. All our Thorndike, Wheeler, and Kennebec Large Print titles are designed for easy reading, and all our books are made to last. Other Thorndike Press Large Print books are available at your library, through selected bookstores, or directly from us.

For information about titles, please call:

(800) 223-1244

or visit our website at:

gale.com/thorndike

To share your comments, please write:

Publisher
Thorndike Press
10 Water St., Suite 310
Waterville, ME 04901